# WAITING
# FOR JULES

# WAITING
# for
# JULES

*Tamara N. Houston*

**ATRIA** PAPERBACK

New York ✦ London ✦ Toronto ✦ Sydney ✦ New Delhi

**ATRIA** PAPERBACK

A Division of Simon & Schuster, Inc.
1230 Avenue of the Americas
New York, NY 10020

First Atria Paperback edition August 2013

**ATRIA** PAPERBACK and colophon are trademarks of Simon & Schuster, Inc.

For information about special discounts for bulk purchases, please contact Simon & Schuster Special Sales at 1-866-506-1949 or business@simonandschuster.com.

The Simon & Schuster Speakers Bureau can bring authors to your live event. For more information or to book an event contact the Simon & Schuster Speakers Bureau at 1-866-248-3049 or visit our website at www.simonspeakers.com.

Designed by Dana Sloan

Manufactured in the United States of America

10   9   8   7   6   5   4   3   2   1

Library of Congress Cataloging-in-Publication Data

Houston, Tamara N.
    Waiting for Jules / Tamara N. Houston. — First Atria Books paperback edition.
      p. cm
    1. Women in the mass media industry—Fiction.  2. Public relations—Fiction.
3. Women—Fiction.  4. Ambition—Fiction.  5. Divorce—Fiction.  6. New York
(State)—New York—Fiction.  I. Title.
    PS3608.O877 2013
    813'.6—dc23
                                            2012041013

ISBN 978-1-4516-9851-0
ISBN 978-1-4516-9853-4 (ebook)

Dear Mom,

You who loves to talk, I mean, HONESTLY,

WOMAN, without pause! Thank you for listening

to pages upon pages—even chapters—with no

regard to the hour or task at hand. I could not have

accomplished this without your support. You are why

God created moms. Thanks for being mine.

Love you!

*"There's only one very good life and that's the life you know you want and you make it yourself."*

—DIANA VREELAND

# Author's Note

I LOVE TO READ and get lost in a moment not of my own making. It has been that way since I was a child in Alabama begging my mom to let me stay up past my bedtime, just long enough to finish the next chapter (or two) of whatever book had so captivated me. The escapism that others fostered also fed my soul and imagination. For that I am eternally grateful, because those authors opened up a world to me that showcased ways of existence far different from the one I knew, that of an only child of a single woman whose great love was not so great—so life for me was not always crystal.

I say all of this to tell you that I have an appreciation for great writers and storytellers, my favorites being Kundera, Z. Smith, Hurston, and Coehlo, but I make absolutely NO pretense of being an ounce of the writers they are. I do hope, however, to be an intriguing storyteller and provide you a good tale to get lost in. A friend once said to me, "You speak like a novel."

I hope that he is correct (thank you, Greg Cham) and that you will embrace what is to come. Welcome to the world of Jules Sinclair.

Sincerest gratitude,
x Tamara

# 1

## THE RETURN

### 2001

AWAITING ME AT baggage claim was a bespectacled middle-aged man positioned near the base of the escalator with *Jules Sinclair* written in a haphazard black script on a white board. He didn't appear too excited to be there, which was perfect for me as I am unclear of what awaits me when I get home, so any forced pleasantries at this point would be exhausting.

Before leaving for London, Marcus and I had the kind of argument where far too many things are said, some of which you just can't take back and others of which you say intentionally to hurt the other because you want them to feel as bad as you do at that moment. Instead of clearing my head, the time away only made two things obvious to me: I didn't want out, and I had no idea of how to get back in—to us. Besides, even if I did have the solution, I'm not sure he'd want to hear it anyway. The answers that I hoped would be miraculously delivered, like how to retract all of the pain and harmful words, eluded me. We had come so far only to end up exactly where we should not be.

On the plane I ran a couple of scenarios in my head so that, no matter the outcome of putting my key in the door, I would be prepared. Option A: He would be there, relieved to see me and in that lovable yet obtuse manner feed me a line to let me know that we would weather this. Option B: He would be out but not gone—

his clothes remaining perfectly spaced on his side of the closet with a few items subletting space on my side. Seeing this I would just wait for him to come back, to come home to me. Option C: A "Dear Jules" note would be on the counter in his meticulous penmanship telling me that it was best if we had some time apart and that he had taken up residence elsewhere—or, worse yet, that he was gone, never to return. While I know that C could very easily be my reality, I couldn't bring myself to consider it without bursting into tears—again. Maybe things would have been different—for the better of us, I mean—if he had told me about the baby, or if I'd never made him feel like he couldn't. Maybe not.

Taking a deep breath, I bring my thoughts current, focusing only on what is before me—identifying my luggage and getting to the car.

"We're going to Beverly Hills, yes?" asks the driver.

"Yes, One North Wetherly."

"Do you have any objections to taking La Cienega down?"

"Any way you want is fine—all goes to the same place," I say.

Normally the drive to West Hollywood from LAX via the main street of La Cienega takes an eternity at this hour of the day, the 10 Freeway is even worse, so I settle into the black leather seats of the town car and allow my thoughts to be lulled into a void. You don't have to live in Los Angeles to know that rush hour traffic here is a terror in and of itself. People enter their cars pissed off at the workday that just ended, armored for the confrontation that awaits them as a result of listless drivers who seem resigned to repeat the habitual routine that has become "adult life": morning commute 8:00 to 8:45 a.m., sitting in the parking garage of your office praying that today will be better than yesterday 8:45 to 8:50 a.m., pasting a smile on your face at 8:55 a.m., "Hello, Bob," "Hi, Shirley," working someone else's job from 9:00 a.m. to 5:00 p.m., getting in car and dropping the facade at 5:05 p.m., evening commute until 6:30 p.m.—welcome home.

What a life! I could never survive it, and yet the infinitesimal details make mine not so different. If anything my wrapping at this point just appears more glamorous and above it all; monthly travel to our homes in New York, Los Angeles, and Bridgehampton, filled with dinners and events that oftentimes end up chronicled in Page Six or photographed for the monthlies. What the rags don't catch are the quiet moments and everywoman experiences that no amount of Executive Platinum frequent-flyer miles, chauffeured cars, or exclusive access will allow me to escape. Basically, as a child of the '80s, I drank the Kool-Aid—with a heaping dose of fairy dust for good measure, as it were—hence *I am woman hear me roar awaiting my knight in shining armor*, that is, if I can, once and for all, put my BS aside long enough to rest in all that comes with the reality of us. *Which clearly I had not done despite past misfortunes.* Try admitting that about yourself and not cringing! To my mind's eye the details of how would always fall into place miraculously, because they always had for me with little or no effort. That is, until I ran full speed into the wall that said, "You can't get what you are not so take a good look princess and be truthful about who is looking back." A frightening proposition any way I slice it, much more involved than maintaining the size 6, five-feet-eight-inch Jamaican-Dutch genetic lotto pool I was fortunate enough to be born into. In the event I ever went north of my regular 135 pounds, the solution was simple: a few spinning classes at Equinox, a horrid regime of salt-free/fat-free/taste-free food, hot yoga, and complete avoidance of the dessert menu for a week or more. Simple enough, right? But this navigating life—getting personal purpose right more times than I fuck up and being brave enough to admit when I do without feeling diminished—I don't know.

In all the commotion of exiting the plane, getting through customs, and worrying that my luggage (like my relationship) might not have made the same flight that I did, I forgot that daylight saving time had ended, so it was completely dark outside. Nightfall with the ever-present charcoal smog overcast was firmly set by 5 p.m., which now seemed fitting. As a child, I could always think better at night. I used to believe that the constellations appeared visible only to hear me talk about the grand life that was to come. Tonight, however, there was not a single solitary star to be found in the sky; *there seldom are, actually, which is one of the sacrifices of living in Lala but I would gladly do without the galaxy, if he will have me.* My hope is that Marcus and I, at the very least, are in the grasp of the half-moon revealing itself amid the smog, so I surrender, lean back and reminisce, allowing my thoughts to return to years prior until my future reveals itself.

# 2

## MEETING MR. MICHAEL
## THURMOND KIPPS?

THE YEAR WAS 1998 and I was trying to return to New York full-time from a stint (forced *sabbatical . . . okay, relationship exile*) abroad when a friend suggested that I contact Michael Kipps as soon as my feet touched U.S. soil again. The intent being to discuss helming the PR department of his restaurant, Carly's, that was now all the rave in the ultrahip yet still seedy Meatpacking District. So I did as instructed *sort of* by preemptively e-mailing him from London, thinking it best to develop some kind of cheeky communication before actually begging for the position.

> *Michael,*
> *    Jules Sinclair here. Blake says that you are utterly lost without me. Luckily I am bored with everything—my life, the Brits, warm beer, peas and mash, etc. I hear you are divine, more important I am told that Carly's is the hottest upstart the NYC scene has encountered in some time. Let's make sure it stays that way. When and where?*
> *                                                      Warmest, Jules S.*

To my surprise his response was immediate albeit short and completely devoid of the witticism that mine had been carefully crafted with.

*Thursday at 8pm. —MK*

There was no inquiry on his part as to when I was scheduled to arrive in New York or an overture to convey that he understood flying across the Atlantic on three days' notice might be an imposition—but it would be great if possible because he had heard good things about me. No, "Thursday at 8pm" is all he said, and so around 10:30 p.m. GMT on a Sunday night I went online to book my travel and pray to the credit card gods.

. . .

It has been said many times over that London is like New York because it has a broad array of cultures and ethnicities inclusive of new money, old money, and no money, all forced to coexist on metros and deckers. Also, it's an epicenter of style and is more than a one-industry town, consisting of banking, publishing, interior design, art, theater, music, etc.—but they are completely wrong. To me New York is a hyperkinetic fishbowl anomaly of possibilities in and of itself; every other global metropolis is but an Off-Broadway production, nicely reviewed but lacking megawatt star power. Emotionally it conjures the innate fight-or-flight impulse for newbies. A rite of passage for all who aspire to re-create themselves on its dense littered streets, as it was for me a few years ago. Everything about New York is a complete affront to the senses, from being sandwiched on a subway multiple times a day and being inappropriately groped, to habitually stepping over trash and being heckled by street vendors, not to mention keeping the requisite pushcart near the door to transport laundry and groceries with no thought to how unnatural it is to be pushing a caged contraption in five-inch heels on any given day.

New York is hard on the body (kind of like sparring a few rounds with Tyson but coming out of it with both ears intact) and potentially mind-altering, but you don't realize it until you leave the island behind and see how life looks on the other side: mini-vans and carpools, chore lists, restaurants that close at 10 p.m., planned subdivisions with oversize, themed shopping malls that could hold Yankee and Giants stadiums collectively with room to spare. But no matter how damaging, the city's lure to rewrite a life, the addiction to "anything is possible if your game is strong enough" is swift. Either you do whatever is necessary to maintain the high or you nearly OD and in a fitful moment of clarity decide to go clean—leaving it forever and relegating the experience to a "when I was younger I lived in New York" story to be dusted off for Middle American friends and relatives as either a badge of honor or a cautionary tale to a wayward child.

· · ·

Touching down at JFK before midnight on Wednesday I imme-diately feel that zing of energy coursing through my veins. The interior of the Virgin Atlantic concourse was sparse with some travelers awaiting takeoff, which made it easy for me to be one of the first people at baggage claim, and since I had used some miles to upgrade to business class, my luggage was certain to be labeled "priority" and descend the conveyer first so I could get a jump on the taxi line before the rush. Luggage in hand I impressed myself exiting the terminal, maneuvering the gypsy cabs who, by the way, are the furthest thing from being actual Gypsies. They are more like West Indian, Caribbean, Russian, and Middle Eastern entre-preneurs with a dream of capitalism, a car, and hopefully a legal driver's license. My first reaction was to put on my best *I am not a tourist so don't fuck with me* face—that is, until I saw that the line of passengers awaiting a taxi in the center partition was wrapped in rows of three. No time like the present to double back and give my sweetest *soooo about that ride into the city* about-face. I was not going to wait twenty minutes or more in 30-degree weather at this hour, even if when compared with London it was warm enough for me to put on some knickers and sunblock and walk to the city.

Greeted by the smell of Hai Karate musk mixed with a distinct middle note of curry, I settled in the backseat and waited for the twilight moment when we would be submerged in the Midtown Tunnel and ascend into the hub of Manhattan. That moment never disappoints. Well illuminated and sleek, the tunnel is a quiet conveyer that ends with the bustle of delivery trucks blocking roads with produce, shopkeepers preparing for the next day's business, and a few late-night joggers, *which I've never understood. Honestly who needs to run that badly (my friend Richard)?* I knew before we exited Murray Hill that no matter the outcome of my meeting with Michael, I needed to be back in New York. Nothing awaited me in London. It had served its purpose. Two years earlier I moved there to do in-house publicity for a new four-star hotel group— and to put some distance in a relationship. Like most things, it was exciting initially *sans the whole emotional despair shattered dreams broken heart of things.* During the week, I worked hard—put on my corporate suit (Chloé by Stella McCartney, of course) and sensible shoes (Alaia or Blahnik). At night, I combined work and even harder play in some of the best private clubs, Soho House and Opium being preferred locations. The weekends, however, I reserved for dropping the "king of the world" pretense and falling down.

The ironic and insufferable thing about a fast pace is that it is the biggest illusion of all. You find yourself so wrapped up in this obligation or that social commitment that you begin to believe your own hype. Mine was that I was living the fullest life possible in the present with no concern for past misgivings despite the obvious (weekends falling apart, h-e-l-l-o?!). Slowly, as the UK scene became habitual, the regimen of my life started to emerge and I found it hard to deny that my past was very much a constant companion in my present. Yes, this is the moment when, if my life were a film score, the music supervisor would cue "Run to You" by Whitney Houston. Instead of running to someone, I was running from someone sans the flesh-colored unitard and wind machine. Each day or so I thought *There has to be more than this. Tomorrow will be better*, and I would wait as patiently as possible for the moment to pass. But like the constantly changing forecast of any given English day—overcast in the morning, sunshine by lunch, only to be disrupted by showers during the evening commute—it just recycled.

Sometimes those moments went easily; other times they decided to battle. And let me tell you they played dirty. Along with their incessant noise reminding me of all that was lacking in my life, they would bring gray skies and make the heavens cry with such intensity that my only refuge was to take to my bed. Thankfully those moments would give way to a classic black-and-white with Ronald Coleman and Greer Garson, William Powell and Myrna Loy, or Cary Grant and Irene Dunne. And there you have it—my life is not a music score but a classic Hollywood movie. The problem is that I live in a modern world and experience has made it clear that none of those archetypes exist anymore with the possible exception of my dad, Charles. There is no dashing man full of ambition with amazing style and comedic wit who is challenged in the best of ways by the paradox of my drive and vulnerability. *So why can't I just accept this fully instead of holding on to a modicum of hope that he is out there, looking for me as well?* I thought of this incessantly as we drove to the hotel until the friction to the car from the cobblestone SoHo streets interrupted my thoughts, forcing me out of my haze.

Two years had gone by since last I was here so I decided to treat myself and stay at the Mercer Hotel in order to be near my favorite haunts: the eats at Café Habana, Balthazar, and Raoul's, the boutiques, and the friends. At check-in the impossibly perfect supermodel-in-training receptionist told me that not only would the temperature reach the mid-50s but that my junior suite was ready due to a cancellation. Initially when I made the reservation I was advised that no juniors were immediately available but would be later in my stay if I wanted to change rooms at that time. *This trip was already starting off much better than expected.* Before going to bed, I unpack and shower, after taking a last glance at some notes on Michael in preparation for our meeting later this evening.

The time difference caused my mind to wake up much earlier than my body desired. Instinctively I reached for the phone to order room service before remembering that the toniest of breakfast experiences was just down the street sans 18 percent delivery charge. Independent of what anyone will tell you or what you may read, Balthazar (noise level excluded) is by far the hippest enclave in the city to observe, be observed, and eat great food any time of the day.

Exiting the hotel I stop on the corner of Prince and Broadway to ogle a stylish day-planner in the window of Kate's Paperie before being accosted by two gusts of arctic wind that chills me to the bone. The first being the actual temperature—mid-50s my ass, more like low 20s without the wind-chill factor. *Mental note: After breakfast come back to hotel and put on anything in my luggage that suggests warmth; cashmere socks, wool tights, and ear covers, despite the fact that I am vehemently opposed to the latter due to chronic hair issues.* The second of course was Cora's name flashing across the screen of my mobile. *What is the deal with mothers and their incredibly poor timing anyway?* Knowing all too well that any conversation with her this early would only bring an unnecessary amount of drama and derailment to my beautifully appointed selfish morning, I ignore the call. Allowing it to go to voice mail instead of pressing the ignore button, which never went unnoticed or unchallenged by her. Snapping back into reality, I continue on my way. I am not here to obsess on the Doppler radar system, Cora's intrusive manner, or even my own gastronomic pursuits. I am here to impress Michael Kipps and get this position. Then and only then can I justify leaving London professionally and afford to move back to the States without depleting my savings (again) in the process.

. . .

I did some homework on Michael and learned from mutual friends that he was a former model in the late '70s through early '80s (actually he was a major deal) who married very well (nice retirement plan if you can get it), enjoys the jet-set life and the spotlight that comes with it, so it was no surprise that he would go into the restaurant business. The shock to many was that he was fucking great at it—front of the house and behind the scenes. So much so that the storied ego of his that was rumored to greet acquaintances before he did worked to his advantage now. Men and women loved to be in his presence and he was an amazing host. In the day-to-day operations he proved to be a skilled businessman, combining all that he experienced from fashion, society life, and dining at the best establishments into the secret of his success.

Carly's was named after his wife and partially funded by her, an older generational wealthy blue-blood type. Carly Spencer Falles, in her heyday, was the standard by which all affairs were deemed a success or failure in New York. Success, if she decided to attend and bring with her a legion of trendsetters known as The Circle. Carly was a one-woman branding machine by virtue of her connections and influence. When she and Michael began dating in '89, most people were amused. Age-wise she preceded him by more than a decade. Anyone with eyes could understand why *she* would want him. The confusion was in his choosing her.

Michael Kipps, at that time in his early forties, remained a divinely handsome man by any standard and, while not having discovered the fountain of youth, seemed to just get better with age. At six feet two, he was blessed with a deep olive complexion that even in the coldest of winter appeared to be sunkissed thanks to his Greek mother, dark wavy hair loosely sprinkled with silver, and a bountiful mouth set against a jawline chiseled by Michelangelo. His dating history read like a prepubescent boy's wish list of the world's most beautiful women, and by all accounts he was financially sound. Knowing these truths, to say that people were surprised by his courtship and subsequent marriage to Carly is a well-documented understatement. To quote a columnist from *The Village Voice*: "For a man who has dated some of the greatest beauties in the world the new paramour of Michael Kipps doesn't seem to share the same looking glass."

True, Carly was not a conventional beauty at any stage—even she knew that. There was no late blooming period where her head would grow enough to minimize those elfin ears or make her nose appear less beakish. Forever lean and tall she kept her flaxen hair long and ethereal as a focal point, since the Nordic thing seemed to be a prerequisite for class distinction in Upper East Side (UES) society for any era. From what I was able to uncover, their public courtship was very brief, about seven months, which only added to the speculation that the marriage would dissolve within three years. She was infamously quoted saying that she felt like "Linda Ronstadt and Michael is my Aaron Neville, together we make beautiful music." Yes, their first official dance as Mr. and Mrs. Michael Thurmond Kipps was to "All My Life," so with all of this for evidence could you really blame the naysayers and skeptics?

Now, nearly a decade later, with a young daughter (the ultimate wedding gift from one of Michael's exes), and having conquered New York on their terms, it seems that they have turned the skeptics into believers as demonstrated by Carly's best-selling book, *Making It Work: A Guide to Lasting Love After 60*. Businesswise Michael had effectively birthed an ultra-chic supper club that didn't feel gimmicky but wonderfully consistent, thanks to a world-class culinary team and marquee live performances. Now in its fourth year, the restaurant has to contend with competitors entering the neighborhood. *This is where I come in.* In order to remain ahead of the pack, Carly's needed to transition from being a novel idea into an institution that is the very essence of New York culture.

On the plane I reviewed the prospectus thoroughly as well as trend reports regarding consumer dining and spending behavior. So much of New York's business depends on a heavy amount of tourism dollars during peak seasons and the cool factor for locals during off-season, especially restaurants. The big question before me was how does one remain all things to all people while maintaining integrity? *Excluding any biblical implications, of course.* Actually, if I could answer that I would be so much further ahead in my life than twenty-eight years of age, relationship averse, hiding in my career, emotionally restless, and looking for the release hatch on my life, not necessarily to jump but just to see the abyss and contemplate *what if?*—but I digress. I had some concrete ideas to make Carly's iconic but didn't want to get too attached to a specific pitch until I saw Michael in the flesh.

As I saw it, going into the interview I had the upper hand, so much information was available on Michael documenting his life, career, and loves. He, however, had little on me. For as much as I am a social ingénue to some, I work very hard to keep my profile quite low, both professionally and personally. If you needed to know me, you did, and vice versa.

# 3

## IF IT LOOKS LIKE A DUCK

FOLLOWING A QUICK stopover at the hotel for those warmer clothes, I started walking to Gramercy Park to get reacquainted with my city. So much had changed, namely Bleecker Street was starting to show serious signs of gentrification with the addition of J.Crew on the corner of Seventh Avenue South. Thank goodness the falafel place, whose name I never committed to memory, next to The Peanut Butter Factory on Sullivan, was still open. I would stop by on my way back for a quick lunch. I wonder if that great vinyl music record store was still there? It wasn't exactly on Bleecker but on one of the side streets whose name I never bothered to memorize. No matter, in the next few days that I am here, I'm sure to stumble across it or a better one.

So lost in my thoughts was I that by the time I got my bearings I was in Union Square standing in line to buy zucchini bread from a vendor at the farmer's market. Hands down the best in the world! Previously, when I lived here and worked at Atkins & Klein doing fashion event—related press, a coworker who was all about buying local and homegrown gave me a loaf. After that I was hooked. Since moving, however, I had not thought about how delicious it was to pop a slice in the oven and enjoy it with a cold glass of milk in the morning before hopping the A or C to my office in Midtown. Today, however, unless I was going to run across the street to The Coffee Shop, there would be no milk at this moment and since the divine zucchini loaf waits for no one I removed a glove exposing my right hand to the frigid elements, all for a delicious taste of memory lane.

"And you're not even going to offer me a bite? I see nothing has changed," he said.

I'm certain that it was not the absence of milk that made this particular bread bite feel exceptionally larger than the previous and lodge in my throat, but the recognition of who owned that voice, Anthony Mason, alias "my heart's greatest despair and UK decision." *Quick invisible prayer and blessing to the Virgin Mary and Saint Peter before turning around.* "Depends on whether it is the first bite or the last," I say, impressed that neither the jet lag nor our history had delayed my retort. *Damn it, I really should have left my hair out—hate earmuffs.*

*Thank you, God, I'll never ever doubt you again! How I have dreamed about this moment and here it is—you know the moment I am talking about, the one where after substantial time you see the man you gave your entire innocent heart to, only to have him completely twist your mind into a riddle of the most epic proportions and the only reprieve after he rips it from your chest and places it in a lockbox to which there is only one key is to put an ocean between you. Well, this is that moment, and I am pleased to report that my legs remain solid and I look as great as one can when wearing fifty layers and swathed like an Eskimo baby.*

"Why can't it be both?" asked Tony.

"Good-bye, An-TONY!" I seethed.

*Fuck no. He is doing it again, the riddles. And to believe that I once thought they were cute? He was never able to give me a straight answer then, so why would I hope to get one now? First bite or last? Beginning or end? Love me or not? Slept with her or did not? And yes, oral does count!*

Immediately spinning on my heels to leave in the opposite direction, he blocks me. I truly believe it was in this moment that I took temporary leave of my senses, all of them because he touched me, I smelled him, and when I went to object I looked up into the warm hazel with hints of emerald flecks that are his eyes. And just like that my heart, which had flatlined, started to beat uncontrollably and I was lost in 1995 again—when we first met.

# 4

---

# THE MAGIC OF RAIN

### New York, 1995

Julesy, DON'T TELL me you are still in bed. Angie and I are at Coffee Shop waiting on you. Snap it into gear, the movie starts in an hour. Oh, bring an umbrella," said Blake.

Shit, I completely overslept, technically not my fault. Every self-respecting Manhattanite knows that Friday is not a "going out party night." It's the night exclusively reserved for the 9-to-5 Bridge & Tunnel (B&T) crowd to overtake the city in celebration of a completed workweek. And yet that is exactly what I was doing last night, playing wing-woman to Blake for her date with some dreadful Wall Streeter—*what is the deal with those guys anyway? Dreadfully immoral pompous bloodsuckers they are. I could never!*—who in an effort to impress her made sure our glasses were never empty. I in return felt it was my duty to at least try to reach the bottom of the glass, which is why I am desperately attempting to pull it together now and failing. My tipping point from buzzed to drunk must have been the two glasses of sambuca after being besieged at Cipriani's by a village of gelled hair and stretch-charmeuse-clad Ginos, Vinnies, and Ginas otherwise known as B&T.

"Ugh—stop shouting. I hear you. Eat without me. I'll meet you guys at the theater." With my eyes closed, my hand clumsily returned the phone to its cradle and began searching the floor blindly for the water bottle resting somewhere in my bag from yesterday's gym excursion; an apt description since I have an aversion to sweating and will stop any activity (well, almost any) at the onset of perspiration.

Earlier in the week I made plans to grab lunch and see *Crimson Tide* with Blake and Angie not expecting to have tied one on the night before. To make matters worse, spring was officially here, which meant rain, rain, glorious "fuck up my hair and slip on my wellies" rain. My only hope in salvaging the day was to see Denzel Washington shirtless or an extreme close-up on his "I am a serious actor and not really trying to be sexy but you want this" lip pout. Union Square being central to everyone, we decided to see it at the little theater across from ABC Carpet. Late for lunch but early for the movie, I bought tickets for the girls as a peace offering. *It would be nice if the sun decided to make an appearance by the time we come back out, but conditions are slim.*

"My God, that man is fine. Tell me about it. I swear they don't make 'em like that anymore. Could you imagine?! I would give him some. Hell, I would give him all," Blake and I cooed simultaneously, talking over each other. The gray chaos of earlier had given way to subtle rays of golden light to create rainbow spurts along the concrete.

"I *know*! *Ge-ne* gets me every time! That voice hmmm all gruff and authoritative. Papi can boss me around anytime. Did you see the way he put that Deezel in his place? Get 'em, Papi."

Dumbfounded, we stared at Angie for a few seconds in utter silence. Thankfully, Blake was not as lost for words as I initially was.

"First, it is DENzel. Second, it's GENE, and third, what the hell are you talking about, Angie? Were you even watching the same movie? Hackman, seriously? The only time he would ever get a glimpse at my cookies is if his Gold Card swiped it."

"Whah? He reminds me of my uncle Ramon. You should see that man smoke a cigar just like Gee-ene. Eeyy Mami it is hot—"

"Ang, please stop, I can't take this. You letting Gene spank it is bad enough, now you want to bring us into your incestuous fantasies. I can't and by 'I can't' I meant *ewh!*" I said finally, after gaining control of my gag reflex, "but it takes all kinds I guess."

"No, it doesn't. That's some Puerto Rican shit right there," said Blake.

"I swear you girls are sleeping. My *abuela* says a good-looking man can bring you nothing but heartache and bad credit. And she should know. She's been married like five times or something, although I'm not sure if Paco is legal. Anyway, Abuela says an average-looking man will work harder and treat you like a que . . . like a—damn . . ." whispered Angie, her words trailing off indicating that she had suddenly forgotten the point she was trying to make or it just didn't matter. Instinctively, Blake and I turned to uncover what had captivated her so. We understood immediately. Anthony (Tony to his friends) Mason, standing with some guys talking, looking like the divine rebirth of what heaven should be, at least to me. I'm not sure if I fell instantly in love with him or if it was lust. Spellbound as I was, one thing was certain, though: I would lose any battle that would ensue over the next year and a half. Within seconds I had taken an entire gallery of photos of him with my mind. Try as I might through the years I still can't seem to delete them.

He was carrying an oversize navy blue umbrella to protect his shoulder-length, sun-streaked, dark brown dreadlocks. Historically, I have never been attracted to men with locks—unsanitary, as Cora would say—but he was so much more than perfectly twisted hair. The rains had subsided, allowing glimpses of sunlight to break through the clouds, and the rays created a halo effect around him, highlighting his golden-honey complexion. A glow so bright that it seemed to emanate from his entire being through the wool pea-coat, ivory cable-knit sweater, dark denims that were loose but not obscenely baggy, on to the camel Timberlands. I stood there transfixed like a child watching a magic show, and he didn't even notice.

At some point he ended his conversation and started to walk

leisurely toward Fourteenth Street. Hypnotized, I followed some steps behind. He stopped to look in at a makeshift music store. Exiting, he came across a homeless woman sitting on the sidewalk and after some conversation placed money in her hands. An oncoming taxi separated us at that crosswalk. Looking ahead, I saw him crossing the street. "Where are you going?" I heard Blake and Angie asking from behind but could not be bothered to stop and explain my actions because I didn't have an answer yet even for myself. I only knew that I needed to see a little bit more of him before the moment passed. As soon as I relaxed, believing I had his pace down, he crossed another street, the abruptness of which paralyzed me. I stood at the corner for a moment watching him walk away, feeling as if a part of me that I would never be able to reclaim was being extracted. The return of rain only heightened the emerging panic of losing something vital. My legs sprinting into action before my head resolved the conflict, I dashed across in pursuit with absolutely no thought of what I would say when I reached him.

"Excuse me!" I said, with an urgency that was startling even to me. He turned as if instinctively knowing that I was speaking to him, rendering me lost for a moment. *Please, say something more than that, Jules. Words. You know what they are—single distinct conceptual uses for language. Select a few, form a sentence, and for mercy's sake don't embarrass us. Come on, girl.* "My name is . . . Hi, I am Jules . . ." *Really, is that the best you got? OMG, it doesn't matter because he is now touching my hand. Dear Lord, I hope he thinks I'm cute and not about to have a heart attack. Okay, say something clever. Ask directions. For God's sake, breathe!* "I am Jules Sinclair and . . . I saw you coming out of the theater, back there, and wanted to say hello." *WTF? Did you just say what was actually in your head? No style, no finesse, that was so amateur. Way to go, little one, way to freaking go. Oh my goodness, did he just smile? He did. Oxygen!*

"Hi. I'm Tony," he said, looking down at me. "Are you a dancer? You hold yourself like one.

Before I could answer, a hint of cinnamon from his chewing gum tickled my nose, giving me permission to close my eyes and inhale the moment.

"No, but thanks for the compliment," I say, slowly opening my eyes, allowing them to linger on every inch of his frame. When our eyes met he was blushing and I knew exactly what I wanted, to be anywhere that he is from now until forever stops being an idea.

Stepping closer and positioning his umbrella so that it shielded us both from the falling rain, Tony said, "So you saw me at the movies?"

"Yes. I was with my friends, saw you, and wanted to, actually *needed* to introduce myself—say hello." Stammering to get the last few words out.

"Your friends," he says, pointing across the street. "You referring to the two girls hiding behind that white van?" Laughing aloud in a way that made me feel as if he and I were in on the joke the entire time, as if it had always been he and I against the world.

And in my very first (of many) "shit that only happens to Jules" moments, Tony invited us to join him for dinner at this Italian restaurant in Greenwich Village just west of Seventh. The décor was nothing to speak of, very clichéd; red-and-white checker-patterned tablecloths with old candle wax–laden bottles on each. I don't even remember if the food was good. The conversation flowed easily and he was more charming than any of us could have imagined. Tony spoke of living in a converted firehouse in Tribeca, transitioning from street dancing to modeling and now photographer. When he did excuse himself briefly from the table, our collective squeal was so loud that I am sure he could not help but hear it in the men's room.

"What would your *abuelita* have to say about *that*, Angie?" Blake asked pointing in the direction of the chair Tony had been sitting in.

"Nothing, because she would be butt naked in the kitchen

wearing only an apron and some heels screaming *ayyy Papi* and cooking him some *paella y platanos, habas con arroz, flan y guava*," I said mockingly in my bad Spanglish. Besides, I couldn't help but go for the big dig here if for nothing more than to shut Angie up a little bit. Over the course of dinner she had gotten a little extra chatty with Tony. "Oh, by the way, missy, you do realize that I not only called this one first but I've already started to name our children, so keep your chi-chis in that enormous bra of yours. *Comprende?*"

"Julesy . . . come on, you know he is not my type. You have nothing to worry about. I would never. Besides, what could a man like that do for me?" she protested. In truth I knew no such thing, since Angie was the newest to our friendship circle by way of an introduction from Blake, so I adhered to a delicate dance with her that I tagged "playfully serious."

"That is the farthest thing from my mind, Ang. I just don't want to have to cut you in front of the future Mr. Jules Sinclair, that's all. Haha."

. . .

In time Tony would admit that he overheard us and was quite flattered by my proprietary declaration of him. By the end of dinner, despite having to share him with the girls, I had a calm about this man that exceeded any anxiety about when he would call or if he would call because I just knew he would. Even if I wasn't sure of how to *be* with one, seeing as though, until this point, I was so used to dating boys. As Blake and Angie headed out the door, Tony placed his hand on my face in a caress that allowed him now to take in the moment and me.

"I didn't plan on meeting you today, Ms. Sinclair, but I would like to know more. How about dinner . . . tomorrow at Odeon?"

# 5

## TONY & JULES

**8:30 p.m.**

WE MET IN Tribeca; our first date setting the stage for everything that was great between us. The conversation was open and intimate, unlike typical first-date small talk. It was akin to a third or fourth date when you know that time is going to be invested in this person, so you go a bit in-depth and open yourself up for a closer look, less afraid of the imperfections they may see. His firsthand experiences mirrored much of what I had only dreamed about at university.

"Yeah, divorce is rough but I came out of it better than most I guess . . . Funny, your escape was the rain, mine was the streets, which just made things worse at home," said Tony. "You know, Jules, if you truly love the smell of the earth after a good rainfall, then you must love Costa Rica. I just got back from there surfing with my brother. The rain forest is amazing. Man, we saw animals unlike anything in the Bronx Zoo. This is our third time there. Have you ever been?"

"No, but I saw a PBS documentary on it last year. It's on my list of must-go-to places," I said.

"Ah, you'll love it. I'll take you," said Tony, to my ears not sounding like an empty gesture but like a heartfelt desire. "It's the best place to get lost and get found in, next to certain parts of Africa. Last year I went to sub-Saharan Africa for a photo shoot and ended up staying a few weeks working with the famine relief to deliver food and vaccines. You?"

"No. I haven't been to the continent yet, but I am an avid supporter of Feed the Children. Okay, *avid* is a little strong. I have supported, would like to do more, and really want to impress you, but it's kinda hard because you have done everything," I said.

"Not true. I've never fallen in love," he said, completing the sentence with a wink, at which we both erupted in laughter. "I can't believe I just said that to you. Did it work? Are you swooning? You are, come on . . . smooth."

With as much seductive sarcasm as I could muster, I replied, "Oh yeah, *something* is seriously rising"—half covering my mouth with my hand to cough out the words—"and it's not the flag in Pamplona but the—" At which we both laughed. "Seriously, don't you ever get tired of the nomadic life and just want a place to call home?"

"On the real, I guess you could say I am a wanderer of sorts. There's so much to explore, and I plan to do all of it," he said. "Besides, being transitory is actually comforting for me. My mom was inconsistent after the divorce, so I learned early on not to get too attached to things or hit the self-destruct button when things get so comfortable that I lose perspective. You learn to adapt. One day you'll reach for it and nothing is there, you know?"

I thought I knew but in truth I had absolutely no idea what he was talking about. I watched the words leave his mouth, heard them in my right ear, and by the time they got to the left I had paraphrased them into an immaculate tale of Scheherazade convincing myself that I was the answer to his wondering.

Every so often the maître d' came over to make sure that "their Tony" was happy, as would friends and neighborhood locals who, like him, considered the Odeon their personal kitchen. I was fascinated watching as he effortlessly transitioned from one to the other; each time never forgetting that I was there and making certain to include me in the conversation or cut a dialogue short when a dim-witted model creature was blatantly trying to blink me invisible.

"I could get used to you at my side, Ms. Sinclair," said Tony.

Officially, he was choosing me. This Sadie Hawkins–esque mentality I reasoned was one of the rare places that Venus and Mars weren't actually so far apart. It's just that women and men approach love and idol worship far differently. As a woman, I acknowledge that I am preconditioned to wait to be selected for the moment "he" will announce to the gallery that I am the most beautiful one in the room. For their part, men—no matter their size, shape, or credit score—seem conditioned to believe that everything they survey is rightfully theirs, be it women or cattle; it is all property, one and the same. The only difference is that cattle can't hold them or build them up when the world around starts to disintegrate. It takes some time before they are ready to hear this truth and fold into a specific woman. I would be foolish to think that I was the first for Tony in this space, but I do believe that I am the most genuine he has encountered, and that in itself could be a frightening proposition over time.

In little to no time we came to know each other's mannerisms so well that the graze of a brow would be a signal to depart, a shortened laugh meant he wanted rescue from an impossibly boring conversation. His hand in the small of my back said, "I'm proud you're mine." Before Tony, I never laughed so much about anything or took myself so lightly. For a while playing Lois Lane to his Superman was enough. But, as much as we were in harmony, there were hiccups that I didn't question, to a great extent because I trusted the strength of our union, until the moments that started as flint sparks erupted into four-alarm fires.

"What are you talking about, Tony? Don't break that! I told you last week that I was meeting Shawn for dinner. I even asked if you wanted to come. Why would I do that if I had something to hide? Why?! Whatever, I guess your boy Jay's word on what he thought he saw is more important than mine."

His quiet moments, the dark ones that were not about waking up late on a Sunday, having coffee, and silently dissecting the paper in bed together—*National Geographic* and *Sports Illustrated* for him, Arts and Style sections of *The New York Times* for me—were the worst.

"Hey, didn't you hear me calling you? What's wrong? How long have you been sitting here? It's past three o'clock," I'd say.

Being at dinner and catching a gaze between him and the waitress, never enough for our friends to notice but just enough for me to feel devalued. My initial thought was always to go quiet and not overreact, but words often found me when we were alone.

"Tell you what, next time I see lipstick anywhere on your person I will be certain not to fall back on the convention of us. You should know better."

Before long I found myself asking him questions I already knew the answers to, only to have him lie to me or avoid the response completely. More nights than I care to admit, I would leave his place in tears and vowing never again. Angrier than necessary at myself for always choosing the wrong corner to try to hail a cab. *Tribeca is a bitch late at night.* And every time we hit a wall he would find a way to reach in and take hold of my heart again. Maybe if I didn't love him as intensely as I did, it would have been easier to make a break sooner.

"Love isn't perfect, Jules. It's not the fairy tale you have worked out in your head. I am trying hard to be *that* man for you, baby, but you have to ride this out with me. I need to know that you will be there."

I was there through everything, even as the tests got harder and harder. I was there when his brother Nathaniel died as they were riding (racing) back from the Hamptons on their bikes. I was there when he said that the recreational white powder was just a temporary situation to take the edge off and was nothing to worry about. I was there long enough to become the enemy so that everything I did to comfort him only infuriated him. I was there for the yelling, the crying, the apologies, and I truly tried to understand it and rationalize that it was not *him*, that he was under great pressure. To my heart's ache I was there when Angie's body held the comfort he needed.

That's the thing about giving a set of keys to your lover; eventually he or she will use them at an unexpected moment. Ours was on a Saturday—October 9, 1996, to be exact, when I received a call from the Conrad Hotel Group in London to join their firm. Tony was the one who gave me the inside information to apply, so it seemed only natural that when they called and offered me the position on a day that was free of any expectations, I would rush to him to talk everything over. And boy, was there a lot to figure out. Could his job be done from London in order to be with me or at least could he split the time since the flight is only five and a half hours across the Atlantic? Should I keep my apartment in NYC or move my things into his? If I were to give up my place, did he want us to get the London flat as a couple with both of our names on the lease? The package they offered sounded good, but what should I counter with? Was the expense package sufficient? Tony held the answers to my future.

. . .

In hindsight it's odd because I sensed my world was crashing before my eyes took in the full scene, but dismissed it. Maybe it was the eternity that it seemed to take traveling from uptown or the uncertainty of what it would mean for us growing to the next level. On entering the main level of his place I smelled a fragrance (freesia and lemon—awful combination if ever there was) that was at once familiar but not readily identifiable. I called his name and immediately upon seeing his form coming down the stairs, I dove right in with my news. I must have been talking a mile a minute while trying to find a chilled bottle of champagne because I didn't initially notice the look on his face or the marks on his back. It was only when I held him again that I felt them accompanied by the unusual warmth of his mouth and that scent (freesia and lemon) in the fold of his neck. This time I didn't need to ask questions. His face was in my hands, so there was no place for his eyes to run in an attempt to escape mine. The story they told me was far more than I could bear, and it was right then that I understood for the first time what real loss was. It was the first moment that I felt I could truly empathize with his losing Nathaniel earlier in the year. I had lost him and unlike the times before, we both knew that I could not take him back, even though I still loved him, and that an ocean between us was the only answer.

It must have been the absence of screaming and dramatics or the unusually long quiet between us, but she called his name and suddenly everything made sense. She was always too eager about any developments about us. I erroneously had become far too open and comfortable in the certainty of Tony and Jules, so I disclosed freely.

"*AN-Tony*, is she gone?"

Well, so much for a long quiet. Somewhere between the first and second landing I met Angie and she met the champagne bottle in my hand. *Damn shame actually now that I think about it—Pierre Jouët rosé was my favorite champagne. I haven't had it since 1996.* All the things that I could not do to him I did to her. Each blow landed only intensified the fury inside. In that moment I understood how someone could take a life, and I would have if he had not grabbed me. I remember him holding me tightly, rocking back and forth. His tears falling down my shoulder, and all I could do was collapse into his arms and mourn us. How odd the whole experience was. When I awoke, we were in the same spot on the floor and in the same cradle position that I so loved to be in with him. Being "in the pocket" is how he always referred to it. I was glad that he didn't wake when I left, for there was nothing else to be said except that I wished we could go back in time and meet all over again, but this time we would be smarter and not hurt each other.

Tony once said, "J, it hurts sometimes to see myself in your eyes. You believe me to be the kind of man that I only aspire to be but fear I will never live up to." Maybe that is why I instinctively held his face in the kitchen, so that he could see my soul and all that he'd destroyed, because in some strange way I knew that it was the only way to reach him. I needed Tony to see what a living death looked like.

I accepted the offer and left for London within the week. My phone met an unfortunate end somewhere along the West Side Highway. Smashing it was the only way I could stop his calls from coming through and my temptation to allow explanation. My office was no longer safe, because he camped out there now in order to explain, so I resigned effective immediately. I left my apartment as is, had my intern forward my clothing, and went to a hotel because I didn't know which of our friends to trust. I walked a lot above Twenty-first Street in the hopes that the city would heal me as it had many times before. But this time she failed me. On the plane I thought of my mother's warning about being mindful of what details one confides in girlfriends about their relationships because instead of celebrating your happiness one will be contemplating how to get what and who you have.

"Baby, watch yourself and these little fast girls you call friends. They aren't happy for you. You better wise up and see who is trying to get what you got."

"Cora, please. My girls are not like that," I said boastfully. "Women today are not like they were back in your day. Besides, Tony would never."

"I prefer when you call me Mommy. Those are the times that I know you really hear the words I am saying to you," said Cora.

"And what if I wanted to stop, hear less. What about then, Cora," I asked, intentionally snarky.

"Nasty little thing you can be sometimes, Julesea. I don't know who you get it from—definitely not from me," said Cora. "Everybody knows the Dutch are extremely civilized people."

# 6

## CLOSURE

### Union Square, 1998

FIRST BITE," SAID Tony, struggling to be accountable in the moment and not divert the gravity of our history entirely with charm. "First bite and I'm sorry for what I did to you, for what I did to us. Jules, if I could . . ."

Feeling my resolve weaken, "I can't do this right now. Not today, I just can't," I said, forcibly releasing myself from his grasp. A rush of uncontrollable trembles started to stir in my chest, only to erupt in my hands. I didn't think I had anymore tears left to cry, but there they were, at the ready and falling freely in front of him.

I've always wondered who those people are that can love someone so deeply and, after a great betrayal, forget that feeling of all-encompassing devotion that was there. I never forgot. I was acutely aware of this disturbing fact whenever a big decision presented itself and my first instinct was to call Tony and get his insight. Our history wallpapered my life, so that in order to breathe, each day I had to place something new and "more important" on a mental Post-it to cover all the pain. Any efforts to peel the paper itself were as futile as the ink now embedded in my skin like a tattoo. Not wanting to lose the moment but seeing that I could not handle all that he needed to say, Tony asked about when I got back into town and if we could have dinner. The tears that escaped were captured by his caress, reminding me of that first night in Greenwich.

For lack of words to save the moment, I closed my eyes to shut him out, get my bearings.

"I have to go," I said and started to walk off. Midstep, the history of us said walking away so abruptly was somehow cowardly and wrong, causing me to pause. Slowly, I turned around to face Tony, still standing there as on the day we first met, with the heavens still shining just for him.

"Breakfast, tomorrow, nine thirty. I'm staying at the Mercer."

Any gesture requiring more of me would have been too much, so I dared not wait for an answer. I knew that no matter what was on his schedule, he would be there. The only thing I didn't know was what I expected, what I needed. Foolishly, I believed I could sashay down memory lane, to all the places Tony and I used to go, and not encounter any of our ghosts. But that, again, is not life and definitely not indicative of *the shit that only happens to Jules*. In some ways I guess the moment is fitting, Manhattan is after all only thirteen miles long and most everyone I know resides below Fourteenth Street. Peering at my watch primarily for somewhere to rest my eyes and resist the urge to look back, I realize it is approaching 3 p.m. My meeting with Michael is at 8 p.m., and puffy eyes and a broken heart do not make a good first impression.

There is no city as amazing as New York. Instead of crumbling on the walk back to the Mercer, I found my stride. The air that before felt cold and biting now felt refreshing. Something outside of myself that reminded me to be in the moment, not in a past that has been written and is at best just a bundle of memories of intangibles. Back at the hotel, a hot bath with my special blend of coconut and lavender bath salts was definitely in order, followed by a quick once-over to make sure that there were no chipped nails, no stray eyebrows, or that telltale mustache that had started to sprout immediately as I blew out the candles on my last birthday cake. If all was good, then I could treat myself to a disco nap and pray the last few hours away.

# 7

## Carly's

**W**ITH THE EXCEPTION of two oversize gilded doors, the simple exterior of Carly's underscored its decadent Hollywood Regency décor meets members-only British club interior. Moments after entering, I was greeted warmly by the hostess, who while requisite supermodel Amazonian gorgeous was further along in years, more like an Iman-type from one of those ravaged African countries that possesses some of the most beautiful humans ever to grace the earth, Somalia or Ethiopia. Her generous nature was not reserved solely for me. There were a few patrons ahead of me, and she was quite accommodating. *Beyond fierce is the Old Guard of glamazons.* Hearing that I was to see Michael, she proceeded to escort me to the main dining room, which was accessible either by twenty or so steps descending into the most stylishly outfitted room I'd seen in some time or by a glass elevator that equally guaranteed you saw everything and were seen by everyone. Deep shades of mahogany, tobacco, and camel furnishings in various luxurious fabrications and skins accented with variations of jade and ivory marble and intricate moldings comprised the room's seating. A stage in the round was the room's nucleus, thereby making every table a great one. The entire layout demanded that I take a moment on the stairs to absorb it all. For the briefest moment I felt as if it were all for me. Immediately I felt ready for my *Sunset Boulevard*-esque close-up. If Michael concocted such an entrance to impress me, it's working.

The hostess, having reached the basin only to notice me stationary, asked, "Ms. Sinclair, is there a problem?" I shook my head no but had yet to move. "Intoxicating, isn't it? If you will follow me." She was right, *intoxicating* was the perfect word.

The room seats about 250 and yet it manages to feel extremely intimate and inviting. On approach I was taken aback to see my table empty. With such an entrance, I expected to arrive at a filled booth greeted by Michael Kipps himself in the midst of an amazing story, surrounded by an admiring court hanging on his every word—but that was not the case. Reluctantly, I accepted my seat as a party of one in a packed restaurant at a time when the last thing I needed was to be alone with my thoughts. After a few uncomfortable moments, I started to regret not wearing my *actually I am not alone but here for an important meeting* T-shirt in order to deflect a few pity-filled stares directed my way. Under different circumstances, I could have given my *watch your man NOT me* vibe, but not tonight, not after seeing Tony and knowing that I would have to face him again tomorrow.

"Ma'am, a Macallan 15, neat," said the waiter as he placed the drink in from of me.

"Actually, no. I didn't order anything yet," I replied, taken aback briefly, "but a scotch would be perfect right about now."

"Yes, compliments of Mr. Kipps. Would you like something else?"

"No. This is fine. Thank you."

Watching him go, I sat there invisibly scratching my head as it dawned on me that Michael Kipps knew far more about me than I'd assumed. Without further hesitation, I took a full sip of the scotch that had been gifted to me. To feel something stronger than the thoughts I was fighting to suppress was highly welcome.

In truth, the disco nap did not help. I was in need of a double but feared turning into a blubbering wreck by the time Michael joined me. Normally, handling my liquor is not a problem. I am well aware of my limits and always mindful to have water between drinks. Actually, I consider the fact that I am not a sad or angry drunk in the rare moments that I take it there to be one of my best traits. Modern Girl Achievements, I call it. At my worst I am quiet and contemplative. Tonight, however, any extra fermented assistance could render me an emotional nutter, so my current plan is to nurse this one drink all evening. Tonight I need to dazzle and convince this man that the continued media development of his business would best flourish under my direction.

"Ms. Sinclair, I hope you are in the mood for a great show"—and with that Michael Thurmond Kipps finally showed himself. Ignoring the formality of a handshake, he slid into the booth alongside me. No sooner did Michael sit down than Alyson Williams, jazz and soul songstress, appeared onstage. Like the clientele of Carly's, Alyson was a New York fixture, known as much for her onstage presence as for being the daughter of legendary trumpeter Bobby Booker. Her personality was as flamboyant and colorful as the black crushed velvet bodysuit with a cheetah cape, matching pillbox hat, and oversize gold jewelry she wore. On the strength of a single note, she could express love's rise and fall with inexplicable clarity.

The performance list at Carly's is not published, so it is the luck of the draw as to who will be performing on any given night. When you call to make a reservation, the only thing that will be confirmed is the time your table will be available and that there will be live music. Quite a useful tool if you have the Rolodex to make each night a showstopper. You are all but guaranteeing that every columnist, "It Kid," society heir, and social climber will be present nightly. For there is nothing more tragic to a self-proclaimed man (or woman)-about-town than not to be in the nexus of the most exclusive goings-on. Even if they are not genuine fans of the music, they are devotees of the scene. *It is intoxicating, remember.*

Throughout the first half of Alyson's performance, I focused entirely on Michael. Yes, in person he was all that the gossips made him out to be: commanding presence, handsome, stylish, and tremendously confident. His choice of dress was understated yet impeccably bespoke. A few times he caught me eyeing him. I could see that he took some pleasure in watching me scramble to look elsewhere when caught. At a moment in "Not on the Outside," he leaned over and said, "I'm the most open cat you will ever meet, so don't try so hard to dissect me. At least not during our first meeting." And with that he affixed a firm squeeze midway up my thigh, just high enough to be indecent. *Oh, great. Does this ever stop?* For this I did not try to avert my gaze but demanded his so that he could see that those male power plays did not intimidate me.

All too often it seems that to be a successful woman in business and not be derailed by unwanted advances, we are to assume the posture of men in an attempt to be invincible—and our femininity invisible. I rejected that doctrine from my first foray into the business world. Yes, my success is a result of the feminist movement, and I appreciate all that was done. However, I reject the belief that every advance by a man in a professional environment is a three-alarm fire sign to cry foul. More times than not I have found it to be a weeding-out process that is part of the game of big business.

As women we are still screaming to be treated as equals, so the easiest—albeit most infantile—way, it seems, for some men to determine if we are ready to play with the big boys is to go directly for the gaping wound of sexual discomfort. *I mean, hell, why don't you just put a Coke can on the table and call me Anita?* The key is how you handle yourself in that moment. Save it—don't waste time trying to explain yourself, because it will fall on deaf ears or be interpreted as whining. Don't bristle either. Hold firm and assert your power with a smirk and a "no" head shake, then move his hand if it lingers and redirect his attention to a better candidate. If they are the daft type, defuse with a quick but serious joke, or mention his wife. And for heaven's sake DO NOT fool yourself into thinking that your sweet nectar will change his life and therefore send you skyrocketing up the corporate ladder of success. It won't. Daddy told me this countless times over the years. "Jules," he'd say, "the only ting dat type of ting will get a woman is a badt reputation."

Leaning into Michael close enough to be within earshot while maintaining eye contact so that even in this dim light he could understand the magnitude of my intent, I said, "You do know it would never work, don't you? I would just be dating you for your money, your power, and social position, only to leave you as soon as a bigger branch presented itself."

Michael smirked. "I like you, Sinclair. You got gumption." Then he patted my knee. "Indeed, I can respect that."

After Alyson's first set, we talked about his business. He spoke about feeling alive in Carly's like it was what he was supposed to do with his life all along and the modeling was just a step to get there. For so long he had been growing other people's wealth, either in editorial, by attending events, or with commercials. Then one day it occurred to him that if his face and name were this valuable for everybody else, then they would be just as valuable for ventures of his own. Now he wants Carly's to become a global destination. For the most part I listened attentively, because it was clear that he enjoyed having a captive audience that allowed him to do all the talking. All in all it was quite informative and impressive. In a much different way than with Tony—in Michael I saw a man I could learn from.

At the start of the second set we began to eat, and just in time too. *I never did get to have that falafel or enjoy the remainder of the zucchini slices from earlier.* I ordered heartily; a beet and goat cheese salad to start, with a petite filet, twice-baked potato, and asparagus for an entrée. Now it seemed Michael's turn to not-so-discreetly check me out. Unbeknownst to me, my ravenous appetite impressed him. *I guess heartache and famine do have their benefits in the right circumstances.* Through bites and head bobs to Alyson's singing, we exchanged some marketing ideas about the restaurant and debated who was a better baller, Vince Carter or Allen Iverson. He was delusional even to have uttered Carter's name, and I let him know it. At that he belted out a laugh that was so robust, even Alyson took notice midway through a song.

The night for me ended around midnight, and despite the time difference I didn't feel like turning in just yet. As Michael walked me to the door, he asked if I could come back tomorrow evening at six o'clock. He wanted to actually see the media strategy I spoke of and give me a proper tour of his burgeoning empire. Next steps in place, I climbed into the back of a taxi and directed the driver to the hotel. For all the things in my life that don't go the way I desire, there are gems—like tonight—that go better than I could ever imagine. The trick for me is to get better at compartmentalizing the storms, thereby always leaving me an open box to identify a great, unexpected moment. This was such a moment. I wanted to savor it, so I rerouted the driver up to Central Park through Times Square and back down Park Avenue so I could let New York know that, while I may have left for a moment, I didn't run away completely. I just needed some time to discover who I was outside its embrace.

# 8

## LAST GOOD-BYES

FOR THE BRIEFEST moment upon awaking, I forgot where I was and how my day was starting. *Breakfast with ex.* Inasmuch as there was immense unresolved pain in the anxiety I felt, everything within me wanted to see him and hear his reasons. I needed closure. Over time I had become equipped in handling that dull pain that never really seemed to go away, the twinge of jealousy and subsequent dismissal that I felt when young love was before me. All the darts and daggers became friends. And while intentional avoidance may not have been the recommended therapeutic approach, I found it useful. I had learned to rebuild my life bit by bit, and in doing so I pushed our relationship so far down that it seemed mythical. Today that fable would leap off the page and become all too real. I just wish I knew if the ending would reflect American movies, with no collateral damage and a neat little bow, or French ones, all bleak and undefined.

8:15 a.m.—The snooze alarm goes off a second time, forcing me to finally concede defeat, withdrawing the covers from around my head but still refusing to open my eyes. I fumble beneath the empty pillow on my left, searching for the mobile or, as I have come to begrudgingly refer to it, "the only bed partner I've had for the past two years."

You have three new voice messages:

Message One: It's Cora. Did you just send me to voice mail? I would hate to think you are standing there looking at your phone, ignoring me.

Message Two: Julesea, why is your phone ringing like that? Are you in the States? Call Mommy.

Message Three: Julesea, it's Cora. Call your father, he is worried.

*My word, what am I going to do with this woman?* Against my better judgment I dial her.

"Hi, Cora—"

"Well, look who finally got around to calling back," said Cora. "You know your father was worried sick about you."

"Was he now? *Good morning,* Cora. I just got your messages," I say.

"How is that possible? I called you at least three times, Julesea. What good is having a phone if you don't answer it? I will never understand. Is this what they are doing over there these days—not picking up the phone?"

I couldn't help but chuckle at her theatrics. "No, that's not what *they* are doing. I am sorry but I was exhausted having gotten to New York on the red-eye and—"

"New—What are you talking about? What are you doing in New York and why am I just hearing about it? Is this keeping secrets from me going to be a habit or . . . ?" *Oh, if only she knew, but let's not complicate things now.*

"Please, stop. It's far too early and there is no caffeine in my system yet. I'm here for an interview but didn't want to tell anyone."

"Well, I'm sad to hear that I am just *anyone* to you," said Cora, combining all of her thoughts into one stealth interrogation. "What interview? Did you get fired from Conrad? What happened? Who are you meeting with? Does Daddy know?"

"No! I did not get fired. I am meeting with this guy Michael Kipps about helming the PR division of his supper club, and no, Daddy does not know, so there is no need for you to feel left out."

"Umph. So you are leaving London to work at a restaurant? What kind of sense does that make? Are you mad, Julesea?!" shrieked Cora.

"A supper club, Mommy!"—*Why am I yelling?*—"You know, the kind of place with cool singers and nicely dressed people. Trust me, you'd like it," I said. "Listen, I promise to tell you everything later, but I really have to go now. Ton-y . . ." forcing the last syllable to silently escape my lips . . . "To a meeting downstairs and I'm not even dressed." Whoa, that was close. Even when we were dating and things were good, Cora struggled to tolerate Tony, always professing that *something about that boy wasn't right.* After our breakup she allowed the floodgates of wrath to open up, never missing an opportunity to highlight the flags she saw or the warnings she gave, all of which I was too naïve to comprehend. I couldn't bear to hear the lashing she would give me, if she knew that he and I were meeting in a matter of minutes. Not today. I need to be as clear and connected to my feelings as possible, not echoing Cora's accusatory yet well-intentioned sentiments.

"Umph. Is this a good opportunity?" she asked.

"I think so," I said, acutely aware of not giving too much for her to dissect.

"And it would put you back in the States, yes? Instead of thousands of miles away? . . . That's good, I guess."

"Yes," I said.

"I just don't know why it has to be in New York. That city is nothing good for you. Just your luck, you'll move back and run into that good-for-nothing wannabe ragamu—." *My goodness, was there any pleasing this woman?!*

"CORA!" I yelled. "I have to go. I will ring you later, promise. Kiss Daddy for me. Love you, must go. Bye," I said, removing the phone from my ear but not actually hanging it up until I heard her mumbling subside. Oh, how I have wanted to hang up on her over the years but I never can. She's an absolute nutter and the very foundation that makes me believe that nothing is out of reach, although I will never tell her that much.

Finally dressed and taking full inventory of myself one last time in the mirror, I think about the kind of woman who I would like to actually be (not a composition of the flaws and unfulfilled dreams that confront me every so often):

*I long to be the woman whom is loved passionately and deeply by a successful man who can provide for me in all ways that matter in this life. A woman who realizes that happiness is not a choice between this or that but an accumulation of moments experienced and shared. I want to be the woman who knows when to let a love go that existed in rose-colored glasses, only to walk into a true love that requires no special frames to be alluring. I want to be the woman whom he chooses to remain faithfully monogamous to and committed to even when things aren't going smoothly. I want to be the woman whose eyes hold his future.*

. . .

Coming down the stairs, into Mercer's subterranean restaurant, I saw that Tony had selected one of the more intimate seating areas. This made me regret not having peeled myself out of bed sooner or speaking to Cora too long, at least I could have controlled the proximity of our bodies. Instead I now had to deal with the forced intimacy created by the booth he selected, which only heightened my anxiety. Seeing me approach, he stands. A proper gentleman. Despite Cora's misgivings, his mama did something right; he always walked on the side of advancing traffic and ordered for me. He knew my food allergies to shellfish and soy. He never complained about my desire always to see scary movies, only to scream and jump from the opening titles to the end credits. Things like that demonstrated why I thought he was a keeper and why then I felt so lucky. In reality, however, nice packaging doesn't always mean that you will like what is inside.

Unsteadily, Tony took the cup from the waitress. "Morning, I ordered you some hot chocolate with a shot of espresso. You're still drinking that, right? Of course you are. It's cold outside. It must be cold in London, huh . . . You look really good, Jules. I couldn't believe my eyes yesterday when I crossed the street and saw you. At first I thought it was someone who looked like you. I've mistaken quite a few girls for you over the years, and then I saw you do the 'first bite of zucchini loaf' dance"—stopping to mimic me with one hand in the air and a heavy-metal rocker head bob—"I watched you for a while, you know, frozen. I didn't know what I should say, I was just so glad to see you. I miss you. Can I say that, that I miss you?" His nerves obviously forcing him to blurt out his confession all in one breath.

I had forgotten what it was like to see him less than composed and how it affected me, so I watched and listened, taking him in. All the while feeling that when it was time for me to speak my truth I would know what to say.

". . . I fucked up, J. I hurt you something bad I know that. There's just no way to make that shit right. I would, you know . . . if I could." Despite the great effort he was making to hold my gaze, I needed to look elsewhere, electing instead to watch his hands dance frantically around the contours of the white linen napkin. "That morning when I woke up and you were gone, everything stopped being a game. It all became too real."

Shifting uncomfortably in my seat, I fought to hold myself at bay and not move to wipe the dam of tears threatening to break over the rims of his eyes. A part of me found this show of emotion endearing. Not in the way that would make all that had occurred vanish, but it validated the fact that I wasn't in this nightmare alone. For so long, in my quiet moments I envisioned him and Angie moving along happily with their lives together and toasting to my broken heart. They would have sex in the bed that he and I had picked out together. In the morning he would gently caress the base of her stomach, as he did mine each day, and kiss behind her ear. Every beautiful memory that we had, in my pain, I extracted my image and replaced it with hers.

"Are you still with her?" I demanded, unable to contain the residual bits of anger that refused to be tempered.

"No! Of course not. I have not seen that girl since that day." Off my disbelieving look he continued, "I promise you, Jules. I have not seen her in years. I did call to make certain that she was okay and made arrangements to cover any medical costs she incurred, but that was all. Believe me."

"Yes," I said, *and I did.*

"She wasn't the problem, Jules, and neither was the other shit. I was the problem. I wanted everything, to have you on my arm and keep the pretense that my life brought. Every time I felt us fold into each other it scared the shit out of me. Automatically I would check myself and run scenarios of how we would end. At first I thought I was crazy and set my mind not to fuck us up. I felt you would leave me at some point if I didn't get it right, so I wanted to be 'that guy,' not just for you but for me as well. It just all came too soon and I wasn't ready, I guess. I didn't want to choose."

Feeling the urge to defend myself, I fired back, "I never asked you to choose, Tony. I didn't even know there was a choice to be made. I never held you back. I encouraged every dream you had, and even when things were tough I pushed through for you, for us."

"Well, damn, I guess you were perfect, some kind of martyr or something, and I was a big fuckup, just lucky to have you, right? I know that's what everyone thought. . . . That's what I thought."

"Let's not do this. You know better. Don't spew your venom at me and I won't do it to you. We both messed this up, Tony. We were both guilty of some crazy idol worship of the other and for all of our intelligent 'ride or die' shit we couldn't make it work and people got hurt. I got hurt . . . and so did you. I am still hurting. I think of you more than I care to admit and I mourn us still every day. I don't want to hurt anymore. I don't want you to hurt any-more." The enormous lump that had returned to my throat was still there but felt manageable. "I want to let go."

We sat talking for hours about things, some reflections about the good times that continued to haunt us both but mostly about the mistakes and do-overs that were impossible to recapture. I don't recall much of the former now because in retrospect they were minor details. What I know for certain is that at some point we were holding hands like old times, crying forgiveness tears in a very public place that held many memories for us. Standing with him at the corner, saying good-bye, I still felt the full impact of us. Had he verbalized all the things I needed to hear? I would have no way of knowing this until time gifts me with perspective. For now I know that I heard the things I wanted to hear. More to the point, I know that I had enough to sleep for the first time in two years through the night—but is it enough to free my heart and love again? A final embrace and Tony walked away toward Broadway. Even now he was the finest man my eyes had ever laid on.

Turning to reenter the hotel, I hear, "Jules Sinclair. *Ti amo, baby, ti amo.*" People on the street must have thought Tony a crazy man, judging by the way they rushed past him. For the last time I cried for us, this time happy tears, and waved good-bye.

"*Ti amo per sempre,*" I whispered loud enough for only my soul to hear.

# 9

## AND YOU ARE?

**M**ICHAEL'S NOT HERE. Let me buy you a drink while you wait," said the man standing behind the host stand at Carly's.

Had I not been fresh off the emotional roller coaster that was Anthony Mason or been so intently focused on landing this job, I would've noticed that this guy was absolutely swoonworthy; mid-thirties, I'd say, with dark blond hair and hypnotic ocean-blue eyes trapped behind the kind of long, sweeping lashes that women, myself included, buy Great Lash mascara to re-create. He was a proper mix of boyish-meets-rugged with a disposition and precise mannerisms hinting of an Ivy League–New England pedigree, possibly, by way of Boston, maybe even spent some time abroad—but not entirely sure, given the limited exchange. Immaculately dressed in a gray three-piece suit and winter-white shirt with mother-of-pearl cuff links, paired with an understated but noticeable vintage Rolex Submariner, and finished with apropos camel Brioni suedes. *If I were looking, this is what I would have noticed—but I'm not.* Like Michael, he seemed to stand just north of six feet two because, even in my Sergios, he towered over me. The circumference of his noticeable egotistical sense of entitlement on the other hand was immeasurable, reminding me of a particularly colorful and *equally gorgeous* emerging Savile Row tailor who, with little to no effort at all, manages to consume 90 percent of the oxygen from any room he is within a three-block radius of. *Obviously, given my asthmatic childhood, it is fair to conclude that we should not mix particularly well—yet despite this insignificant little detail he is the prototype for the beloved of my "grown woman imagined," but I digress.*

I ask current cocky man of mystery for the time to ensure I was not confused about the hour only to realize that I was correct. "He said six o'clock. Do you know how long he will be?" I asked, unknowingly biting my bottom lip as he stared at me with an amused look on his face, making me all too aware that I was at a disadvantage. "Did I say something particularly funny? Maybe he left a message for me. Can you check? My name is Jules Sinclair and Michael said for me to meet him here." I continued feeling myself getting a little flustered, and rightly so. I felt bare and exposed, like he wanted something from me that I was in no position to give or even entertain.

Satisfied with himself for having gotten unsolicited information, he replied, "And so you are. Michael unfortunately is not here. Par for the course, really. However, when he does come, you will have to wait until he and I are finished." Devilishly smiling to reveal a slight upturn indentation on the left corner of his lip, the kind that frequently results from a childhood sports injury, he said, "I mean, it is only fair given I was here first. Now, where were we? Ah yes, I'm buying you a drink while we wait. Between sips you can ask me anything you want, assuming, of course, I have piqued your curiosity as you have mine, in which case don't be bashful, ask me anything."

Debating whether or not to take him seriously, in any manner, even briefly, I found him impossible to resist, and that irritated me all the more. "You dropped something," I said, causing him to pat his pockets, then look around the floor to uncover what could have possibly fallen. After a moment or two of allowing him to search in vain and feeling quite satisfied with myself for having leveled the terrain, I said, "Your *r*. Where are you from? I hear, what, Boston—Toronto?"

"And so I did. You've got a good ear," said cocky mystery man before ushering me by the elbow toward the bar area.

Once seated, he slid his chair uncomfortably close to mine and asked the bartender for a Pimm's cup and an herbal tea. "You're meeting with Michael because of why?" I asked, thinking that he could very well be here interviewing for the same position as me. I mean, let's be real, men only dress like this in magazines or for job interviews, so I am guessing it is the latter.

With a slight pivot of the head in my direction only to stop before facing me, he pauses for maximum effect before responding. *Seriously, I have never!* "And here I was hoping that you would want to know about me as a person. Such is my lot, I guess. Women see me in this package and somehow it's still not enough. It's always who do I know? What do I do? What can I do for them? When am I going to be enough? When?"

For a split second I was taken aback and thought that just maybe this guy might be slightly off. That was until the bartender placed the tea down in front of me and started to laugh. "Are you shining me?" I asked. "You said to ask you anything and so I did."

"Correction, I said to ask me all the questions you wanted, assuming that I had piqued your curiosity as you have mine. The expectation being that we would get to know each other better, not make another man the focus of our relationship, which is never a good move, by the way. It's tantamount to us being on a first date and talking about some dreadful ex who broke your heart and slept with your best friend. Is that what you want?" he asked, lowering his head in resignation, leaving me speechless again at the bull's-eye. "Sadly I see I was mistaken and find myself in this all alone. I guess it's better that I know these shortcomings of yours now instead of later when—" Before he could finish his soliloquy, Michael blew in.

"Marcus, sorry to keep you waiting. I got stuck uptown with the missus—you know. Jules, hang tight. Have a drink. Raymond, take care of her." He said all this in one sweeping movement that not only took my asthma-inducing companion but also left me in limbo to wait on him for an undetermined amount of time.

The long dial on my watch indicated that it was about twenty minutes to seven o'clock, so I picked up my phone to ring my friend Jessica to notify her that I would most likely not make dinner but surely be there for dessert. Tonight was the big group introduction, as she had recently started dating this finance guy and was now ready to have him meet her friends for final approvals.

Removing Marcus's drink, the bartender said, "You should not have canceled. You'll make dinner, maybe not the apps, but you'll make the entrée for sure." He was a slender gentleman with soulful eyes and the most amazing unblemished deep mocha skin that, like my father's, made his age hard to pinpoint—but I'm guessing midforties.

"Really, what else can you tell me? Do I have this job? . . . Am I really doing the right thing in coming back to this freaking city now? Was this the right suit to wear? Am I falling apart with a total stranger or is this just a really bad dream?" I said, sick with anxiety. "Oh God, please don't tell me that I am sitting in front of you totally nude right now!"

With little more than a raised eyebrow to convey that he was well equipped to deal with the brand of meltdown I was displaying, he offered, "Maybe I should put a little something in that tea to warm you up. Rum?"

"Sorry, it's been one of those days, you know. I do that, tend to ramble on when I'm out of sorts."

"It's all right, drink this. It won't put hair on your chest but it'll give you courage," he said, sliding the improved drink in front of me. His easy demeanor had an immediate impact on me, which I guess is the prerequisite for bartenders, especially since my grasp on reality was still not as strong as I would have liked it to be. From the enormous mirror hanging over the bar I watched as Michael and *Marcus* conducted their meeting/interview at a table behind me, the emptiness of the restaurant enabling me to hear every fifth word or so of their conversation.

After a few minutes it was obvious that *this* Marcus character was not some random guy trying to steal the job I had claimed. His interaction with Michael was far too casual. Although, the more I studied Marcus, the more I couldn't shake the feeling that I knew him, like maybe we had met before through someone significant, but for the moment I could not place him. Shortly thereafter they stood up, did the obligatory man-hug, and said good-bye. I chuckled to myself slightly, a combination of disbelief and disappointment, in seeing Marcus exit. That after all the work he had put in earlier to get my attention, now he made no effort to come over and say a proper good-bye. Well . . . *Total wanker.*

"Jules, thanks so much for waiting. Did Marcus try to pick you up?" asked Michael, and didn't wait for my response. *I could see now that this would be an underlying theme of our relationship and declined to accept it.* "Of course he did. Don't worry, he's harmless. Besides, you're a good girl and he wouldn't know what to do with someone like you. Hell, I didn't at his age and let me tell you I met many a good girl," said Michael, releasing the same hearty laugh as last night. *Officially, they were friends.*

In lieu of the formal meeting I understood we were to have, which was why I came equipped with three Kinko's-printed PowerPoint copies of the proposal, Michael gave me a tour of the restaurant that included a state-of-the-art kitchen that would make Jacques Pépin proud. The offices, to my delight, were not located in the basement or behind the kitchen as they often are but on several upper levels on the other side of the elevator, accessible only by key card. The rehearsal and recording studios with discreet sleeping chamber were located in the bowels of the building—*so very Marvin Gaye of him.* He introduced me to the staff on hand. The Imanesque hostess I now knew as Lidia. Michael's girl Friday, Simone; at first glance one can see that she is highly efficient and not in the

least bit fuckable (i.e., threatening to an aware girlfriend or insecure wife): tight bun, kitten heels, bare face with the exception of
some rouge and a mouth that seemed turned down even when she
was smiling. Clearly the answer to why she had been with him longer than any woman in his life aside from his mother. Next there
was chef Grayson McClovoy, a James Beard winner who preferred
diner food to the five-star meals that were his trademark. By the
time he formally introduced me to Raymond, the gravel-voiced
bartender, I felt as if we were old friends. And like a proud papa
who was too easily distracted, Michael announced that this was his
humble little core team and he was sure I would fit right in.

"I want to open the summer season strong with some Brazilian
Corcovado shit while those other motherfuckers are on holiday,
you get me? I'll need you set up in the office by next month . . .
Walk with me," said Michael as he moved toward the lobby. "I won't
be here, but I am reachable to you through any number of privacy-
killing methods of technology—just don't video-conference me. I
hate the way I look on that thing. If for any reason you can't get
me, go to Simone. She actually runs this place. The missus and I
will be in the Mediterranean. All right, that about does it. See you
in a few weeks."

"Michael, Miiichael," I said as I struggled to gather my things
and follow him to the elevator, only to have the doors close in my
face with him smiling on the other side like the Cheshire cat.

Alone, standing at the base of the stairs, breathless, I ran aloud
the catalog of unanswered questions in my head: "What just happened? Did he just offer me the job—but how? What is my salary? Oh my gawd, who can pack up their life and move to another
country in two weeks? I mean honestly, who? Me! Oh shit, am I
really doing this?!" *I may have been caught off guard but clearly not
lost for words.*

"You sure do ask a lot of questions," said Raymond. "That's
Mike. You'll get used to him. I have worked for some of the biggest

and best but he is the perfect mix of Sinatra and Dean. By comparison everyone else is a Bishop or Lawford."

Surely, I must have looked at Raymond like he had two heads. What the hell is he doing talking about the Rat Pack when the limbo that is my life just got a little crazier and no one is forthcoming with the most precious details of HOW? I gather my things and grunt something inaudible that was meant to be "Good-bye and thank you for the tea" before racing up the stairs to try to get one last moment with Michael. Much to my dismay he was already being abducted by a bustling set of diners. Having canceled my dinner with Jessica, I decided to return to the hotel and just come back to the restaurant around 6 p.m. tomorrow for details.

. . .

When the state of your life is undergoing great reconstruction, the most desolate place to be is a sparsely decorated hotel. *Oh, excuse me, contemporary-decorated hotel.* Aside from Jessica, the only people to know I was in town were Blake and Richard, both of whom were unavailable tonight. And even with time to spare I didn't want to show up at Jessica's midcourse, only to interrupt the flow of her dinner. Thankfully I always travel with candles, bath salts, a classic movie, and a cashmere blanket Cora gave me one Christmas—you know, all the essential accoutrements to make any place feel homey. Opening the door to my room, I was greeted by the most decadent floral scent before laying eyes on the large bouquet of tulips sitting on the coffee table. *Ah, Tony. It's just like him to do this. Sending an arrangement of my favorite flowers was a beautiful bow of sorts to our story. Ending of a relationship or not, they are gorgeous.* There had to be at least fifty stems of various marigolds, purples, whites, and pinks. I could not help but smile and closed my eyes for a moment to just enjoy meaning enough to someone to evoke such a gesture. Obviously, I was wrong:

*Welcome to the team, Jules. Call Simone to work out your move.*
                                                        *MK*

Okay!!!!! This is one of *those* days (and nights) apparently. You know the kind, where you feel that everything was already in motion before you even got out of bed and no matter how hard you try to catch up you remain behind everyone else. So you resign yourself to accept that the deck is in fact stacked in another's favor and, although you may want to dissect Sun Tzu's army ball one soldier at a time, there are far too many of them and only one of you. I won't even ask how it is that Michael knew my favorite flowers were tulips, because it was obvious that I would be grasping at straws. *When the hell did my life turn into a Cathy comic strip where I'm frazzled and scratching my head?*

Next to the flowers sat an oversize white envelope thick enough to hold a contract. Given all of the surprises of the last twenty-four hours, I was apprehensive—*okay, downright panicked*—to look inside immediately; for all I knew, the results of my recent gyno exam might have suddenly been telegraphed across the pond, made their way to Michael's office, and now he was the bearer of my female news. Who was to say? So, instead of opening it, I returned it to the exact same position I found it, tiptoed to the bar, poured myself a sizable glass of wine, and ordered room service. My food came quickly, allowing me to focus on something other than the magic envelope that had mysteriously levitated and found its way to the bed under the left pillow next to my phone. Soon all that remained were a few spoonfuls of butternut squash soup with truffles, a half-eaten burger, and an ivory puddle that once was apple pie à la mode. All in all my belly was filled and my spirits soothed but my mind was a jumbled, singularly focused, erratic mess. I needed to know what was in that envelope. Was Michael making me an offer competitive enough that I could make this move back to New York in style and silence any potential objections from Cora in the process? Or would I be forced to exist on a salary far lower than what I am currently making with the Conrad Hotel Group, and have to live in some modified efficiency (translation: small enough that I could shower and flip bacon on the stove simultaneously); or a "conventional" one-bedroom walk-up in the sketchiest part of Alphabet City that would force me to wear track shoes on any given day in order to avoid stepping on a stray heroin needle or coke blade? *I need this!*

All my life it seems I have been adjusting to everyone else's playbook of priorities and deferred dreams. I went to undergrad at BU (Boston University) because my dad said he had the best years of his life there in grad school. I came to New York the first time to live out my mother's dream, because she was deprived of her Mary Tyler Moore life by getting married and starting a family so young, a not-so-little detail she mentioned more than a few times over the years, namely when Daddy would criticize her spending. I went to London to escape Tony and, in the process, found me. Now I just want to return home, on my terms, wiser and more aware than before.

Using my soiled napkin to wipe the remnants of mayonnaise and ketchup off the butter knife, I sliced the envelope open while saying the most pitiful prayer ever heard: "Dear God, I promise that if you make this offer good I'll never ask for anything else . . ." With only one eye open, I scanned the letter for the important points. "HOLY SHIT!!" I screamed, loud enough, without question, for adjoining rooms to hear. Not only was the offer good, less than $10K or so difference from where I expected my raise to be, but it came with serious perks. It allotted for proper moving expenses, an apartment in the city for the term of my employment (with an option to rent it at fair market value should I no longer work at Carly's), and a sizable entertainment account to be used for any number of things. Officially, I am moving back to NYC and, unlike my last move, this time I am not running away from something or someone. I'm running to my future!

Riding high on the fumes of possibility, I was unable to sleep, so I stayed up making lists of all the things I could do over the next two days. Priority No. 1 is to get reacquainted with the city by doing all of the things I had once found a volume of excuses not to do when I lived here or missed when I was in exile: visit the Met, have a banana smoothie at New World Café on Columbus, visit the Museum of Natural History, walk down to Coliseum Bookstore, take in an outdoor movie at Bryant Park, go to the Paris Theatre, and even hop the Staten Island Ferry to people-watch while getting a glimpse at Lady Liberty. *Shoot, I just may go over to Ellis Island—if it's open.* On Saturday I would dine at Cafeteria with a hardy group of friends and then head out for a night of dancing as if there were no tomorrow. Sunday I reserve as the perfect day to get lost in a marathon brunch down the street at the Cub Room with Richard, one of my nearest and dearest, before heading to JFK for my return.

In addition to being one of the best political speechwriters in the business, Richard Boulton has the distinct honor of being the only Ivy League gay Black American card-carrying Republican I know. *I mean really, who in their right mind is not pro-Clinton right now? Bill or Hillary? Really, who?* His heart and capacity to love is more expansive than anyone else's I know. In the tough times he was always there for me and never outwardly judged my decision to stay with Tony during the initial onslaught of not-so-perfect moments that was clear to everyone else but me. When I escaped to the hotel to hide from Tony, Richard was the only person I called. Not to mention that the man can cook his ass off. *It's a fact.* In the beginning, when I was trying to impress Tony with my culinary skills, it was actually a Richard Prescott Boulton home-cooked meal, prepared in my kitchen of course, so that I could have evidence, by way of dirty pots and delicious smells filling the space.

I remember his first words at the start of dessert. "Damn, girl, my mama don't even make cobbler this good." He bakes cakes from scratch and spends his weekends in a place named Mantoloking. *I mean, have you ever?* I worship him and needed to bask in his goodness.

"Darling, when are you coming home? London is absolutely dreadful and the men are even worse. Come home. We miss you. I can't continue to carry the reins of fabulousness all by myself. Well, actually I can, but I don't want to," Richard said at brunch.

"May thirteenth," I said. "I'm just going back to give notice and pack my things!"

"I'll drink to that," said Richard.

"Of course!"

# 10

## HOLLAND PARK

**W**HAT IS THE deal with that five-and-a-half-hour flight that just knocks me forever on my ass? Standing in what had to be the slowest of the Customs and Immigration queues at Heathrow did not help matters as my head was splitting, which could have had something to do with the two rasmopolitans and two celebratory Bellinis that Richard and I had before my airport transport arrived. Too much sugar, *I need to lie down.*

My flat is located in Holland Park, in a whitewashed Victorian town house, and of all the things that I do genuinely treasure about London it's at the top of the list. When I first settled on the location it was with the expectation that I needed something calm and far removed from my previous existence with Tony. Whereas we were modern and fast-paced, I wanted old-world and serene, the kind of location that would allow me to get lost in some well-deserved soulful moments. The interior had been restored to the original architecture, with intricate crown moldings and expansive built-in bookcases in the main room and bedroom. The only drawback is that it was a fourth-floor walk-up. One would think that coming from New York I would be used to that, but my building then had an elevator. *What can I say?*

Initially when Blake told me to contact Michael, it was in response to an offhand suggestion I had made.

"You know, I should move back to New York. There is really

nothing here for me in London. Lord knows I have not had a decent blowout since I moved here. What's the deal? Is England anti-Dominican or something? You would think that with all these Africans, Jamaicans, and Middle Eastern people there would be one on every corner, especially in Brixton."

Laughing, Blake responded, "You do know you are stupid, right? That's not a bad idea, though . . ."

"And how would I go about importing a Dominican, Blake?"

"Not the Dominican, crazy. You moving back to New York, it's not a bad idea. We are ALL here and the city is hot again. You could easily find a great position. I will make some calls."

At the time I did not give much thought to it because it was not realistic in any way, or so I thought. Blake and I always talked a mile a minute, and the ideas flowed faster than Niagara Falls, mostly from her.

"Let's open a B&B in Vermont. I am over NYC."

"I am ready to start my own clothing line. You and Jessica should join me."

"Did you read about such-and-such's new club? They asked me to come in as an equity partner. I think it is a good move, don't you?"

"Let's go to Kenya and import some Maasai fabrics."

Many, many ideas we've had over the years, and it never matters who originates them because 99.9 percent of it is just hot air and we know it. So when I hinted at coming to New York and she vowed to make some inquiries, I allowed it to be another grand illusion and didn't think to speak to my superiors at Conrad about desiring to move on, even when Michael confirmed he would meet with me. Undoubtedly my decision will come as a surprise. I wonder who they'll pick to replace me? Most likely that cute little pixie Rebecca Ryan, who transferred to PR when I joined. Initially I had reservations when tasked with the responsibility of starting a new position and training someone with relatively no marketing/special events training—*or style for that matter*—but she proved to be a quick study and hard worker. I was glad to have her on my team, that's for certain. After a few work lunches at Selfridges and Harrods, she even started to show the signs of becoming a burgeoning fashion plate with her own style.

On Monday Mr. Conrad (Hershel to his friends) called me into his office to express his regret at my impending departure. He wasn't happy about the imposition but said he understood. In appreciation for the work I had done he let me know that should New York prove too naked of a city, I could return "home" at any time. It felt good to know that he valued what I had done, so I didn't have the heart to tell him that New York was home—I just ran away briefly to gather myself.

At the risk of pushing Hershel's generosity, I asked to work half days in order to pack up my flat and be available to all things New York as soon as the city awoke for business. Michael's secretary, Simone, proved invaluable in the transition, sending me shipping account numbers, paint samples, and even selecting my assistant, Jacklyn (pronounced Ja–clin) Travers. *I'll bet anything she is one of those combo babies—you know, dad's name + mom's name = what the hell?!* Jacklyn, a recent grad with impressive internships at Condé Nast and Ralph Lauren in the Special Events and Marketing departments. In time those skills would be put to the test, but for now her most important job is to oversee the painting and setup of my new apartment.

Located on the Upper East Side—not my desired location, but hey, who am I to complain—the apartment is a few blocks down from Michael and Carly's penthouse. Actually it's one of theirs. *That's right, my new boss and his wife, whom I had yet to meet, are also my new landlords. Oh, the smell of incest in the morning!* Michael's rationale being that with only a few weeks' notice there is no time to secure a proper residence and focus on learning the ropes of the job. And even if there were, given the nature of real estate in

Manhattan, after an exhaustive and lengthy search, I'd end up living unhappily in DUMBO or Hoboken all the while running up a very sizable hotel tab on his dime. Let's be real, even with my raise there is absolutely no way that I could have afforded an apartment like theirs, so I'd be a fool not to take it.

Listed as a two-bedroom, it was much larger than my current flat, complete with an open-plan living room/kitchen, butler's quarters (i.e., guest room mini), a separate family room (i.e., my office and TV room), a decent-size dining room, and two full bathrooms. The only drawback that I could foresee was its proximity to the street. Apartment 8A is a corner unit with more than half of the property's living space on the Fifth Avenue side (too much freaking traffic all the time) instead of Seventy-third Street. An influx of images of New Yorkers leaning incessantly on their horns no matter what hour of day or night as if their lives depended on it made my ears hurt. Maybe I would have Ja-clin make sure the windows are double-glazed, or maybe I will just shut what they call the hell up, count my blessings, and finish with the last load of boxes.

. . .

Despite this move being of my making, there were moments, fleeting at best, that I found it hard to fathom the little life I've built here coming to an end. London taught me how to breathe again. Had it not been for the pond at Kyoto Garden in Holland Park or the destinationless (obviously not a word but let's pretend) strolls down Regent Street, allowing me to be consumed in a voyeuristic moment, I would remain emotionally adrift. Feeling pity for myself because I decided that my personal best was left behind with Tony—*actually, that he had taken it.* That is, I think, the cruelest thing about losing intimate love—when in it, I truly believed that I was giving not just my realized best but *my all*, and when that love came to a bitter end, all that was left was a victim in place of the heroine I once envisioned myself to be. I felt as if I had been robbed of everything that made me meaningful. Eventually I accepted that it was me and not Tony who recast me as a secondary player in my own life.

My rebirth coincided with a fertile season, Tudors boldly blooming, the most breathtaking roses in vibrant colors that defied belief for anyone who saw their bare branches during the frost, I no longer felt the need to hide from my own image or believe the barrage of negative things about myself that my subconscious dispensed freely. Even when I had a relapse emotionally (and I did from time to time), it immediately felt wrong in some major way to dwell in pain when the world around me was screaming with such beauty and vitality. For the first time in what felt like forever, I could appreciate the beauty of simple things, the sun's warmth on my face, establishing eye contact with a passing stranger without the protection of oversize sunglasses, or taking a huge breath not because I was trying to stop time but because I wanted to feel life course through my system and with my exhale release any fragments of the reservation that was trying to block my happiness.

For the first time in my adulthood, I knew that I could depend on me no matter the terrain as long as I had my work to fall back on. And so, bit by bit I started to open myself up to conversations with people on my outings to Notting Hill, be it for carnival or to shop. At the Blakey and May Fair for drinks (because, no matter how depressed, one should never drink alone . . . too often), I left the book at home and smiled. I met people who through their stories taught me the invaluables I hoped not to forget once the geography was but a memory. The trick, as I was told, is being able to move on quickly and purposefully when the union brings more innate grief than joy. The next was taking responsibility by identifying the lessons learned and finally dreaming a bigger and better reality by painting a vision on a much broader canvas where I was neither the victim nor the damsel but the author.

Labeling the final box, I took heed of the flashing red sectors of my life that I was not ready to advance toward. I've never known how to be okay with just being me until now. From the moment I arrived in New York, I was in a relationship, be it with Tony or the city itself, despite my cries of independence. Moving to London, not knowing anyone and not having a partner to spend countless hours on the phone with about the issues of transition, showed me just how codependent I was. So if I look at things from that perspective, I must admit that London gave me far more than I gave it. I am stronger like those trees over the way in Hyde Park, changing with the season. When it appears they are at their most vulnerable, dry, brittle, and weighed down with ice from winter's chill . . . a change of season comes, and they blossom from the inside.

# 11

---

# WELCOME HOME—
# I'M BACK

Had it not been for an accommodating bearded doorman in a green stitched felt hat with matching topcoat and white gloves standing at the ready when my taxi pulled up, I surely would have continued questioning if I was in the right place.

"Good afternoon, ma'am. Let me help you with that."

"Thank you. I believe this is my new home," I said.

"If that is the case, then that would make you Ms. Sinclair in Eight A."

Impressed more than surprised at the level of service, I responded, "Yes, it does, and you are . . ."

"The name is Percy. Been here nearly twenty years, so I know everything that is to be known here."

"Well, in that case you can tell me if I will be happy here," I said.

Taking a moment to evaluate my person before presenting me with an envelope containing the keys to the unit, Percy said, "Yes, ma'am, I do believe you will be."

"Then tell me where to go."

The photographs Jacklyn sent of the apartment did not do the space justice. Location notwithstanding, it was loaded with the kind of potential that would perfectly complement my interior aesthetic for all things bohemian chic and contemporary. Pungent still was the smell of fresh paint from earlier. *I should have thought of that and told her to come by and air the place out so it wouldn't be so overwhelming, but that escaped me in all the commotion.*

The main door opened onto a long hallway with bare walls ideal for displaying some of the art I planned to collect (item 2 on my *"all the things in New York I wish I had done before but didn't do and now would"* list—right behind making better girlfriend choices). Similar to my flat in London, there were expansive windows, built-in bookcases in the family room/office but not in the living room or sleeping areas. The teak floors played well against the café au lait walls and white crown molding I had had done. Unlike London, the kitchen and baths had been completely remodeled with granite, stainless steel, and exposed cabinetry. The only noticeable drawback was that my unit didn't have a washer-dryer, but there was one in the basement.

Unpacking proved far easier than I expected, a major advantage of traveling light to get over heartache and of treasuring little. With the exception of the clothes on my back and those in my carry-on, the remaining evidence of my life had been sent a few days earlier. Aside from a few fabulous flea-market finds—clothes, shoes, and purses collected as part of my self-prescribed therapy regimen—everything else would have to be new. The majority of the furnishings I bought in London were more about function than form and reflected a part of my life that I needed no reminders of. Lying in between a Vuitton monogram bag and a vintage Kamali romper was a holdover sweater from Tony's closet that managed to survive the shredder that ate our photos. Now, looking at it against the blank canvas of my emotional landscape, it feels ill placed and no longer necessary. No more did I need a memento of what it felt like to belong to someone in order to know that I was of the world. The fact that I awoke now each day not initially thinking *how quickly can I get through it and come back to bed* was more than enough.

. . .

With less than a week to get fully settled and no welcome wagon in sight, I need to make this place livable or at the very least sleepable in a day. I mean, the expansive hardwood floors were nice enough to look at but not optimum for R&R. The sheer volume of windows alone guaranteed me no protection from the elements of sun and car horns when trying to sleep in late on a lazy weekend morning. Had it not been for Richard and his masterful OCD blueprint on the best one-stop shopping locations to purchase all things home-related, I would have been a sad sack of domestic ignorance.

> *Darling,*
> *Welcome back to civilization and the land of men with straight teeth. Obviously, much has changed and you will need to get adjusted. Here's a little list of some stores to get you started.*
> *Yours truly,*
> *Richard*

Topping his grid was Bed Bath & Beyond—the latest mecca of all things home furnishing and less draining on the purse strings than ABC. Richard's craftiness went beyond bold script, bullet points, and highlighting; he even supplied street addresses of stores and cross-referenced the locations by inventory. The only thing missing was an in-store directory detailing which items could be found in aisle 5 as opposed to aisle 3.

The magnitude of the store was more than a bit intimidating, but easy enough to maneuver, enabling me to find the most divine 400–thread count Luxe Versailles Jaipur cotton sheets and Bailmour comforter along with enough pillows to make me forget that I still slept alone. *The Sofitel dream bed I'd preordered from*

*London would be in perfect company.* Luckily, I was able to make it to checkout moments before the store's same-day delivery cutoff took effect. With a three-hour window before everything arrived, I made my way to Carly's only to find the doors locked. Its entrance accessible only by a keypad requiring a code I had yet to memorize. Instead of returning home and staring at my watch, I walked over to Pastis for a late lunch.

Back in the day this was my default kitchen, a little piece of France in the heart of the Meatpacking District. The crowd was always relatively the same: West Village neighborhood patrons and hip Upper West Siders who braved the C or E below Midtown to mingle with the artsy set for a bite of braised beef with carrots and sips of Côtes du Rhône with lively conversation. In all my years of coming here I'd never made a reservation, which was crazy, considering the place was always packed, and yet the staff always managed to find me a table. Today, however, may be the one time that lady luck was not on my side. As far as I could see, every table and bar stool was taken. My hopes of ensnaring one were rapidly evaporating. Of course I could use the wait time to people-watch, which was one of the major draws in coming here, but what fun could be had standing alone twiddling my thumbs, overtly staring at people? The whole idea of inconspicuous observation is to have a decoy or distraction method—i.e., the menu, a magazine, food, a glass of wine, a semi-interesting companion—while positioned comfortably, blending into the fabric of things, and not literally standing out. As I stood contemplating the best location to wait, a familiar but not readily recognizable voice greeted me.

"You know, it was rude of you not to give me your phone number, but I forgive you," he said.

Turning around to see who was speaking and make certain that I was indeed the recipient, I came face-to-face with Michael's friend from the restaurant, Marcus. Temporarily I was lost for words. *Apparently I am still doing that at the sight of attractive men.* He was more handsome than I recall; definitely a James Bond–esque panache about him, if Bond were ever to be blond, tan, and smoking hot with a come-hither stare. I recognized his cologne immediately, Clive Christian, a brilliant blend of success and power in every conceivable way. Also a clear sign for me to make haste and just feign ignorance. About a year ago I discovered it at Browns while engaging in some much-needed retail therapy. The spray guy was supercute and I was in desperate need of some male attention, so I walked over and freely gave him my wrist. In return he gave me a bill for £210. Desperate times, I say. The scent conjured up the image of the man I longed desperately for but fear I'll never find, having mucked it up so badly already, so I did the next best thing and handed over my credit card. In the times that I was sickened to be sleeping alone, I'd spray some on to usher in sweet dreams of coupledom.

The Achilles' heel in my selection of men was that I definitely preferred Type A's (emphasis on *A*)—attractive, alpha, arrogant, ambitious overachiever *just shy of asshole*—and this guy checked all those boxes and then some. I still didn't know exactly what he did for a living, but I KNEW HIM and his type all too well—*flashing red lights!* Actually every man, starting with my first love, Adrian Perry, was some variation of him—natural-born swagger. So, having been down that road far too many times before with only my battered heart to show as proof that I had loved and lost, it seemed best to neutralize this advance from the onset and pretend to not remember him.

"Excuse me," I said, coolly detached, "but I think you have me confused with someone else. Sorry to disappoint."

"Quite the contrary, I can't ever see you being a disappointment," said Marcus, seeing through my staged performance of selective amnesia. "You wore a pale pink pantsuit, almost blush, with a graffiti top. Your hair was tousled in one of those intentionally messy yet completely fussed-over updos like a morning-after. But what I remember most is that you smelled of Opium. My mother wore it when I was little, so I am entranced by any woman who can carry it off as she did."

"Well, don't you have a great memory?" I responded, devoid of expression.

His disbelief obvious, Marcus responded, "Amazing. You don't like me, do you?"

"I don't know you."

"Which means what? You would like to? You'd like me."

"Listen, as touching a comparison as that is—the bit about your mother—I try to refrain whenever possible from talking to men with poor manners. I mean, honestly, who puts in that much effort and then leaves without as much as a good-bye?"

"So you do remember," Marcus said triumphantly. "I knew you did." The smirk on his face was just enough to reveal a dentist's wet dream. Clearly he was more than up for the challenge and quite enjoyed hunting his prey before conquering.

"Vaguely."

"If I gave you inside information, would that make us friends?" he asked.

As I opened my mouth to respond, his leggy companion arrived. *Completely typical, why am I not surprised?* If I had to guess, I would say that she was requisite factory-grade SBA—Super Blond Amazon—hailing from some region in the Eastern Bloc where the grasp of the English language is just enough to make men (who should know better) turn over the keys and security codes before any talk of a prenup is had. Marcus, on the other hand, seemed undeterred by her presence, continuing, "Michael said you were a beast at PR/marketing and that he would be a fool not to hire you."

"Well, that's cool, I guess?! . . . It was lovely to see you again with your girlfriend."

"Yes, *Marcus*," he replied, slowly and demonstratively, as one does when teaching a toddler a new word. Not taking his eyes off me. "That's my name, Jules Sinclair. Should you forget again, Marcus."

I can't be certain, but I think I broke into a slight run when the hostess appeared to show me to a table, anything to put some distance between Marcus, his SBA, and whatever little flutter occurred in my stomach as I looked at him. True, I may have been off the emotional (and intimate) market for the past few years, but I didn't forget what butterflies felt like or their significance—although I was starting to question if I would ever know what sex felt like again. *That's right, I still had yet to put another man, no matter how superficial, between Tony and me with a proper screw.*

When not consumed with the emotional loss, I thought of nothing else in lucid moments but the physical deprivation of my body. In the middle of the night, my back would unexpectedly arch as if preparing to receive him. Showers and mornings proved the worst, when my fingers would automatically trace the contours of my body as if Tony still had possession of it, starting from the nape of my neck to the roundness of my breasts, only to linger between my legs until I was near explosion. With Tony I learned to appreciate the wonders of my body with the lights on, oftentimes with him watching. He always complimented me in bed, and that made me feel like the best he'd ever had. It's hard when you have been with the best to risk returning to average or unappreciative, so I pushed all that desire to the deepest crevices of my mind and went on with my life.

If anything, the time unavailable had only intensified my awareness of how few and far between those genuine feelings of interest and desire are. True, I met many men during the course of work or personal outings, some of which could have justified having a quickie. None sparking the slight tickle in the base of my stomach on sight or memory of him, or the faint twinge of disappointment that occurs in parting; none to date except this guy, Michael's friend, and that has trouble written all over it.

During the cab ride home my thoughts did briefly—*hence, the entire ride*—return to Marcus. Throughout lunch, I caught sight of him, and indeed he proved to be a fascinating one. Easily, his self-possessed nature allowed him to own the room without overpowering it, a feat in and of itself. His mannerisms were purposeful without the appearance of trying. He was even personable with the staff. *According to Daddy, one can tell a lot about a man's character based on the way he interacts with serving staff: waiters, maids, doormen, drivers, salespeople, and the like. If he is dismissive of them, then no matter how gracious he may appear to be on the first few dates, soon, asshole tendencies will emerge.* Of course, if I was interested in him, then this would be a positive, but since I am not, then it is merely an observation. Much like the one I made in concluding that he and the SBA were together but not *together*. From my POV *in the adjacent corner along the far wall* it was easy to see that she was working a bit too hard for his attention. I mean, honestly, if this Amazon tosses her hair one more time I just might have to say something. And don't even get me started on the gratuitous, definitely vulgar use of food around her mouth. *Seriously! Eat the damn french fries already!*

Somewhere between my being transfixed on their body language and wanting to snatch her off to the bathroom to give an albeit rusty yet decent tutorial on "How to Be Comfortably Alluring During a Lunch Date," Marcus looked up squarely in my direction and raised his glass as if to say, "I know you're watching," leaving me once again to conclude that proper people-watching cannot be done alone. Caught and having no other recourse, I smiled back meekly and flagged down the first waiter I saw to get the check and leave. Clearly not the best day for Pastis; the strawberry shortcake would after all be there far longer than he would. I'd just come back when they were not present.

Exiting the taxi back uptown on Fifth, I saw there was time, not much, but a few minutes or so to spare before the deliverymen were scheduled to arrive, so I popped across the street at the park entrance to grab a vanilla soft-serve cone. Percy was still on duty.

"Ms. Jules, deliverymen from the Sofitel are in the maintenance lounge for you," said Percy, as I entered the building savoring the final remnants of the ice cream.

A few steps into the lobby I stopped midstride, acutely aware that I had absolutely no clue where the maintenance lounge was, so I doubled back.

"The maintenance lounge . . . what is? Where is?" I asked.

"Ah, yes, ma'am. See you need to take me up on that tour of the building. The maintenance lounge is in the rear of the building down this hall to the left. It's a holding area for delivery and service staff."

"Really now? Fancy," I said.

"Yes, ma'am, only the best round here. You go on, I will send them up."

"Thank you, Percy, I think I am really going to like it here if everyone is as nice as you. Oh, by the way, you don't have to call me 'ma'am.'"

Reaching up to tilt his head at me, Percy responded, with great affect, "Yes, ma'am, I do. It's my job and I like it."

Over the next couple of hours the delivery from Bed Bath & Beyond arrived as well, allowing me to put everything in its place before complete nightfall. Between the jet lag, the day's field trip, and unpacking, I was pooped. Before going to sleep, I fired off an e-mail alerting the gang that I was back.

*Hello Lovelies*

*It's been a while but the wait is over. I's here and in need of my fam. Before anyone asks, yes, the rumors are true, I am on the Upper East Side, so YES you must venture above Midtown at some point and let's bypass the fretting. No stateside number yet but am reachable on the UK mobile. It feels good to be home.*

*A zillion X's & O's*

*Jules S.*

. . .

Pleasantly, Sunday morning arrived without the intrusive horns and sirens that I expected. Though not completely inaudible, the street noise was far less than I feared and didn't wake me through the night—or maybe I was just so freaking tired that I could have slept through an AC/DC concert at Madison Square Garden. With no food in the house and no desire to go purchase any, I dressed for breakfast and headed down to my SoHo destination, Cub Room. En route I grabbed a few glossies and city magazines to get an overview of what the evening dinner scene was in print. This would undoubtedly be the resource for visitors to the city. I wanted to understand what they were seeing and whether Carly's was part of that dialogue. Of course I would get the local intel from friends and casual "about town" hipsters soon enough.

. . .

The Cub Room's interior remained the same as that of a ski lodge, but that was it. The staff I knew was long gone. I didn't recognize anyone but did see a friendly face among the diners, semihidden behind a newspaper.

"And you didn't even call to say you would be here. Honestly, I am hurt, appalled, and lost—lost for words at the utter disrespect," I cried.

"Oh dear," Richard said in an exaggerated Savannah drawl, "I can see your mouth is rested but the rest is delusional. Sit, your drink is lonely."

"*Merci*," I said, and settled in for a marathon Sunday. Yes, it felt great to be home again, to be a part of something that is always good. Richard and I are one of those always-great things. Although I must say I often take more than I give.

"Now, darling, tell me, when did it become okay to leave the house looking like this? I mean, what, are you rapping now or something? A tracksuit? Tsk tsk. Is that what the queen is wearing these days?" Shaking his head with disapproval and hissing, he said, "I don't think so. It seems we have a lot of work to do now that you're home. Let's make a list."

"What? It's Adidas," I exclaimed, tugging at the label name strategically sewn below the left shoulder.

"Honey, I don't care if it's Valentino. It's still wrong."

"You're an elitist," I said, ending with an exaggerated furrow of the brow.

"Hmm, I am glad to see that at least you still remember how to do the pout 'n' furrow," interjected Richard between sips of his Bloody Mary and while still pretending to read the *Financial Times*.

"Of course, I just wish you gave a workshop instead of wasting your time writing speeches for a bunch of boring politicians. Yesterday after Bed Bath & Beyond I went to Pastis for lunch and observed this guy who should know better with an SBA severely in need. Dreadful."

"Ewh, they are back in force, you know. For a moment I thought the Asian girls were going to be the dominant dames on the scene but someone unloaded a freighter full of Nordics and God are they ever in need."

"Heinous creatures, they are," I offered.

"Which reminds me, by the way, I must take you to Pravda. It's cavernous, filled with Russians—part of the room likes boys, the other half likes your kind and they all speak in code so repeat nothing. In any event we will have a ball! Cheers," said Richard, folding the paper in half and placing it atop the already explored stack.

"Interesting, but I'm not sure if I am ready for all that just yet," I confided.

"Oh dear, don't tell me you are still pining over that Bob Marley wannabe Antonio, are you? Darling, an ocean, two years, and a few decent lays later . . . let's move on."

I could not help but respond, completely deadpan, "I see your job at Hallmark fell through. Too bad, really you are so amazing with the whole sensitivity thing. No, I am not still pining over Tony. I just have not found anyone to fill the space in between is all. I saw him, you know, when I came in to interview. He smelled so good!"

"Oh, yes, there is nothing better than the scent of 'rip my heart out of my chest, Rasta betrayal' in the morning to get the juices flowing. Honey, tell me you are not going back down that road. We lost you for far too long. Last time everything happened so fast. We all stood by and did whatever we could to support you, but this time you have to know better. Don't you?" asked Richard in a surprisingly fatherly tone, complete with disapproving head nod.

"Relax yourself there, Boulton. We saw each other. I almost choked on zucchini bread. We had the long-overdue talk. I inhaled deeply *probably for the last time* so I could lock the smell of him into my memory, and then we said good-bye. He finally gave me the closure I needed."

"Well, that's imagery. My dear, one day you will learn that you are the only one who can give yourself closure; no one else. I'm a wise old owl, so I know what I am talking about. In time you will accept that you hold the keys."

"My goodness, what the hell have you been doing while I was away—reading Confucius or something! Enough now, enough," I said. I heard Richard loud and clear. He knows it as well, but I was far from ready to live in the reality of those words, so I offered, "I missed you, my friend."

# 12

## MEETING THE NATIVES

Being the new kid on the block when the boss is away definitely has advantages. It gives you the time to form your own relationships without an overseer, forcing people to conform and mingle. Initially Michael was due back within a week of my arrival but decided to extend his trip for two additional weeks after he and Carly ran into Lord So-and-So Hoity-Toity in Capri, who asked them to join his entourage on one final jaunt up north to Croatia. *I mean, who in their right mind could possibly say no to that kind of invitation? I would like the option to, though.* For the most part the team at Carly's was nice. There was no apparent divisive line between the kitchen, front of the house, and executive office the way there often is in places like this. The only noticeable tension arose when Simone Phillips—aka Girl Friday—ventured down from her ivory tower for inspections. After some well-heeded watercooler conversations, I choose to engage Simone rather than evade her despite her obvious lack of warmth.

"Afternoon, Mrs. Phillips, a beautiful day, isn't it?" I'd say.

"That would depend on how you got here, now wouldn't it? For my part I was stuck in the freaking Lincoln Tunnel for nearly an hour because of all that dagnabbit construction. I swear to you that creep Giuliani is going to be the death of me yet."

Where does one go after that? Nowhere, so I offered a half-hearted "Yeah" and kept it moving.

In the encounters that followed I let her set the pace and always referred to her as Mrs. Phillips until the day that she told me to call her Simone. It seemed we had reached something of an accord.

. . .

Everyone I've met in the apartment building falls firmly into one of three categories: ancient, married, or fabulously gay. In "single woman" terms this means that the common areas (hallway, laundry room, elevator, library, etc.) are tantamount to Switzerland; completely neutral, an unexpected perk that says "no primping required when roaming the halls" on the off chance that Mr. Right, Mr. Possibility, or Mr. Scratch My Itch are on the premises. There is Mr. Leon Sol, who has to be as old as the building itself. I see him every morning on my way to work with one of his many verbally abused nurses. Each time I smile and offer up a chipper "Good morning. How are you today?" In return he grunts, sucks his teeth like a West Indian, and cuts me a sideways glance. *A nasty habit he obviously picked up from one of his helpers*. On exiting the elevator, his nurses always shoot me the embarrassed sympathy gaze, as if trying to apologize for his lack of social graces.

Then there are the married ladies who lunch at Fred's and Le Bilboquet daily as if it is a career to be mined for societal advancement defined by seating placement. For the most part they range from midthirties to late sixties and are totally insular. Their names fall somewhere between Muffy, Kinsley, and Taylor. Their collective identity is validated each time they can find someone to exclude, and at present that person is me. Within days of moving into the building I had my first encounter with one of them, Mitzy Bloomfield.

"Jules, right? The girls and I heard someone new was coming into the building, so I guess that is you," she said in all of her fake-enthusiasm, Lily Pulitzer glory. *If this were Connecticut and not New York, I would swear her last name was Stepford.* "Normally, we have a full background on whoever moves in as they have to come in through the committee, you know. My husband, Randall, is the cochair, you know. This is after all a building of families with strong lineage and extensive ties to the city. We are very selective. Whereabouts did you and your husband come from?"

"Virginia by way of London. Single—me. I'm not married." Judging by the way she shrieked in horror, I feared for a moment that she was experiencing a shooting pain up her left arm.

With gravely exaggerated compassion she recovered to say, "Ooooh well, it's not for everyone, is it now?! So I take it you're one of those career girls on the fast track or something—so intriguing. I assume your boyfriend finds that attractive, yes? You know there is something to be said for that, I guess going against convention."

*Okay, Mean Girl. I get it loud and clear. You were sent here by the legion of Bitter Betty Sisterhood to put me in my place.* Had this been another time (actually a year and a half ago because I still needed a place to deposit the anger and pain), I would feel the need to break your face or mind-fuck your husband just enough that he accidentally called you by my name over breakfast or in bed just before you can think to fake a headache. Lucky for Mitzy and her kind I am still operating at half-mast.

"Messy Missy, is it?" I asked, knowing full well that it was not her name but enjoying the tense little pinch in her face just the same. *Mental note: even if she redeems herself in the future, call her Missy.* "Surely you could give the ladies a much better report on my life situation if you made good use of yourself and helped me bring these bags inside."

On the way home I had stopped by D'Agostino's to pick up a few kitchen essentials but forgot to get one of those cart thingies downstairs in order to bring the bags up, so extra hands—even hers—were needed.

"I have always been curious about this unit, such great views. When Randolph—that's my husband—and I were looking to purchase in this building we tried to see it but were told it was not on the market, although it was obviously empty and had been for some time. Apparently it was part of Carly Spencer Falles's portfolio. I can't believe she sold it. You do know who she is, don't you?" asked Mitzy, leaning in as if sharing highly classified information.

Honestly, I know that I should have taken the high road here but why disrupt things now? "Hmmm. Not really. I know of her. It's her husband I know best—he's just too divine."

In hindsight it is more than fair to identify this comment as the one that put me at immediate odds with the wives in the building. Had Mitzy asked the proper follow-up question (How do you know Michael?), the gray area would have been cleared up instantly, but she didn't and I didn't volunteer. From that moment forward, anytime I entered a common area where they happened to be with their husbands, octopussy ensued. Suddenly they developed more arms than visible to my eye and began to twist, turn, and maneuver their men in any direction but to be in direct contact with or in sight of me. Sometimes I pretended not to notice, but if they caught me at an especially feisty moment, I forced interaction.

"Stuart, saw you yesterday headed out to play a few rounds. Looking good. What's your handicap?" Flick the hair, cue laugh, and stroke his arm. "I am totally taking you up on those lessons."

"Larry, when you get a chance, I would love to read that book on Goldman Sachs that you told me about the other day."

"Randolph, looking good . . . real good."

Oh, fun times, not just for me but also for the doormen (whom the Stepfords regarded as *the help*, with no life beyond getting the door and walking their pampered pooches) and the few boys in the building who loved boys and who formed their own little protective unit around me. It's like I was the most unruly one in the litter and they made it their duty to have my back no matter how many times I put my foot in it. My favorite was Gary, "the gay," who lived across the hall in 8B.

. . .

Gary and I had the pleasure of meeting on a Wednesday afternoon in early October as I was checking the mail. The Brazilian Corcovado series was bringing rave reviews to Carly's. I was completely exhausted. Michael was beyond excited and rightly so, taking full credit for the earth, the stars, and all creation that comprised the parties and this new positioning. Somewhere along the way he did manage to squeeze out, "Good work, young'n, now let's see what you have planned for the holiday." In all the commotion with work, a few personal things fell by the wayside, domestic upkeep being at the top of that list (note to self: call Richard and get a housekeeper referral to come weekly, stat), checking my mail a close second. Had Ivan, the evening doorman, not reminded me of the overflow of my box, I would have put it off another day. Gary discovered me there sitting on the floor in the lotus position, surrounded by piles of mail and unable to tear myself away from the image of Oprah, aka Glamour-puss Winfrey, sprawled out across the October cover of *Vogue* magazine.

"I *know*, could you *just* die?! Look at Ms. Thing on that chaise looking all kinds of sexy. Honey, I do the same thing—only upstairs in my apartment in a green dress. You seem comfortable," he said in an animated tone that was peppered with a shade of disapproval for my loitering in the area. "Nice shoes, by the way. Gucci?"

Ignoring the bit of gay snark, I conceded that the heels were in fact Gucci vintage, not Tom Ford, and found myself in conversation with, surprisingly enough, the guy who lives across from me: Gary "the gay," *until I learn his last name*, contributing editor for *Decor* magazine. Over the course of my nearly five months of living here, with the first month and a half spent as quiet nights at home cradling with Häagen-Dazs, I couldn't help but notice that whoever lived across the hall entertained regularly. Actually, there were a few nights I pulled a chair up to the keyhole in order to watch the procession of spirited revelers come and go. From what I could see they were all quite trendy dames and dandies who were well aware of themselves. Basically, the kind of people I would be friends with if I were social.

"I can't believe you are just reading that. I ripped my issue open as soon as it arrived. Can you believe that Anna put her on the cover!" exclaimed Gary, *definitely more of a statement than a question.* "You know the old girl had to starve herself to make that happen or they did a hell of a job in Photoshop . . . My money is on Photoshop. For real, look at those arms! Now, you know and I know that's not possible . . . I'm an editor, you know, so they can't hide nothing from me. I mean, come on, Mommy didn't look this good when she was dragging those mounds of fat in that sad little wagon with all that hair on that deprived body. You have great skin, by the way. What's your secret?"

By the time Gary came up for air, he was actually sitting on the floor next to me and had commandeered my magazine, flipping feverishly through the spread that he knew all too well, providing page-by-page commentary like a live sporting event was unfolding.

"Cetaphil or Leaf & Rusher to wash, pure cocoa butter at night, and light moisturizer in the morning. Normally I would also say 'all the sex I could handle' as part of a successful clear skin regimen, but that is a sadder state of affairs than Oprah dragging that fat across the stage," I replied. Judging from the blank expression on his face, Gary had forgotten that in the midst of his rambling he had asked me a question, so we just continued on into our love fest. *If there is one thing I know well, it's the gays. What can I say, they love me and I them. Apparently, there is a burgeoning diva inside of me that appeals to them. That and the fact that I have an amazing set of natural breasts, not a nibble or a bite but a perfect mouthful of perkiness that is every man's (gay or straight) and woman's weakness.*

"So you are the little thing that's got these women around here on high alert. You know, I heard all about you, Miss Thang! That

Mitzy Bloomfield told us you were a husband-stealing piece of work with no respect for social seniority who probably slept her way to the middle. Of course you immediately became one of my favorite people, sight unseen. Poor Carly Falles. How did you do it?" asked Gary.

"Ouch! All that just for little ole me," I asked, faking injury. "Well, let's hope that Messy Missy is not called to testify to my character in a court of law anytime soon."

"GYRL, did you say Messy Missy?" Gary cackled. "I am dying!"

"Honestly, Gary, she gave me no choice. I saw her one day in the elevator and instead of rolling out the welcome wagon she came at me with some antiquated insecure junior varsity high school cheerleader nonsense. It was like she had been sent out by the old crow's society to put me in my place . . . so I decided it would be a shame not to send her back with anything but a scintillating report for the very hens who clutch their chubby, balding, new-money husbands whenever I am around."

By this point he was totally engrossed, so I continued to plead my case, knowing full well that he would report every detail back to the old girls, which would be helpful. As much as I enjoyed being the topic of conversation, those women would surely have spread word along the UES soon enough that Michael and I were shagging behind Carly's back. That in itself would be absolutely scandalous and plausibly true if it touched her ears, so I had to set the record straight.

Carly and I had yet to meet. Michael and I worked much more closely now that he was back full-time and soon would do some traveling together to heighten his business profile. The few appearances that she made at the restaurant always seemed to come when I was away. However, there was not a moment of the day at work that I did not feel her presence. She was in the paper, or on the phone with Simone, and in every nook and cranny of the restaurant's décor. Wanting to put a living face with the legend and feeling the urge to kiss the ring, I rang her up one afternoon, only to learn that she was out for the week at a health spa retreat, so I left word with her social secretary proposing high tea at the Peninsula when she returned.

From the Oprah-Messy Missy encounter, Gary and I became fast friends. He took it upon himself to oversee the decorations on my flat, less as a solid to a newfound friend and more as an empty canvas to present to his object of carnal desire, Jean Pierre (no known last name), a totally cute, up-and-coming interior designer whom he wanted to bed repeatedly. Thankfully Jean Pierre's work actually appealed to me despite its being decisively more glam than my usual. *Oh well, what's one more mirrored piece of furniture coupled with Mongolian fur pillows and a sparkly chandelier when it is free!* In success, Gary promised a lovely profile on the apartment showcasing Jean Pierre's work with a requisite photo of me as the hip young Manhattanite. *J'adore!!* If all things remained on schedule, the piece would run near the top of the year. I gave them both keys, sat back, and watched the magic unfold.

# 13

## MASTERS, THE MAN . . . NOT THE TOURNAMENT

**K**EITH MASTERS (QUITE the accidental encounter) was managing partner of a pretty significant boutique advertising firm in the city. The first time I saw him was at Carly's while standing on the other side of the main one-way mirrors overlooking the main dining room. He came in with about five or so Midwestern types. The dynamics were obvious: he was the "big city" executive showing the good ole boys a proper New York evening. Once they were seated, I allowed my eyes to linger a bit longer before going back into the office to work on the task at hand: finalizing preparations for the last two major post-Fashion Week parties and locking in a private party; my first serious pressworthy events for the venue. Initially, Michael was against the ideas of catering to the fashion kids, as he now felt the scene had become too common and considered renting the venue out to Russian oligarch Nikolai Abramovich as his playland. Sadly, he, like a few others in the know, just could not get past the previous season's oversights of grunge and heroin chic. As for the Russian with a never-ending cash flow, well, that was far easier to finalize—but only after chasing Michael for a few days about it and hijacking his office.

"Listen, Simone, I know that Michael has told you to tell me that he is not in, or that he is on a call, or is attending to something extremely important in some area of the restaurant that I am not in, so don't even bother. I am just going to sit here—right next to you—until he comes out of his office or gets off that elevator. Ah, before you protest, you know and I know that it is paramount that I sit next to you—how else can I ensure that you don't send him some encrypted message or tap the little warning buzzer that I am told is somewhere on your desk?" I said, wagging my finger, to chastise her as if she were a wayward student. "I've been watching you, lass. I know how you two work, Batman and Robin, Lone Ranger and Tonto, Mr. Roark and Tat-t—"

"Jules, if you finish that sentence and make me Herve Ville-chaize, from *Fantasy Island*, I promise you that all of your vacation requests will be mysteriously lost in the vortex known as my shit list pile."

"Ouch, I love it when you bite. Grrrh. It just makes me feel all warm and tingly."

"Stop making me laugh. I have a reputation around here to keep up, you know. Some people are actually afraid of me," said Simone, trying to regain her composure.

"Yes, you do," I said, nodding in mocking agreement. "Believe me when I tell you that everyone is aware of Superbitch. Instead of leaping tall buildings in a single bound, you can wipe out an entire service staff and a few creditors in a single glance."

By this time Simone and I were laughing so hard that Michael came out of his office motivated by sheer curiosity alone. Other people have a sixth sense about impending danger; his alerted him anytime fun and frivolity were going on without him.

"Simone, what's going on out here? I was gonna ask for . . ." But then, upon laying eyes on me, "Oh Jules, I should have known. I thought the English were incapable of laughter yet here you are, kee-keeing and laughing it up outside my office. Glad to know that I am paying you so well to languish about."

"Actually, you are paying me to do exactly what I am doing, creating great press opportunities for Carly's. However, in order to get an answer for some key requests, you force me to become duplicitous, chasing you down, attempting to bribe poor Simone, which by the way failed miserably, so in desperation I had no choice but to set up camp outside your office and, well . . . what can I say, I'm funny and you know I'm not a Brit. Just have not been able to shake the accent is all."

Realizing he was cornered, Michael attempted to make a fast break into his office, but I had anticipated the move because he is anything but original and had already used it on me a few times successfully. So while speaking I made sure to position myself within two steps of him; close enough not to invade his personal space but not far enough away to have the door closed in my face, which he had done before as well. Michael's office is the only area in the entire restaurant that Carly had not taken her interior decorating ambitions to. It was once again indicative of their most interesting relationship. She was often looking for any way to have more meaning in his world, while he was keeping strict hold on the depth of engagement.

"The key to any relationship, Jules, is allowing a man enough space to be a man and to determine his own course of action. I had to learn that and when I did I found a woman who also knew it to be true." Michael said this to me one day when I was forcibly trying to coach him to say specific things for an interview. "Your job is not to direct the tide but to ride it out. I'm a great wave, let me do my thing."

Michael's office was an extreme ode to the Ralph Lauren Man, that is, expensive hunting lodge complete with thousand-dollar beverage coasters, tufted leather sofa, authentic deer horn magnifying glass, and letter opener—*poor Bambi's mama*. Whenever I was inside I felt an overwhelming urge to light up a stogy and make some derogatory comments about women while leaning back to admire my boots made from the skins of endangered animals, just after calling PETA to say bugger off. Sometimes the feeling was so overwhelming that I would actually lose my train of thought, but not today.

"Why aren't you giving me an answer on this Abramovich party buyout?" I asked. "The deadline was two days ago, and if we don't respond today, surely they will secure another venue."

"And the problem with that is? Let him throw his money around to someone who needs it."

"Honestly, Michael, I don't understand. He is one of the wealthiest men in the world and is known for being an ultimate tastemaker. In selecting Carly's as the location for his event, we become an international destination, officially. Doesn't that mean anything to you—hello?!" Passively sitting there looking at me as if I'd asked him to pass the stapler. "Fine. If you don't want to do it, then just tell me and I can take it off my list. Otherwise you have to give me something more—like a yes, right now."

"Jules, you're good at publicity and events, but you don't know people like him yet. Not the way you should. Not the way you will. Your life experience has not afforded you those kind of years yet. I know people. I know Abramovich's kind all too well; new money—enough to last for ten generations and save a few ravaged countries along the way. He is used to getting exactly what he wants when he wants. Afterward he tosses it aside with complete and utter disregard. Now he wants to come here and use my baby as his playground. I won't allow her to be disrespected. I know the deadline passed two days ago and I know that his team is still calling you, which raises the question of why is my space so important to him and how much is it worth to ole Nikolai?"

Michael's state-of-the-union speeches, as I had started referring to them, were now par for the course. The revelation that he knew the exact nature of my talks with a prospective client was surprising and showed on my face. He silenced me with a raised right hand.

"Don't ask. I know that the same way I know that it would do you good to actually go out some nights with your friends instead of curling up with Häagen-Dazs and Black and White cookies from Googies. No one wants a skinny fat woman. It looks bad in bed." Pausing to shudder at the visual, "Now, where was I . . . oh yeah, Abramovich. He selected my place because he knows what I have created here, told his minions, and expected this to be done ASAP. Now they have undoubtedly gone back and told him the details for his big U.S. party are not secured. Despite the fact that he has far more pressing matters at hand, this will become the annoying fly in his day, which he will handle directly. When he does, I will be here."

With those final words, he buzzes Simone and tells her to have the car brought around. I, on the other hand, am still sitting there trying to process what I just heard—the part about the ice cream and the cookies more so. *Is there a camera in my shower that feeds directly into Michael's office? What the hell!*

"Relax yourself, Jules, I don't have your place bugged. I just know people. I also know your doormen very well. Ivan and Percy are my guys, they tell me things from time to time about my new tenant." Now up and pouring himself a drink. "Honestly, though, you should go easy on the snacks." Michael seems to have forgotten that his driver was patiently waiting downstairs, because he just continued to talk.

"I'll take that under consideration," I said.

"Do you know why I hired you? Not because you were the most qualified. You weren't. But you came as a referral by way of someone I value. Then we met and I saw myself in you as I first started in this town; hungry, ambitious, and naïve enough to believe that I could play by the same rules as the other kids. Early on, life gave me a few hard knocks that would have broken a lesser man's constitution, but I rebounded quickly and quietly. I saw that in you," he said, taking a sip of the bourbon he had just poured. "People, especially men, are easy to understand. We show you exactly who we are within ten minutes. Be smarter than the rest, Jules. Remember, if you are a quick study, then there is not enough time to invest too deeply and lose. Now, as it stands, I have something Nikolai wants in the short term. An association might not be a bad thing, so let's reel him," said Michael.

Finally he headed for the door, with me glued to the chair trying to absorb, prioritize, understand, and cross-reference all that he just said. Before walking out, Michael says, "I almost forgot, Carly will see you for lunch on Tuesday at the house. Simone will give you the address. Don't embarrass me; I've been talking you up."

Seriously, the extra pressure I did not need. I was already on edge about meeting this woman, the icon, the legacy, the namesake. Meeting Noriega had to be less stress-inducing. Seeing that Michael left a sizable pour of bourbon behind, I downed it in one massive gulp. The trail it burned through my body left me off-balance, clutching the sofa for support until my chest stopped burning. *Damn it to hell, too much testosterone in this freaking office. I don't even like bourbon—I know this!*

· · ·

Later in the week I was out for dinner with Blake and Joy, at Indochine, when I literally bumped into Keith Masters. I had never thanked Blake properly for the referral to Michael, so tonight was in her honor. The place was packed with the usual clientele of models, artists, music guys, club kids, and a few bankers. As I made my way through the crowd, someone turned and pushed me hard enough to knock me off-balance. Before I could fall, a hand grabbed me firmly around the waist and pulled me up. Mere inches apart from his sun-kissed glory, I recognized him instantly as the *big city* guy from Carly's.

"Are you okay?" he asked.

"Yes, thanks to you," I said, somewhat breathless. "I don't know what I would have done if you weren't here."

"Lucky for me I was. I'm Keith, by the way. And you are . . . ?"

"Jules Sinclair," I responded, without realizing that I was biting the inside of my bottom lip and trying to speak between clinched teeth. Always a telltale sign of arousal. *So glad the ole girl is back!* Keith was still holding me around the waist with one arm as he told me that he liked my name because it made birthdays and anniversaries a no-brainer. By the time Joy came over to redirect me to our table, I couldn't hear anyone else in the room but him. I didn't have visions of happily ever after or a baby carriage, but every nerve ending in my body was telling me that this was the man to officially put sexual distance between Tony and me.

Apparently, I was not the only one who saw the sparks. At the table Blake and Joy began grilling me about who he was, how I knew him, and what I was going to do about it. Before I could start fumbling for answers to their barrage of questions, two bottles of Moët & Chandon arrived at the table. The first bottle said "For now—because I loved meeting you." The second, "For later— because I want to know you. Keith Masters 917-409-6640."

"J, oh my gawd, that is Keith Masters, damn! I thought he looked familiar." Looking for a sign of recognition on my face, of which there was none, Joy continued, "Listen, I read about him constantly in *Adweek*. He is hot shit."

Joy is more like a half sister than a friend. She is the official Cuban in my life, and knows my heart and its failings better than most, so I always take her words as authority. Born in the U.S. but sounding as if she just got off the boat, raft, tire tube, whichever you prefer, yesterday. She works downtown in finance at Merrill Lynch and lives the American Dream inclusive of WASP husband, unruly prodigal son, a golden retriever, and local neighborhood watch. I firmly believe that had she been raised outside that little North Bergen enclave of Cubans and Dominicans, where they speak nothing but Spanglish, sounding imported despite being born in the States, listening to soca/salsa, and shopping primarily at bodegas while reminiscing about the Old Country, she surely would be further up the corporate ladder by now. She is whip smart, as evidenced by the bonuses that her boss gives her annually in lieu of the promotion she so rightfully deserves.

"Aaaah, so *that* is Keith Masters. I have heard about him but didn't know he was so damn hot," cooed Blake, spinning around to uncover what direction the bottles could have come from. "I wonder if that stops anyplace south of . . ."

"Listen, blondie, hands off and stop twirling your hair—this one's not for you. This one's for Jules," cried Joy, wrapping a protective arm around me as exhibit A. "Besides, isn't he like forty years too young and a hundred million or so dollars too poor for you or something? Our Jules needs to get her stride back before those gates are rusted shut."

"What???!!! I was just looking. No harm in that, is there?" responded Blake with a faux innocence that even she didn't believe.

At this point I had to interject, if for nothing more than just to fend off the first line of piranhas; and make the first rule of Girlfriend Code crystal clear: *Thou shall not cockblock.* As it pertains to my girlfriends, I have learned that no saying rings truer than "To know you is to love you." In Blake's case, to know her is to understand that her gray area as it pertains to men is vast, with a sliding scale. Just because one of us may have seen him first, gone on a date with him, slept with him, or dated him for a few years but parted amicably, doesn't really register for her *if* he has the power and financial means to support her lifestyle. There are, however, attributes that make her essential, namely that she is up front in her motives (sometimes she will say things so matter-of-factly regarding her intentions that I wonder if she even knows what a filter is), extends the same courtesy to her girls—she had no qualms about one of us dipping in her pool (although I would never)—and she is ride or die in her love/support for her girls (as long as it does not interfere with plans to land Daddy Warbucks).

"Blakesy, you can try but you will fail on this one. I mean, let's face facts. We both walked right by him. He allowed you to pass and keep walking. Me, he stopped and now has sent over drinks. Hmmm, actually, bottles. Yeah, not so much, sweetie, but I'll be sure to give you a full report." *TMI—Heaven forbid I would ever tell her that the only reason Keith stopped me is because he stopped me from falling.*

We were laughing so hard that I didn't even notice Keith approach our table. This was definitely another point on his scorecard. Most men (outside of a sports bar and properly liquored up) would never have the chutzpah to approach a table of cackling women.

"Hi, again. So I realized that it might have been presumptuous of me to just send over my number the way that I did. I hope I didn't offend you, Jules Sinclair." *If heaven had a light, hmmm, I am thinking it could be this man.* I opened my mouth to respond but didn't recognize the voice that was coming out.

"Not at all! As a matter of fact, it was quite nice of you, Keith." Ahhhh, I love it when mama–Cuban bear comes out of my Joy. It's sweet that she thought I needed it, but I didn't. In his presence I felt renewed physically. My body just responded to this man, so I took Keith's hand as he stood over me to make sure I was his only focal point.

"No offense taken at all. The thought of any man besides you sending his number over seems wrong, wouldn't you agree?" *Oh gawd, that sounds so cheesy coming from my mouth. Damn, I hope it's working.*

"Indeed," he replied, holding my gaze while stroking my hand. "Ladies, you seem to have me at a disadvantage. You know that I am Keith, and you are?"

Blake offered only a limp handshake and dismissive nod in his direction as if to imply "why are you breathing my air." In the years that I have known her and seen her for who she truly is, I recognize this move and appreciate it. In Blakesy speak, it is a clear sign of surrender, love, and respect. Translation: I honor the code and will not jockey for position by blocking the cock. To the poor guy on the receiving end, he just thinks she is an uptight narcissistic shrew. He is partly right.

"Hi, Keith. I am Joy. I was just telling Jules that I was reading about you last week in *Adweek*. Great campaign, by the way. I am at Merrill in wealth management. We have many of the same clients."

Knowing that Joy can gab on endlessly without coming up for air, I placed my left hand under the table and squeezed her leg. Hey, sometimes a squeeze is a love pat. Other times, like now, it's a shut-the-hell-up.

"Ah, nice to meet you both. I do have to get back to my table." Now looking squarely at me, he instructed more than asked: "Tell me you will use that number, anytime."

"Promise," I said.

.   .   .

Under normal circumstances at some point in the evening our tables would have magically merged and dinner with the girls would have turned into dinner with new friends and new man prospect. That's part of the storied NY magic. Tonight, however, that was not the case. The place was standing room only.

When time came to leave I had lost sight of Keith. His night out with the boys had long since turned into a raucous affair, far different from the civilized work evening I'd observed at Carly's. Gorgeous girls were abounding and doing their best to captivate. Obviously, he was not hurting for female company, so I pressed onward to leave. Having said good-bye to Joy and Blake, I stood in front of Indochine for a moment debating the merits of walking a bit to enjoy the crisp evening air or hopping a cab. Reaching the corner, I heard my name and turned to see Keith running in my direction. Amazing. Despite the commotion at his table, he had seen me leave.

"I had hoped you would at least say good night," he said.

"I thought about it but, ah, you seemed a little busy," I confessed.

Dismissive of the company inside, he replied, "I can see why you would think that, but no."

"I see. Did you receive the bottle that I sent back over?" I asked, hoping that it had been delivered, since my phone number was written in lipstick on the label.

"I liked that—made me the hit of the table. The last number was smeared," said Keith. Liquid courage in place and too impatient to let the moment pass, I looked up and kissed him on the lips. Instinctually he responded with such passion that I almost collapsed again in his arms under the streetlights of Lafayette and Astor. The warmth of his tongue fondling mine tasted of berry sorbet. Pulling away I said, "Three. The last digit of my phone number."

"I won't forget," he responded, and placed me in a cab with a final, shorter kiss good-bye.

# 14

## A NEW ATTITUDE

THERE IS NOTHING like a hot new man prospect to put the pep back in one's step. A few days after our encounter, Keith and I had our official first date. I must confess that it was not without incident. The plan, as it were, was that we would meet at 147. Located in a converted firehouse, 147 was NYC typical: velvet rope, dimly lit, dinner reservations starting at 9 p.m., people dressed for a stylish evening out, and the dancing afterward sanctioned by the likes of Biz Markie or Q-Tip on the turntables. When I arrived, Keith had left word saying that he was running a few minutes behind and would be there shortly, so I took a seat at the bar and ordered a vodka martini. Unlike London, the bartenders at 147 were absolutely scrumptious, offering plenty to keep me distracted until Keith arrived, specifically Franco. Tall, olive skin, dark hair, *probably Italian*, with an air about him that said he was a bad boy so little girls need not apply. By the time Keith arrived, Franco and I were moments away from arranging to say "good morning," at the end of his shift.

"Something told me to send security ahead to watch over you," said Keith over my shoulder. Swiveling around, I immediately cupped his face and said, "Never," sealing the things that need not be said with a soft kiss.

"I can't stop thinking about you, Jules. Today I was in a presentation and found myself thinking about the other morning. It came much to soon."

I had to agree. After Keith put me in the taxi the night we met, he went back inside to say good night to his friends and then proceeded to come to my apartment. There were absolutely no pretenses about why he was there. Immediately upon my opening the door, my skirt was on the floor and by the time it closed, so was his shirt. *Two years is a long time to deprive a body from the nourishment that it needs.* Our first location was the far wall in the entrance hallway. Afterward we made our way to the kitchen and finished off a carton of ice cream. Between bites we got to know each other better. I learned that he hailed from Newport Beach, hates surfing, and played baseball in college. Keith was recruited by a major team, but quit during training camp, finding the future lifestyle at conflict with his personal goals. He, like countless others, *myself included*, came to New York for the sole purpose of creating his own identity instead of the prefabricated one his parents had constructed. Once here he started working with a dot-com and excelled quickly through the ranks. When the company folded—*they all do*—he received an offer to join an advertising firm from a most unexpected contact: an exec he knew from the club scene whom he used to do blow with. One thing led to another and before he knew it, Keith Masters had found his calling. His charisma and quick wit were extremely advantageous, so his star continued to rise. On the personal side he was aware enough to know that he wasn't ready for a long-term relationship but didn't like coming home from a long trip to an empty home either. Keith was an open book. I found his candor quite refreshing and even surprised myself in response, so there was no pressure this evening now that we were dressed, off my kitchen floor, and out in public. I felt as comfortable with him as I did with Blake or Richard (sans ever having the desire to rip their clothes off).

Instead of playing some antiquated role by telling him what it was that I thought he wanted to hear, I allowed my dialogue to be as bare as my body intertwined with his. I told him that I escaped to London after a bad breakup and had just returned. That in my heart I did not know if I was ready or even capable of loving another man as I had Tony. *Hadn't even entertained it, although I did miss the familiarity that comes with togetherness.* The mere thought of it—loving another so hard—scared me, so I tried never to entertain it any place other than on a film screen in the context of actors portraying characters. *How much more distance can one get than that?* I told him that I had no guarantees or expectations about us past tonight. To which he responded, "Let's discuss that in the morning."

Well, that morning came, as did many nights thereafter over the next couple of months. My every other Saturday was now his, but we were *not* in a relationship; sitting at Café Gitane, talking about the goings-on of life with casual acceptance, no hope for more, shopping together, no agenda, dining with friends of his and mine. Sundays remained as they had always been: quality time with Richard. Depending on whose house I awoke in, Keith's or mine, Richard had the following to say:

"Looks like someone forgot creepin' etiquette. Darling, how many times have I told you to always have a clutch big enough and dress small enough for a quick change? The world need not know that you are doing *The Walk.*"

"There is no shame to my game, Boulton, I shall have you know. Not only did I shower and refresh but I even picked up fresh panties from Vicky Secrets before joining you," I responded.

"Well, I guess that is something. Lord knows there is nothing worse than day-old fish. Ewh," he said, slapping the table to emphasize his pun. "So tell me, when is lover back and what is the story?"

"Lover is in Chicago for the week. The story is the same as before: I like him. I like him a lot, but beyond that I don't know. For example, I know that he likes me and shows me, but I don't see our story in his eyes, you know? Not in the long term."

"Good girl. Keep those tacky rose-colored glasses off and see a man for who he is. In doing so you will learn who you are too. What he has to offer will appeal to you or it will not. The moment you start to justify is the moment you say good-bye."

"Honestly, you should write a book or be the first fab gay rapper," I said, slapping Richard a high five.

# 15

## ENCOUNTERS

IN SPITE OF myself, I had to admit, there was a bit of melancholy that accompanied the physical absence when Keith was away, but I dared not tell him—*or say it aloud,* as I knew it had more to do with enjoying being part of a pair again. We spoke or e-mailed often, if only to keep the lines of communication open by making an observation about something odd that occurred within our respective days. I'm quite sure that I started this habitual dynamic when I e-mailed him.

Subject: URGENT!

Why is it that if another human being is doing something truly disgusting in public I am destined to be the only one who sees it; picking their nose, scratching their balls, or picking their nose while scratching their balls? I mean, honestly, you would think they are lying in wait for me to cross their path or something. How is your day?
x Jules

Subject: Re: URGENT!

Hi Princess—consider yourself lucky. I was in the restroom before the first meeting and had the displeasure of seeing Mr. Cornell take a piss, handle himself, and exit the restroom without looking at the faucet.

Entering the room I was wishing like hell that he was Japanese so we
could bow instead of shake hands.
Masters

Keith was due back in town on Friday morning so we made
plans to grab an early dinner and catch a movie, the same day as my
long-overdue lunch with Carly after having it rescheduled twice.
The first was her doing—"hair appointment with Domenico from
Milan who is only in New York for the day." The second cancellation was my, or better yet, Michael's doing. He wanted to sit down
and go over the holiday lineup I had put in place, specifically the
money he would have to put out to have the likes of Lauryn Hill,
Cassandra Wilson, and/or Terence Blanchard take up a limited
residency at Carly's. Fan of the latter two or not, he was not excited
about investing in three costly acts for an extended amount of time.

Awaking that morning, I found myself surprisingly antsy at
the thought of spending time with Michael's wife. I had shared so
much time with him that in some strange way it just seemed odd
to now be meeting Carly. It was as if, since a meeting did not happen within the first couple of weeks of my arrival, then it shouldn't
happen now, at least not in this very staged way; high tea at their
penthouse on Seventy-eighth Street between Fifth Avenue and
Madison. Not wanting to deal with the whole uptown-down-
town transit thing, I decided to take the day off, electing to work
from home, not just because of this appointment but because Jean
Pierre and Gary were coming over shortly to oversee the finishing
touches on the apartment.

I must say that the outcome far exceeded my expectations. Jean
Pierre completely ignored my request (thankfully) for a chocolate
and ecru palette in favor of shades of charcoal silver, iced blue
velvets with royal purple, chartreuse, and brushed gold accents.
When I described it to Blake, she said that it sounded more like a
Gypsy-inspired brothel than a pending feature in *Decor*. Her part-

ing words were "a *Decor* Don't—I cringe." The reality of it, though, was quite striking. My favorite room of all was the bedroom, complete with a king-size four-poster bed. Hanging from each end of the bed were the most sensuous pewter dupioni silk drapes. The foot of the bed featured a powder-blue chaise, a coffee table, and two Louis *someone or other* chairs. The whole thing just seemed so civilized, in spite of the bold striped wallpaper that I still had yet to come to terms with. When Gary arrived, I was in the throes of dressing: options A through E on the bed or floor as I walked around in only my bra and a black pencil skirt, which would soon become option F.

"How I do love your chi-chis, darling. They're like mocha clouds of perfection. Can I borrow them sometime? You know, either as pillows or just cuddle buddies," he asked, standing behind me in the closet, proclaiming the merits of my cleavage instead of discussing the blouse options I asked his opinion on.

"Funny, you do know that they are part of a package, don't you? Wherever they go, I go, which means you would find yourself sleeping with a woman." I gasped, covering my mouth for effect.

"Oh dreadful, I would never! No offense, honey, but I've never had the desire like some of the boys to play in the *shallow* end of the pool. I mean, I hear it can be lovely but just not for me." After a beat, Gary had selected a completely new outfit for me and was shimmying me out of my skirt. "Although, I must say, you do have a tight little body. Who knows, one day we may talk about you carrying my kids—obviously by artificial insemination."

I halfheartedly nod in agreement, "Obviously!"

*When did it become so en vogue to just loan your womb out or lay claim to someone else's? I mean, shouldn't there be a more extensive process to it, like drinks, dancing, expensive gifts, a small island, and not just a five-minute assembly of a day outfit?*

A few hair flips and perfume spritzes later I was primped and ready, wearing a pair of blush full-legged natural-waist trousers and a matching oversize silk blouse with a huge bow at the neck. The look achieved the desired sentiment, conveying, "I am fashionable, yet I respect you and am not a threat."

One thing I know for sure is that the more accomplished, beautiful, and successful the woman, the more easily threatened she is. No matter how secure and pulled together she may appear to be, it's just window dressing—underneath she is a hotbed of insecurity who would gladly chew off her own arm if threatened. *Okay, that may be taking it a little far, but close enough.* I have also learned that being shortsighted—i.e., needing to show the world how attractive I am—is the quickest way to make an oversight or misstep. At this age, coming into my own and now feeling on top of the world, I want to show it every moment possible, just not today. Not with Carly. I like my job, love my apartment, and would like to keep them both. So for today I am a great student, and Carly is my guide.

# 16

## HIGH TEA

IN NEW YORK there are three levels of High Society status. The first is New Money, often characterized by its lack of subtlety. The typical demographic consists of Wall Street traders, recording artists, and record label executives. The second is the Nouveaux Riches, which is just New Money but well traveled and of international origins. These are the second generation or so, known as trustfund babies. For the most part, they are still trying to gloss over the famine, ill-gotten gains, and messy bloodlines of their heritage. Their sole ambition is to be part of the social elite. This brings us to the third, and most illustrious, category: the Blue Bloods. Their fortunes are so vast that no less than six generations can live off the interest of their great-great-great-grandparents' fortune. Their names adorn skyscrapers, medical institutions, and museums the world over. Their history of exclusion is almost as extensive as the endowments that they provide to support the arts, bankroll political campaigns, and implement medical research programs. Walking into the entrance hall of Michael and Carly's home, it was clear to see that she hailed from the last category.

The main elevator opened onto a foyer that was larger than most New Yorkers' entire apartments. Ringing the doorbell, I was greeted by a butler, who escorted me past the receiving level (the art gallery) through three additional levels (living area, bedrooms, and recreational, respectively) before reaching the solarium, where

I would have tea with Mrs. Kipps. She arrived just as I had expected, immaculately put together, clad in covet-worthy 1920s deco jewels, and precision-dyed hair. Having elected to embrace her age, she wore a silvery maven cut like Carmen Dell'Orefice, every strand of hair meticulously painted to silver low-lights and highlighted perfection. We exchanged a few pleasantries. I commented on how lovingly appointed her home was. We glossed over travel, art, and the lack of style in present-day New York. She in kind responded that I was far more impressive at my age than she ever was. The only thing I seemed to be lacking, according to Carly, was a vice.

Between sips of tea, I could feel her eyes on me in an almost unnerving kind of way, as if she wanted to know what made me tick. No sooner had I thought this than she leveled me. Eerily her tone never changed in delivery, so I questioned if I was hearing properly.

"You are indeed a young woman with potential, Ms. Sinclair. I can see why Anthony fell and self-destructed."

Surely she could see the mechanics of my brain trying to make sense of the words coming from her mouth and put the pieces together, so Carly went directly into her story.

"I met Anthony nearly two years ago in Costa Rica. Our daughter, Kaylin, was in her terrible twos or threes, which seems to have extended to her fours and fives. My nerves were at their absolute end, and I needed to get away. Michael was in such awe of her that every little tantrum and screech was a source of sheer delight. All I could think was that the 'gift' from his ex was more like a cursed life sentence that I would have to find a way to deal with. To get some perspective, I decided to go on retreat to one of those marvelous resorts in Costa Rica where they do yoga at sunrise before a waterfall and at night offer candlelight meditation accompanied with champagne. The first few days were blissfully beautiful and silent. You will find it's the simplest things that you miss when there are children to consider, which is why I never wanted them—but for Michael. Like sitting alone, awaking late, being indulgent, and deciding how hard you want to love but I digress. Where was I? Oh yes, coming back from the trails one day I saw this divine specimen of a young man. The next day, around the same time, I saw him again and thought what an ideal distraction he would be. I was faking a slight injury, entirely possible given my advanced yet extremely well kept years, and he assisted me back to my bungalow. He was so attentive, and initially I was blind enough to believe it was indeed my charm that had elicited such a response from him. Then I looked into his eyes and I saw tragedy of immeasurable despair. Quite Greek, one would say. Understanding the other sex the way that I do, I didn't dare ask him but was intrigued, consumed even, to find out his story. Over the next week or so we spent a lot of time together, nearly every waking hour of each day." Feeling the intensity of my stare, Carly clarified her last statement. "For my part I would have loved nothing more than to *explore* him, but such was not the case. He touched my heart in the most maternal way. The way that Kaylin should have touched my heart when she was placed in my arms for the first time—but did not. I never wanted kids, you know. Did I mention that? Just not the type. I have since grown to adore her incrementally and will continue to *appreciate* her, but it is not the way I instantly loved Anthony—like a son. I wanted to protect him, to heal whatever pained him. It was not until the fourth day or so that he told me that he had lost everything and came to Costa Rica to lose himself and see if anything was left to salvage. He spoke of his brother and of you, both losses of unimaginable depth. The whole thing was just far too tragic to be real. I needed to know more about you, so I made some calls."

Having heard more than enough, I was overcome with anger. Trembling, I railed, "Who in the hell do you think you are, lady? You don't have the right to play with people's lives like this. You don't have the right to play with my life like this. What's next? Is he waiting downstairs for me on one knee, with a ring? Will he come to the restaurant one night when I am in the middle of a million things and obliterate my whole world?" The tears were now streaming down my face with abandon. My mind was running a million scenarios at this point; under normal circumstances each would have been more outlandish than the next. But this encounter was anything but normal. "What did you think, you would tell me this story and I would run back to him? Heal him? Forget everything? Well, you are wrong. You're dead wrong. I won't! I don't think of him anymore. I have moved on with my life, and now you are telling me that the cornerstone of the life I am building is an illusion. All constructed by some deranged old woman in heat with nothing better to do than play fucking Geppetto with other people's lives, with my life? Well, fuck you. Tony is not the victim here. I AM. He shut me out long before *he broke my heart*, and no amount of quiet walks in the middle of a fucking forest will change that."

I hastily gathered my things to leave without regard for the china that I knocked over and sent crashing to the floor. Carly remained sitting, as calm and observant as when she began her tale. Reaching the door, I was empty, bereft of any fight. My shoulders and head collapsed into the door for support. I just wanted to disappear again. The loneliness was back and I was exposed.

"Jules, I did not ask you here today to hurt you anymore than you already have been. You must believe me. Initially, I did have this grand fantasy in my head that I would bring you here unbeknownst to Anthony and the two of you would miraculously find your way back together; with a bit more help from me, of course. I know that is not the case, at least right now." Carly walked over to me and held me with a tenderness absent of maternal instinct but filled with female compassion and empathy of what it feels like to love and lose. "It took me nearly a lifetime to find Michael, to allow myself to be vulnerable to him and accept him as he is, trust him to accept me as I am in total. It was wrong of me to dream that you kids could be smarter than us at such a tender age, when neither of you truly even know what love is; that is, until you lose it, as you both have. I do think of Anthony now as my son, and I hope to help him be a better man. The same way that I know Michael is coming to adore you."

"Was Michael a part of this as well?" I asked, having just thought of his potential involvement.

"No. As I said, I did have some intel done on you. Initially, I gave no thought as to what I would do with the information. I just wanted to know what kind of woman could bring a man like Anthony to such an emotionally barren place. I guess you could call it envy more than curiosity, really," said Carly, taking my hand in hers. "Jules, for all the great loves and whirlwind romances of my life, I have never touched a man's soul as you have. Not even with Michael. Yes, he loves me now, but that is because he has played extensively with wild abandon and has made a conscious decision to have an easier, more peaceful life, and that is what I offer. But he is not passionate about me. So I was curious." Searching my face for agreement, as if pleading with me to believe her, Carly continued, "When the position at the restaurant became available, I knew that you could do the job and suggested you. Next thing I knew, everything was happening so quickly and you were here to meet. You miraculously ran into Anthony and subsequently charmed my husband. And here we are. I do hope that despite my meddling, we can be friends."

My tears had stopped, leaving behind only a nauseating feeling in my soul. The overwhelming scent of roses that filled the room only made matters worse—*always hated roses, most overrated flower ever*. I just needed to go. Removing my hand from Carly's and composing myself, I felt compelled to tell her one last thing before leaving:

"If you know Tony so well, then you know that he will hate

you if he finds out what you have done. In loving him you must tell him, today. He will be mad, but it won't last long."

Despite all that had happened between Tony and me, the thought of him hurting because of some crazy-ass, bored, rich woman was not what I wanted. In moving on with my life, I needed to know that he was okay. Saying good-bye to him at the Mercer earlier this year, I had that assurance. Now I was not so sure, but what was I supposed to do about it?

My intent had been to go home, but instead I found myself walking across the street to the park. I was in a daze, so I sat on the nearest bench and tried to drown out the incessant audio in my head, hoping to lose the previous two hours somewhere in the exhaust fumes of traffic. I knew that I would not contact Tony as a result of this meeting. Would I have to contend with him calling me to apologize for the nutter? If so, how would I respond? Did this revelation change things for us? I had no idea, but I felt sick. Sick in my heart. The kind of illness that makes it abundantly clear that for all the forward movement I truly thought I had made, there was one glaring omission: my heart still belonged to him in some crucial, infinitesimal kind of way, and would forever. Suddenly, I just felt overwhelmingly tired and needed to go home.

I managed to pull myself together enough to walk the few blocks home, but not before nearly being hit by a black Mercedes. *Completely my fault—stepping into the crosswalk the way I did absentmindedly.* Percy was standing out front at his post and saw the entire thing.

"Ms. Sinclair, everything all right with you? That was a close one. You have to watch out for these here drivers, sho'nuf. They ain't like London, no ma'am. They'll run you over before they think to stop."

"I don't know, Percy," I said, my voice trembling as I tried to hold myself together. "I'll be more careful." Tears streamed down my cheeks.

"Aw, nah, miss. You're okay now. Just a little shaken up is all."

"It's not that. The car. I just—one of those days, you know?"

"Whatever it is, the good Lord will work it out for the better. Always does. You just hang in there. Get yourself upstairs and rest."

"Thanks, Percy." I smiled weakly.

As I turned to go inside, the doors opened on a black chauffeur-driven Mercedes like the one that nearly struck me.

"Welcome back, Mr. Crawford. How was your trip, sir?"

"Good, thank you, Percy. It's good to be home. You're good?" were the last words I heard before the elevator doors closed—*glad to know someone is good.*

# 17

---

# REFUGE

ONE DAY OUT of the office turned into three unexplained sick days, days that I had yet to actually accumulate—a minor detail that I couldn't care less about. Once surrendering to the safety of my apartment, I undressed immediately, turned the shower on full blast, and prayed that the water would wash away all the feelings of pity and insecurity that Carly had conjured in me. *In this moment I missed so much the rains of London that seemed to cry for me daily.* There was no use pretending anymore, the grand illusion of reinventing my life in New York had come crashing down like an elaborate deck of cards. The fail-safes for healing that I had established across the pond, like watching *Random Harvest*, no longer worked. I could not calm my mind enough to watch old movies. Every time Paula entered Charles's (Smithy's) office for the first time in her new clandestine role as his secretary, I ached and yelled at the screen, rewriting their dialogue and demanding that she confront him in the moment and say:

*Charles, you fool. I am your wife. Don't you remember our little cottage in the countryside? We had a lovely life. We had a child and then you went away for a job interview and apparently bumped your fucking head, you dumb-ass motherfucker. Now you're allowing this little prepubescent twit to sink her claws into you when I am the one who brought your ass back to life. Why,*

*I ought to bash your damn head in until your memory comes
back and then I will leave your sorry ass broken and destroyed
the way I am.*

Yeah, it's safe to say that watching old movies was definitely not
helping matters. Food and the occasional spliff, on the other hand,
definitely were. My kitchen was littered with containers of takeout
food from nearly every vendor in the neighborhood. Under normal
circumstances I probably would have felt guilty or overly conscious
of potential weight gain, but considering that my anxiety would
not allow me to keep anything down, I had no fear of an emotional
five or ten pounds.

There was no proper context in which to place things, so I allowed them all to coagulate in one big ball of crazy. *In feeling the
way that I do, does this mean that I am still deeply in love with Tony,
even though I know that we are not meant to be? In truth I don't think
we ever were—in love, that is—as much as we were codependent. But
I do love him.* I care about him but never really knew him. The man
I knew would never conspire to do what he did. The man I loved
would not have let me go to London without being hot on my
heels, standing across the street from my flat, awaiting my exit in
order to plead his case. The man I envisioned him to be would have
fought for me. And that is where the insurmountable problem was
in all of this. *I still had never accepted that Tony was just a man, not
a superhero.* True, I no longer viewed him through rose-colored
glasses but it was still, to some degree, Old Hollywood. The illusion of flawless perfection created by a lens smeared with Vaseline
no longer was sufficient. It worked for the young adult that I was
when we met, but it fell severely short of the woman I have become
in the past couple of years.

It had never occurred to me that my very foundation had
changed, that I had grown in principle. I spent so much time saying Tony's name, asking about Tony (indirectly yet directly), avoid-

ing Tony, learning how to exist without Tony, that I never took the time to notice Jules Sinclair. And my, how she had changed. No longer was she playing dress-up going from one homecoming ceremony to the next. She was the main event. She is me, far from perfect but not as naïve.

The final two days were a lighter version of my sabbatical, not so much an open gaping wound, but not fully healed either. Gary was out of town with Jean Pierre, recouping his "favors," so there was no concern about an impromptu visit. The only people who dared to cross my doorstep were the delivery guys with my eats and the FedEx guy who erroneously delivered a package for Mr. M. Crawford in 7A. On the third day I received a call from Michael via Simone, which I answered.

"I have Michael," Simone said matter-of-factly.

"Jules, how you feeling? Hey, Simone, jump off this call. Carly told me what happened. That's wild, kid. Only the kind of perfect storm that my wife can create, always got her hands in something. Her heart was in the right place, you know, if you look at it from a specific geometric angle through an official NASA telescope." He paused for a moment to see if his attempt at humor actually registered on me. "That's life, though. Some motherfucker is always pulling the strings like your ass is Pinocchio or something. Your only choice is to handle it and keep your priorities in check. We have a full season to prepare for. Your neo-soul artist is already becoming a pain in my side."

"Michael, why did you hire me?" Among the many questions I had been wrestling with over the past few days, this is about the only one that I actually stood a chance of getting an answer to.

"Like I said before, you came at the recommendation of someone I value deeply, Carly, but that is not why I hired you. I met with you because of her. I hired you because I liked what I saw when we met, so I offered you the job. Jules, why are you making me repeat myself? You know I hate that. You're ambitious and a fighter. More important, I don't mind you breathing some of my air. Hell, if we had met earlier, I might have had to add you to the harem."

"Thanks, Mike. I needed that. Maybe not the last part, but—"

"Who's Mike? You've been hanging around Raymond too long. The name is Michael and you are out of sick days. I'll see you tomorrow."

"Correction, thank you, Michael. See you tomorrow."

# 18

## EMERGENCE

**D**AY FOUR AND I was ready to return to the world. And none too soon. The morning air, thankfully, was cool but not unseasonably cold. I checked the forecast with old reliable: my body and an open window to feel the breeze; *goose bumps denoted a scarf, perky nipples meant a sweater or light jacket, a full-body shimmy inclusive of goose bumps and perky nipples meant head-to-toe North Face coat and gloves.* Today was a perky nipple, so I put on an oversize cashmere angora-blend sweater, a military coat I found in a surplus shop off Shoreditch High Street, and black riding pants with over-the-knee boots, then headed out.

"Miss Sinclair, glad to see you on this fine morning. I was 'bout to send a rescue party, but the cadre of deliverymen gave me the distinct impression that you were still with us," Percy said jovially as I exited the building.

"You're quite cheeky today, Perceville," I said, winking. "It's a good day to be seen."

"Can I get you a taxi?"

"No thanks, think I'm going to walk a bit and allow New York to do her thing with my soul."

"That's the spirit," said Percy. "Nothing better than a good walk. Keeps you young. The missus and I do 'em frequently. We even got a little group in the neighborhood and walk on the weekends at night down to the local . . ."

Oooh, Percy and that gift for gab that seems to know no con-clusion! Seizing a lapse in his story, I offered my final salutations and departed. Time permitting, I could make my way up to Fifty-eighth Street before crossing over near the Plaza and grab a quick bite at Rue 57. In spite of Carly's meddling, Tony and I *had* met and said whatever needed to be said, on our own terms and in our own way. The rest, at this point, was anybody's guess, but I could handle it no matter what.

Reaching Sixtieth Street, I wait for the light to change and join the other commuters entering the crosswalk. The roundabout was already filled with horse-drawn carriages and their handlers grooming them for tours through the park. Making way for an advancing pack of schoolkids, I step off the sidewalk, only to be accosted by the loud blaring of a horn. It's shrill, so loud that I nearly jumped out of my boots; so close that I could feel the heat from the engine before it ground to a halt. I mimed a profuse apol-ogy before walking on, in the hope that we could all agree to just let this little incident pass without a public spectacle. Continuing on my way, I had the unnerving feeling that despite the hundreds of people on the sidewalk with no thought of me, I was not alone, which in and of itself was crazy. Rationalizing that I was just being paranoid—nerves having been frayed for days and such—I keep walking. A few steps onward, I glance to my left, only to see the front bumper of the car seemingly keeping pace with me, so I pick up speed and maneuver myself to the inside of the sidewalk, far-thest from traffic. Firmly enveloped in the sea of people, I relax and allow my mind to drift again until my thoughts are interrupted by a familiar voice.

"You do know that you are about to give poor Carlos a heart attack, don't you? This is the second time in less than a week you have walked out in front of him. You got to go easy—space your collisions. He's an old man, the reflexes aren't always so sharp," said Marcus. "Tell you what, why don't you make it easier on everyone and allow me to give you a ride? At the very least it would be less than the increase in my insurance, should he actually hit you next time."

"Sorry about that, but no. I'm fine to walk."

"Well, in that case why don't I join you," replied Marcus.

"Honestly, I'd prefer if you didn't," I said. The last thing I wanted or needed was company, especially his. The sheer fact that he was male, breathing and daring to interrupt my solo pilgrimage, rendered him persona non grata.

"You know, this is the third time we have met and the third time you have rebuffed me. I'm starting to get the feeling that you *really* don't want me around."

"Really, you're getting all that, are you? Maybe you should listen," I said.

"I know you didn't mean that. Probably didn't have your morning coffee or something. I know how you girls can be at certain times."

His last comment stopped me cold in my tracks. "Seriously, you didn't just say that. Rude, actually, very rude!"

"No less rude than you refusing my sincere generosity when all I am doing is trying to protect you from becoming roadkill."

"Listen, I said *sorry*. I said *no thank you*. I will even apologize to your driver if it will make you go away," I said, unwilling to disguise my annoyance. "What else could you possibly want from me, Marcus? There must be a zillion women who would love nothing more than to be aggravated by you at any time, but as for me, *no thanks*. The last thing I need right now is another person trying to barge their way into my life and arrange things."

"So you're not a morning person. Got it," said Marcus, seemingly unfazed by my animosity. "Let's just walk, shall we?"

"Whatever," I replied, as it seemed easier at this point just to keep pressing forward. Reaching Avenue of the Americas, it was clear that he was not leaving my side anytime soon, so I mentally redirected my path, in the hope of coming across a subway stop without looking obvious. Surely there must be one on this side. The red and orange lines were never familiar to me, but I was prepared to hop anything moving and cab it from anywhere in order to put some distance between him and me.

"Do you mind telling me where we are going or don't you know? Carlos has been trailing for about seven blocks and pissing cabbies off."

"Marcus, I don't want to be rude to you anymore than you want me to, so I beg you—go away. I am not interested. I am seeing someone."

"Well, forgive me for saying so, but it doesn't seem to be going so well just by the looks of things."

"What do you know? Besides, it's not him—just got blindsided by some old ex issues is all. Never easy, but I'ma be okay. Shit happens, right?"

"That it does. So is that what we're doing here, walking to recover?"

"Something like that," I said, feeling a flash of relief at the sight of a subway entrance ahead on Fiftieth Street. "Just thought certain things—feelings and such—were in the past. I mean, you would think there was nothing left, right? I left the country, for Christ's sake, even saw him earlier this year, and all was okay, and then this woman meddles . . . Anyway, who cares, right? We were young. I'm fine . . . and this is my stop," I said, gesturing to the subway.

"Sounds complicated."

"Unnecessarily so," I say, extending my hand. "Thanks for the walk."

"Jules, we're not all bad, you know—after the maturation process and all, we can actually be something great to call home about," said Marcus.

"I'll take your word for it. Sorry about before, really," I said, realizing that there was no justifiable reason for me to be so harsh to this guy, other than the obvious, my attraction to him in spite of myself.

"You sure I can't give you a ride? Not for me, for Carlos—you can make nice."

"No thanks, another time—Carlos," I said over my shoulder as I went into the station.

. . .

Jacklyn was the first person I encountered at the restaurant. I hadn't noticed it before but she too is quite the little chatterbox of unsolicited information. "Hi, Jules. Feeling better? You sounded awful on the phone the other day. I think you and my friend Kelly had the same thing. She was sick too—sounded like death. We were supposed to go to the Roxy and she canceled, so not cool. At first I thought she was ditching me for some guy, because she does that, you know, but then I realized, after speaking to you, that seriously she was sick. You both sounded the same—awful. Also, Lauryn's people called. She needs to do a morning sound check. They should be here within the hour. I tried to reach you when they called earlier, but your phone went to voice mail."

*I seriously doubt that Kelly and I were suffering from the same illness.* There was no need to stop and give her my full attention; as it was, Jacklyn always seemed to be a step or two wherever I was until dismissed. I continued into the elevator and waited for her to come up for air so I could tell her we would resume this after my morning coffee.

"How do you do that?" I asked, staring at her in complete bewilderment.

"Do what?"

"Talk for that long nonstop without breathing. I swear, I'm just waiting for you to pass out."

"I do? Didn't know. Should I stop?" Jacklyn asked.

"No, just an observation. I must've been on the subway when you called," although she did not need my affirmation, seeing as how she knew the routine of my life better than I did most of the time.

"Yeah, that's what I thought, so I went ahead and rescheduled your morning appointments so you can remain on site. Mr. Kipps has already called to find out what's going on. He is coming in early, I think. I asked Simone in order to make sure, but she is crankier than normal, so I guess it's true."

"Of course he is. The Love Boat would never set sail without Captain Stubing." Off her utterly clueless look, I decided it best not to explain and just buy Jacklyn a box set of 1980s television shows for Christmas. "Let me see the set list and her rider," I said, scanning the papers as I walked into my office, only to stop immediately in my tracks. "Are you pulling my leg? She wants to be called Ms. Hill?! What the—? Lordy. Alrighty then, let the games begin. Grab me a latte and meet me back downstairs in fifteen minutes."

Despite whatever storm cloud could be brewing with this earlier sound check, I felt good being back in the office. Here the rules were abundantly clear and incapable of forcing me to take to my bed. *The customer is always right and in some cases so is the entertainer if ultimately it will make the customer happy.*

From a comfort perspective, my office was the next best place to be other than the apartment. Because of the configuration of the building, there was no corner unit to be campaigned for. To compensate, Michael had placed all the executive offices with the exception of his on the top levels facing the street, each with floor-to-ceiling windows and discreet little patios. "I only have one rule: no smoking in the offices," Michael had said within the context of one of his random daily e-mails regarding team and office protocol, which were sent more out of boredom than as mandates. A rule that apparently applies to everyone but him.

I thought of this briefly as I laid eyes on the exquisite crystal and gold-plated ashtray that was doubling as a vintage paperweight. During the course of decorating my apartment, Jean Pierre found a few pieces that demanded to be in my office: an antique Italian desk, duo-toned Moroccan carpet, an amazing RMID sofa, and a coffee table.

There is no way that I could have afforded such luxuries on the modest decorating budget Michael approved, but with Jean Pierre's discount and an extra helping of charm, they miraculously found their way into my space without too much damage to my bank account. To complement, I added fresh orchids and vintage black-and-white photographs of my music and fashion inspirations. Taking a quick moment to flip through the phone sheet and monthly booking report before rushing downstairs, I came across a Post-it from Simone affixed to the second page that read, "In case Michael doesn't tell you immediately. Looking good."

The restaurant was booked solid through the winter season, with an extensive waiting list to compensate for any cancellations. This was indeed promising. When I originally proposed the idea to Michael back in September, he made it clear that his only focus was the flow of the restaurant and being the most liked man on the island, "so you better make sure everyone is at their best so I can be at mine," he had said.

"Jules, glad to see you could be with us today," Michael said, poking his head into the office and forcing me to look up. "Good thing too. I hear your first one is already making demands. Ms. Hill, huh? Maybe you should start calling me Mr. Kipps as well," he said, pausing briefly as if to decide whether he was going to enter or just keep on moving. "You ready for this?"

"Real funny, Michael. Real funny. No worries, I am fine," I said, but judging by the look on his face, it was not the most convincing of deliveries. "Seriously, I am fine. What are you doing in this early? Trying to get an autograph or are you worried about me?"

"No, and you are delusional. Today is a heavy delivery day and we had to order more than usual in anticipation of the reservations. The restaurant will be filled throughout with service staff and outside people."

"Uh-huh."

"Usually I leave this to Raymond, but every once in a while I take a more hands-on approach. It keeps the troops motivated and engaged."

"Well, look at that. Here I was thinking you were Captain Stubing when in fact you're a modern-day Bonaparte," I replied, in a much lighter tone to let him know that my wits were about me and that I was indeed joking so he should take it as such.

"And you will be in Waterloo if your big idea doesn't generate enough money to recoup me on the enormous fees I am paying these singers to perform and the additional staff," said Michael, not missing a beat while still straddling the doorway.

"Well, based on the reservations—" I attempted to say.

"And before you tell me about a full house through December, tell me how many of them will be drinking hard liquor, ordering bottles, and how often we will be turning those tables over. That's the restaurant business, Jules. Those are the things that keep the lights on and me bespoke in Savile Row. Where is your assistant?" asked Michael. "Oh, there you are. Jacklyn, call my office and have Simone set up a call for me with Marcus and Simon. Afterward she should meet me in the restaurant."

"Yes, Mr. Kipps, I'm on it." The syrup dripping from Jacklyn's every word was laughable. Her crush on Michael was completely obvious to everyone, especially him, yet she would never admit to it and was too naïve to know how to conceal it properly. Even the one time I asked her about it. "Absolutely not, Ms. Sinclair. I-I-I, why would you even think such a thing?" That is the moment I figured out how to tell when she was lying, from her stuttering and being overly formal. I couldn't blame her, though. When I was twenty-two I only had eyes for older men and if one like Michael crossed my path, all jet-set debonair with a bit of edge, I surely would have been swooning. Thankfully, that phase was brief and lasted only a year or so until I met Tony.

As light and witty as his delivery might have been, Michael's point was abundantly clear. In business as in life, *always know your break-even point*. In doing so, you know how much you can risk and recognize when it is time to walk away or cash in. Two years in another country, three days in seclusion, and I still could not succinctly state this: five minutes with Michael and it seemed like common sense. "I am going downstairs to check out the stage and Laur—Ms. Hill's dressing room. Take Keith off my phone sheet. I will call him back later."

By later, I meant today within the next hour or so, but one thing led to another and before I knew it the phone call became a hastily typed e-mail.

Subject:

Hi you,
Temporarily fell down the rabbit hole. Might I ring you when I resurface?
x Jules

His response was quintessentially Keith.

Subject: RE:

Princess
Nothing you can't handle, I'm sure. Get back at me when you're ready.
Masters

In the week that I allowed to not-so-subtly slip by, I was conscious of the fact that I was purposefully avoiding inviting Keith immediately back into my life. Not because of anything that he had done and not for some grieving or pining over Tony. Before the whole episode with Carly, I was clear on our dynamics. He was my Transition Guy, our chemistry (in bed and out) amazing, we enjoyed each other with no expectations of a future. But now the line was threatening to get a bit blurred because moment to moment my desire to just fall into him, to fall into any man and be rescued, was as pressing as Rapunzel's need to escape that tower. What can I say? It was a pattern that I could never seem to shake, so I kept busy.

* * *

I still had not found a cleaning woman of my own and Richard's seemed to be unavailable whenever I needed her, so on Saturday I decided to clean the apartment and do laundry, all four loads of it. It seems impossible that I could live here alone with no pets and yet accumulate so many dirty clothes in a matter of a week or so. After taking down the final two loads, I collapsed on the sofa and got lost in an episode of *ER* before realizing that the time had long since expired on the first load, so I rushed to the basement to place them in the dryer before someone in the building complained or rudely removed them from the washer and placed them on the folding table for anyone to see. Opening the door, I heard the phone ringing and decided it was probably best to pick it up this time. After all, Cora had phoned twice already and would probably continue calling until I answered. *That woman was relentless.* Saturdays were our day to have an extensive one-sided conversation, always in her favor, whether I wanted to or not.

"Hi, Mommy," I said.

"Hi, sexy. Sorry to disappoint, but you can call me Daddy if you like." My goodness, I love the sound of his voice. Most people's phone voice is uneventful, monotone, or nasal—not Keith's. His was authoritative and rich with no reverb. He could probably make the Annual Crop Report sound desirable, which was no small feat since my eyes glazed over at the mere mention of stocks and such.

Noticeably caught off guard, I said, "Hiiiii," making a valiant effort to recover. "The name is vaguely familiar but the specifics are a bit cloudy. Is this your new number? It is not in my phone."

"No, I'm just at the office putting the final touches on a presentation for Monday with the Japanese. Why don't you save me from this slave ship and let's grab a drink. Say, Amaranth in twenty minutes?"

"Are you sure we could handle an impromptu drink on a domestic Saturday, and by impromptu I mean me showing up looking more casual than you have ever seen me?" (Bare face, yoga pants, and a well-worn sweatshirt that I snagged from a college boyfriend many moons ago.)

We agreed to meet within the hour. He would still arrive in twenty starting off with a solo Dewar's, and me shortly thereafter. Despite the time cushion, I still found myself rushed for time. Thank goodness the restaurant is only a few blocks down the road on Sixty-second Street, just behind Barney's NYC.

Turning the corner from Fifth onto Sixty-second Street, I was immediately reminded that Saturday night is a "going out" night for many. Normally Amaranth is filled with locals who over time become friends. It's comfortable, easy, and delicious. Tonight, however, it was packed. There were tons of people standing in front awaiting a table. Initially, I feared that Keith would be among them, but then I remembered that he and Gianni, the manager, were good friends. Sliding by a young couple who screamed, "Connecticut date night," I saw Keith ahead at the bar.

"Did someone write an article this week about this place that I am not aware of? There's like fifty people outside waiting for less than ten tables," I said.

"Well, I'll say. Thank goodness Gianni had the chairs in the back or we would have been with them," Keith said, standing to kiss me. "Welcome back from Wonderland, Miss Alice. I was beginning to think that you were lost for good."

For the first time *we* felt a bit strange to me, or maybe it was just the fact that I was still hypersensitive in my own skin and overtly aware of my failings, as it were. Some people were fine with a one-night stand to provide them the distance and security required to exorcise the demons of a former relationship. I preferred the composition of a full-on relationship, despite this casual exercising in "just dating" that we were doing. Eventually, I reasoned, I would find my knight, shining armor optional but sword essential. Looking at him now, I had this overwhelming need to apologize for the absence but was not quite sure of where or how to start.

"You look great."

"Really? Thanks," I said, a bit self-conscious and thinking that I should have put more effort into my physical appearance for him.

"I didn't want to crowd you, but I was getting concerned, you know?" Keith said, preferring to focus his attention on the bottom of the nearly empty glass of whiskey than on me, ensuring that the "keeping it light" boundaries remained.

I confided so was I, the first day or so, but once the initial shock of things passed, I was better than I had thought, which was great. My only concern was the epiphany that maybe just maybe Tony was not the love of my life, despite the immense pain that I had endured or the lengths to which I'd sought to escape. That part I still had yet to come to terms with, and in trying to do so I came face-to-face with old patterns, which is where my head lived right now. I wasn't ready to elaborate on specific tendencies just yet.

"Keith, am I a masochist or something?" I blurted out, wanting a real answer and not to be pacified.

"No, baby, you're not. You're just on the later side of twenty-eight with Saturn's return in your house and it is having one hell of a time with you."

"Huh? What is that, Japanese or something?" I offered, half serious. In response, he explained that the emotional roller coaster that has been my life for the past year and a half was more than normal as this was the astrological time when everyone's cosmic house was thrown into disarray by Saturn going retrograde.

"Think of it as the universe's way of making order out of the confusion your life until now has created, by showing you what you are made of so you can live on your terms. No one gives us a guidebook into adulthood, so we enter it boldly and unapologetically. Our parents long since forgot, so they only warn us of the obvious physical danger. The rest is left up to us to figure out or fuck up. In the arrogance of our youth, we are certain that we have all the answers, so we make career, life, and love decisions all from a place of sheer naïveté. Problem is, the overwhelming lot of those choices are not our personal truth. They are more conditioned precepts and societal brainwashing as to the life we are programmed to have instead of the life we want to have. So as we chronologically get ready to enter a stage of true adulthood—at about thirty years old—everything goes to shit in order to clean house and put us on the right track. Chaos into chaotic order is what I call it," he said, pausing only long enough to finish the last sip of his drink and signaling the bartender for another. "The fucked-up thing is that while we are going through it, we vow to remember, but at its tail end, most of us are so happy to get through the shit that we immediately delete it from memory, forgetting to pass on the wisdom. Now here is the kicker: if you do remember to warn someone, understand that it is a waste of time because it will fall on deaf ears. Even if I knew you at the beginning of your cycle and told you what was about to happen, you would not have believed me."

"Yes, I would!" I said incredulously.

Unconvincingly he replied, "Sure you would have if I came to you and said, 'Jules, for the next two years or so everything that you thought you knew and thought you had firm hold of in your life is about to be pulled from under you and no matter how hard you try to hold on, to fix it—everything will fall apart.' Would you have believed me?"

"Or would I have told the bartender to cut your drunk yet completely fine ass off immediately?"

I knew Keith was right. I would not have believed him if he had tried to explain that the chaos in my life was necessary. *Tomorrow I would talk to Richard about this. I wonder what his retro-cycle was like.* "Or maybe I would have told you that you were on some Southern California surfer vibe and should put down the pipe."

"True. Unfortunately, you can't force this to pass, Jules, just because you want it to. If you allow it, you will be much better off in the long run than you can ever imagine. Seriously, I know this firsthand."

I could feel his sincerity and was grateful. Nearing the end of my second glass of scotch, some parts of his dialogue escaped me—or at least that is what I thought.

"Until twenty-seven I was the golden boy, came from the right family, captain of my high school football team, played college baseball, and got recruited into the majors despite the fact that I was marginal at best. Everyone was so proud, and in the beginning, so was I. Maybe I was just riding on their fumes and never stopped to own my desires because I didn't know I could. My all-American life was figured out for me at birth. Once out of the protective family enclave, I started to go off track but not enough for anyone to wave a red flag. My mom never wanted to see a problem, so she dismissed the drinking and partying. When undeniable, I remember trying to talk candidly with her about things I was feeling, but it was too much for her to hear, so she sent me to her therapist to be fixed. Much to her chagrin, the very therapist she sent me to forced me to dismantle my world in order to understand that I wasn't broken, that it wasn't a phase, and eventually the boundaries of everything in my life had to be redefined in order for me to write my own story. Leaving baseball for prospects unknown disappointed my dad, but we got over it soon enough. He is proud of my success. Accepting that I like men and women devastated my mom and put a wall between us that we are still recovering from. If someone would have told me at twenty-seven that the very foundation of my family life and my identity would be shaken to its core, I would not have believed it." Leaning in to emphasize his last point, he said, "Jules, I only tell you this because the whiskey may now be talking but—your man cried like a little bitch more than a few times. That's how intense everything was. We should really eat something or tomorrow will be rough. Steaks? I'm starving . . ."

The walk back home was rough, but not because of the endless pour. Scotch I can handle. Learning that the man I am seeing is probably attracted to the same kind of men as me was another matter indeed. So, from Amaranth to the shower later that night, and on the subway Sunday to meet Richard in SoHo, I replayed the latter part of our conversation/Keith's confession a million times. But was it indeed a confession, an impossibly late disclaimer (by the way, I too like boys), or a point of fact?

# 19

## SWITCH HITTING

**D**ARLING, ARE YOU certain you heard him properly?" Richard calmly asked within minutes of our meeting at the Cub Room and my immediately spilling the details of last night with Keith. "Before you go and get yourself into a huff, know that I am not doubting your account so much as I want you to be absolutely certain before we go down this murky road."

"Richard, in case it's lost on you, I am having orange juice and not a cocktail, not a mimosa. Orange juice! Doesn't that tell you that something is seriously wrong?" Knowing me as he did, even Richard had to concede that my starting our Sunday brunch with just juice was cautionary. "He told me all this stuff about Saturn and Uranus, which I was going to ask you about, but then he levied the wallop about baseball, his mom, men and women, Aaron or Erin. WTF!"

"Wait, wait, honey, are you sure of the context? Lord knows, with how creative people are today in naming their children, anything is possible. It could be Aryn, Erin, or Aaron. All of it is unisex now. I blame Calvin Klein. Would it kill anyone to just stick to the King's English?"

"Ugh, stop, you are making my brain hurt more than it does already. I know he said A-Erin-Aaron-somebody, and I know I heard the words *men* and *women* after sumtin' sumtin' drinking and partying. And before you ask, NO. I did not stop him midsentence to get clarification. I didn't even realize I needed it until I was halfway home, and what was I supposed to do at that point? Besides, that's why I have you. Help meeeee!" I whined.

Watching me dissolve into a squealing tantrum suitable for a three-year-old was not exactly what Richard had in mind, so he attempted to soothe me as only he knew how. "Here, take a sip of this. Before you speak again, take another. Then calmly tell me how he spoke of him/her?" he said, stuttering out a correction at my horrified expression. "Darling, I meant *her*. Drink more, improves clarity."

"They met in college freshman year in a public speaking class. You know, that one random course that requires an *x* and *y* credit. Please refrain from making the obvious chromosome dig here, please. Anyway, one thing led to another and they became friends, hanging out partying, and ultimately it became uncomfortable for Keith because he was having feelings about Aaron, Erin, Aryn. *What the fuck!* They started dating, sort of, first love, and Keith felt as if he was living a lie. *Oh gawd!* He had a lot of pressure on him and they broke up, but not because Keith didn't love him/her. Eventually, he spoke to his mom and she sent him to therapy. The flip is that, instead of 'curing' him, the therapist helped him own his truth."

"Oh, dear. I bet that is not what *Mommy* had in mind." Richard could not help but laugh at the irony. His shoulders animatedly bounced up and down as the spasm of laughter subsided. He knew this terrain all too well, as he had to contend with a disapproving mother when he came out.

"Honestly, I need for you not to be savoring the demolition of my pseudo-relationship as much as you are that drink. What am I supposed to do with this? Isn't there some type of law or something about this?"

"Like what, honey? As far as I know there is no law for a knight in knight's clothing with a questionable sexuality who is not trying to hide it from you, as some do."

"Richard, we have slept together many times, and he responds to me physically, and I am not talking about the alcohol, the E, or 'blue pill' type of response. I mean, I know that we are still in the 'getting to know each other' phase, but this is just too much information and I am not sure I am equipped. This just introduces too many things into my world that are impossible to comprehend."

"Okay, first things first, tomorrow call your doct— Oh, dear."

Before Richard could finish what he was about to say, he'd laid eyes on Blake entering our sanctuary, looking all things equestrian city chic—the Ralph Lauren version, that is. Her hair fell below her shoulders, the same golden wheat color as the turtleneck she wore, with matching riding pants and a blue denim jacket accessorized with an oversize paisley scarf in earth tones.

"Hey, kittens. I knew I would find you both here," said Blake, looking around to see who else was there. "What is the deal with this place and both of you anyway? It's like you have this little Sunday sandbox with a standing reservation for the two of you. Anyway, I woke up and decided I was crashing this little party." Searching for a space to sit at our cramped two-topper, she added, "Couldn't you find a better table?"

"No, this is the only table I like. If you want something a bit more on the fringe, then I suggest you grab a lonely table of one," Richard instructed.

For as long as I have met him here, this table, located in the center room, directly across from the bar, has been his fixture. I have actually arrived on Sundays ahead of Richard to a wait list with every table in the restaurant filled with the exception of table 16, Richard's table. It awaited him, come rain, sleet, or shine, or standing room.

Choosing for the moment not to be goaded into an early round with Richard, Blake continued, "By the looks of things, it's a sad sack of a party and I probably would have been better served just staying home."

"Don't you worry, Blake, all is well here. Jules is just going through the relationship weeds."

"Not again. I thought we were done with the Tony thing. Carly is a meddling old bat. I swear, Julesy, you have to let that whole history go. He is great to look at but honestly, he is not the sort you build a life with. Tony is the kind of guy you meet in your twenties, fall head over heels for, surrender the last part of your innocence to, do some 'shrooms with, and in return he strips you down to your emotional core and obliterates your entire world. You grieve for a bit, pull yourself together wiser and stronger now, setting your sights on the guy who looks good but not as good, who loves you far more than you love him, and above all has the financial trajectory to keep you in the comforts you deserve. By all accounts I would say you are right on track, wouldn't you?" said Blake, conscious of the dumbfounded expressions on our faces as she spoke: "What?"

"Just when I thought I had you pegged as a gold-digging social climber from the womb with a shovel in her shoe, you astound me," said Richard, causing Blake to do a double take. Because Richard handles me more with kid gloves, I oftentimes forget that he can be rather biting if need be. Much of his ire seems to be reserved for Blake, although I wouldn't daresay it was out of spite as much as it is a reflection of his former self. Somewhere in a world that only the two of them can comprehend. This is their way.

"Thank you. By the way, am I the only one who can make your inner cunty queen come out or do you use that kind of language with all the ladies? If so, I can see why Jules is still such a sad, sad sack."

"If this were the eighties, I would cut you," said Richard, with butter knife in hand.

"Richard, if this were the eighties you would have to find me, and by my calculations Salt Lake City, Utah, is a far cry from Studio 54, where you were most likely twirling. And I do mean 'twirling' in all connotations," said Blake.

"Stop it, you two! First, this is why you are not invited to brunch, Blakes. You and Richard can never seem to play nice, even for my sake. It's like you both went through some horrible divorce and I am the poor child stuck in the middle. Anyway, it's not Tony, so save it."

"Oh, thank Gawd," said Blake, gulping down the remainder of my juice.

"I think that Keith is bisexual," I said.

"And, what? I'm not following."

"Are you listening to me, Keith is—" off Richard's look I felt the need to amend my statement—"Keith and I had talked over drinks last night, and he told me that he is attracted to men and women."

"Welcome to New York! If they are not bisexual, they are bi-curious or bipolar—at least he's in the affirmative. If you like him, ride it out. What, why are you looking at me like that? I swear, you have been hanging around Richard too long. You're starting to get that same ole uppity scowl. Listen, I know you have not been on this island for a few years, but sweets, let me tell you, you will be hard-pressed to find a man of Keith's stature and age who is not dabbling. Seriously, forget difficult, it's nearly impossible in this town. The only question you need to ask yourself is, What's your endgame? If it is to have great sex—and I assume the sex is good because he is too damn fine for it not to be—then I say keep at it. If your intention for this one is marriage, babies, country homes, and beach club memberships, then you might need to find out which side of the pendulum he is most inclined to."

"Either I have had more drinks than I can recall or maybe my sugar levels are low, but dare I say you made sense *again*." Richard's backhanded compliment was not lost on Blake or me.

"I know. I do that, you know," said Blake, reaching across the table to take an unsolicited bite from Richard's omelet. "Hmm, I don't like this. You should have gotten French toast."

"Well then, maybe *you* should order French toast and leave *my* food alone," said Richard.

"Oh, yeah, I could do that."

"That would be progress."

"What's wrong with her? Why is she just sitting there like a lump? This *can't* be what you both do every Sunday. If so, I will take that table for one," Blake said, in reference to the two-topper in the far corner near the kitchen—clearly the worst seat in the place. The kind of table reserved for rude customers.

Mischievously, Richard responded, "Stop it, Blake, can't you hear the wheels churning in that pretty little head as she tries to process all that you have said?"

"Now that you mention it, there was a faint smell of smoke moments ago. I thought it was from the kitchen." Both snickering at my obvious despair.

Exhausted with being the pun of the joke, I spoke up. "You are both quite cruel human beings when you want to be. You must know this. No more brunch trios. You bring out the absolute worst and snarkiest in each other. Yes, Richard, I know that 'snarkiest' is not a word in *Webster's*. So be it," I said, glaring at both of them equally.

For the next fifteen minutes or so we ate in silence, until Richard placed his hand on top of mine, offering, "Honey, things aren't always so black and white, you know. Based on what you have told me, there appears to be no malice, so you can't cry party foul per se, but you must know if you can handle all that comes with being involved with someone who is hitting for both teams." Looking in Richard's eyes I could see that he did not take my predicament lightly, despite the earlier quips and jabs.

"That's what I said," Blake chimed in, midway through devouring a healthy bite of her French toast. You would think she had not eaten in days by the gluttonous display.

"Next time, can you please wait to swallow before enlightening us? I already feel ill," I said.

"Speaking of that, I hope you took your own advice," replied Blake. "By the way, you should go and get tested tomorrow if you haven't already. The virus just isn't reserved for the boys who love boys, you know."

"The virus?" I asked before understanding. Fuck, *HIV*, the one variable I didn't even consider in this whole equation. It is dangerous enough in this day and age having protected sex with a new partner who is heterosexual. There is always a fear of a condom slip and accidental pregnancy until the much-welcomed appearance of moodiness, bloating, and cramping that precedes a monthly visit from Mary. To my knowledge, four of my close girlfriends had abortions before they were twenty-five, and that was big news— drastic even. Two of them occurred in college, and if I am correct, their parents still do not know. Now let's throw into the mix an incurable, fatal, easily transmitted disease that is highly prevalent in the gay community. *I think I am now going to pass out.*

My mind was reeling and I could not bring myself to tell Richard and Blake that there was indeed *that one time* Keith and I did not use protection. It was the first night, when I allowed myself to live too greatly in the moment of not having any for so long. A few days afterward, over dinner, Keith was the one to bring it up, more a preemptive discussion to unexpected fatherhood than anything else.

"Hey, I just want to let you know, in case you're worried about the other night, don't be. I don't have any diseases and shit. My fellas are great swimmers, though, so ya know."

"Relax yourself, Masters. While I am certain our fictitious children would be absolutely gorgeous if that was the case, it's not. I am still on the Pill. Never got off, actually. Having always lived by the 'what if?' factor, it just never made any sense for me to stop taking them. Now, obviously, I didn't know there would be a substantial drought in the forecast."

"And your decision had absolutely nothing to do with the documented weight gain that happens to women after they come off it?"

"Your parents should never have encouraged you to read," I teased, pinching him lightly. "All I will say is that it could have been a deterrent."

It seemed so light and trivial then. We laughed it off and all was forgotten. Now, sitting here, I can feel Blake's and Richard's eyes on me, and I can't decide if I am to look up and meet their concerned stares or look away and change the topic. I opt to just lean back and squeeze my eyes closed as tight as possible. Surely, I would awaken any moment to see that the drama being played out was not my own. Not so. Instead, a few air kisses and hugs later, Blake, Richard, and I were making our way down Prince Street so I can catch the N or R train on Broadway. Even if his apartment weren't located a few blocks east of Broadway on Mott, Richard would walk me to the subway or a taxi. To hear him tell it, "Papa would turn over in his grave if I didn't see you girls off properly." It was part of our dynamic that I always looked forward to and, truth be told, looked for in the guys I date. Keith is chivalrous also.

"It's such a pretty day, but can we not do this again? I don't quite like being the center of all the drama, you know. That is not what our Sundays are supposed to be about." My body was now as tired as my mind, so it seemed only right to descend the steps into the subway, where there were fewer people to contend with, than on the streets where it seemed like the world was out and jovial.

"What we must never do is give our location to that dreadful Blake."

"Stop it, I know you like Blake. Admit it, she has grown on you."

"Honey, psoriasis also grows on you, but you don't see me inviting its discomfort into my life, now do you? Our Sundays are about enjoying each other's company, being a sounding board and reflecting on the week that was. Not an obnoxious free-for-all. Now, arguably, this one just happened to be a bit more complicated than most." Wrapping his arms around me tightly, Richard said the words I so needed to hear: "We'll get through this. *You are fine, don't worry.*" Pulling away to look at me, he added, "As a precaution, though, I want you to call my doctor in the morning and see him immediately. If you wish, I can meet you there. Just tell me what time. Then we can decide what to do about Mr. Masters."

Escaping into the subway station, I knew only two things for sure. The first was that Richard was still standing at the entrance looking after me, more concerned than he would like for me to know, so I dared not turn around. The second is that I didn't need the results of my AIDS test to help me decide about my relationship with Keith. At this point I know a few things about myself well enough to understand that I am just not that modern of a girl to be with someone with an affinity for both sexes, no matter how amazing the package is or how much he appears to adore me.

Truth is, on a deeper level, if pressured to address this publicly, I would have to admit that I am not 100 percent comfortable with the whole intimacy of homosexuality, which seems like an enormous contradiction given my circle of friends, but it is true. With my friends I can compartmentalize things—focusing only on their happiness, but not with a man I am intimate with. I am not proud of this, but such is the case. *With each and every day I must admit that I am definitely my mother's child. You can take the girl out of Jamaica but some parts of Jamaica stay in the girl.* Right now, the major problem, aside from the obvious, was how to handle things with Keith under these conditions. In my heart of hearts I felt that he was not the sort to cavort with such disregard if he knew there was a life-altering problem. Hell, Keith loves himself much too much. More to the fact, he is open and honest with me with no seeming agenda, which is new, in a manner of speaking, especially as it pertains to my romantic entanglements. The worst-case scenario cannot be my fate, it just can't.

# 20

## THE VOICE IN MY HEAD

SADLY, AFTER I returned home, the remainder of the day got progressively worse. As much as I attempted to calm myself and rest, the panic within me grew. Was I being delusional? Was I dying and didn't know it? *Yes to the latter, because it is inevitable—obviously.* My overwhelming immediate concern, to be specific, was dying before the natural occurrence of events I envisioned claimed me; old age after having lived an amazing life as a media guru, traveling the world with my debonair überamazing husband, jetting between our homes in Manhattan, Paris, and Lake Como while raising a beautiful family of two—potentially being the bane of my daughter's existence because that is often the way of mothers and daughters, the apple and aspiration of my son's eye because that too is the way of things, and becoming the coolest grandmother ever. Then, after celebrating my ninety-fifth birthday, where I am fit as a fiddle and can compete with any sprite of a seventy-year-old, my house filled with family and friends collected over the years, I would go upstairs to rest and peacefully exit this world. Nowhere in this vision does it say that I am to contract a fatal, painful illness and die alone without even the most basic of comforts and support. I don't even have pets. *Maybe I should get a cat! Hate cats—hateful animals they are.*

Around 4:43 a.m., after the umpteenth infomercial designed to help me zap blemishes, lose belly fat, and tone my thighs—*am*

*I the only one who finds the ThighMaster unsettling?*—I just couldn't take it anymore. Having left the solitude of my bed long before and repositioned myself in the living room on the sofa, I needed answers.

"Mommy, you up?"

"Yes. Why are you, Julesea? Insomnia again?" Cora asked, without much regard, because my nonsleeping bouts by this time have become sort of legendary for their duration and frequency.

"Why do you insist on calling me Julesea, Mommy? You know my name is Jules."

"Well, when I pushed you out of my body and signed the birth certificate, it was Julesea Isabel Sinclair. I don't know why *you* choose to keep forgetting that little fact."

"Well, if you would have asked me first, I would have told you that I prefer Jules."

"Really? And I was to wait how long for this *personal identification* preference, Julesea? A few months on the hopes that miraculously your first words would be something other than 'mama' or 'dada' or maybe just maybe I could have waited a couple of years. In the interim I would call you 'hey you' or 'the only fruit to have come from my womb' when strangers asked."

"Mom!!!!!!"

"No, seriously, you're right. Of course you are. I have only been in the world slightly longer than you. Here I am thinking that giving you a name, an honorable name, your grandmother's name, would be a sense of pride for you and, if nothing more, save you from being picked on in school, but what do I know? I am just your mother."

By this time I was sitting up and laughing uncontrollably, nothing like one of Cora's ill-timed rants. A much-needed reprieve from the past few hours of mental torment. While it is true that we (okay, I) may not speak as much as we (okay, I) should, my mother has always been the one true constant in my life. A presence that, regrettably, I take for granted much too often and whose counsel I always seek at my darkest hour, even when I think that the decision has been made. I always want her final sign-off.

"I knew you would be up. Why don't you sleep, woman?"

"I have not slept in thirty years, Julesea. That's your dad's job. The man can sleep through a tsunami. Mothers keep vigil. We pretend to keep ourselves busy with the minutiae of work—*if we are lucky*, social engagements, and home to distract us, but all in all we are just waiting for the phone to ring and be needed again."

"Mommy, I'm twenty-eight. Please stop rounding up. It only makes me older and in doing so, you too."

"I look good. Always have. Let's hope you take after my side of the family. Did I tell you that I saw your Helen last week, and let's just say that time is not being a friend, but who am I to judge?"

"Woman, you are shameless."

"The truth is always without shame, Julesea—something I learned a long time ago. Now, what drama is plaguing that mind of yours and how can Mommy fix it? Let's be quick about it. Daddy will wake up soon and I still have not put my face on."

"Incredible! Has Daddy ever seen you without the face?" I asked. Cora is a naturally beautiful woman, so her devotion to makeup borders on insulting to the rest of us. Her skin flawless and glowing, encases large chestnut eyes set high on Elizabeth Taylor–type cheekbones, a telltale sign of her multiracial, Dutch-Spanish-African heritage *and a blueprint to the Jamaican history*. Her hair, the deepest mahogany, is fine yet thick and wavy; when loose it cascades down her back like one of those Spanish women from Seville who inspires men to paint *and commit suicide*. Growing up, I used to love just staring at her, specifically her mouth, full and bountiful, the most evident feature of her West African ancestry.

"Of course not, why do you think I don't swim?" said Cora. "Men should never see what's underneath. Kills the illusion."

Oh dear, she was firmly basking in her element. Humor was spot-on, with a healthy heaping dose of cynicism best served at twilight. How could I ever tell her everything?

"Um, well, you know I'm seeing someone new, right?" I said, my eyes racing to the ceiling for the right delivery.

"The advertising guy?"

"Yeah, Keith. Well, um . . ."

"Dear, I am certain that Catholic school taught you actual words. If not, Daddy and I deserve a refund. Chop chop, now you're starting to make me nervous. Is he dead? Did he break up with you? Did you find him wearing your lingerie? What?" Then she paused only long enough to work herself into a proper frenzy. "Lawd Jesus! Are you pregnant, Julesea Isabel Sinclair?! Ya betta say nah, child, and it bets ta be the truths, gyrl!"

Oh shit, whatever internal radar she has has gone postal, because her well-nuanced middle American dialect had now given way to her Jamaican upbringing, which is reserved strictly for family reunions and three-alarm, red-alert situations.

"Shhhhhhh. No, MOMMY! Stop yelling, you'll wake Dad," I said, looking over my shoulder frantically as if he were in my apartment instead of hundreds of miles away. "I am not pregnant, I promise" (I hope not, but it would be more welcome than the current proposition), "and Keith has not broken up with me. We're fine—sort of. Not really. I'm just not sure I want to continue is all."

"Lawd, why didn't you say so in the first place, gyrl? Calling me first ting tis mornin' all mealy-mouth. What was I ta tink? You know my pressure is bad."

"Lady, you don't have high blood pressure, so stop . . . Mommy, Keith is gay."

"I think I would have preferred you telling me you was pregnant."

"Really? Not funny, Cora. Well, to be fair, he's *not* actually gay. He's bisexual and—"

"And the difference is what? The man is a bati boy! Drop him immediately and change your numbers. Didn't I tell you to be careful in that city? I did. I told you. I know." She was so elevated, there was no reining her in.

"Cora, what's wrong?" said Dad in response to the outburst.

"Oh, my Lord. Mommy, did you wake Daddy up? Where are you?" Hearing him rustling in the background, I realized that this entire conversation was in fact being conducted from their bed. Not in the kitchen, where I thought she would be at this hour, making herself some tea or in the bathroom luxuriating over a multitude of creams, perfumes, and emollients.

"Charles, it's nothing. Hush up now and go back to bed," said Cora.

"Tat is what I waz tryin ta do, Cora, but ya so loud, all the tyme. Just loud. Who you talking to at this hour? Is it Helen? Tell her ta go ta bed and let us be." My father has never been the kind of man to make any airs about himself. To describe him as simple would be far too easy and erroneous, because he is anything but. Charles Barrington Sinclair, a kid from the slums who got a break, took it, and did good. Being a pure Jamaican made him proud and being from Kingston made him the third cousin twice removed from Bob Marley—or so he said, but aren't we all? Cora is the great love of his life (by both of their accounts) and as such he allows her a lot of leeway to be grand, because it makes her happy and that's all he ever wants—to make her happy. I have been searching for this type of man (age-appropriate and nonincestuous) my entire life. Most girls grow up wishing for Prince Charming. I only wanted my dad. Freud would have a lot to say about that, I am guessing.

"No, Charles, it's not Helen. Now stop making a fuss and go to bed," she said, admonishing him to a slight rumble before returning all her attention to me.

"Hold on, dear, I am getting myself up. Okay, now where was I?"

"Before or after calling Keith a derogatory, homophobic term, Cora?"

"Listen, dear, don't get snippy on me. I am not the bati-homosexual who has lied to you and God only knows what else."

Interrupting her before the cycle of events fueled by her imagination became fact, I said, "Keith did not lie to me. In fact, he told me of his own free will and unsolicited, I might add, about his life preference . . . situation, you know, I mean. I just don't know what to do about it is all."

Animated and muffled now, Cora said, "You don't know what to do about it?! Well, I will tell you, Julesea Isabel. You are going to break up with him and go get yourself tested. Lawd knows what kind of tings he could've given ya. I can't believe this! Did you not see it? I mean honestly, dear, we raised you better."

"Seriously, Mommy. It is not like he was wearing pink sequin hot shorts, twirling down Fifth Avenue, and I intentionally went over and said, 'Date me, please.' Of course I didn't see it. Keith is a well put together, successful man who likes sports. Hell, he even played professional baseball. He drinks beer, out of the bottle. So, no, I didn't see it." Unbeknownst to me, my tone had risen slightly.

"What did I just say? Watch your mouth, Ms. Thing. I didn't go through eighteen hours of labor for you to take that tone with me."

"Sorry."

"It's okay. You're not yourself. What cold cream are you using these days? I am trying some new organic something or other that cost seventy-five dollars, and I swear Noxzema works just as good and it is only four ninety-nine."

"Mommy, please focus."

"Honey, I am focused. I know exactly what this is. Keith is one of those metrosexuals. I was watching Sally Jessy Raphael a few weeks ago and know all about it. It was on Oprah's show too. They want their cake, yours, mine, and Daddy's. Walk away, Julesea, you aren't that New Age. Walk away."

"I know, and I am. I just wasn't prepared is all, and now my every sensibility is in knots," I confessed.

"Honestly, I don't know how you girls do it. In my time the only thing I had to worry about was making sure your daddy wasn't dumb enough to fall for that cheap Rosalyn Bradshaw before I was ready to be with him. The gay boys were easy to spot and they were run out of town. This is indeed a different time, and I am current, but some things just aren't to be, especially where my child is concerned."

"Mommy, you do realize that it has been more than thirty-five years since Daddy dated Rosalyn? It's pretty safe to say you've won."

"Never let your guard down, Julesea. You know, she lives in the States now. Just last week Aunt Helen told me she saw her sometime back. Big as a house she is—big as a house."

I couldn't bring myself to confess to her that Keith and I had unprotected sex once at the beginning of the relationship and that I was, in fact, going to be tested as soon as possible. Cora Madeline Augustus-Sinclair may be poised and sturdy, but she is also hot-tempered and irrational. To even hint that I was concerned at this point about anything other than his sleeping with men would have her hopping a plane to New York right now with poor Dad in tow, demanding to see the doctor's credentials and have a proper sit-down with Keith. No, thank you.

"Mommy, it is nearly six o'clock, and I need to try to get some sleep. Thanks for listening."

"That's what I am here for."

Before hanging up, I remembered something. "Oh, I haven't used cold cream since college, Mommy. I use Leaf & Rusher Green Tea Cleanser. It is *amazing*. I will have Jacklyn send you some later today."

Sucking her teeth in resignation: "Tsk. And that one! Girl scared of her own shadow, she is," said Cora.

"No, she is scared of you. Treating her like a slave, Mommy. Umph, I wonder."

"Don't be nasty about the Dutch, dear. Unfortunate incident, it was, without which we would not be here," responded Cora.

"Incredible," I say.

"I know. I love you, Julesea. I do."

"I know. Thanks, Mommy."

# 21

## NEW LEASES AND RELEASES

"Jules, you're here early. I haven't had a chance to get your coffee yet."

"Don't worry about it, Jacklyn. I picked one up on the way in. Just bring me a copy of my schedule for the week, an updated phone sheet, and then come in so we can go over it."

"There is one from Friday night already on your desk. I'll check the voice mails from the weekend for updates."

After hanging up with Cora, I tried to go back to sleep, but it was impossible, so I got dressed and walked.

"Jacklyn, why am I meeting with Michael this afternoon?" I yelled from the interior of my office after a quick glance at the calendar.

"Simone said it's some kind of investor meeting."

"But you're not sure?" I asked, irritated.

"Not really," Jacklyn responded in a casual, resigned manner.

"So you just put it on my calendar? You need to find out. Also, I need you to call Dr. Katz first thing and get me an appointment for today . . . I haven't been feeling well since the weekend . . . Might be coming down with something."

"Jules, I checked the voice mail and applied all the updates to this phone sheet," said Jacklyn, replacing the old phone log on my desk with the new one. "Nancy from Dr. Katz's office called to confirm your eleven thirty appointment today. Do you need me to change it? Your mom called and said to call your father."

"No, I'll do it myself." Despite how slowly events were registering for me this morning, I knew that the osmosis gods had not miraculously gotten me an appointment with Dr. Katz. "Change my dinner with Keith until the end of the week and get Richard on the phone for me."

"He called too. It's also on your phone sheet . . . in your hands," said Jacklyn.

"Who?"

"Keith . . . and Richard."

"Well, what did he, Keith, say?" I asked impatiently.

"The meeting went well. He's sorry but has to cancel. He has to leave for Tokyo tomorrow and will call you when he returns. I already took him off the phone sheet."

A slight agitation was evident in Jacklyn's voice and, try as I might, instead of overlooking it, it just incited me enough to push back from my desk. Suddenly I saw Barcelona shades of red.

"Am I disturbing you? Or is it no longer your job to assist me?!" I said, staring at her with an intensity that dared not be contradicted. "Well, what did Richard say?"

"He just called to say that he will see you today at eleven thirty."

"Okay," I said, partially scanning my schedule. "This week will be insane, so we should try to . . . change my Wednesday with Gillian to her next avail. I need to be on-site all day. On second thought, keep Gillian on. Just have her come here so she can see Jill's rehearsal. We need that review in the *Post* this week. Why is my Thursday evening still blocked? I thought you took Keith off?"

"Yes, but Simone just told me to lock it in for a dinner with Michael and the financial team."

"Listen to me. Why am I in that meeting? I don't even know their names. What am I supposed to do—take notes?"

Shrugging her shoulders, she replied, "Dunno."

"Did you not ask?"

"Yes, but Simone just dismissed me, so I figured I—"

"You figured what? That you didn't need to get all the information?" Not bothering to wait for her response, I continued, "I know that Simone can be a bit brisk"—off her look—"Okay, downright rude sometimes, but she does her job at all times and protects Michael's ass. She never sends him into anything unprepared. You have to do that for me as well. That is why you are seated out there, not to look pretty and flirt with Michael. Understand? Your job is to be my gatekeeper, to protect me and keep me organized. Right now I just need every fucking thing to be okay. You are supposed to protect me, get it?!" Midtirade I became aware of Jacklyn flinching and thought it best to quiet myself. Leaning forward slightly to relieve the pressure on my temples, I feel my eyes burning, but I refuse to cry under the weight of things. "Go back to your desk."

The air in the office was thick, almost stifling. To stop my hands from shaking, I continued to rest my head in them and took some deep breaths. I was wrong for yelling at her, but I needed not to apologize right now. I needed to own the rage and sense of helplessness that had built up inside me. How could I possibly be expected to focus—much less care—about a group of wealthy, overprivileged bankers with a hard-on to see their names in print now that Carly's was a bona fide hit, even if they are ultimately the ones who pay my salary? My life is in the balance, and I swear as I sit here I can feel my glands swelling, accompanied by an onset of fever. When I did look up, Jacklyn was still standing before me like a deer in the headlights. Thinking it better than to try to defend herself against my verbal thrashing, Jacklyn said the first thing that came to mind and neutralized me.

"I'm sorry. I don't know, but I will find out."

"Okay."

"Jules, are you sure everything is all right?" she asked. "You're reminding me of Mrs. Sinclair."

"I hope so. Go back to your desk. We'll finish this up later . . . Oh, Jack, order me a car for an eleven o'clock pickup and have them wait for me until I am done."

It didn't take a genius to know that something was more pressing than a bout of not feeling well over the weekend. The doctor had already phoned. Richard was meeting me there, and to top it off, Cora had called as well. Since day one, Mom had clearly positioned herself as the unofficial horrible boss in Jacklyn's postcollegiate career. To me, she is my assistant, efficient and moldable, but to Cora, Jacklyn is the docile child who answers the phone with no spirit, takes only partial messages, shipper of things, and reservations sorter that she could easily do without but will tolerate. Early on I had thought to intervene but reasoned that she could use the stiff real-world training that only Cora could give her. Since she just completed NYU and was fortunate enough to work for a mostly relaxed boss, like me, it seemed only right that I allow her the opportunity to earn her stripes as I did through the Academy of Cora, otherwise known as the "Jamaican hazing fury!"

I wouldn't classify staring out the window or surfing the Internet on all things HIV/AIDS-related as working, but it's how I spent the next few hours until the car arrived. Exiting the office, Jacklyn attempted to give me a dossier on the investors.

"I can't look at this right now. Highlight the key points of interest and put it on the desk. I'll look at it when I return."

My ability to focus on anything other than the immediate prognosis of my health would be heavily skewed over the next couple of hours. Within the fifteen minutes or so that it took to go up Eighth Avenue to Dr. Katz's office on Sixty-fifth Street, psychosomatic or not, I swear that I could hear my T cells decreasing, screaming, "Save me," accompanied by a spontaneous inflammation in my throat and sporadic bouts of nausea. That night with Keith was several months ago, so if there was anything to be detected, it should be as clear as the Great Wall from space.

## 22

## AND YOU ARE?

Standing in front of the cream-colored four-story brownstone of Dr. Katz's office, in his uniformed wool overcoat, blue Brooks Brothers blazer, striped dress shirt with cashmere sweater vest, and crisp camel-colored khakis, was Richard. The sight of him always makes me smile. Even in the most formal of settings, he always appears to be more composed than the rest, which is to say nothing of how we first met: years ago in the private room of Lot 61, surrounded by club kids, happy pills, and high-finance mergers *of a different kind*. Richard was with the new face of Versace, a dear friend of his whom I only dared to drool over, much less believed I would meet one day. Through my girlfriend Emily, a fierce club promoter from Philly, we found ourselves at the same table. For one reason (too many drinks) or another (nerves that were soothed with drinks) I couldn't speak. Richard took pity on me and the rest, as they say, is history.

"Darling, love the look. Did you pick out this smashing ensemble or did the old girl from across the hall come over to save you?"

"His name is Gary and noooo! I put it together myself. The turtleneck is new, Bergdorf sale last week. I've been dying to wear it, and the pencil skirt, oh well, it is . . ." Instantly aware of what I had just said, I added, "Well, not *dying* to wear it. I mean I can very well not. I can actually *live* to wear it?"

"Oh dear, you sound like that little anxious pixie of an assistant of yours. Breathe."

Before I nervously rambled anymore off the deep end, Richard took me by the arm to usher me inside.

"Hello, Nance. We have an eleven thirty with Gerald."

"Hi, Richard. Come on back. I didn't know you were coming in until this morning, when Dr. Katz told me to make the time work. Hello, Jules, I'm Nancy. You have a concerned friend here," she said, gesturing at Richard. "I'm going to put you guys in Room Seven. Remove your top and put this on. The doctor will be right with you."

Arguably the loveliest courtroom in the world, the inpatient suite was appointed in warm marshmallow and ecru shades of rattan furnishings from Kreis, with Ansel Adams framed landscapes decorating the walls. Had the examination table not been in the center of the room, or the official apparatus lining the countertops been absent, I could have forgotten where I was—but they were there and I was acutely aware of why I was, a fact that I had tried poorly to shield when seeing Richard outside earlier.

"Are you scared?" I asked Richard, as I continued to search every bit of square footage for a sign of hope. The silence in the room was deafening, so I had to say something. Why not ask the obvious?

He replied, "Not at all. Are you?"

"A bit. I wasn't yesterday when we spoke but somewhere in the night I became afraid about the real possibility that doesn't seem like it belongs to me, which is dumb because I am sure no one thinks that they should have this death sentence."

"We are not going to speak about this disease like you have it until we know. You hear me, Jules?! In the late eighties I lost some dear friends to this disease, and I don't relish going through it again with you . . . If anything, this is just a wake-up call in your otherwise long and youthful life," said Richard, who was cupping my face like my dad used to when I was little and troubled by a problem.

And, as I had with my dad many times before, I willed myself to believe, in that moment, that the world just might bend to his will, on the strength of nothing more than his love for and belief in me. Since our first "real talk," Richard had claimed never to want children, but I believed different. He is one of the most instinctively loving individuals I know. I always held it to be true that, as he said, he didn't want kids because adopting them as a single gay man, even in today's world, was nearly impossible, even when importing them from a Third World country. Feeling all the fatherly love he had given me over the years, I wanted so much to be a big girl for him always, but especially now.

"When did they stop using the fabric gowns? These paper things are vulgar," I said, to introduce some levity into the moment.

"Vulgar, honey, but far more sanitary."

With a soft knock on the door, Dr. Katz entered. He was not as old as I had expected, mid-forties or so, and much cuter, though not dreamworthy. By now Richard was seated in the chair to my left, mumbling something to himself about the mind-numbing nature of the weekly magazines available to read.

"How can anyone expect to focus on anything other than the obvious when all they give you is garbage to read? I must speak to the good doctor about this."

"Richard. Good to see you. Hi, Jules, I'm Dr. Gerald Katz. How are you?"

With a bit of nervous laughter, I said, "I hope much better than the last forty-eight hours of mind games tells me I am."

"Yes, Richard told me you had a scare," he said, nodding in Richard's direction. "Why don't you tell me about it?"

"I guess you could say that." The moment itself just felt so overwhelming that I could not help but get flustered and tear up a bit.

"It's okay. Take your time," Dr. Katz implored, taking firm hold of my hand.

My voice noticeably quivering, I said, "I met someone about three months ago and allowed myself to get swept up in a moment. A stupid moment, you know, because I didn't really know him at all and now, as of Saturday, I learn that he is not entirely who I thought he was and I just don't want to be sick. I don't want to be one of those statistics." The tears were now falling freely. Richard, usually averse to extreme displays of emotion of any kind, had positioned himself at my side and was holding me around the shoulders.

"I understand. You are worried you may have been exposed to HIV. Is that correct?"

"Yes. The guy, Keith, told me over the weekend that he is bisexual, and it's just sent my head into a tailspin. I mean, he's very hetero and healthy . . . not that I'm saying AIDS is a gay disease because it's not . . . I know that, but to be confronted with this . . . you know, so I never thought, but with that lifestyle the possibility suddenly seems real in a way that it never did before . . . I just don't want to be sick," I blurted out in one extemporaneous thought.

"First, I want you to breathe," said Dr. Katz. "It was good that he told you about his sexual identity. Now you can make the best decision for you. Jules, the fastest-growing demographic for new HIV infections is the heterosexual community; specifically, women thirty-five years of age and younger. Falsely, many people still think on some level that AIDS is a disease reserved for the gay community or drug-addicted—it's not. It is a human disease. It doesn't discriminate by sex, income, race, or education." Studying my eyes for any sign of recognition, Dr. Katz continued, "You had unprotected sex with him about three months ago. Have you engaged in any other risky sexual practices before or after this? Have you been tested for AIDS before?"

"No, we were safe after. About two years ago, I was tested, but there's been no reason to since then—until now."

"Bad breakup," Richard chimed in, the disapproval of Tony still obvious in his tone.

"Yeah, bad breakup. He, Tony, cheated." The Kleenex in my hand had been properly torn to smaller pieces with each nervous twitch, so that it fell to the floor in noticeable chunks like the imitation snow displays that lined department store windows. "I got tested then and was fine."

"That's good. Since you have been tested before, then you know that it takes about twenty-five days for HIV antibodies to appear in the blood."

I nodded in agreement but was still as foggy today as I was then about what that part of that statement meant. Dr. Katz continued, "When the body is introduced to the Human Immunodeficiency Virus (HIV), it produces specific antibodies in response. These are the antigens that we look for in order to determine if a patient is positive or negative. Now, since your last test, there have been great advances to expedite the results and accuracy. Results can now be determined from blood and saliva. Blood tests of course are still preferred unless you have an aversion to needles."

"No, I'm fine with that," I said.

"To be doubly clear, we will do both tests today. I'd also like to do a pregnancy test, while we're at it. Okay?"

"Okay. How soon will I know?"

"Within an hour or less. Doesn't that sound better than the week it used to take?"

Words failed me, so I just nodded and squeezed my eyes closed, still trying to wake up from this nightmarish moment. Feeling a hand on my upper arm, I opened my eyes to see the nurse who brought us in from the waiting room standing by the counter, preparing the syringe for Dr. Katz, who was applying an alcohol swab to the crease of my right arm. I couldn't bear the moment, to see my potential liquid death being extracted, so I turned to the left to look at Richard. For the first time I saw the fear of "what if?" in his eyes that hurt more than the needle's prick breaking my skin. Without thought I found a bit of strength and mouthed, "It's okay," smiling weakly.

Within a minute or so, Dr. Katz had given the crimson vial over to her. "All right, that's it. We will know in a little while. You are both welcome to stay in here. Go out, grab some coffee, and come back, or we can call you when the results are in. Whatever you would like to do."

Knowing that Richard would take my lead, I spoke up: "We'll stay here, as long as someone can bring Richard some less offensive reading material. I mean, it is bad enough having to do this, but worse is doing this and hearing him complain about the rotting of American values that you are perpetuating with these weeklies."

Directing his response now firmly at Richard, the doctor said, "Touché. I'll send in my private stash."

"Dr. Katz, thank you for allowing me to tell you about me instead of just looking at the chart. It makes this all better in some way."

With a smile and a tender pat on my shoulder before exiting the room, he replied, "We try. If you need anything, ring the front."

．．．

My head was still throbbing, but I dared not ask for aspirin. Instead, I positioned myself near the window and watched as people went about their lives, completely unaware that mine was in purgatory. When Dr. Katz and the nurse came into the room together, about forty-five minutes later, I thought I was going to pass out.

"Jules, we ran both tests and there are no antibodies present in your system," Dr. Katz began.

The sight of both of them spoke volumes of dreams deferred and lifetimes limited, or so I thought, still standing there immobilized in the same position, arms wrapped protectively across my stomach, not daring to breathe. And while I heard everything that was being said, the accompanying emotions boiling inside were too much to express, so I just focused on the one that I had been withholding for the past hour.

"My head is splitting, can I have an aspirin?"

"Jules, did you hear what I said? You're negative. Given the incubation period, if there was an infection, there would be some indication by now, and there is none. I can't say if you are in great health in all areas because we have not done a full work-up, but I can tell you that you don't have HIV. As a precaution, however, I would like you to come back in a few months for another round of tests. Nancy will contact you with date options. Jules?"

The last thing I remember was nodding before everything went out of focus and then dark. I awoke some time later to see Richard hovering above me.

"Honestly, did I teach you to be this dramatic? I don't think so," he said.

Wearily, I replied, "I'm okay, right?"

"Yes, my dear. You are fine. Now promise, let's not do any part of this again. You know I'm old."

"Deal!"

Dr. Katz reentered just as Richard was about to help me off the examination bed to stand up.

"Here, let me give you a hand. Glad to see you on your feet, Jules. Don't be alarmed by the fainting. Given the considerable amount of stress you have been under the past few days, it's to be expected. Thankfully, Richard caught you before your head hit anything or else we would be running a different set of tests."

Teasingly, I said, "Who knew the old man's reflexes were so good?" Despite the jab, Richard knew the admiration was implied, so he opted not to protest. Dr. Katz continued, "I am happy the news is great. Let this be a lesson about the choices you make and their potential impact. No more is it just an unexpected pregnancy that can derail a life." Reaching into his pocket, Dr. Katz's left hand displayed a rainbow of surprise that was the gold-seal confirmation that all was healthy in my world. "Normally, I reserve these for my younger patients."

"And me," Richard said incredulously, tapping into his inner child.

"... and Richard, but I think you deserve one today for being so brave. Don't choose the orange; it tastes like medicine. The green is my favorite but don't tell Nurse Nancy."

"I hope it's sour apple and not that fake apple," I said triumphantly.

"Young lady, what kind of operation do you think I am running here? Of course it is."

For the lollipop and for the green light on my life, I threw my arms around Dr. Katz. "I'll see you in a few months for follow-up."

Outside on the sidewalk with Richard, everything was justifiably better than before. The sun had broken through the clouds enough to create pockets of "warmer than over there." There was scattered movement in the streets but without the blare of horns and erratic energy. In total, the whole scene was cinematic. I was not entirely sure of how to express my gratitude to him for being the one to endure all this with me. Slipping my gloved hand in his, I asked, "Do you want to sit in the park for a minute?"

"Only if that park is Café Luxembourg and the bar has an unlimited pour. After the morning you have put me through, I must implore that it is after five p.m. somewhere on the planet and therefore perfectly fine for me to have a drink or three," he said, his laugh breaking the calm of the bustling street and seemingly igniting the sound of horns and life that was all around.

In fact, it was barely 1:15 p.m., but I had to agree.

"Martini? My treat."

"Honey, after the gray hairs you have given me, you will be buying for the next year. And you know I only drink top shelf, so you get your checkbook ready."

"Richard, you do know checks are so passé, don't you? I have an expense account, you know."

"Don't make fun of the old, dear."

# 23

## BATTLE LINES

**E**N ROUTE BACK to the office, I stopped at Magnolia Bakery on Ninth Avenue to pick up a much-needed peace offering for Jacklyn. From the elevator I could hear her fielding a persistent caller. Her day had obviously not improved,

"For you," I said, presenting her with the box of sweet treats. "I am sooo sorry for being rough on you earlier today. I was in a foul mood but all better now."

"It's okay, Jules, I guess," Jacklyn replied, quickly dismissing any residual skepticism that may have existed in favor of sinking her teeth into a vanilla cupcake. Mouth filled with cake and icing, she said, "All in all, you're awesome. My girlfriend Elisa is over at Sui and she gets yelled at *all the time* for looking Anna in the face. I mean, how could you not look someone in the face when you're passing them in the hall or they are asking you a question? That's just weird, right! You being mean to me because of your *situation* is totally expected. I mean, I would be completely freaked out if I thought I was knocked up and—"

"Whoa whoa whoa, rambling sister! Lower your voice. Who said anything about being knocked up? I'm not pregnant. In fact I am one hundred percent fine."

"Well, you had to see the doctor, and then Cora kept calling and asking about Keith, and well, I just assumed."

"First, stop listening to Cora. That woman will have you believing that she is the result of *The* Immaculate Conception. Secondly, you know what happens when you assume, don't you?" We nodded in unison. "That's right, *you* make an *ass* out of *u* and *me*, so knock it off. Now, if you would like to apologize for your gross mischaracterization, one of those vanilla cupcakes will do just fine!"

"Indian giver," said Jacklyn. "I knew you were going to take one."

"Hey, hey, simmer down, little Jackie. That is Native American giver to you!"

"Well, look who decided to stroll in today and grace us with her presence," said Michael, standing on the opposite side of Jacklyn's desk, nosily leafing through the papers strewn about Jacklyn's in-box, a stark contrast to the paper-free workspace of Simone's always immaculate desk. "Is someone having a birthday or something?"

"Good morning, Michael," I said. "No."

"Correction, Jules, good afternoon."

"For the record I was here at eight thirty this morning. I had to leave for a doctor's appointment that ran longer than expected."

"Everything okay?"

"Yes!" Jacklyn's voice shouted, causing Michael to do a double take as if he hadn't noticed her sitting there—next to the cupcakes.

"Jacklyn"—he nodded, then indicated he would like to speak to me in private—"you are aware that we have a meeting today at four thirty, correct?" And I was ushered into the office.

"Yes, I was just about to review some notes on the partners before calling you. Just curious, though, why do you want me in there? With the exception of Carly, I don't know your partners."

Once inside the office, Michael and I occupied opposite ends of the sofa, enabling me to sit in the lotus position and him to recline, extending his legs onto the coffee table. Our formality had long since given way to a casual ease in private. I had the Carly upheaval to thank for that. It wasn't the same brotherhood relationship he shared with Raymond, and it wasn't the same Obi-Wan/

Papa Bear one that I shared with Richard, but enough so that I was no longer inexplicably self-conscious or overly eager to please *the Big Boss* every time I was in his presence. *I really like Michael and never want to disappoint him.*

"I want to expand the restaurant into some other territories starting next fall. Been looking into London—your old stomping ground—and a few others. They, the investors, don't, not right now. I need you to provide impartial evidence reinforcing my position," said Michael.

"So you're thinking a brand strategy and maybe a comparative analysis as to the benefits."

"Exactly. The market is ripe, and if we don't dive in now, we're going to miss out. I can't have my hands tied right now. Carly's is my baby as much as Kaylin is. I know what's best to keep her sexy. These dudes are just money guys who were supposed to be silent, but now that shit is hopping and we have some momentum, they want to flip it like they know. I can't let that happen. Not right now."

"Am I wrong in thinking that you and Mrs. Kipps held the majority interest?"

"Collectively, yes, but one of the investors has the largest single share and is a close friend of the family. I don't trust him. He has been leading her, so to speak, for some time. Got her to thinking that the best decisions for the business are the ones that keep me close by, like keeping Carly's New York–bound, under her watchful eye. So he's dangling the platinum gift—freeing me up to spend more time at home with her. Well, you know how that translates. Not happening," said Michael, shrugging off the possibility of being ready to stay home and live a quiet life. "We're about to do something epic here, and that requires vision," Michael continued, patting his pockets for a match to spark his cigar. Although I didn't want him to light up in my office, it seemed best to let this one slide. I could just open the windows and air the space out as soon as he left.

"With all due respect—are you certain that's her intention? Maybe, if given the chance, she'd want you to spread your wings. I mean, after all, it is your dream and no one wants to be a dream killer," I said. *Lord knows what calamities could be avoided if only Michael would include her in parts of his professional life instead of leaving her home alone to rattle about, orchestrating havoc in other folks' lives.*

"After how she has infiltrated your life, can you ask that question with a straight face?" asked Michael, erupting into one of his big laughs. "All in all, mixing business and home is never a good idea—that is, if you want to keep your personal life intact, and I do. Besides, it's not time to play that card yet." Michael's gaze was now steely, fixed on me with a determination that suddenly made me feel as if we were in NATO talks, the couch having been transformed into a small island. He was now the Dominican Republic and the investors were Haiti. Unwittingly, I had the responsibility of holding the title, as it were, to the land in the center that both sides wanted. "When the time comes I will handle Carly, but until then I need those cats to be tempered down long enough for me to figure out what it's worth to them. If I need to, I'll cut the head off the damn dragon before I let someone come into my house and tell me what it is that I can do with it."

As stimulating as it was to see Michael going all General Custer, it was also a bit disturbing. I can't shake the feeling that there is far more to this story. Not only was he asking me to side with him against his partners, he was asking me to align myself with him in a potential battle that would surely pit me against Carly, and that is not a fight I was looking forward to. If the encounter at her home confirmed anything, it was that you don't get to be the legendary society gatekeeper Carly Spencer Falles without being formidable. I just wasn't sure if I was ready to take her on so quickly. Judging by the resolute look on Michael's face, I would say, ready or not, it was time to start shining up my sword and shield.

"I understand," I said, rising to retrieve the dossier off the desk. "Okay, let's see who we have here. There is Simon Kleinman of Barrett, Browning & Fisher."

"Good ole Simon. He isn't much of a concern. A conservative securities investor with a diversified personal portfolio. For clients, he isn't risk averse. With his own money, however, he prefers to err on the side of caution."

"Okay, then there is Marcus Crawford of Chimera Capital. Wait, isn't this—"

Watching Michael move about the room, I could see him running the catalog of what history between the two he wanted to reveal, given that I already had a frame of reference, *far more than he knew but enough:* "I forgot you two met here. He's the key, Wall Street's boy wonder. You'd think he has more to do than telling me how and what I can do with this place. I guess that's what too much success early on does—deprives these upstarts the opportunity to learn humility and respect. You know what they say, Jules, it's not the enemy you have to watch out for, it's the pupil."

"Is that right? I'm just wondering who named their firm Chimera," I said.

"Ha! Me. I gave him the name—seemed like a good one at the time," said Michael, now seemingly lost in thought, standing at the window and speaking more to the history of a relationship that preceded me. "I know this dude all too well. Hell, that was me about twenty years ago, an overly accomplished, unapologetic thirtysomething badass. Everything about him is strategic. The expansion of Carly's isn't his endgame; it's the means to an end that I don't know yet, and that is the mind fuck. Marcus is not going to put one over on me."

"Michael, if we are going in within the hour, then I need to get busy."

Stumping out the final drag of his cigar in the vintage crystal ashtray on my desk—*purely for decorative purposes*—he said, "So it is. You know what I need. Make me proud, Dorothy. This shit ain't Kansas."

As if the scenario were not heavy enough. I felt as if I were being thrown into the middle of an old Western shootout right before someone yells "Draw!" Time permitting, I want to know more about Marcus, because clearly there is far more to him than being a Super Blond Amazon modelizer and random morning walking companion, which in and of itself is in conflict, but given the constraints, that would have to wait until I could get Michael all that he needs. It was most important in the immediate time frame to know the published business about our competitors who had succeeded and failed. Picking up the line and dialing, I said, "Jacklyn, give me a search report on the top-niche restaurants launched in the past five years and then whatever information is available on members-only clubs, à la the Supper Club, Soho House, the Groucho Club, et cetera. Also, time permitting, pull up some information on Marcus Crawford of Chimera Capital and *don't* ask Simone, just show me what is available online."

After a few minutes she came in with printouts. "I glimpsed at this but didn't get a chance to proof everything. Also, do Fashion Café and Planet Hollywood count? They are niche, have entertainment aspects, and are expanding rapidly. I added a few facts about them as well."

"Actually, yes, they're good examples of what not to do. This is good. Listen, I also need information on the Rainbow Room and Cipriani. Also, get me the actual investment numbers here and the annual operational costs. For those you will need to go to Simone, *sorry.*"

"Okay, I'll try." The regret for the blasé response showed on her face before it settled. "She hates me, you know."

"Don't *try*, Jacklyn, *do*. One last thing, what is the name of that restaurant on Forty-second in Hell's Kitchen, a few doors down from Chez Josephine's? They occasionally have musical performances."

"You mean Soul Café. They opened about a year or so ago. I go there all the time. They have this roasted chicken with sweet potato mash that is crazy good."

"As if I care. Forget it. They haven't been around long enough to help my case."

Minutes later, after exhaustive speed-reading, I gathered my red-leather-bound Smithsonian notebook and headed off to the conference room. Just as I reached the door, Jacklyn came running down the hall.

"Simone is on the line for you. She said the meeting has been canceled," said Jacklyn, out of breath.

"What do you mean canceled? It's supposed to start in less than ten minutes. How can it be canceled?" I turned abruptly on my heels toward the direction of Michael's office.

"Where are you going?"

Annoyed, I barked, "Learn to ask better questions, Jacklyn," and I marched off to find the battle.

Utterly defeated with the course of events, she exclaimed, "I did, promise! Simone wouldn't answer me."

Arriving at Simone's desk slightly winded, I wanted answers. "Simone, what's going on? Why is it canceled? I just sat with Michael about this."

"An emergency came up with one of the partners, so it is being rescheduled."

"And you couldn't tell Jacklyn this?" I said, eyeing her skeptically. "Come on, what's the real story?"

"Shhh," she said, frantically waving me to be silent. "Lower your voice. Michael is inside talking to Carly." Leaning over in order to speak as low as possible, she added, "From what I can gather, Mr. Crawford is not going to be in the meeting."

"Oh," I said, involuntarily grimacing at the possibility of having to come face-to-face with Carly sans the benefits of a boardroom table and witnesses.

"No, there's more. Carly is here to convey his wishes."

"You mean like his proxy," I said.

"Yes, can you imagine?" responded Simone.

"Shit. This is sooo *Dynasty*."

"Shit is right. Michael hit the roof. I have never heard him lose it like that, especially with her."

"What about Simon?"

"Redirected. Mr. Kleinman's office called to say he was running a few minutes late, so I told her not to bother. He has already called to speak with Michael."

"Shit."

"Jules, you already said that. Say something else."

"I know, but this is some crazy . . . ish. I mean, it's like having Blake, Alexis, and Dex live-action figures—insane!" From behind the closed doors I could hear loud muffled voices climbing in varying degrees of intensity, with the most irate one clearly belonging to Michael. "So what am I supposed to do?"

"I don't know. What do you normally do with yourself?"

"Stop being snippy, Simone. It doesn't suit you."

"Touché," she countered.

"I'll be in my office if Michael needs me. Okay?"

Jacklyn was away from her desk when I returned, most likely downstairs with Raymond complaining about me. I couldn't blame her for not wanting to be in the line of unnecessary fire. *Next time I'll get her cupcakes and a kickboxing certificate.*

Nothing would please me more than to know that this day would soon be coming to an end. I desperately needed to recharge. My plan had been to leave the office immediately after the meeting and have a decadently decompressed night at home cooking, having some wine, and watching a flick. Now, however, I was not certain what time that was going to be possible. On the off chance that Michael would want to speak with me after expelling Carly, or if he decided to pop into the office, I needed to be there. Looking around, surely there was work to be done to pass the time. None, however, seemed more pressing than reorganizing the neat piles on my desk. After two hours or so, I was nearly stir-crazy and had to ring Simone.

"Oy! What time is Michael leaving? They can't still be arguing. Sadat brokered peace with Israel in less time."

"You are odd, Jules. Michael left over an hour ago."

"What?! Why didn't you call me?"

"Was I supposed to?" asked Simone.

"Yes!"

"You didn't say anything."

"It was implied," I said.

I could have wasted my time engaging her in a fruitless war of words, but why? Hanging up, I logged off the computer and gathered my already packed bag, complete with grocery and movie rental lists. Yelling from the interior of my office, I said, "Jacklyn, go home."

"About time! I thought this day would never end."

"You're telling me. Why don't you come in tomorrow at eleven a.m."

"Boy, you must really feel awful. Cupcakes and now this."

Stopping in front of her desk, I conceded, "Yeah yeah yeah, only because it wasn't your fault, but you rode it out. Good job."

"Here, don't forget this."

"What's this?" I asked.

"The information on Marcus Crawford that you requested."

"I'll never read it tonight. Put it on my desk. I'll look at it in the morning."

. . .

Seeing me approach the apartment building, Ivan stepped forward to open the entrance door.

"Evening, Ivan."

"Miss Sinclair. No delivery tonight?" he asked, eyeing the grocery bags in my hands.

"I know! It seemed like a good idea to give them the night off, at least from me."

"Cooking is a lost art today. My Elizabeth is a great cook. It's why I married her."

"Really?" I said. "In that case your wife may have to give me lessons. My skills are limited. And by limited I mean three or four key dishes." He shook his head, more in recognition of the mass exodus my generation has taken away from the kitchen. "Don't laugh. I'm serious."

"At least you try. It's better than most."

"Ivan, do you mind if I put these down somewhere for a moment? I need to check the mail."

"Of course!" he said, reaching to take them, "Where is my head? I'll take those."

Walking toward the postal boxes, I said, "It's been a few days." Off his look, I relented. "Okay, a week or more."

"I'm not judging, ma'am." Placing his hand across his chest to emphasize his point, he added, "It's my job to notice is all."

"Of course, Ivan. I can only imagine what you don't notice."

Trashing the circulars and junk mail, I walked back over to the doorman's stand to get my bags filled with pasta, salmon, wine, cheese, fruit, flowers, ice cream, and vegetables.

"Anything important?" Ivan asked.

"No, just the usual—bills, magazines, bills, and more bills."

"That is capitalism. You pay in this country just to breathe the air."

"Isn't that the truth."

"Would you like some assistance upstairs?"

"No, I should be fine. The hard part was the five blocks getting here. I can manage if you place them in my hands."

"You should get yourself one of the carts. They're convenient," said Ivan.

"Yes, I should, and I would if they weren't so gawd-awful-looking. Besides, could you imagine me pushing a cart in this outfit?" I said. "Exactly. Travesty."

Walking to the elevator, I realized that I did not have a free hand to press the call button. Without looking back, I called to Ivan over my shoulder.

"Ivan, can you get the elevator, please?"

"Here, let me do that." *Nice voice, definitely not Ivan's heavily accented German, and he smelled good. Seriously, I must stop fixating so much on smell.*

Stepping aside so that I could enter first, he held the doors at bay. Feeling the bags slip a bit, I thanked him while trying to readjust them without looking up to see the owner of the voice.

"What floor?" he asked.

"Eight, please," I said. *Nice shoes.*

Entering, I moved aside, allowing room for the nice-smelling gentleman, only to come face-to-face with Marcus! *If I had a free hand it would have been used to pick up my face.*

"You've got to be kidding me. What are you doing here?!" I said.

"I was wondering when we would meet again."

"What are you doing here?"

"Heard you the first time," he said, winking and turning his gaze up to the level indicators. "I live here, unless you know something I don't." Leaning closer to me: "Did Mitzy Bloomfield have me voted out of the building?"

"You live here?!"

"Yes, Seven A, and you"—he scanned the bags in my hand—"you're cooking me a well-deserved welcome home dinner, I see."

"And why would I do that? We are not friends."

"Not yet, but we should be. I knew it from the moment I saw you—that we would be friends. What's on the menu?"

Shaking my head to reorganize my thoughts, I said, "Spaghetti vongole with a pear and arugula salad . . . Ugh! Why am I telling you this?"

"Because I asked," he said.

"Nothing for you. I've had an impossibly long day. Started as the worst day actually and . . . wait, YOU LIVE HERE!"

"Yes." Laughing while clearly amused at my discomfort, he continued, "Why is this such a point of confusion for you?"

"Because I live here."

"Yes, I know," he said, smiling. "We've established that. You're in Eight A."

"How do you know that?"

"The walls talk here, didn't you know?" Holding his stare to determine if the line was sufficient, he continued, "Besides, Carly told me. Earlier this year I wanted to purchase the unit from her and have it connected to mine, but I couldn't because Michael gave it to you—his new hire."

The elevator doors opened right on time, because there was not much left to say after Marcus's revelation. "Well, this is my stop," he said.

"And so it is," I heard myself reaffirming, as he turned to leave, "Officially, the worst day."

Placing his hand on the door sensor before fully exiting, Marcus said, "The worst day can often be the best day in disguise. Remember that."

# 24

## WHEN IT ALL FALLS DOWN

**Present day—2001**

THE WORST DAY did become the best day," I say to myself softly.

"Excuse me, ma'am. Were you saying something?" asks the driver.

"Oh, nothing. Just remembering something is all."

Looking out the window at the random oil rigs lining the Ladera section of La Cienega told me we still had a ways to go before reaching West Hollywood.

"Shoot, we passed Starbucks, huh? I could really use a coffee," I say.

"Yes, ma'am, but there is another one coming up just after Rodeo. Should I stop there?" asks the driver.

"Yes, please."

At this hour, the ordering line was short although the store itself was filled with people at tables on their computers or in the oversize chairs reading the newspaper.

"Welcome to Starbucks. What can I get started for you?" asks the barista.

"A grande nonfat vanilla latte, a tall Americano, and a slice of zucchini loaf, please."

"What's the name?" Seeing that I was distracted, the cashier repeats himself. "Miss, what name can I put on the drinks?"

"Sorry. Jules. My name is Jules."

In the metal wire stand by the counter lay copies of the *Los Angeles Times* and *USA Today*, each with ghastly images of the 9/11 World Trade Center attacks from last week. The entire world outside me, as within, was in upheaval, leaving no place for the mind to rest. On the morning of September 9, after a horrible fight with Marcus, I left L.A. on a flight bound for London after he stormed out. My schedule called for a day's stopover in New York before continuing to London on the morning of September 11. It wasn't until I landed at Heathrow that I learned of the attacks. Walking through the terminal, although it was packed with thousands of people, I was overcome by a feeling of quiet morbidity and despair. It felt as if the life-force had been separated from oxygen. Knowing my state of mind, I chalked it up to a myopic vision of things and emotional despair over the row with Marcus and the anger I felt at him, at me. Not until I settled in the car and turned on my phone to retrieve my voice messages did I learn of the attacks, giving me another reason to cry.

"Julesea, this is Cora. They done blew up the World Trade. Lawd, what is dis world comin' to, child? Call your father, he is worried about you."

"Jules, honey, it's Richard. What a dark day for the world. Don't be alarmed, we are all as good as can be expected. Joy was not in the office yet. She was on the ferry from Jersey when the first plane hit. Poor dear, saw both collisions. Pray for everyone. Call me when you are settled."

"Jules, Daddy here. Have a safe flight and call me when you are settledt at the 'otel."

"Hi, young lady. Didn't you fly out today? I hope it was not on United. Call me. I'm fine. I'm worried—can't find some of my friends. Love you. It's Joy. Please call me."

"Julesea, it's Mommy again. Your father is worried. I keep telling him that you are fine and that you were on Virgin Airlines. You were on Virgin, right? I like that Richard Branson. Lawd knows why anyone would fly United, such ugly interiors they have. Call your father."

"Hi, Jules, your driver will await you at baggage claim on landing and take you to the Sofitel St. James. I was able to upgrade your room to a junior suite. Everyone, your mom twice, Richard, Marcus, Joy, and Michael, have called. No worries. I'm on it."

"Jules, it's me. I spoke to Jacklyn, so I know you're okay." My hands began to shake hearing his voice; I replayed it three times before pressing Save.

Hearing Marcus's voice broke me down. I didn't have the energy to battle the contents of my purse for my sunglasses. Nor did I care that the stranger at the wheel saw me openly sobbing into my sleeve. It required only a small leap of faith on his part to deduce the nobility of my tears, being for the victims and not for the selfish concerns of my relationship. The emotional distance in his voice, where days before there existed such closeness, chilled me to the core. I tried to rationalize that, because he called, he still felt something more significant for me than obligation, but the absence of subsequent communication made it very clear that our relationship remained in a kind of peril that even a tragedy such as this could not repair.

At the hotel my television was set to BBC news in order to see the coverage of the attacks. Each time they showed the unfathomable images of the first and second plane crashing into the towers, I saw our life together crumbling into the great rubble that was left; our happy memories heavily shrouded like the soot that cloaked everything in the immediate radius. To say that my heart was heavy was an understatement. To say that I wished all of this to be another bad dream was accurate. That night I dropped to my knees and prayed the most heartfelt prayer possible for us, for all of those who had lost their lives to this war that we didn't start, and for all of those loved ones left behind to pick up the pieces. No one should know such tragedy. Marcus and I should not know such despair.

Despite the World Trade attacks, the business at hand did not come to a grinding halt. It just continued with more suspicion. I remained in London as planned for the week to oversee the media rollout for Carly's UK, each day starting and ending seemingly the same, eyes closed. I would awake with morning amnesia and instinctively reach for Marcus to my right, only to find the bed empty. Initially, when I returned in the evenings, I would either go to the front desk to retrieve my messages or check the hotel phone when I came into the room. In the absence of a blinking light, I would phone the front desk just to make sure that no oversight or phone malfunction had occurred.

"Hi, this is Ms. Sinclair in 704. Are there any messages for me?"

"No, ma'am, there are not." After putting this charge to the same night clerk a couple of times, he inquired dutifully, "Is there a specific call that you are expecting?"

"Oh, just the rest of my life is all."

But my life was an ocean away, and if I knew how to stop looking outside myself for answers, I could tell him that and get out of my own way. A few times I did pick up the phone to call but always hung up before completing the number. *What would I say? I'm sorry. I'm scared. I thought I knew more about me. I'm learning. Please don't leave me?* I wanted to say those things but just could not. *I would sound so pathetic, and besides, after everything that I now knew, I didn't want to be* that *girl.* I should have said those words during our fight, but I felt cornered, so I pushed back, because it was easier and less intrusive. Each solitary moment found me reliving fragments of that fateful night.

◆ ◆ ◆

## Los Angeles
### September 9, 2001

"What do you want from me, Marcus? You want me to say I'm sorry? Well, I am!"

"That would be the least," he said, stomping off toward the kitchen.

"Don't walk away from me," I said, giving chase after him. "Tell me what you want. You said it was okay! I'm trying to understand everything."

"Well, it's not, but what was I supposed to say? No, Jules, you can't go? Okay, you want the truth? I don't want you to go. I want you here with me, not half a world away or physically here, subconsciously waiting for an excuse for us to not work."

"I'm not. *I haven't been.* I'm here! What do you think I have been doing for the past year zipping back and forth? I have been here for you as much as I can, in a place where I don't know anyone and the women treat me like crap but you pretend not to notice. I have been here at your side, event after event, smiling like some mute as everyone tries to figure me out."

"That's what you think?" Marcus asked incredulously. "Is that what you call spending more time at dinner on your BlackBerry than socializing? Being downright prickly to our friends? Leaving an outing to take a call . . ."

*That's the thing about arguments—no one listens, feeling in the heat of the moment that the only option is to talk over the other. Arguments like this never follow a logical order but always guarantee to reveal all holdover irritations that lie beneath in the most ugly and desperate way possible.*

"I can't believe this. I put my life on hold for you," I railed back at his blatant indifference to my sacrifice. "Without any assurance, do you know how scary that is for me?"

"Appearing less emotionally invested in this than anything back East."

"I don't see my friends at all in order to be here whenever possible, and it's still not enough . . . I should have listened to Cora."

"I'm not going to do us on Cora's timetable or anybody else's for that matter! What does she—"

"Don't you dare," I said, feeling protective of her more as a point of contention against Marcus than as actual defense of Cora's meddling.

"There are two lives I care about right now, and you are controlling both of them, or don't you see that?" asked Marcus fiercely. "And now you are off to London for God knows how long!"

"It's my *job*, Marcus, so yes," I said.

"Well, I guess that makes it all right now, doesn't it? Your *job* is publicity, not being someone's patsy, Jules. You can't possibly be serious. Try, just once, having the same reverence for my well-being and what I am offering as you do for Mike's. How about that?"

"This is not Michael's fault, Marcus. This is about me making the right decisions for *my* future. This is about you keeping secrets, lying to me."

"That's where you're wrong. This whole situation has been orchestrated by Mike, yet you refuse to see it. Damn it! You asked that I leave him with something. I gave him London, and this is how the son of a bitch repays me, by trying to take what's important to me?!" said Marcus, erupting with anger unlike any I had imagined him capable of. Sensing himself dangerously close to being uncontrollable, he abruptly stopped in an attempt to contain his burgeoning rage. "How else would you have known about her situation, if not for Mike? If you had just come to me immediately, asked me, I would have—"

"You would have what, finally told me what you should've volunteered? That she was carrying your child?"

"My God, Jules. It's *not* my baby! Do you want to see the damn test? It's impossible. How many times do I have to tell you that? How can I make you understand that I was blindsided and needed to figure things out before I could tell you so I knew what we were up against?" pleaded Marcus, unclenching his fists and walking over to me. "Why is it you find it so difficult to just trust me, to rest in me—especially about this?"

"How can I . . . ?" I knew the words without full completion— *when try as I might I still have battle scars of Tony and Angie doing a number on my head and it's overriding the life with you that is right in front of me*—and knew they were wrong as soon as I heard them stumble out of my mouth, but I couldn't swallow them up and back away from the road they led down. Using all his strength, Marcus slammed down the nearest object he could find into the granite countertop, causing me to jump.

"Look at me! I'm not Tony," he said angrily, roughly taking hold of my face and forcing me to see the details of him as clearly as possible. Eyes inflamed and exhausted, he said, "Jules, you are the love of my life and I am trying harder than I ever have not to fuck us up. I know you better than anyone ever will. I know what you think. I know what scares you. I know what makes you happy. I would never . . . You shouldn't need a piece of paper to know my intentions. If they aren't clear by now, then I don't know what the hell to tell you."

"Make me believe you," I said, my voice reduced to a whisper from the screaming and crying moments earlier. "Make me believe that this is real, that I don't need a backup plan, that I can trust you forever. That I won't wake up one day alone in this to find you gone—emotionally at first and then physically—like him."

"Are you serious? I have been as transparent as possible with the good and bad of me. It's the most valuable thing I have to give," said Marcus, with more tenderness in his words than my heart could stand. "What more do you need to get out of your own way, baby, and let us grow? What more do you need?" he asked, before resigning himself to the gravity of our predicament. "Julesea, we share a home. Was I crazy to think that we were building a life?"

Words escaped me, so I shrugged and averted my eyes, prompting him to release me but not before saying, "If it's that difficult for you, then why are we here fighting this hard for this? Better yet, why am I here?" he asked, and walked away toward the door.

"Where are you going, Marcus?! Come back here," I screamed, overcome by inconsolable grief as I watched him grab his keys off the corridor table and walk out the door. *Wait! Wait! I didn't mean that I couldn't trust you. I just don't know how to confront the bullshit in my head and fight for us. PLEASE wait.* But all of this was in my head. I continued standing there stunned, defiant, desperately praying that he would storm back in to resolve things—but he didn't. When 5:45 a.m. came, I awoke alone to find his side of the bed untouched, as were the guest room, his office, and the living room. His cell phone went straight to voice mail. *I didn't dare leave word. What would I say?* So at 6:30, I snapped the locks closed on my last bag and got into the waiting car for transport to the airport, all the while convincing myself that the momentary indifference I felt was real, that I could let go of the trapdoors in my head and move on with my life, with or, if need be, without him.

· · ·

### Back to Present Day
### 2001 Los Angeles

Walking back to the car, I was very much aware of my failings and the courage it would take just to be present in the life I covet. Giving the driver his Americano, I debate asking him to detour through Hancock Park. I feel the need to see its tree-lined streets with beautifully manicured lawns and kids playing a game of tag as a reminder of the future Marcus and I had discussed before everything got so out of focus, anything to delay knowing our fate.

"Here's your coffee," I say. "How long do you think?"

"Not too bad now. You should be home in about fifteen or twenty minutes."

"Some people can live a lifetime in fifteen or twenty minutes, you know," I say.

Evaluating the merits of that statement, the driver replies solidly, "I guess they can."

Leaving me alone again with only my thoughts, trying to uncover the definitive moment my short-sightedness mucked everything up.

# 25

## THE PAWN

### 1999

**H**OW'S MY SOLDIER?" asked Michael from behind the hostess stand the next morning.

"Save it, Kipps!" I seethed. "Why didn't you tell me that Marcus Crawford, your partner and nemesis, lives in my building?"

Staring at me blankly, as if the location of Marcus's residence was common knowledge, before deciding whether to be dismissive or defensive, Michael selected the former. "You've been in the building long enough. What have you been doing if not getting to know your neighbors? I know you met Mitzy already. She's a pill."

"Well, I didn't know, so to run into him last night after the day I had . . ." Immediately remembering that Michael had no knowledge of my health scare—and never would—I said, "I meant *we* had, and you going all last stand on me."

"And?" he asked, not understanding the great injury. "What is the deal with you and these Confederate references?"

"I wasn't prepared is all," I say, partially reenacting the carrying of the bags scene. "I mean, I walk in bags in hand. There he is all smiley and flirty and—"

"And what? Did he ask you out?" he said, a sudden sense of interest piquing in his tone.

"No, of course not, but—"

"But nothing. Remember what I said, Jules," Michael admonished, using his index finger to drive home his point.

"Michael, you said a lot and I am still trying to process half of it."

"All you need to remember is that he is the key and not to be trusted."

"Yeah, yeah, that part I remember. I just don't want anything to be complicated," I said. "I mean, not only do we have the meeting coming up, but now I have to worry about potentially dodging him afterward once you push him out the sandbox."

Walking from behind the podium and taking me under his arm, Michael responded, "Who says it has to be complicated? Just do your job. Got it?"

"Yes. Although that hand is making me curious about my 'job' description," I said, fixated on his hand now resting sinisterly on my right shoulder.

"I like you, Jules. You're quick," said Michael over his shoulder as he began to walk down the stairs into the dining area of the restaurant.

"Apparently not quick enough. What the hell?" I murmured under my breath, purposefully loud enough for him to hear.

"Never what the hell, Jules. Always what the heaven! Just when you think the deck is stacked against you, you get an ace." His declaration stopped me in my tracks. Had there been eyes in the back of my head, I would have clearly seen the wheels churning in Michael's. With two days until D-day, I definitely needed to plan accordingly for the partners' dinner on Thursday. Undoubtedly the wolves would have their teeth sharpened, and I was determined not to be the lamb.

The elevator doors opened to reveal Simone. "Morning, Jules. Have you seen Michael?"

"That's Ace to you."

"Huh?"

"Nothing. He's in the restaurant."

. . .

Having given Jacklyn permission to come in late earlier in the week, I decided to reward myself in kind on D-day, Thursday morning. I knew the day itself was going to be excruciatingly long. My look needed to be flawless, and yet, try as I might, fashion inspiration was eluding me, so I did the next best thing to having Tom Ford on speed dial.

"Gary, I need you."

"If only you had a cock, that would be the news."

"Once again, too much information. Seriously, woman, down! Can you come over?"

Living across the hall has its advantages. Less than two minutes after hanging up the phone, Gary was ringing my doorbell. While discarding elements of another poor outfit choice, I nearly tripped over my own feet rushing to let him in after the second extended bell. "Why didn't you let yourself in?" I asked, out of breath.

"Left the key with Jean Pierre."

"Oh," I said, tilting my head to the side to take in his modest sleep attire. "Interesting. Not what I envisioned. Good, though."

"What did you expect, a silk kimono with a big butterfly and velvet slippers?" Gary asked.

Conceding that his description was spot-on accurate, I nodded with an affirmative yenta shrug-sigh combination.

"Are you sure you're not Jewish? That was unnerving. The head nod, the judgmental eye squint, and concave shoulder. Reminds me of home."

"Ha! You want coffee? I picked up an amazing kona from Dean & DeLuca the other day," I said, leading him into the kitchen. "So how is the boy?"

"Yesterday's news, honey! I was looking for a yacht and he was more of a schooner, if you catch my drift."

"Ewh! I do and TM motherfucking I. TMI," I said, playfully pinching him. For a split second I thought of asking Gary about how best to exit my relationship with Keith—but opted not to, for once heeding the warning that Cora had given me years ago about not sharing too much with people. "Scone?"

"Well, aren't you a chipper little Brit. Is there clotted cream as well?"

Turning my head to the side in faux modesty and pleased with the association, I said, "I did pick up a few charming habits and phrases across the pond. The clotted cream, however, was not one of them, nor was the blood sausage. Some good old American butter is just fine for me."

"Such a shame . . . passing on a nice long big sausage," Gary said salaciously, half submerged in the refrigerator. "Where's the ice cream, J?"

"Middle shelf, praline and rum raisin. I polished off the rocky road on Monday."

"You're better than Baskin-Robbins," said Gary. "Ah, this is what I'm looking for."

"Are you seriously having ice cream and scones for breakfast?"

"Ice cream, butter. All the same; creamy and it goes down smooth. If you catch my—"

"Once again, drift has been thrown and caught, so let's please end the erotica portion on this segment of 'Breakfast with a Gay.'"

"Boring little lass you are this morning. How can I make it better?"

"What was that, Irish?" I asked. "Obviously dress distress. Tonight I am having dinner with Michael and his investment partners inclusive of the missus."

Clutching his invisible pearls, he said, "Oh, honey. If your last romp with Lady Kipps was any indication, you're gonna need more than just a hot outfit. You need a shield and sword to survive."

"Obviously," I said, throwing myself across the counter in feigned defeat, "but it's not just Carly who I have to deal with. Michael has this partner who thinks that—wait, correction, who *knows* he is hot shit. A Wall Streeter with a penchant for supermodel accessories and Italian fineries."

"Hmmm, sounds like a contender for yours truly."

"Fan club, maybe."

"Meow," said Gary, fake clawing at me as we entered the bedroom. "You better save some of that side-eyed kitty mix for later tonight with Carly."

"Seriously, this guy has her ear, which is most inconvenient for Michael, since he has specific views about the direction of the restaurant," I said, standing before the mirror, evaluating the merits of the charcoal Calvin Klein suit.

"Sounds like a player."

"Understatement. The first time I met him was during my interview. When I arrived, Michael was not there and this guy starts hitting on me hard, asking to buy me a drink—flirt, you know. Eventually Michael comes, they talk, and the guy leaves," I said, turning away from my reflection to face Gary, "without even saying good-bye to me."

"Sounds like someone made an impression," said Gary.

"Noooo, I just thought he was rude is all. Besides, I am not even close to being his type."

Now standing behind me to see the mirror's truth, Gary reached for the suit with his left hand and replaced it with a denim trousers, dress shirt, and blazer combination. "And how do you know that? Has he seen the gold coast yet?"

Giggling. "Why do you always do that? You know being gay does not give you free rein to fondle me, at least not the way you're doing it."

"Maybe not, but being your resident man-of-style does." He switched out the dress shirt for a purple silk camisole. Admired his work. "Much better. Put that on," he instructed.

"I ran into him and his token Eastern Bloc model girlfriend at Pastis last year when I moved in," I said, tugging to raise the straps on the camisole to minimize the revealing neckline. "You don't think this is a bit too casual?"

"Jules, you work in a supper club, for Christ's sake, not an accounting office," retorted Gary, slapping my hand away to loosen the straps so that the front revealed a bit more. "There we go. If Miss Thing is going to hate you, let's give her a reason. At least you will have the boys on your side." Admiring his work: "Stop squirming. So he was with Nadja Auermann . . ."

"More like Esther Canadas," I said.

"Oh, girl, mommy is fierce—talk about lips made for sucking," exclaimed Gary.

"Which was beyond annoying."

"If I didn't know better—"

"But *you do*," I said, narrowing my gaze on Gary's reflection to discourage what we both knew he was about to say.

"Jealousy," sang Gary under his breath. "Try those shoes on."

"Focus. The point is, he lives in the building. A little detail no one bothered to tell me until I ran into him a couple of days ago in the lobby."

"Wait, he lives here in this building?" I could see Gary's photographic mind taking inventory of all the residents. "With the exception of yours truly and the Crypt Keeper, Mr. Sol, as eligibles, that leaves only *Marcus Crawford*. Nah nah, Ms. Thang, you have been holding out! Dish now."

"Ouch, stop poking me. There is nothing to dish about. He is . . . you know, and I am—whatever. It's just incredibly odd, don't you think?"

"I knew there was something wrong with you . . . You're odd,

Jules. Marcus Crawford is one of New York's top bachelors and dare I say my future baby's daddy."

"Oh gawd, is he bisexual also? What the hell is going on in this place? It's like an epidemic of some kind. Maybe we should just rename the Big Apple the Big Rome." Only I found the humor in that remark.

"Umph, I wish he was. Trust! I have visions of how I can turn him, but he is strictly heterosexual," said Gary as he placed different purse options near me to determine which looked best. "Poor thing, he has no idea what he is missing."

Fidgeting with the blazer, I said, "Are you sure this isn't a bit too risqué? I love the skinny jeans with the blazer, but the top just seems a bit too Garment District, don't you think? I look like one of those Betsey Johnson girls."

"Here's the thing, Jules. You're never going to win with Carly, so stop trying to dress for her and man up, so to speak. Besides, from what you have told me, I can't see how she is against you. I mean, in my humble opinion, if anything she's just a philandering relic who occupies her time meddling in other people's lives because her husband has yet to make her a priority despite the sacrifices she's made to raise his love child and finance his dream. You were just an unexpected distraction—perk, if you will."

"You think all that, do you? Humbly, I mean?" I ask, clutching my invisible pearls.

"Ignoring you—yes I do! Take her out of the equation completely and just do you." Holding up the winning Ferragamo oversize clutch, he said, "What you should do is focus your efforts on captivating that divine specimen of availability, Marcus Crawford, so you can give me all the details."

"Yeah, right. Are you not listening? I am totally not his type nor am I interested."

"Trust me, honey, you're interested, just too stubborn to admit it," said Gary, stepping back to take a final look at the outfit. "Don't take yourself out of competition before the game is in play." Now turning his attention to my curly mane, pulling it back, then up and off my face in search of the right placement, he said, "Hmmm, no . . . maybe, yes, we need to blow this hair out and put it up in a sleek ponytail with some oversize hoops."

# 26

# D-DAY

"Hey, it's Jules," I said.

"Hi, Jacklyn, it's Simone. Is Jules around? Hold on. Yes, Michael, I am calling right now."

"Simone, stop multitasking, and focus. It's me," I said.

"Oh, where's Jacklyn?"

"On lunch break, so I am manning the phones."

"Well, that's a role reversal. Must be nice. Maybe I should work for you."

"Ha, that would be the other way around, Mrs. Phillips."

I could hear Michael, barking orders in the background: "Simone, I'm not paying either of you to be friendly. Has Davis arrived yet? I need to go."

"Hold on, Jules." Off receiver: "Michael, he will be here in five minutes. I am preparing your bag right now. Kaylin is aware that you will get to her in twenty minutes or so. I spoke to the nurse myself. Sorry about that, Jules."

"Hey, is everything okay?" I ask, getting a quick overview of the source of Simone's distraction.

"I really wish you would stop using the word *hey*. It's very unattractive, dear."

"Lordy, have you been speaking to my mother?" I asked. Sensing that now was not the time for cheekiness, I quickly interjected, "What do you need?"

"Hold on again." Simone off receiver: "Yes, Michael, yes. Correct, it will be there. I put those numbers in your bag. I'm getting it right now. Jules, you still there? Hold on."

*Pet peeve—boss or not, I find idling on the phone just plain boring and a waste of perfectly good time. Talk about improper.* "Simone, it's still me, holding."

*Why am I even trying?* The sarcasm in my voice is completely lost on her. "Sorry, Jules. Hold on one more— Michael, Davis is downstairs. Yes, I am on with her now."

"Simone! Obviously you are trying to tell me something, but between the incessant ringing of the phones and Michael barking, I'll never know."

"Jules, where is the research you compiled for the meeting tonight?" Michael demanded, breaking onto the line.

"Michael, that is what I was asking her," Simone said in her most diplomatically efficient tone.

"And yet, I still don't have it," Michael bellowed from his office, forgetting that he had us both on the line.

Clearly he was on a rampage today and anyone within earshot was in the line of fire. Wanting to deflect this as soon as possible, I looked down to see the haphazardly written notes on the report I was reviewing, quickly determining that it was in my best interest to give him this set, scribbles, smudge marks, and all. "Michael, I am on my way to you now." En route to his office I could organize them into something halfway presentable.

"Well, get a move on it," he said.

By the time I reached the end of the hallway, Michael was waiting impatiently at the elevator.

"Is everything okay?" I asked, worried in the off chance that it would impact my duties.

Stroking his temple, indicating that awaiting Davis's arrival was not the only thing causing him pain, he said, "Katy-kins is sick. I need to pick her up from school."

"Ah, so sorry. Sucks to be sick. Is Carly meeting you there?"

"That's not her thing," he responded.

Thinking it best not to break the flow of conversation, I stepped inside the elevator when it arrived and accompanied Michael down to the lobby.

"Oh"—*surely there was a better, less simplistically judgmental response I could offer up*—"my mother isn't great with medical emergencies either." A total lie that I am sure Cora heard on some superhuman maternal level, despite being thousands of miles away. In truth, she was amazing in medical situations. It's one of the few times in my childhood that she was singularly focused on doing whatever was necessary to make things better entirely for me. My dad, on the other hand, tended to fall apart, which was unnerving considering he is always so strong and assured in day-to-day affairs so that my mother and I don't have to be. After one rather unsightly wrist fracture in junior high school and witnessing him faint at the sight of a needle, I stopped leaning on him in matters of illness.

"Um. How is she, your mom, at the mothering?" Michael asked rather intensely.

Beaming with pride, I confess, "Relatively great, in her own way, but I'll never tell her that. She has a special way of showing it but she does." Our relationship has never been transparent. If I am to believe Freud, then I accept that it never will be—such is the case with mothers and daughters, I guess.

"Well, that would seem to be the minimum expectation, now wouldn't it?" Michael responded.

Knowing firsthand of Carly's deign to accept Kaylin's presence in their lives, I knew exactly what Michael was insinuating. More important, I knew that it was a door that I did not want to open. So I quickly rebelled against the uncomfortable moment by thrusting the papers I held toward him: "Here are the comparable restaurants in the U.S. and Europe. It is primarily made up of supper clubs and theme restaurants in the U.S. and private members only clubs in England. Also, you should pay close attention to the expansion rate of each—that seems to be the key. The ones that have forgone mass expansions seem to fare the best. I've already started putting some notes in the margins but—"

Shoving the papers into his leather attaché, he said, "Got it. Thanks," just as he got into the car and signaled Davis to drive on. Walking back into the building, I saw Simone going in the direction of the dining room, so I followed.

"Whoa, what was all of that about?" I asked, pretending to be oblivious to the overall specifics, but in reality, just wanting to gossip a bit.

"Kaylin has the mumps or something. Anyway, when she calls everything else takes a backseat for Michael, as you can see."

"Clearly an understatement. I have never heard him be so unglued and terse *with you.*"

Simone responded offhandedly, "I've grown used to it. Carly gets to abdicate maternal responsibility and I get the wrath."

*Great, another Carly-laced bomb for me to sidestep.* "I gave him a copy of the research I'm using for tonight, my copy actually. I'll get you—"

"Oh, honey, that meeting is canceled," said Simone, between sips of black tea. "You need to know that Michael Kipps will stop the world for only two things, Kaylin and this place. In the rare event, like now, that they decide to compete, the little princess always wins." *So much for that number one–selling book that Carly wrote about their storied love and family. By my calculations, that put her at a distant third. I guess fairy-tale endings, at least for her, are just that.* "I'll let you know when he puts it back on the books."

· · ·

Satisfied with the knowledge that Michael's attention would be consumed by Kaylin, I decided to make it an even earlier day and leave at 5 p.m. Now I could make that meal I never got around to. In retrospect, the encounter with Marcus a few nights earlier had somehow overshadowed the gravity of all the preceding events; the negative AIDS test, *a forgone conclusion to a well-heeded warning,* deciding how to address matters with Keith *sidelined until his return—breaking up via e-mail even from a nonofficial relationship is bad form,* preparing a meal—*shelved.* I had even thought about Marcus in my dreams to some degree, although I can't recall exactly what he was doing or what I was doing for that matter, but I'm sure he was there nonetheless, because I awoke with a smile and hearing him in my head.

Within an hour of arriving home, I was fully immersed in domestic bliss. My very skinny jeans and barely-there cami replaced with baggy cargo pants and a basic white tank. The Tahitian vanilla and gardenia scented candles, which I purchased from the same Portobello apothecary as those in the office, were lit throughout the apartment to complement the Anita Baker CD playing. Wanting the experience of cooking but not that of being a slave to the kitchen, I opted to roast a chicken and finish it off with a simple pear and arugula salad.

"The perfect companion you are," I said admiringly to the glass of Chardonnay resting in my hand as I stood by a window in the living room, watching the traffic steadily move down Fifth Avenue. The lights from the cars made every night seem like a Christmas parade. *The horns at times make it sound like the Puerto Rican Day parade.* The unexpected ring of the doorbell startled me back into the present.

"Just a minute," I said, leaping off the sill and rushing to open the door without looking because I was certain it was Gary seeking a full recap. Instead it was Marcus, standing before me in dark gray jeans and a white V-neck T-shirt that revealed a thin silver chain with dog tags. "What are you doing here?" I asked. *Honestly, it must be criminal to be this fine!*

"Not exactly the greeting I was hoping for but better than before, so I'd say we're making progress. Hi, Jules," he said, mischievously smiling down at me.

Unfazed, I responded, "You fancy yourself quite a bit, you know?"

"That has been brought to my attention before. Why don't we discuss it over dinner? And before you say that you're busy, remember we were supposed to have dinner tonight, so there should be no one else on your calendar," he said, trying to peek inside the doorway to make certain that his assumption was correct.

Stepping to the right to block his view inside, I ventured to correct his perception of the evening. "You shouldn't be here. And for the record, *we* were not having that kind of dinner. I was meeting my boss and his partners, of which you are one—apparently not a nice one, I might add, during which time food might have been served."

"Character assassination aside—exactly, dinner. Obviously not the way I would have preferred our first date to be, with onlookers and such, I'm quite private myself, but if you prefer chaperones—it's a start."

I shook my head in disbelief. *Clearly, reasserting the specifics was futile.* "What are you doing here?"

"I thought I just answered that," said Marcus. "Are you going to invite me in?"

"No." *You inside my apartment would only mean trouble and that is never happening.*

"Well, that isn't very neighborly of you, now is it?"

"The same could be said for you, stopping by uninvited and without a gift. I mean, who comes to a person's home for the first time empty-handed? Not very neighborly, Mr. Crawford," I said.

Looking down at his bare hands as if they had betrayed him by not spontaneously producing a gift, Marcus conceded his faux pas: "I'm sorry."

*Totally forgiven* is what I was thinking but not what I was saying.

"Well, well, it looks like your meeting went far better than expected." I didn't notice Gary coming down the hall. "*Marcus*," Gary said with innuendo dripping all over his former comment.

I can't be certain if Marcus was purposefully ignoring Gary's comment, oblivious to it, or just plain indifferent. In either case, Marcus turned to shake his hand and engage in small talk as neighbors often do. "Gary, it's been a while. How are things at the magazine?"

"Too long. When are you going to let me profile your Bridgehampton home? I heard from Edward and Cecilia that it is amazing." I wanted to interrupt and find out the social relevance of "Edward and Cecilia," but Gary was now firmly in pitch mode. Gone were the exaggerated gestures of femininity that accompanied my fashion makeover this morning. In their place now were decisively more masculine movements that mimicked Marcus's own.

"Soon, soon. I didn't get a chance to spend as much time there as I would have liked this summer, a weekend here and there. You know?"

Gary nodded, "Of course. I would think that a property of that size located on the water is beautiful year-round. A winter story would be magnificent—'On Frozen Pond.' I could allocate a number of pages to it before the season passes."

"Good to know," said Marcus. *Ah, now I see it. He is clearly indifferent, and poor Gary is working so hard to make him care.*

"I would even go so far as to guarantee you the cover." By this time my presence was purely a matter of happenstance, at least for Gary. Marcus's nonchalant air prevailed despite Gary's refusal to acknowledge it. He was determined to seal the deal here and now. The reason for such urgency eluded me, but I was surely going to find out. "Did you see the great coverage we did on Jules's apartment?" Bingo! Gary, finally, said something that interested Marcus *and annoyed me.*

"Did you now? Somehow I missed that issue," replied Marcus, switching his gaze to me instead of Gary. "Would love to see how the photography compares with the actual space."

"Say no more. I have an issue inside," said Gary, pointing in the direction of his apartment across the hall. "I'll bring it over."

"Perfect," said Marcus, with an all-knowing grin that his pawn had captured my queen. "We'll wait for you inside," he said, pushing past me into the foyer only to step aside and smile down at me with those piercing blue eyes. *Checkmate—king's pawn.* "You coming? I'd love a tour."

Despite the masterful play, I was not ready to concede any ground to Marcus, at least not the kind he was looking for. *Sure, he had managed to gain entry into my apartment—so what? It means nothing.*

As he followed me inside I could feel his eyes searching every inch of my body instead of the apartment's décor. *I only need to prove a gracious host and provide Gary some time to wrangle Marcus. No big deal; this is not even about me. I'm just being neighborly. I'm not betraying Michael, just being a good neighbor is all!*

From behind Marcus asked, "Should I ask you now what specific unflattering things our Michael has been saying?"

"No, you should not. All deserved, I'm sure. Can I get you something to drink?" I asked.

"I'll take that as a compliment. Whatever you have open is fine."

"Of course you would! I'm having wine. Is that what you want?" I insisted.

"Not really. Been one of those days. I'd love a martini, but if you don't—"

"No problem. Gin or vodka?"

"Bombay, if you have it."

"Okay, Bombay it is. Have a seat, I'll bring it out."

From inside the kitchen I made a beeline for the telephone and called Gary. Marcus had been in my place less than ten minutes yet it felt like an eternity. My previously relaxed vibe was steadily being replaced by a subtle anxiety in knowing that he was there and not knowing what to do with him. At this moment he could possibly be looking at my photos and any manner of personal effects that I was not comfortable sharing with my colleagues, especially him. *God, please don't let him venture into my bedroom.* It was still nuclear from this morning.

Cupping the phone's receiver with both hands, I said in a rushed and desperate whisper, "Gary, where the hell are you? Changing! For what? You're just showing the man a magazine, giving him a quick look about, and then getting the hell out so I can enjoy my evening. Get over here now."

"It smells great in there," Marcus said from the living room over the music. "You have good taste."

"Thanks. I love candles, especially mixing scents to come up with something unique," I said, without being certain if he was talking about the aroma from the chicken or the room scents, so I opted for the latter. "Do you want an olive or lemon?"

"Lemon is perfect."

*Whoever invented martini glasses must never have had to carry one across a room.* Coming in from the kitchen, gingerly balancing his drink and my newly refilled glass of wine, I found Marcus standing near the Bose system, going through my music collection. Since working at Carly's, I had come to appreciate great sound quality. Not nearly as much as a pair of Dior heels but enough so that I felt the need to invest in a good audio system.

"Here you go," I said.

"What do you know about Corcovado?" Marcus asked, taking a cautionary sip, only to have his taste buds come alive with the perfect balance of vermouth, gin, and lemon, chilled to perfection. "Cheers. Oh man. This is perfect."

"Fifteen shakes is the key," I said. "I'm a music lover, Crawford, or hadn't you heard?"

"So I see, Van Morrison, the Stones, Tribe, Grace, Miles. . . . whoa, is this the Upsetters? What do you know about Scratch Perry?" I could tell he was impressed, but, like me earlier, not ready to concede too much ground. "Nice selection, but I am not convinced. What is the best yet lesser-known Marvin song? If you know that I'll—"

"Too easy. Take a seat and prepare to be impressed," I said, stepping in front of him to locate the song in question. Once it was loaded in the player, I turned around to face Marcus and savor the moment. Hearing the first few bars of "Funky Space Incarnation," he made a quick gesture, unexpectedly spilling a portion of his drink.

"So sorry. If you have something, I can—" he said, indicating that he wanted to clean up the small puddles of cocktail now on my wood floors and coffee table.

"I will take that as a sign that you are thoroughly impressed," I said, laughing. "There are towels in the kitchen." Laughing felt good. I hadn't done that in a few days.

"Actually, I was referring to 'Symphony,' but this will do."

"You so were not!" I said. "What are you going to say next, you cry sometimes?"

"No, I wasn't. Look at you, Jules Sinclair, audiophile. Does Michael know you're more than a pretty face yet or is he still seeing the world through his glory days?" asked Marcus, kneeling to clean the spill.

"Not addressing that," I said. "Come on into the kitchen, let's get you a refill."

"Don't say you weren't warned," said Marcus.

We spoke effortlessly about music, both of us harboring a secret love for Tim McGraw and Euro pop. Soon we were playing the music equivalent of Confession.

"No way, I have you beat. My most embarrassing song moment is Diana Ross's tribute to Marvin," I said.

"'Missing You'? Come now, how is that worse than not understanding the meaning of 'Love Come Down'?" asked Marcus. "I was a ten-year-old kid in South Boston singing about female masturbation! You have *any* idea how embarrassing that was—"

Putting a hand before him to signal "wait for it," I took a courageous sip of wine. "I can't believe I am telling you this. Okay! So obviously she is saying 'since you been away I've been down and lonely,' right? Because Marvin is dead, left her alone, and she misses him."

"Wait, wait, why are you closing your eyes?" he asked.

"Because I don't want to see your reaction," I said, squeezing them extra tight.

"All right now."

"So I thought—remember, youthful ears and I was in Catholic school at the time. I thought she was saying, 'Sister Benaway, I have been down and lonely. Sister Benaway, I've been thinking, 'bout you.' I thought the song was about having confession with her favorite nun. I was jealous that I didn't have a favorite."

The silence that greeted my confession made me open one eye to make sure Marcus was still in the room. He was there all right, face scrunched up, lips pursed tightly as if trying to decide whether to get up and hug me for my extreme naïveté or allow the volcano of laughter to erupt. Within seconds, loud riotous laughter ensued. My injury clear, I was trying to pretend that it was more funny than thoroughly embarrassing, when I accidentally sprayed him with the wine in my mouth, sending us both into full-on uncontrollable hysterics. Any notions I had of being graceful quickly dissipated. By the time Gary arrived, we were somewhere between old friends and new prospects.

"Glad to see y'all didn't wait for me before getting your party on. What's so funny?" he asked, looking from me to Marcus. "Why is his face wet?"

"Diana Ross and Catholicism," I offered, because Marcus was on the last wave of hysterics. Clearly the moment was too far gone to bring Gary up to speed and he had other matters to attend to.

"What are you cooking? It smells good in here," said Gary, looking in the fridge for grapes.

"Roasting a chicken."

"Great, I'm starving. What else is on the menu?" asked Gary.

Taken aback at the implication that I would now have dinner guests, I stammered, "Um, I was just thinking to make something simple—for one, but, um, we could do some sides, maybe an arugula salad to start."

"Sounds delicious," said Marcus. "You got some potatoes and buttermilk? I'm pretty famous for my garlic mashed potatoes."

Slapping him on the back, Gary said, "Well, then, get on it, instead of sitting here watching me suck on these damn grapes."

I took a seat at the island alongside Gary as Marcus went about procuring ingredients as if he had been in my kitchen a million times before and knew what was located in every cabinet and drawer.

"Marcus, where does a man like you find time to cook?" asked Gary.

"College. You either starve, eat ramen, and risk getting high blood pressure, ration care packages from home, or learn to cook. I learned to cook. Calling my nan for simple recipes here and there. Soon I found I enjoyed being in the kitchen. The whole process seemed to free my mind up so I could think about exams and stuff."

"Where did you go to school?" I asked.

"Brown," said Marcus.

"Oh, Providence," I replied, as he affirmed some of what I thought upon first meeting him.

"Yes. You know it?"

"No, but Cora, that's my mom, is hopelessly obsessed with Newport. So I know all things Rhode Island."

"So, Marcus, could we get some shots of you cooking in Bridge-hampton? Our readers would love it, and for the people who know of your reputation, they would never think—" Gary said, gesturing to the kitchen. "It would be an amazing give."

"And what is your reputation?" I asked.

"Only one of the most enigmatic and stylish corporate raiders to emerge in recent years," said Gary in his eagerness to impress Marcus.

"Investment banker," corrected Marcus as he went about combining ingredients in a large bowl.

"Isn't that the same thing as a venture capitalist?" I asked.

"Yes, but VC has an ugly connotation in today's market. IB is more PC than VC," said Marcus.

"Whatever you call it, he is a wonder and everyone wants to know what's behind the transcontinental bravado," said Gary. "I just hope one day to have enough money for him to play around with."

"For the love of heaven, *please* put this man out of his misery and allow him to shoot your house so we can enjoy dinner," I said, getting up to start the salad and asparagus. "Or else he'll continue shining you on, and I in turn just might lose my appetite."

Removing the mixing blades from the potatoes and offering me a taste, Marcus said, "Only if you agree to be there. Something tells me I need a team around me to protect my interest or Gary will have carte blanche."

"She'll be there," Gary insisted, shooting me a look that begged not to be contradicted.

With that out of the way, Gary allowed himself to relax and enjoy the evening. Marcus and I busied ourselves putting the final touches on dinner; Gary kept the glasses filled and the music pumping. Formality and duplicitous agendas had long since gone out the window, so no one made any steps to move to the dining room. Instead we settled nicely around the island, spoke freely, and ate heartily. Dessert, like dinner, was impromptu, so a store-bought peach cobbler with heaping scoops of ice cream finished the meal off. Without ever intending to, I had hosted my first dinner party in New York since my return, my first actually in three years or so. I forgot how much I enjoyed the easiness of great food, good people, and home comforts. Marcus was the first to leave. He had vowed to stay and help clean up, but the constant ringing of his cell phone made it apparent that he was expected elsewhere.

"See, dinner with me wasn't so bad after all, now was it?" he said at the door.

"No, dinner with you and Gary was great."

"Maybe next time just you and me."

"You and I both know there are a million reasons *that* dinner will never happen. Chief among those is that you are my boss indirectly, and I'm dating someone—remember?"

"You don't have to be, you know. As for Carly's, it's just an investment," he said.

Remembering the charge Michael had bestowed upon me, I said, "It's much more than that, Marcus. There is something great there if it is allowed to grow and expand. You'd know that if you looked closer at the long term."

"We'll talk about it over dinner," he said.

As he reached down to raise his ringing phone (exhibit A), I said, "Right?! We'll make it a lovely group event, you, me, and the woman who is not content with leaving a message or allowing time for a proper call-back. Good night, Mr. Crawford."

"Good night, Jules," he said as he backed away slowly down the hall to the elevator.

· · ·

Unbeknownst to me, Gary was standing on the other side of the door eavesdropping as I turned to close it.

"Holy shit!" I screamed, clutching my chest.

"Shit is right," he said. "You have been holding out."

"Have not," I protested.

"Oh, hells yes! That man wants you."

"Well, that is not going to happen."

"Listen, honey, you know I love you like a new sister from a wayward father, so let me tell you, be careful. Marcus Crawford is better than Midas. He always gets what he wants. The problem is that his attention span is legendary ADD, if you get my drift. Why do you think he is so good at financial raiding? He goes in, assesses the situation, manipulates control, and then destroys it before it becomes a fixture."

"That makes three times today, G, that you have 'thrown me a drift.' Loud and clear on all," I said, "but you have nothing to worry about, I've been a fool already and irresponsible once, not again. I have no intentions there."

"Good girl," he said, crossing the hall to his apartment. "Stupid girl . . . *lonely* girl."

Before his door closed fully, I playfully yelled, "You know I can hear you, right?! Just know that you owe me, Mr. Editor, and I will collect later."

"As soon as it goes to print. I'll see you in the Hamptons, *lonely girl.*"

Exhausted, I collapsed into bed, but not before replaying the evening in my head. I had such a great time and hoped for a redo—in general, not necessarily with Marcus, although . . . and Gary. In the move back to New York and diving into things with Keith, I didn't realize that I had forsaken some simple, essential things—like just being me with people. Nothing more, nothing less. After Tony, I built a wall around myself that even my closest friends had not been able to truly penetrate. Richard had even commented on it: "Honey, at some point you will have to let it all down"—but he had not pushed the issue. Had tonight gone as planned, I would not have known what I was missing. Further indication that the transitional relationship with Keith, even without the scare, was not what I needed.

. . .

Keith had been back from Tokyo for a few days by the time we actually saw each other. While away, we communicated via e-mail once or twice. The first was an e-mail he sent.

> Subject: What's the most coveted commodity in Japan?
>
> Attachment: Photo of Keith in all of his bronze, statuesque glory and a cipher of commuters blatantly checking him out.
> J—one of my coworkers took this. Who knew I was such a big deal just for being?
> Masters

> Subject: RE: What's the most coveted commodity in Japan?
>
> Here I was thinking it was Michael Jordan sans the mocha tan, of course;-) Glad to hear you arrived safely. See you when you return, would like to chat.
> x Jules

After clicking Send, I read the e-mail a few times. Why on earth did I say "Would like to chat"? It is the relationship equivalent of a siren in the middle of the night—you know there's trouble coming but are clueless as to what it is. Since that fateful brunch with Richard and Blake, I had accepted that we could not go on being a romantic item. What eluded me was the perfectly strung sequence of words that would convey this without making him feel judged for his lifestyle. More than anything I didn't want to hurt Keith in any conceivable way, and yet it was inevitable. Rejection never feels good, even when done with compassion and sincere regret. The thought crossed my mind *more than a few times* to seek advice from friends, but it always felt like a betrayal, so I did not. My expectation was that I would surely know what to say when the moment presented itself.

"Jules, Keith is on the line for you."

"Put him through, Jack."

*Well, I am about five minutes away from the moment and no closer to knowing the bottom of the third or fourth act of this production.*

"What's the sexiest girl in Manhattan doing?" said Keith.

"Honestly, where did you learn to talk like that? It's very Dirk Diggler, you know."

"I could be offended by that remark, but I am choosing to find the compliment, in a seventies porn kind of way. So, how have you been?"

"Dodging grenades, as it were. Michael has found himself—Hold on a minute," I said, placing my hand over the receiver and yelling to Jacklyn. "Hey, Jack, jump off this call if you are on." As a matter of security and a sometimes selective memory, I have Jacklyn listen in on some of my calls and take notes. The downside of this is the resulting paranoia that makes me think she now listens to every call, especially the personal ones, and transcribes everything I say. "Okay, where was I?"

"Michael, grenades," said Keith.

"Oh, yes. Michael is on the warpath, so I seem to spend my days in trepidation fearing the phone and smell of cigars."

"Sounds like my timing is perfect then."

"It's something," I replied.

"Go look out your window."

Walking to the window half expecting to see John Cusack standing below with a large boom box above his head, instead there was Keith, or at least someone who bore a striking resemblance to him. He was standing near the streetlamp wearing a fitted dark blue wool dress coat, a camel houndstooth scarf knotted high on the neck—and a dapper newsboy cap, talking on the phone.

"Just as I thought, you look good, lady," said Keith, looking up to the window and revealing his face.

"Obviously—you know how I do," I said. "When did you start wearing hats?"

"You like it? I had a stopover in London and picked it up," Keith said, his hand tracing the parameter of the brim.

"Well, look at you," I said, overwhelmed at the sight of him, and the physical response it still conjured in spite of everything.

"If you come down from that ivory tower of yours and join me for a coffee, you could look much closer," he said. "Before you look at that calendar and tell me that you can't, know that I only have about twenty minutes or so but wanted to see you."

"In that case, how could I not?" Flirtation with Keith is easy. His come-what-may manner made me happy even when there was no cause for celebration—like now.

"Jeez, it's colder out here than it looks. Were you standing out here the entire time?"

"No, I had a meeting a few doors down and dialed you from there," he said, switching to the outer side of the walkway. "Let's go to Petite Abeille. Do you mind?"

"Not at all, but if you only have twenty minutes, then maybe not."

Searching the immediate length of the cobblestone streets for an alternative, he said, "You're right. In that case, let's do Pastis. It shouldn't be too bad at this hour."

With the exception of a few tables in back and two guys at the bar, Pastis was abnormally bare.

"You have a preference?" asked Keith.

"No, you choose," I replied.

"We'll take that one-top by the window."

"Perfect, I normally sit in the back. It's the best for people-watching, you know," I said.

"So I've heard; however, I've always found that the best way to know people is to observe their habits and listen to what is left on the table, between the lines. You'll have enough for a novel," said Keith.

"Really, I've recently learned that sometimes observation can fail you. Sometimes it's the overt statement that tends to pull the rug right from under you."

"Perhaps. I just have not ever heard anything from another person that I didn't observe beforehand."

"Then you're lucky, but I can't say that." Now fully engaged in the dance, I decided to just jump right in.

"Michael got to you that bad?"

"No, not Michael," I said. *Deep inhale, hold it . . . now go.* "You seriously threw me for a loop last time, Masters."

"I know, the whole Saturn in retrograde thing is a hard pill to swallow."

"True, but that came in a distant second to me hearing you like men as much as I do."

"Really?"

"Yes, really," I said, my eyes purposefully drifting to the intricate stitching on his lapel for a place to rest in order to avoid any conflict apparent in his eyes.

"Shit, Jules, I thought you knew."

*Leave your hand exactly where it is, J. Don't remove it from the table or else he will think you don't want to be touched by him.*

"And how would I know that? You and I had never spoken of it before and I'm not a mind reader, so . . ." I trailed off 'cause the landing destination was unknown, even to me at that point. *Look at him, Jules. You need to see his face. More important, he needs to see yours. God, I'm going to miss those lips.*

"Damn, Manhattan is small, you know, and I am anything but closeted or low-key for that matter. Besides, your friend Joy seemed to know a lot about me, so I just guessed that was inclusive of the girl talk. I'm sorry, baby. I had no idea you didn't know."

"If she knew, she didn't tell me, nor should she have been the one. You're the one I'm sleeping with." *More of a statement than an accusation. Yes, a statement. Let's hope.* "Besides, I am not a fan of hearsay, even from friends."

"What can I say, J, I'm not disputing that if—Listen, I am sorry. It was not my intent to deceive you. I would never. Please don't be mad. We can figure this out."

"I'm not sure we can. Keith, I'm not mad. I still don't know specifically what my entire position on all of this is. The two things I am absolutely clear on is: I want us to be okay no matter—I've gotten used to talking to you, and second, that we can no longer have any kind of sexual relationship." *Damn, those words just breezed out. I hope he heard the first part.* "I'm not saying that I am going all Terry McMillan or anything, but I'm just not sure I am that modern, you know? I mean, I'm still battling through a mountain of insecurities every day: Am I smart enough? Am I pretty enough, fit enough, engaging enough to keep my man's attention? Not to mention how difficult it is just to not feel constantly like somewhere along the way, in the big picture of things, I fucked something up royally as to the course of my life—twenty-eight years old and still single, hello?! Keith, it's hard enough to be a woman in this world with the statistics that are drilled into our brains every single day about being more likely to be somebody's baby mama than a wife. Living under all of that and now having to watch my back with the next man, about his attraction to my man, is much more than I want to deal with right now, you know?"

Leaning back from the table, smoothing the invisible wrinkles on his herringbone twill trousers, he said, "I hear what you're saying, Jules. I just don't like it. Can we discuss this later? I really have to . . ." His eyes followed the dial on the Roger Dubuis timepiece far more closely than necessary, before searching the room without success for our waiter to bring the check.

"I know you have a meeting. Go, I'll get this," I said.

Standing in front of a bistro in the Meatpacking District with a less-than-ten-minute conversation is not exactly how I envisioned everything coming to an end, but that was the case, life seldom provides a perfect moment. Had I even said what I needed to? Walking back to my office, I convinced myself that the warm hug Keith gave me before disappearing into his taxi was a sure sign that we would be more than ships passing. *If, however, we were passing, I could stride much better with a new pair of shoes from Jefferies.* Besides, it's not as if we were in a serious relationship or anything. He was just some guy I enjoyed sleeping with, talking to, e-mailing, laughing with, and texting. No big deal, right?

# 27

# BOUNDARIES

Turns out Kaylin's mild fever was the precursor to a nasty case of bronchitis. For a week, Michael kept vigil over her. It was the first time in his life that he felt absolutely helpless, and Michael Thurmond Kipps did not do helpless well. If he could not will the infection out of his daughter's body, then he would shift his focus to the one thing he could control, his restaurant, even if from afar.

"Saddle up, baby girl. Mike is on the warpath and is looking for you," said Raymond as I took a seat at the bar.

"Again? I have been yelled at, hung up on, and blamed more in the past two weeks than I was in my entire adolescence when I actually was guilty of occasionally sneaking out the house and lifting money from my mom's purse."

"Well, I don't know what to say about all that, but I can tell you that my man's looking for you, so be ready."

"Warning signal heeded. Pass me the phone." My day had been consumed doing media previews of the renovated upstairs recording studio that we were now opening up to certain musicians, i.e., those who Michael felt qualified as *real musicians* or those with insane recording budgets. Given all that was going on, I didn't think it necessary to send Michael my schedule. Normally Jacklyn would have been able to inform Simone of my whereabouts, but like Kaylin, she was home with a fever (thankfully not bronchitis) for a few days.

Somewhere between yelling and near convulsion, Michael attacked on hearing my voice: "Jules, what in the hell are you doing having dinner with Marcus behind my back? Do I need to be concerned about where your loyalty is? You know we are on opposing sides right now. Why would you do that and NOT tell me?"

My intent had been to tell him about the dinner with Marcus—innocent enough, right, but something inside told me not to. In the two weeks that had passed, I had not seen hide nor hair of Marcus, so I considered the encounter not worth mentioning. Michael's accusations came so quickly and were so venomous that I didn't have time to understand the complete root of his ire.

"Michael, I don't know what you heard, but Marcus and I did not have dinner."

"Are you saying that he is lying?"

"No, of course not, but—"

"But what, Jules? No means what, yes, you did have dinner with him. You need to tell me something or else I need to evaluate who's on my team. It's like this slick motherfucker has Carly's ear and now yours. Who in the fuck has my back? I'm fighting for my family here."

I could feel Raymond's eyes on me, watching my face go from pensive to defensive. If I tried to interrupt and argue back, my points would get lost and things would surely go from bad to worse, so I waited for Michael to settle down. "Is there anything you have to say for yourself or do I need to consider making some changes?"

Taking a deep inhale, I closed my eyes to center myself before speaking. "Michael, I am now and have always been on your side, never question that." I looked up to see Raymond nodding in the affirmative, indicating that I was responding appropriately, and continued, "I should have told you about the dinner with Marcus and Gary, but Kaylin got sicker and I didn't want to burden you with superfluous information about nothing—music and trivia."

"What? Who in the hell's Gary?" he asked.

"My neighbor from across the hall. He is the editor in chief of *Decor* magazine. You've met him—he did a piece on you and Carly years back." After hearing him grunt something inaudible that gave the impression this was information he did not have, I continued: "If you recall the day Kaylin got sick, we were supposed to have the partners' meeting. With the meeting canceled, I went home. Marcus knocked on my door and asked me to dinner. I said no. While he was standing there, Gary came home and, upon seeing Marcus, began to pitch him heavily for a feature in *Decor*. One thing led to another, and the both of them ended up in my place talking about the feature and eating. Marcus left and then Gary."

"And that's it?" Michael asked.

"Yes," I said, having glossed over the fact we spoke all of five seconds about Carly's. "We were never alone, so even if he wanted to speak of other things, he could not because of Gary." *Jeez, I hate lying, I don't even know why I am right now, but did Michael really need to know about the fun we had when Gary was away or could I just keep that for me?*

"And you didn't say anything about Carly's?" The emphasis Michael put on the question felt more like an inquisition, so I quickly replayed the evening in my head before speaking.

"Um, when he was leaving he mentioned something about Carly's being an investment opportunity. I said that it was much more than that, that Carly's was something great, and if given time he would see it."

"And that's all you said? You didn't say anything else?" repeated Michael.

Of course there was more. I had not given him the full context for this line of dialogue, fearing it would serve only to falsely imply my disloyalty. I couldn't bring myself to tell him that Marcus had asked me out on a date (again), and that in declining (again), this conversation came to be. By this time Raymond had given up any pretense of polishing glasses and was firmly attuned to our conversation. Michael may have not been there in the flesh, but his spare eyes were clocking my every response.

"Yes, that's it," I said.

"Umph."

Nervously tapping my pen on the table, I needed more than "umph." *Am I cleaning out my office? On probation for withholding? Forgiven?* In the most neutral, nonantagonistic tone I could muster, I asked, "What does 'umph' mean, Michael?"

"It means don't ever keep anything from me again, no matter how insignificant *you* think it is. You don't have that luxury—especially when it has to do with Marcus. I deal enough with that at home. I look up and the same motherfucker who is rallying to change the direction at Carly's, who has been mysteriously out of the office for the past two weeks and not returning calls, is suddenly at my living room while my baby girl is upstairs."

"Oh, I didn't know."

"'Oh' is right. Thankfully, I was well versed in trumping anything he and Carly had to say. There I am in my own home, at my own damn table, talking about there being something great here at Carly's—in full fight mode. That's when he sucker punched me by saying you said the same thing over dinner."

"But didn't he say anything else? Didn't he give it context?" I asked.

"Nothing. He didn't need to say anything else. His jab landed squarely where he intended. Here he is bending my wife's ear and now letting me know that he was making ends with one of my employees as well."

*Wow, is this the same guy who sat at my table and laughed with me? Talk about me being naïve. Well, I'd sort my feelings about that later. Right now, I need to save my job.* "He said it like that to get a rise out of you, Michael. You know that, right?"

"Yes, and it would have worked had he not finished by agreeing there was potential there. It would just take a capital infusion that neither of us has to explore things."

"Wait, so this is a good thing," I said.

"In a manner of speaking, but it's far from over. That was a warning shot. He made it known that he can circumvent me—a coup d'état. If he thinks that his carrot will stop me from moving ahead, he's got another thing coming. Not only will I expand Carly's but I'll find the purse strings to bankroll it, buy him, and hold on to what's mine."

"And you guys can't work together?"

"It's about more than that, Jules. A man has to be in control of his destiny at all times—can't let some other motherfucker that I showed the ropes to come in and start making the rules. Soon he'll run out of maneuvers, and I'll show him who he's dealing with. Marcus Crawford needs me far more than I need him. That's for damn sure."

*Clearly no love lost between these two, but how could things seemingly go so bad in a year's time? For anyone to dig their heels in the way Michael was and react as he did screamed of far bigger issues than deciding when and where to open new locations. It's as if the pupil had now become the teacher—only problem is that Michael wasn't ready for forced retirement.* I understood more than Michael gave me credit for. True, I should have told him about the dinner, but my words and time spent had somehow influenced Marcus, which was good. Marcus's being invited to his home at a crisis moment by his spouse, whose attention should have been on their child, should have been the issue. *Once again a glimpse into their dynamic that left more questions than answers—at least in my mind.*

Hearing him calm and knowing now exactly what he needed to hear, I said, "I understand. You're right. It won't happen again."

Hanging up the phone, I vowed to speak with him about my presence at the impending *Decor* shoot when the time presented itself. Raymond, having observed the entire exchange, placed a single shot of tequila in front of me as soon as the receiver touched the cradle.

"You handled yourself well," he offered.

Feeling more vilified than vindicated, I replied, "Thanks, Raymond," and looked down at the cup. "Wrong *T*, though. I'll take a chamomile tea instead of tequila."

. . .

"Michael is full of hot air, just fall back and let this partner drama fade, or next time you may have to let him touch more than your upper thigh to keep your job. As for Keith, cut your losses and kiss the sky instead of mourning something that was nothing more than a glorified booty call."

"Blakes, you can be incredibly crass at times. Correction, more times than not," I said between bites of salad. "Remind me again why it is that I called you and not Joy."

"Because she will placate you and tell you a bunch of bullshit to continue the pity party you have going instead of helping you to live in the truth," said Blake.

"And what would that be, exactly?" I inquired.

"The truth, little Julesea . . ."

"Uh, really, you must stop that," I said. Once upon a time, maybe over cocktails or the sort, I told Blake my full name. To my dismay she actually has the ability to retain much more than credit card numbers, because whenever she needed to emphasize a point and silence me momentarily, it was total recall.

"Whatever." Blake was in full stride and not about to be deterred. "Truth is, not every person who enters your life is supposed to be there for the long haul, even when they have the ability to make your toes curl. In reality, most of them are temporary transients. Keith was a 'jump-off' because you needed desperately to get lubed. Now that squeak has been properly knocked out and you can get back on the highway of life."

"Why is it I feel like a 1979 Volkswagen Beetle?"

"It's better than the spider/cobweb metaphor I was going to use." She snickered at her quip. "Seriously, though, Jules. Don't create a problem where there is none. Listen, I have to jump, weekly staff meeting, but let's go out soon. We'll go to Life. You're always good Big Daddy bait for me. Who knows, maybe I'll even invite the old girl—Richard could use some loosening up."

Hanging up the phone, I wondered if Blake was right about people and partners being transient. Sure, Keith and I had never spoken about our future, as a couple, but there was something—*feels like melancholy*—to be said for no longer having the option to explore "What does this mean?" Now, in spite of everything, all that's left are a few memories of "What could have been if." Those are the worst; like little leprechauns, always filled with promise at the end of a fictitious rainbow that will never deliver a pot of gold. *"Mama knows," that's what Cora always says. She also says that bad things, like good things, come in threes, just at an accelerated pace. Maybe that is the feeling of discontent stirring inside.*

It was a little after 6 p.m. when I exited the 6 train at Seventy-seventh and Lexington, but nightfall had yet to fully engulf the city, so I allowed myself to stroll and window-shop. The tips of the trees seemed fatter this evening, despite the mounds of dirty snow scattered about the sidewalk. A clear sign that warmer weather was around the corner. At least that was my hope. *I wonder if anyone told that groundhog? Lazy ass.* Approaching my building, I didn't expect to see Percy standing outside under the heat lamps placed discreetly along the awning above.

"Hi, Percy, when did you start working evenings?"

Tipping his hat as he pulled the door open, he said, "Miss Jules, I normally don't, but Ivan couldn't make it tonight, so here I am."

"You sure are. It's a cold one tonight. Hopefully there won't be much foot traffic that keeps you outside."

"I can only pray, but you know I don't mind. No, ma'am, I do what is needed to get the job done 'round here," said Percy.

"True. Well, take care," I said, escaping into the building before he started to run the laundry list of all that he does daily to make our lives easier. In the course of our regular interactions, I had come to realize that everyone has this incessant need to be a star in their contribution—especially doormen.

Rounding the corridor from the mailboxes, I glimpsed Percy talking to Mitzy—*clearly strike one*, and I didn't know which one to feel sorrier for on this eve. *Definitely Percy.* Time had not made Mitzy and me any closer as cordial neighbors go. And try as I might, the sound of her voice and her prissy mannerisms just brought out the worst in me. So much so that on the day I had the misfortune of running into her in the fragrance department at Saks, the image of fucking her husband in her bed was the only reprieve from a positively mind-numbing conversation. *Obviously, I would have to be really drunk, popping E, and he would have to shed about fifty or so pounds.*

"All right now, Mrs. Bloomfield, you have a good night and let me know how that is coming along," said Percy, to my chagrin.

Darn it, where in the hell is this elevator? Seriously, all the freaking money in this building and it must have the slowest elevator on the island. Maybe she'll check the mail first and I can just avoid her . . . or maybe not.

"Well, hello, Jules. It has been *forever*. The girls and I were starting to think you had left us."

"No such luck, Mitzy. I'm here."

"So I see," she said, sizing me up as if it were the first time we had ever met. "In that case, how are you settling in?"

"Just fine," I respond, keeping my eyes fixed on the ascending lighted numbers of the elevator panel: 2 . . . 3 . . . 4.

"The girls and I saw the piece on your apartment in *Decor*. It was quaint, not exactly my taste, but seems fitting for you," said

Mitzy. "Was that Marcus Crawford I saw walking with you some-time back? There I was, out for my morning run through the park, and surprise—you and Marcus. At first I wasn't certain, I mean, after all, I normally see him with the tall, glamorous girls, one after the other—funny, isn't it? I can't believe I remembered such a thing after all this time."

*Damn, why does she try me every time? One day I will be mature enough to ignore her kind. Today, however, is not that day.* "Mitzy," I say, looking at her admiringly, "what moisturizer are you using these days?"

"Chantecaille, of course. It is the best! Why do you ask?"

"Last time I saw you there were all of these lines around your eyes and mouth. *Far* more than there are now. I was just wondering. I thought it was La Mer. Stuff works wonders, wouldn't you say? Like spackle, it is." *Ding, talk about perfect timing. Thank you, elevator.* Stepping into the empty car, I turned to see Mitzy, still on the opposite side of the threshold—mouth open and pearls clenched. I thought to reach down and hand her back her face but opted not to. *Why try being a considerate person now? Let it stay on the floor.* "You coming? No? Have a good night then." *Oh yeah, that was much better than envisioning sleeping with her chub of a husband. Much better.*

# 28

## A GIFT HORSE

*To the woman who knows her way around a kitchen and a music catalog, you are full of surprises. Jules, I really enjoyed dinner (and the walk). Sorry it took so long for me to tell you.*

*Soon,*
*Marcus*

"Well, he certainly has great taste in stationery and nice penmanship. What is this, Cartier?"

Snatching the note, I said, "Richard, I need you to focus. Like he *really* wrote this! Who does this guy think he is? Like some candle and note will—"

"Not *some* candle. Diptyque, dear," Richard corrected, sniffing the contents of the box again.

"Focus, will you?" I repeated. "It's just some wax and a wick in a sixty-five-dollar box. A candle and a note—"

"*Cartier*, my dear, not *a* note. Will what? Make you accept his heartfelt thank-you and express his obvious good manners?"

"You know, that is the problem with you, Boulton. You get caught in the gestures. Let's not forget this 'beacon of etiquette' almost cost me my job, and is a bully."

"Slightly exaggerated, don't you think?" asked Richard. "I assume that last bit was about Michael? You need to focus on how this man is with you and let Michael fight his own battles."

"Maybe, maybe not," I said.

"What did he have to say for himself?"

"Nothing. I haven't seen him since. I come home a few nights ago and this package is sitting at the door," I say, raising the gardenia-scented Dipytque candle and note in each hand as exhibits A and B.

"So, basically, you are being irrational because what? Because you still have yet to decide how many shades of pissed-off to be. Or maybe you are flattered but too stubborn to admit it. And maybe, just maybe, you want a talking point. Where's the cornmeal?"

"I reject all of the above. Cornmeal, left cabinet above the stove."

After opening and closing just about every cabinet and drawer in my kitchen, only to come up empty, Richard pleaded, "Please tell me you have a cast-iron skillet."

"Of course. They were on the list you sent Jacklyn, weren't they? Look in the oven."

"Gawd, you are from the islands—your people. These haven't been seasoned," said Richard, removing the still-wrapped trio from the oven and placing them in front of me with a bottle of cooking oil. After a beat or two of me making no motion toward them, Richard instructed, "Don't just sit there looking at me all lost. Get to rubbing oil in each. Those pans won't season themselves."

For years I have said that Richard is going to make a great wife when it is legally permissible to be such. Tonight was but another example of that, and I reaped the benefits of his nesting tendencies. As payback for accompanying him to some dreadful intellectual event at the Princeton Club, he had agreed to cook me a meal of braised short ribs, macaroni and cheese with cauliflower, green beans, and corn bread. Provided we were not in a food coma afterward, a tryst at Life with Blake was in order.

◆ ◆ ◆

Since my time in London, Life had become the hottest nightclub in town, making the Village a nighttime haven once again. Word

had spread throughout the boroughs that if you were about anything—New Jack Swing, high fashion, or otherwise—then you
were a Tuesday or Thursday fixture. What was not discussed as
much was the delineation of being "in." Entrance was gained only
through one source, Kane, the Pimp Daddy–clad doorman. His
eye for spotting supermodels and rock stars rivaled his awareness of less recognizable publishing and financial scions whose
power was represented only by their title as seen in *WSJ, Vanity
Fair, The New York Times, Harper's Bazaar,* and *Forbes.* When
a patron made it to him, they were directed to one of two locations: the curtain on the right (for the majority) or the discreet
staircase located behind the hostess (for the aforementioned
models and scions). The rule of thumb was pretty simple: If you
had to stand in the line that wrapped around Sullivan Street,
then you went to the right. *Although away for only a brief time, if
it were not for Richard and Blake remaining fixtures on the scene,
I might have found myself in that line.* "Out of sight, out of mind"
*is the decree of New York club culture.* If you walked directly to
the front, never taking notice of the revelers in wait, shivering in
their skivvies only to have Kane lift the ropes, kiss your cheeks,
and stamp your hand, then it was down the stairs you went.
Once during a rush to the loo I ventured upstairs wondering
how crowded the line to the bathroom could be, considering everyone of note was smashed downstairs. Grossly mistaken! The
vibe was decisively different, more pedestrian, with pop music,
and packed, so I completed my business and headed back to the
subterranean level.

Those lucky enough to go downstairs found a dark, narrow
maze of little alcoves that prohibited anyone from reminiscing
about Studio 54. DJ Mark Ronson's lithe body behind the turntables—*or maybe his volume of crates loaded with vinyls*—was the
first thing one saw at the base of the stairs. The dance floor and
aisles always melded into one. For, in a city like NYC, "those in the

know" could pack a hundred rooms of this size many times over, yet somehow they all made do with these cramped quarters. On this night, Blake had arrived before us and secured a prime table across from Mark, ensuring the best location to watch people arriving and be watched.

"Hi, kittens," she said, unlacing her supple limbs from the current big spender captivating her attention. *And paying handsomely for it, I might add. Meow.*

"Honey, I love it," exclaimed Richard at the sight of Blake in an emerald strapless silk jersey jumper accented with a chunky gold belt, earrings, and cuffs.

"I was worried you guys weren't coming out," said Blake.

"We almost didn't. Richard threw down in the kitchen. I couldn't stop eating," I said.

"No worries, though. I forcibly removed the fork from her hand to ensure she would fit into that dress," said Richard.

"Thank goodness, or all of this would not have been possible," I said, gesturing to my long-sleeved, black lace minidress with nude lining and black suede pumps. Not wanting to contend with deflating hair, I pinned it in a purposefully messy chignon, finishing the look off with a pair of diamond studs.

"Well, you look great," said Blake's date. I couldn't be sure if his compliment was genuine or as a point of entry, because more than five minutes or so had passed and Blake still hadn't made introductions. With Blake, whether it was purposeful game play or absentmindedness was anyone's guess.

"And you are?" asked Richard, extending his hand.

"Peter Emmanuel, you?" *Nice. He has the right amount of salt and pepper that is clearly perfected by some overpriced stylist who only makes office visits because a man like this would never go to a salon unless it meant waiting out front in his chauffeur-driven car for his lady fair.*

"Richard, and this one is Jules."

"Good to meet you, Blake has told me a lot about you both," said Peter.

"I bet she has," Richard said, cutting a side-eye in Blake's direction.

Leaning over to Peter, I said, "Don't mind them. It's their way, like vultures to each other they are. Consider it constant entertainment or an extreme example of bitches marking their territory."

Quickly Peter established himself as the host of the evening, making certain that the bottles kept coming. He and Richard found themselves in talk of financial policy and fiscal responsibility that bored Blake and me no end. Thankfully, the initial bars of Michael Jackson's "Baby Be Mine" came to the rescue, transporting us out of our seats and to the dance floor.

"Peter seems nice," I say.

"Huh?" said Blake, mid-two-step and finger pop.

Moving closer to her ear and yelling, I said, "Peeeeter seems nice."

Nodding, she said, "Oh yeah, he is nice enough, but you know"—she glanced in the direction of the table—"not perfect."

"Lord, Blakes, give him a chance," I implored.

"We'll see," she said, wrinkling her face before being overcome by the melody. "I love this song. *Wooo, baby-be-mine. Woooo.*"

Mark's masterful selection of songs made it impossible to leave the dance floor for the next thirty minutes or so. Had it not been for the beads of sweat forming on Blake's décolletage, I would have remained, but public perspiration is a party foul of unforgivable magnitude for her. I'll never forget the first time she told me, "Jules, the only time men want to envision a woman sweating is when she is on her back, *comprende?*"

"Time to do a twirl around the room," she said, grabbing my hand. The purpose being to see who in the room was potentially more interesting than her date. *Squeezing through tight groupings of partiers is like the game Operation. How close can you get to the edge*

*of grazing a boob or an ass before the buzzer goes off and someone
calls party foul?* We stopped a few times to greet friends. On the
final loop back to our table, Blake spotted a table of substantially
more potential and gave the signal to say "target identified"—two
firm hand squeezes translates to "stand in view of the target and
mentally will him to approach." For Blake this normally happened
within minutes of assuming the position. In this case, I could not
be sure if the target was one specific person or the entire table,
however big it was. With bodies everywhere, I only got a glimpse
of a right shoulder and French cuffs.

"Is he looking?" asked Blake.

"I can't tell. You're closer than me."

"Damn it. Okay, here goes," she said, spinning around.

"Ouch, watch the ponytail, sister. I am standing here," I said,
after receiving a mouthful of hair.

Through clenched teeth, Blake mouthed, "Sorry, J. He's watching, game on. Bingo. He's on the move."

In the moment that Mr. Potentially More or the representative
approached and whispered the magic words that would bring us
to his table, my eyes caught sight of Angie—*strike two*—standing less than six feet away. I had not seen her since the scene at
Tony's apartment, when I discovered them together, and while I
had made peace with his betrayal, I had not even begun to deal
with hers. For what it's worth, Angie was a friend. Not a bestie
but a friend . . . *A friend who was fucking my man while smiling in
my face, mind you, but a friend nonetheless—or so I thought.* Maybe
not in the Richard, Blake, and Joy kind of way but a friend who
was in the circle and expected to abide by the Code. Somehow she
lost all meaning the moment Tony wrested the bottle from my
hand, and yet in this very instant, the weight of her is too much to
bear. She is all that I can see, all that I can feel. Unable to breathe,
I need to get the hell out before she sees me and forces a situation
beyond my control. Freeing my fingers from Blake's, I don't wait to

explain. She would discover my absence soon enough, shake it off, and focus on her prey.

Forcibly pushing past people with abandon, I needed to make it to the surface. The dress prevented me from scaling the stairs two at a time. Richard called my name. I could not stop. Reaching the top, I was besieged by a large group awaiting entrance to the curtained room, providing enough time for him to reach me.

"Honey, is everything okay? I was calling your name," he said. When I turned to face him, my hands were shaking. Clearly I was far from all right. "Oh, dear. What is wrong? Did something happen?" For a minute or so I only nodded.

"She's here," I said, mistakenly expecting immediate recognition.

Searching the room blindly, Richard asked, "Who? Who's here?"

"Angie. She's here. I saw her on the other side."

"Did she see you?"

I shook my head. "No, I don't think so."

"Oh, dear."

"You said that already. Say something else."

"Do you want to leave?" asked Richard.

"I don't know. I don't think so, but I don't know what I want to do to her. Do I cuss her out? Do I leave? Do I finish what I started two years ago and beat her ass?"

"Definitely not the first or the last. You know how much I detest social scenes. Besides, penitentiaries give me hives. The uniforms are awful and the last thing this ole girl needs is to claw some tacky bitch." After a beat, Richard offered, "But I will if that's what you want. You know what, I may even enjoy it. It has been a long time since I checked somebody." Fully taking him in, standing before me in a dark bow tie, checked shirt, and seersucker trousers, brought a smile to my face that was a precursor to sidesplitting laughter. "What's so funny? I could scrap back in—"

Still laughing, I helped him finish the sentence: "—the day. Ohhhhh baby, I bet you did, but not today. Not over that," I said. "I'm okay. I promise. Just a little caught off guard and shaken is all. I'm okay."

"Are you sure?"

"I promise. I'm great. How could I not be? I am here looking pretty good. You've got my back and that is my song!"

Extending his arm, Richard escorted me back down the stairs. I may have exited like Carrie but I reentered like the Homecoming Queen. "Honey, where is Blake?" he asked, steps away from the table where Peter now sat in the company of a baby-model creature. "Her man is great but may not be hers for long."

"She's shopping but not to worry. It is Blake, after all."

At the table I guzzled a shot of Patrón with urgency. As the lime splashed each taste bud, I lived in the awareness that Angie was never the problem. She was as much a by-product as I was a victim. *Now thankfully a by-product whose Latina predilection for rice and beans and pastelitos de guava had transformed her once cute hourglass figure into something more science fiction, almost lava lamp–esque. But I digress.* The reason I forgot her immediately is because, whether or not she had slept with Tony, he and I still would have ended because we were never meant to be. She was just an excuse to prolong the hurt. *I am sooooo damn done with hurting and done with running.*

"And what do we have here?" Blake said on returning to the table to find Peter fully engaged in a rather intimate conversation with the baby-model creature. Definitely not a man to be played, he threw Blake a look to say, "I don't wait, ever." To which she pronounced "Closure" and sat on his lap, creating an awkward moment for all except her and Peter.

Toward night's end Blake confessed that she was not worried about Peter in the least because true to form she had found Mr. Potentially More at that table and he was even the right age to go half on a few babies. After which she would have a surgeon repair whatever childbirth stretched or lowered. Saying our good-byes out front, Richard was the first to stumble off, vowing to catch the late crowd at Raoul's before calling it a night. Peter's car was in front.

"Jules, would you like us to drop you home?" he asked.

"Thank you, but no. I'm going uptown and you're just down the street. Don't worry, I'll take a taxi."

"In that case, allow me," said Peter, stepping into the street and stopping the only available taxi in the cluster of cars cruising Bleecker Street. "Here we go."

"Perfect. I do hope that I will see you again, Peter," I said, giving both him and Blake the same amount of intensity, as they were truly birds of a feather.

"Of course," Blake said, hugging me tightly but not releasing until she whispered in my ear, "Maybe—we'll see."

. . .

Exiting the taxi put me face-to-face with the third strike, Marcus. It was too late for him to be leaving, so I assumed that, like me, he was just getting in as well from who knows where. He was standing at the doors in conversation with Ivan, who was now back on night duty. Seeing them, I debated hailing another cab and heading to Raoul's, where Richard was, but I feared it would draw too much attention, as Ivan was preconditioned for yellow. Then I thought it might be better to walk around the block, giving Marcus ample time to wrap up his conversation and go inside. That is, until the wind swept down Fifth Avenue through my barely there dress, making my final inebriated option seem most plausible: rush past them, in the hope that they would be so engrossed in conversation I could make it into the building onto a waiting elevator and into the safety of my apartment without having to engage Marcus. *Hmmm, it's possible. Head down, shoes off, direct my energy elsewhere—anyplace other than on them—and walk softly yet briskly. Nice, a few more steps and you're inside. Yes, quiet mind, focus. Yes—damn doorman!* "Evening, Ms. Sinclair," said Ivan. *I'm going to remember this come Christmas when you are looking for a gift.*

*Shit, I am so busted. Makes no never mind, just mumble something, nod, and keep walking. Maybe I can make it to the elevator before—*

"Ivan, I'll catch you later. Jules, hold on," said Marcus. Quickening his pace to fall in step with me, he said, "Jules, did you hear me?"

"I heard you. I just wish you would stop speaking and saying my name is all."

"Whoa, not sure what I did to deserve that, but okay . . . I guess. Did you get my note? I know it's a couple of weeks late but—"

Stopping abruptly to face him, I said, "Seriously, you have no clue? I pegged you for a lot, Marcus Crawford: narcissistic, indulgent, arrogant clearly, but clueless? Not so much."

Trying to make sense of my attack and clear his head from earlier festivities, he said, "Okay, I'll bite. Whatever it is that you think I did, I apologize." The seductive whiskey notes of spice and vanilla still lingered on his breath. Ivan was now standing inside the lobby by the door fully within earshot of our conversation, although he was pretending not to listen.

"You know exactly what you did. I expected more from you. Much more," I said emphatically. "Was that part of your plan all along?" I continued not leaving the space for him to respond or defend himself. "To come into my home, gain my confidence, pretend to be my friend, and then use whatever little crumbs of information you had to hurt me. Oh wait! What am I talking about? Hurt me? You don't even know me and could care two cents about me. Hell, I'm just a pawn for you to get one over on Michael. I'm shocked you didn't tell him about our walk or running into each other at Pastis while you were at it." I could see the intoxicated clouds in his mind parting in order to allow the light of recognition for misgivings to become solvent. "It doesn't matter that I could have lost my job over nothing, an innocent freaking dinner. It doesn't even matter to you that my boss now questions my loyalty."

Reaching out to quiet me down, he said, "Jules, shhh, shhh, my bad. It's not what I meant to happen. Honestly, you have to believe me."

"Did you just shush me? Don't touch me. I don't believe anything you say," I shouted, now drawing the overt attention of Ivan, as I pounded the elevator call button again. "Who do you think you are anyway—shushing me like that? You can't just go around—"

"I did shush you, I was wrong. I'm sorry truly. Forgive me? I didn't think it would impact you like that," said Marcus, lowering his head as the full weight of my situation washed over him. "Mike is just so damn smug sometimes and I thought—"

"Next time keep me out of your thoughts, okay?" Stepping into the elevator with the expectation of watching the doors close in his pompous face, I turned to find Marcus within inches of me. For a moment I was overcome by the sheer magnitude of his presence towering above me, and the all-consuming fragrance it created, rendering my senses temporarily inoperable. I think this is what they call chemistry. *If you kissed me right now, I would let you. No! N-o!! This guy is not . . .*

"That's hard to do, Jules. I've thought about you since the day we met—been thinking about you even more so of late."

"Like I said, I believe nothing you say," I said, moving to the opposite side of the elevator car.

"Well, it seems I will have to work harder on that."

"Don't trouble yourself on my behalf. Trust me, I'm not that important to the games that you men play."

The elevator doors opening on the seventh floor signaled the much-needed end to our conversation. "But you are. You'll see," said Marcus, placing his body between the doors, freezing time until he was certain his overture was clear.

Later, as I was lying in bed drunk and alone, clad only in a bra and panties, my heart was beating far faster than the swirl of questions running through my mind. It's just the culmination of the three strikes, I told myself. Problem is, when it comes to the last, to Marcus, my head and my emotions are sending mixed signals. The incessant blinking on the answering machine proved a much-needed distraction, sort of.

"Julesea, it's Cora. Call your father. He would like to come and visit you on his vacation this year." *Worst timing ever that woman has.*

The clock on the nightstand said 2:51 a.m., far too late to phone her back. Just as well, I was so freaking tired. Reaching over to turn out the lights, I felt my phone vibrate under me—*clearly a cosmic joke.* The caller ID said *Blake.*

"Shouldn't you be having sex or something of the like so I can live vicariously through you?" I asked.

"Not tonight. Peter could have got some if he played his cards right but the baby-model creature changed all that."

"Oh yes, I forgot how territorial you can be. Poor guy has no clue what he is in for."

"Poor him? Poor me! I met the most amazing guy tonight and couldn't even thoroughly enjoy it because of Peter. I mean really, what gives with that?"

"You can't be serious, Blake."

"Oh, am I ever," she cooed. "He's not like the guys I normally go out with."

Sarcastically, I said, "In what way? He's not in the midst of divorcing his second wife and replacing his current paramour with you?"

"Exactly."

"Seriously, Blakesy, you are a piece of work."

"And you are spending far too much time with Richard. Being snide is becoming far too easy for you, Julesy. So the thing is, this guy didn't immediately fall over me, although I could tell he was interested. He made me work for it. He didn't even ask for my phone number. I had to give it to the representative who came over initially and do the ole bait-and-switch . . . I'm intrigued."

"Wow, I would have paid money to see that," I said. "Maybe you've met your match."

"Speaking of which, where in the hell did you dip off to? I turned for backup and you were gone. I really needed you to engage the friend, who was far too eager in the details of me but clearly standing on a slimmer wallet. What gives?"

"Oh, my. That is definitely not a conversation for the phone, especially at this hour. I have an early day tomorrow, so I need to get some shut-eye. Allow me to get through this kick-off, and we'll discuss," I said.

# 29

## PLAUSIBLE DENIABILITY

**W**HAT KIND OF name is Punxsutawney Phil, anyway? He saw his shadow all right, and took me right back into the burrow with him. It's as if I went to bed last night, in the dead of winter, only to awake and find myself in the midst of New York's emotional prespring alert but oblivious to the details in between—with the exception of work and home. Sad as it might be, the most consistent man in my life of late has been Michael (*and Daddy, of course, but he's perfect for the most part*), for whom I have much respect but had caused great injury to. I wanted nothing more than to repair things with him, even if it meant an entire chunk of my life had gone missing. So, as a show of solidarity, I lived and breathed Carly's.

The holiday music series had been a smashing hit. We made a profit and got amazing press out of it despite the diva demands of some of the performers—or should I say their handlers, who were oftentimes far worse than the artists themselves. As a result, Michael had a "life is too short" epiphany, as I like to call them. Sure, being sold out every night with a wait list was fantastic, but the headaches and erratic energy that resulted underscored the elusive magic that was Carly's. In return, Michael charged me with the task of securing a single performer to do residency. To paraphrase him: "It's not enough that she can sing or has sold some records. I need a motherfucker who can keep this place packed, bring in some special guests, and impress me enough to sit and watch every night for the next four months like it was the first time." It was the latter that I feared would prove my undoing. Was he insane? We were in the midst of a hip-hop revolution. He was describing the Spice Girls—not a jazz or soul singer. The way I saw it, the only game in town that had accomplished this was the Carlyle, and they already had Bobby and Eartha with a decisively older crowd and much smaller room. Carly's was hipper and less antiquated. Its crowd wasn't still living in the heyday of Jackie O, Warhol, and Maria Callas. The Carly's patron was living for Kate Moss, Keith Haring, and Russell Simmons, so who was out there with enough swagger and gravitas?

The answer actually found me one night, thanks to Cora. After much debate, she and Dad had come up from Virginia to spend the week with me. Daddy, who seldom takes a holiday, had wanted—as I learned—to return to Jamaica to spend some time with friends. Cora, as I had thought, was not having it. New York held the lure of endless shopping, Broadway shows, and an up close and personal look at my life, emphasis being on pointing out all that is lacking. In typical Cora fashion, she had their entire stay planned to the smallest detail. The only saving grace for me—*poor Daddy*—was that my days were consumed with work, so lunch at Tavern on the Green, with all those camera-happy tourists, and walks through Times Square, bobbing and weaving through more camera-happy tourists and TRL audience members, was out for me. My nights, however, were a different story indeed.

"How much work can a woman do?" asked Cora, when I thought to use it as an excuse for why I would not be available a couple of evenings. "This is exactly why you girls today are single. You work far too hard for nothing and have no time to focus on finding a husband." One of her favorite tirades when it benefited her. Daddy sat across from me with the same compassionate look that he has given me since I became old enough to be Cora's reflection. More for him than for myself, I felt sad. Normally he was the one with work to escape to, but this week—his only week of rest—it was either him or me in the crosshairs of the Santa Ana wind known as Cora Madeline Augustus-Sinclair, aka Mommy. When viewed from that vantage point, it seemed only fitting that with him taking day duty, *being pulled around the city like a poodle to look at a whole manner of things he could care less about and nothing he was actually interested in*, I would make myself available as much as possible.

On this particular evening Cora had music on her mind and made plans for us to see Nancy Wilson at the Blue Note. Everything about Nancy, from her voice to her command over men, pleased Cora, and had for more than thirty-five years. To hear her tell it, Nancy was the first great love of her life "in a respectable, decent way," and then came Daddy. For it was by Nancy's example that she was able to lure him in the first place. Being a child in Jamaica, where the caste system still prevailed, it was rare to find images of beauty in a package that looked like hers. True, Cora may have been half Dutch, but that was relegated to her bluish gray eyes and "good hair," which made a striking contrast to her molasses-colored skin.

I grew up hearing stories about the first time she saw Nancy on television with Sammy Davis Jr. It was magical. Any woman who could hold her own with the Sammy and not be billed as a bimbo was someone to admire. Tonight, however, was Cora's opportunity to live her dream and be in the same room, breathing the same air, with her hero. Earlier in the day, following one of my uncontrollable nuisance spats with Cora, Daddy made it known that tonight was hers, so we (I) was to play nice, at least for the evening. *My, how I love the way he loves this woman and makes the way for her easier, even when she thinks she is driving.*

"Julesea, stop fidgeting, you'll mess up your hair," said Cora.

"Would that be so bad?" I asked, having been reduced to child-like tendencies days earlier—a record, really.

"Not if you would prefer to look like one of those hooligans off the street, no," she insisted.

Catching a glimpse of myself in the mirror near the entrance of the Blue Note, I found that particular leap impossible. Heeding Daddy's plea for peace, I had allowed Cora to dress me for the evening. And while she resisted the urge to turn me into her clone, she could not resist cleaning me up properly in a manner she thought befitted the occasion. Feeling much more like we were attending Easter Sunday service than a jazz club, I chose to engage in an all too apparent battle with my clothes, as children often do when being forced to be presentable. *When did Escada become appropriate for a twentysomething—albeit a late twentysomething—to wear? Maybe I missed that memo.*

"The hatpins in this thing are sticking me," I said.

"Well, go to the ladies' room and adjust it, but don't ruin your chignon. Took me forever to get it right. We must get you a deep condition before I leave . . . The girl's hair is unruly, Charles. Always has been. She gets it from your side."

Exiting the bathroom, giving one last tug to my skirt, I ran into Marcus—or should I say, crashed into him.

"Research or going over to the other side?" he asked.

Our last encounter aside, out of mind, I had to admit I was happy to see him—a familiar face to endure the torture. "You wish. Neither, I'm here to see Nancy, just because."

"Really?! I didn't know you were a fan. I don't recall seeing her music in your little collection," he said.

"Still hating on my musical stylings, I see. You know you were impressed," I said. I pointed in the direction of the table where my parents sat. "I confess. I'm a total novice. My mother is the biggest Nancy fan on the planet."

"Cora, right?"

"Yes," I said, flattered that he remembered her name from that one dinner so long ago. I can barely remember the name of a person I met five minutes ago.

"Nancy is something. I try never to miss her when she's in town." I found myself smiling easily with Marcus, and for a brief moment it was as if there were no one else around. All that existed was now, a dimly lit room filled with the smell of cigarette smoke, chicken, and ghosts of music past. *Not exactly the most storied of images but accurate nonetheless, and it was nice just like that—no bells, no whistles.*

"Really?" I admit, I hadn't pegged him for the type.

"Oh, yeah. I think she was my first great love. With my friends I was drooling over Sheena Easton or Janet Jackson. Secretly, I was lovin' hard on some Nancy Wilson."

"*Good Times* Janet, *Diff'rent Strokes* Janet, or *Fame* Janet?"

"*Diff'rent Strokes*, of course. Charlene was *the most*," replied Marcus incredulously.

"Well, I hate to tell you this, but my mother beat you to the punch, albeit from afar."

"You don't say," he said, looking over my shoulder in the direction of our table.

"Yep, she's been crushing on Nancy from back in the day in Negril."

"Well, I have never minded sharing, especially with a beautiful woman."

"I'll keep that in mind," I said, inadvertently flirting. Had I time to think beforehand or prepare myself for seeing him, surely my responses would have been more measured.

"I was hoping you would." The musicians' appearance onstage signaled the imminent start of the show and an abrupt end to our conversation.

. . .

"And who was that *nice*-looking man you were talking to, Jule-sea?" asked Cora when I returned to the table. "Him look like Paul New-man."

"Oh, Marcus. That's just my boss . . . sort of. I mean, he is an investor in Carly's is all, so he's like my boss but not really, whatever." *Clearly I'm rambling—why? I can hear myself and it sounds peculiar. Just stop talking, Jules. Stop talking.*

"Don't look like any boss I have ever seen," said Cora, taking one last inventory of Marcus before turning her attention back to the stage.

"Well, that might be because you have never actually had one, Mommy dearest. Bosses, you know, are reserved for people with jobs," I said, unable to resist the open door. Even Daddy had to break character and laugh at that.

"Oh, hush up, Charles. You know I work. I have worked for the past thirty-one years keeping you together," she said, placing her hand on my forearm. Then, loud enough for Daddy to hear: "The man would be lost if it weren't for me."

"Of course I would, dear. Of course. Who knows where I would be now, probably living in Delaware marriedt to Rosalyn wit a couple of . . ." Daddy trailed off.

"A couple of delinquent children who are a menace to society. That is exactly where you would be if you were with that . . ." replied Cora, sending them both into full-on hysterical laughter.

Their dynamic never ceased to amaze me. I used to think that her jealous cries were just for show but have come to know much better; they are part of the romantic dramedy that makes them the ultimate couple. From any distance it is clear to see that Daddy loves her from here to infinity. Her behavior, on the other hand, requires closer observation and analysis. But when you get it, *Eureka!* You realize that her love for him is her very essence—without it there would be no reason to exist. Charles was *the one* before even she knew there was a choice.

. . .

The lights dimmed to reveal a single spotlight, in which Nancy stood. Having been familiar with her music did not prepare me for seeing Nancy. Mind you, I am not a fan of velvet and am often hard-pressed to acknowledge it ever works, in any construction, but this night, on her, it was magic: a bordeaux mermaid-cut gown with an open back, and it draped her body like silk. Her hair, short and layered with enhanced silver streaks throughout the black mane, created the perfect frame—or halo as it were—around her face, of which I am a major fan. This woman owned the room and every person in it with her sultry style and melodic voice. The way she glided around the stage as if she were entertaining at home and not to a room filled with fans mesmerized me.

The whole scene felt voyeuristic, especially regarding Cora and Charles, who, like Nancy, I felt like I was seeing for the first time. In the dim club light, Cora's eyes sparkled like diamonds transfixed on Nancy, but her heart was firmly in Charles's hand. With tender discretion, he was stroking her leg under the table, and she leaned in to kiss the side of his face, eliciting a secret smile whose meaning was only for them. If wearing this sorbet-colored knit suit and matching pillbox hat was the price to be paid for a front-row seat to true love, then so be it. As the evening progressed, Nancy transitioned from song to song with the fluidity of the greatest storyteller, even making loss beautiful, almost enviable.

"As many of you know, last year was extremely difficult. I found myself to be a child of the world without the two pillars of my world. Tonight is one of my first performances in a long time, so to tell you that I am overwhelmed with gratitude is, well . . ." An explosion of applause and whistles drowned out whatever was to come next. "Indeed, tonight is about firsts, first loves and first times, so I would like to dedicate the next song to Cora for the first time, '(You Don't Know) How Glad I Am' that you are here tonight. Thank you."

The force of Cora's nails digging into my flesh for stability caused enough pain to tell me that I was not having an out-of-body experience. Nancy Wilson had just said my mother's name and dedicated a song to her. Cora screamed, drawing the attention of the room, and then she went into some type of catatonic state that only melted as tears rolled down her cheeks, streaking the immaculate face that took an hour to put on. At that moment the entire world may not have existed for her, but I was quite curious to know the identity of Santa. Instinctively, I looked to my father, trying to read his mind and determine how he made this all possible. His eyes still bulging in bewilderment said to look elsewhere—but where and how? Turning, instinctively, to my right, I found the answer. My eyes locked on Marcus's. There was no excessive grandeur in his presence, just immense sincerity. Overcome with emotion, I tried to mouth "thank you" but feared it was too little consolation to express what I truly felt, so I smiled, cupped my heart, and tried to keep the mass in my throat from spilling out. *Thank you for the candle. Thank you for making my mom's reality surpass the dream. Thank you a million zillion times over. I'm sorry for being such a pain—honest.*

At night's end, once the lights came up, I searched for Marcus but couldn't find him, a fact that did not sit well with Cora. She wanted to see him, thank him properly. Unable to deliver him in person, I caved under the pressure from both of them and shared that he lived directly below me, should she want to thank him in person. *Clearly, I was not lucid. Giving Cora this type of information, no matter how innocent, was like giving Kim Jung-Il a partial (and by "partial" I mean a completed) blueprint, sans physicist, with all the details of our nuclear program.*

*    *    *

Friday was their last night in town before returning to Virginia, so Daddy could finally get some rest before going back to work. Cora found it hard to believe that he felt he had not rested the entire time they were there. "Something must be wrong with that man. All we have done is relax. We have gone to the Met, the Whitney, Central Park, SoHo, Saks, Bendel's, had tea at the Plaza, seen four plays, Alvin Ailey at Lincoln Center—*Revelations* is just the best, Julesea—and taken a boat around the island. How can he possibly be tired? And we didn't even get to see MoMA or go to the top of the Empire State Building."

"Are you kidding? I'm exhausted just listening to that list, much less being forced to do it all in only a few days, considering that many of them I haven't done in the entire time I have lived here," I said.

"Well, you know what I say," she began—*or, as I have come to call it, "the answer portion of Cora Says" during which I often remain quiet, knowing that every time she will respond before I can search for the answer. Selfish player she is.* "You only live once."

"Mom, I don't think you coined that phrase."

"Who cares, dear. It sounds best from my mouth. Get home early tonight. I am cooking all your favorites."

Since I missed being home for the holidays over the past couple of years, this was indeed going to be a treat. Despite the fact that it is only for Dad and me, Cora has always cooked as if for a football team. From the foyer I could hear the familiar competition of the television and the music system. *Some things never change.* Cora always cooking to music, Dad transfixed by a continuous loop of sports. Independent of the space, they can have both systems going simultaneously at rather high levels without irritating each other. *Odd as all hell it is, unless you grew up in it.* Tonight, Stuart Scott and Lionel Ritchie were in a serious battle.

"Mom, Dad, I'm home."

"In here, Julesea." Placing my purse on the hall table, I followed Cora's voice into the kitchen. "What took you so long?"

"I know, sorry. I tried to get out earlier but couldn't. Michael has been on me to find a permanent act for the restaurant, which is proving difficult considering what he is offering. And of course, he is not the . . ." My words trailed off as I realized that Cora had absolutely no interest in the minutiae of my work life. She seldom does, be it work, studies, friends, unless it relates to beauty, a current relationship, or the man who could be her future son-in-law—she just zones out after two minutes or so, and that's being generous. *I could force her attention by confessing that I made an offer to Nancy Wilson earlier, but why tempt fate? A premature confession of that kind would only set me up for ridicule of some sort in the event that I can't deliver.*

"Everything looks so good. What can I do?" I said.

"You can unload the dishwasher and put those in," she said, gesturing to the numerous pots and mixing bowls strewn about the counters, covering every available counter surface. There were trays of meat patties on the island, stews and beans brewing on the stove, tins of foil awaiting ackee and saltfish, fresh coco bread, and more, so much more. All that was missing was a steel-drum band playing "One Love."

"Mommy, who do you think you are cooking for? I won't be able to finish all of this in a month, much less retain any hope of fitting into my clothes after."

"That's the idea. You're too skinny. You know me, I didn't want to say anything."

*Since when?* I said, but only to myself.

"That time in London, with all that bad food, has you wasting away. Now, if you had been blessed with a curvy figure like the women from my side of the family, that would be fine, but you take after your father, lean and long with n' ass at t'all, really, so we have to be careful, don't we?" *That is always a statement more than a question.* "How will you ever be able to catch a man when you giving him nothing to hold on to? Thank goodness I'm here." *Yes, thank goodness you are here, Cora, or else I just might start to feel a little too good about my entire day, a little too comfortable in my own skin. Thanks so much for reminding me of my genetic misfortunes.*

"I guess looking like you counts for nothing, huh?" I said sarcastically, hoping in vain that maybe, just maybe, she would suddenly develop the empathy to understand the power of her words, even after all these years riding on my psyche.

"I t'ank God for it every day," said Cora, raising her hands to the sky and looking up to give holy recognition of a prayer long answered. "Heaven forbid you come into this world with a boy body, looking like your aunt Helen. Like I always say"—*pause, wait for it, hold it*—"a person walks forward not backward, so a beautiful face will get you farther in this world than having a big casaba melon for a booty. Remember that."

"Hence the problem, Cora. I remember too much, so it shocks me every day that I am able to wake up on my own, feeling good and somehow remembering that you do love me—in your way."

"You're welcome." With her free hand, Cora grabbed my chin, admiring her greatest work. "You are such an exceptional young woman, Jules. Mommy loves you every day, all day. Don't be nasty."

.  .  .

The music in the kitchen did little to drown out the heated conversation Daddy was having in the living room. "Mom, who is Dad screaming at? Doesn't he know that Stuart Scott is broadcasting from a studio in Connecticut somewhere and cannot hear him?"

"Oh, ignore him. He and Marcus have been going at it like that for over an hour now." *Yes, I think this is when the room started spinning, but I'm not sure, entirely, because I temporarily lost my hearing.* "What?! Don't stand there looking at me like that. You heard me. Your Paul New-man boss-friend is here. He is in the—"

"Shhhhhhhhh . . ." I said, creeping to the dining room door, attempting to peek outside so my eyes could confirm what my ears were hearing. From my vantage point, I could only see two half-empty beer bottles on the coffee table and the shadows of the TV screen, nothing else. I didn't see my dad or Marcus, although I could hear them. That is, until I turned around and there he stood in my kitchen, getting a spoonful preview of Cora's oxtail stew. To an outside person this whole scenario would seem completely plausible and wholesome, sweet even, but it's not. *UGH . . . damn that Cora. I should go over there and shake the shit out of her, or at least until one eye rolls back. Why, why, WHY?* Dad was the first to acknowledge me.

"Bunny, when did ya get in? Cora, why didn't ya tell me she was here?" he asked, crossing over to kiss my cheek before opening the fridge for another beer. My eyes raced back and forth erratically between him, Cora, and Marcus, silently pleading with one of them to speak up and explain what in the hell happened to normal. Marcus, of course, was the one to break ranks.

"Jules, you didn't tell me your mom was such a wonderful cook. Now I know where you get it from," he said. *Was that a flash of color? I think Cora's tail feathers just spread. Unreal, this woman!*

"Apparently you are not the only one who is not told things," I said, cutting my eyes at Cora. "What are you doing here?"

"What does it look like, chyle, he is havin' dinner," said Dad.

"Okay, but where?"

"Here wit us. Is there a problem?" asked Daddy.

"No, of course not, but um . . ." I tried not to be an embarrassment to Daddy, who must be as mortified as I am at the imposition Cora has put us both in. "I mean, I'm sure Marcus has other, better plans for the evening than to, you know, hang around . . . here . . . with us."

"You okay, bunny? Why you talkin' all funny and nervous-like?" asked Dad. *Not the response I was expecting, but let's ride with it.*

Marcus offered, "True, I did . . . have other plans. That is, not better, just other, but I canceled them when your dad came down and asked me to join you guys."

"W-h-e-n my *dad* came down and asked you to join . . . us," I said, bobbing my head up and down with each word as if it would help the cerebral process. Cora stood off to one side with her arms folded, silently admonishing me for immediately placing the blame on her.

"Dear, what did I tell you about being repetitive?" asked Cora.

"Good ting too. Did ya know he loves Jamaican food, even been to the Blue Mountains where my people's from? Small world it is, small world indeed," said Dad.

"Apparently," I said. My need for rescue thoroughly transparent, Cora ushered Marcus and Daddy from the kitchen, citing the need to put the finishing touches on dinner and leaving me free to scratch my head and wait for the ground below me to get firm.

"Mommy, how could you let him do this? Why would Daddy go to that man's apartment and force him to come to dinner? Did you send him?" I'm sure my eyes pleaded with her in a manner that gave far too much away.

"Which question would you like me to answer?" said Cora, returning to the stove.

"All of them! This makes no sense. It's like I can't escape this guy. I walk in the lobby, he's there. I come out of the bathroom, he's there. I come home, he's here. Whyyyy?"

"Ummm. I see," said Cora, now giving me her full attention, which only made me feel more trapped, and needing desperately to push back, against anything.

"You see nothing, so don't start, woman."

"More than you, Julesea. I see everything. Now listen to me, pull yourself together and freshen up. I'll finish up things here. Go! Been laboring over this hot stove all day anyway."

My bed had been made from the morning, but was now covered with freshly washed and pressed clothes that Cora had collected. I collapse to the floor, staring at the ceiling, dazed and still confused—surely the antithesis of what Cora had in mind when she said "Pull yourself together," but that is what I am doing, and I plan on remaining here until someone tells me what in the hell is going on! The problem is not that I don't enjoy Marcus's company, because I do, in spite of myself. It's just that his presence in my life defies logical categorical placement, complicating things when what I need above all right now is easy, breezy, and uncomplicated. I need logic in the form of neat little bowed boxes with identifiable labels. In the beginning he was a cocky, well-coiffed guy I'd met out on a job interview, then he was a typical modelizer I ran into at lunch who, unbeknownst to me, is a partner in the company I now work for, and my neighbor *and*, while not so silent in his interest (in me and in the company), is in direct opposition to my boss and mentor. Then he goes and does that thing for my mom with Nancy. Most damaging of all, he is the first guy since Tony who makes me pit-of-the-stomach-near-faint nervous, to which the only defense is distance and total, complete avoidance.

A quick shower to clear my head did assuage matters slightly. *Although I did expect much more from the Holy Trinity—maybe they were taking the night off.* Putting on a pale pink cashmere sweater and white Hudson denims improved matters more. As Neon Deon Sanders always says, "When you look good, you feel good, and when you feel good, you do good." But I needed to do more than good if I was to keep my wits about me tonight. Before leaving the room, I saw a message from Blake:

Drinks tonight? Suddenly free—don't ask. xo Blakes

More than you know but can't. Parents' last night in town. xJules

Love THE Cora—total riot!!! xo Blakes

You can have her. Seriously, take her and Daddy too! :-? xJules

I must have details. TTFN. xo Blakes

## 30

## A HEAP SEE
## BUT A FEW KNOW

Tʜᴇ ɢʀᴇᴀᴛᴇsᴛ ᴀʙsᴜʀᴅɪᴛʏ of the evening had to be the moment Marcus and Daddy started singing 'Whatcha See Is What You Get.' I mean, they really thought they were the Dramatics or something. Insane."

"Darling, absurd is three adults, me being the most senior and knowing better, on a party-line call like it is 1986."

"Stop it, Richard. Three-way calls are the best. Don't listen to him, Jules. It sounds like a great evening. Keep going."

"Joy, I think I heard something drop on your line," said Richard.

"Huh, really? I wonder what," replied Joy.

"Your pom-poms, dear," said Richard.

"You are not as funny as you think."

"How would you know? We haven't seen you in forever," said Richard. "Is that what happens when one leaves civilization and moves to Jersey? Now *that* is absurd."

"No. That is what happens when one has a full-time job, a husband, two children, PTA meetings, bake sales, and peewee football to contend with. Something that our Little Miss right here may be knowing soon enough," said Joy.

"Unless he is walking up to my door and ringing the bell, I don't see that happening anytime soon," I said.

"Darling, I hate to break it to you, but it sounds like he already did. As a matter of fact, not only has he rung twice and left a gift, your father invited him in and welcomed him to the table. I mean, unless I am misreading something . . ." said Richard.

"Seriously, don't you have a speech or something to write? You know, utilizing that big brain of yours, less lip . . ." I said.

"Play daft if you want, Julesea, but I find it all too interesting the way you and this young man are intersecting. Stop trying to fight the obvious."

"What is it with you? Have y'all been talking to Cora behind my back? Stop calling me that!" I said, far from ready to have a direct "What does this mean?" conversation about my interaction-attraction to Marcus. "We live in the same building, so that is bound to happen. Mystery solved."

"Joy, take over. Even if I didn't have to put the finishing touches on the finance speech, I am not in the mood to play 'hide and go get the truth from an emotionally stifled Jules Sinclair' tonight," said Richard.

"Would love to but can't right now. Jackson has taken off all his clothes again and is streaking through the house."

"Isn't that normal for a four-year-old?" I asked.

"Who knows? And he is six," said Joy.

"Who?"

"Jackson," replied Joy.

"Oh, definitely not normal!" I said.

*Emotionally stifled seems a bit harsh, I believe. Emotionally reserved is fair; emotionally conservative much better and quite fiscal even. True, I was playing a game of cat and mouse with myself about this man and fooling no one who was aware of the situation. Thing is, my history tells me rather explicitly that falling in like, even in love, is the easy part when I meet someone who is the physical representation of everything I desire. Being acutely aware of how that actual manifestation impacts my life (voluntarily losing myself in the illusion of him as I do) is a far different matter. Right now I need a guaranteed leap of faith that I will not wake up one ominous day and realize I am exposed in this like-love that is unbearable alone. Besides, it was just dinner and dessert, at my home, with my parents, and it was . . . kinda glorious . . . nothing major, so why is it that I just can't go to bed and stop replaying the events of the other night?*

. . .

"You know what your problem is, Julesea?" asked Cora, once I finally sulked out of my room to help put the finishing touches on dinner.

"I love that you think I only have one, problem that is," I said. "Give me ten minutes and surely I can rattle off a solid fifty or so, forty at minimum."

"You don't know how to live in the moment. I don't know where you got that from. Surely not me."

"Of course not. Nothing bad ever comes from your side, Mother."

Thinking it best not to encourage my dissent and remain on message, Cora continued, "Look at you. Your father and I are here, a nice *single* handsome man is in the living room, who is obviously smitten with you. Daddy is happier at this moment than he has probably been the entire trip, but that seems to escape you, because you have decided, for some ungodly reason, to be unhappy. Well, I will not have it, you hear me? I didn't raise a child to be rude and inhospitable."

"This coming from the woman who dragged the poor man around the city like one of those purse dogs as she indulged herself. Of course he is having a good time. He's on estrogen overload, having mucked about with the two of us for the past week. Poor man'll latch on to any testosterone he can get."

"That, my dear, is the trade-off of marriage. It's in the fine print. If one day you are blessed to get out of your own way and actually live in the now, thereby gaining a husband and giving me some grandchildren—trust me, you will do the same. Now, put these plates on the table and fetch Daddy and Marcus . . . ay ay—with a smile, please."

It was much too early in the proceedings to do the quick shot of something I desperately needed in order to medicate myself into pleasantry. So I opted for a more acceptable approach. The way I figure it, whatever the wine doesn't soothe, the rum punch will. Dad led us in grace with one of his comically brief blessings that underscored the labor of love Cora had put into making each dish, forcing her to do a not-so-subtle sucking of the teeth. *You know what they say, you can take the girl out of Jamaica but you can't take the Jamaica out of the girl, no matter how well coiffed her weekly blow-out might make her.*

"Mrs. Sinclair, everything looks so amazing. I don't know where to start," said Marcus.

"Well, start wherever your eyes lead ya and your stomach will follow," said Daddy. "My Cora is one of the finest cooks 'round, and that's no lie."

"Thank you, Charles. You know I do what I can," said Cora, badly feigning a truckload of modesty.

I swear, even in replaying the whole evening from the comfort of my bed is like a scene from *The Twilight Zone* or some parallel universe: Cora pretending to be demure while silently commanding me, with laserlike glances, to speak up; Daddy and Marcus getting along as if they were old chums. *What is it with this guy and his eerie ability to assimilate?*

"So, Marcus, tell me," started Cora. *Oh boy, that is never a good start to anything.* "Why is it you don't have someone special to cook for you at home?"

"Mom!" I shrieked in horror at her brazenness, causing me to cough uncontrollably and choke on my last bite. While recovering, I placed the napkin over my face and prayed for the quickest death possible.

"What, Julesea? I am asking him a simple question. Good-looking, successful young man like him. It makes no sense."

Laughing and far from rattled at the inquest, Marcus said between bites, "I hate to tell you this, but women today, at least in New York, don't cook like this. If they did, I'd be home."

"Sad but true, y'know. Girls today don't put a premium on family and making a good home. All they concerned wit is competin' in a man's world. Makes no sense," said Daddy. "Never has."

"Daddy, how can you say such a thing? I work," I said.

"And I would prefer it if you didn't," he stated. "Don't go lookin' at me like dis is the first tyme ya hearin' me say dis. You know why I work so hardt. So you and ya mother don't have to. Always have."

"And we appreciate it, Charles," said Cora, absentmindedly touching the new diamond-and-gold timepiece on her left wrist, which Daddy had purchased earlier in the week. "Home triumphs over all when the commitment is there."

"I'm not saying I don't appreciate it, Daddy. I am just saying that one does not necessarily denote the other. I work and yet I can cook—and will one day embrace balancing career and family."

"Ya listening to dis, Marcus? Balancing family," said Daddy. Having been out of the house for so long and for the most part having Cora as our intermediary, I forgot how chauvinistic Daddy could be about sex roles. *I guess that is also a latent Marley trait.*

"It's a fine line, sir. The values across the board on relationships have shifted. Men no longer seem to have the intrinsic desire to protect and provide for women as they once did," offered Marcus, to the complete surprise of Daddy, which made for an uncomfortable moment prompting a very pregnant pause before Marcus raced to do damage control. "At least as far as I can see, sir."

"Is that all men or just you, Marcus?" asked Cora, sounding more like a federal prosecutor than a housewife. *Oh shit, I guarantee he is wishing that he didn't cancel those other plans.*

Unapologetically, Marcus said, "My peer group, for certain, and

myself. But you must understand that like anything else it is a matter of perspective."

"How can it be perspective when it is tradition?" Cora asked
impatiently.

"Well, in my defense, I have never experienced it, traditionally
speaking," said Marcus.

"Unless your mother was invisible, then I don't understand,"
said Cora.

"To the greatest degree she was. She left early enough for me
not to remember anything specific about her other than her smile
and perfume. My father and my nan raised me."

"Oh, I am sorry. I did not know," said Cora. "I just assumed
because you seem so well brought up . . ."

"It's quite all right, really. My nan is a great woman. Between her
and my pops, I wanted for nothing. If anything, my mom's absence
motivated me to be the best. As a kid you think—I thought—if I
was the best, then she'd come back. That kind of thing can give you
fuel; did for me. Don't know why I said that."

Moved by Marcus's revelation, I placed my hand atop his. "I'm
sorry too," I said, unaware of the unspoken exchange between my
father and mother at witnessing the innocence of this gesture. *Cora
later commented that she perceived this as my first act of civility that
evening.*

"You know, last week I saw the same thing on *Sally*, but not
*Oprah*," said Cora. Feeling the scrutiny off our blank stares, she
said, "What? I did. Sally could probably help is all I'm saying."

"Cora, what does ya' blasted daytime shows have ta do wit the
boy never having a mother?" asked Daddy, echoing the sentiment
that was in my head. "I swear, woman, sometimes I just don't know
'bout you."

Ill-timed or not, the table erupted in laughter. The tempo for
the evening was now set. Marcus was no longer a visitor to be
danced around or cajoled. As for my need to put him in a box, well,

that too was of no importance. He was, at least for the duration of this dinner, a Sinclair and treated as such. *That'll teach him.*

Maybe it was learning about his mother or my finally acknowledging my own inappropriateness, or maybe it was the second glass of rum punch, but all was good and no thoughts of "what if" or allegiance to Michael underscored the evening. There was more than enough laughter to be had at everyone's expense, which leveled the playing field considerably. Marcus learned quickly that Cora's flair for the dramatic extended far beyond tabloid television and that Daddy's Old World conservative sensibility made him risk-averse.

"I, for one, have never been comfortable playin' round wit my own money, much less having the responsibility for other people's," said Daddy.

"Yes, that can be daunting. However, it can also be an adrenaline rush all its own. To know that in one hour I can gain or lose more money than my ole man will make in his lifetime is lunacy. Temporarily, anyway. After a while, Charles, it becomes par for the course, and the amounts become ordinary, so you have to find the next rush."

"Marcus, that's easy ta say, when you are not the one on the losing end of a life savings, or an IRA," said Daddy.

"True, sir, but I have been, and knowing that feeling of grief, firsthand, is what makes me great at what I do. I know what it feels like to lose everything." Shaking his head in reflection of the amateur trap that the man he is today would never have fallen victim to. "At the beginning, I invested all that I had, which wasn't much, mind you, into a sure thing, that was suppose to split. My intel being the best available so what looks crazy now seemed perfectly solid then," said Marcus, reaching for another serving of stew. "Well, the stocks did split, more than tripling my investment, but I got greedy, stayed in, reinvested, and lost everything when they bottomed out just as quickly. From that moment on I said never again."

"See, so you don't even play the market."

"Hmm, not entirely true. I don't, from a personal position anymore, I do it only for strategic gain," said Marcus. "I set clear long-term goals, remain objective and alert. The outcome is strictly business."

"Is that why you are in the restaurant business?" asked Cora. "People love good food and music, so that is always a money earner, yes."

"Actually, my business is about global acquisitions, and restructuring of companies with a more austere purpose, if you will. Of everything in my portfolio, Carly's holds the greatest risk because the decision at that time was not purely a business one. In general, restaurants are not very stable. They require an immense amount of start-up capital. Their success is subject to a number of factors, which only increase the potential rate of failure, and loss on capital put in."

"So, then, why would ya do such a thing when . . . I don't see it," said Daddy.

"When I just said, strategic gain and never again," Marcus said, shaking his head in recognition of the contradiction this posed to his earlier assertion. "Let's just say, I owed a favor to a friend."

"Carly," I asked, feeling it was a query well within my right to ask, given the course of conversation and my relative silence until this point.

"No. Michael, actually," said Marcus, between mouthfuls of food.

"Really? I didn't know that," I said.

"After all the years that Mike kept me on track, it was the least I could do. Without him, this town would have gotten the best of me early on."

"Oh, I thought you were Carly's friend, not Michael's," I said, noticeably puzzled.

"Actually, Mike was the friend. Carly was and still is the client and, well, you know what they say about business and pleasure."

"Bad idea, never mix them," said Daddy.

"Right you are," responded Marcus. "Learning that right now—"

"Surely there are exceptions to any rule," said Cora, looking from Marcus to me, and then back again, to make herself abundantly clear.

"Clearly, an exception is always possible given the proper motivation," said Marcus, taking the bait.

"Indeed," boasted Daddy.

"Okay, before the night gets any weirder, I am going to excuse myself and take a breather from this table while I can still walk and not roll away," I said, more concerned with the nonverbal covenant seemingly being forged.

"Good idea, bunny," said Daddy, patting his protruding, well-fed belly. "Dat was some fine cooking, Cora. Fine indeed."

"I second and third that, Mrs. Sinclair," said Marcus.

"Well, don't go getting all tired on me just yet. We still have dessert to look forward to," said Cora. "Why don't you two go into the living room, Julesea and I will bring everything in."

Forever the gracious guest, Marcus began to clear some of the dishes from the table. "Well, at least allow me to help."

"Nonsense, now. Put those tings down. Come have a cigar with me. Cora and Jules will handle that," said Daddy. *I can't be entirely certain, because it rarely happens in my presence, but I could have sworn that Cora cut her eyes at Daddy briefly; definite side-eye. Making it all the more odd really, how when the night started, it was Cora whom I thought I would have to push down, muzzle, and lock in a closet, and yet here we are and it's Daddy—or should I say "Benedict Charles"—who is in serious need of a gag order and restraints.*

Safely secured in the kitchen and out of earshot, I hissed to Cora, "What in the Hades has gotten into him?"

"What are you talking about?"

"Daddy, that's who! He's all women's role this and strutting about all broad-chested, not to mention is about to smoke in my house when he knows I have upper-respiratory issues. What gives? And don't tell me you didn't notice because I saw you throw him a side-eye."

"Dear, I hate to break it to you, but that has always been your father. He's a man," said Cora. "Where do you keep the coffee again? I don't know how you find anything in here," she said absentmindedly, while rifling through the cabinets. "Imagine how much worse he would be if left to his own devices. Like I always say—"

"Oh, please, not another one of your—"

"A man needs a woman to tame the beast, otherwise they'd be eating their feet and smelling all over the place," said Cora, putting the finishing touches on dessert. "How else can they grow? Now, what about that Marcus?!"

"What about him?"

"Don't play dumb with me, Julesea," said Cora, standing in front of me with her hands on her hips. "You like that man and he likes you. Why else would he be here putting up with the jibberish from your father and me? Get the berries out of the fridge."

"Trust me, Mom, I am not his type."

"How many times do I have to tell you that men don't have a type? They have ideas that are quickly dispelled when the right woman comes into the picture. You want him? Make it known, and like that," she said, snapping her still immaculate French manicured nails, "you are his type, end of story. And, for the record, you might as well stop walking 'round this here kitchen acting like you aren't listening to me. I know you, Julesea Isabel Sinclair. I know every thought you have before you do, so hear this. You like this man but he scares you. Get over it."

"Mommy, stop. You're making my brain hurt."

"Your father likes him, you know."

And so Benedict Charles does, as evidenced by their multiple sing-alongs. *Another latent trait of Daddy's Marley gene is the desire to sing whenever the mood is right, wrong, or there just happens to be enough Red Stripe and some good music around.* Who's to say what preconceived time notions Marcus may have had about joining a Sinclair family dinner, but if it was anything less than a full night's affair, then he was sadly mistaken. Whether Daddy schooled him on this fact earlier during their sports showdown or at the time of extending the invitation is anyone's guess, but not once did I see Marcus look at his watch or go over to the console table to check his phone. *Yes, I was looking.* I saw him notice when it lit up a few times, but he didn't advance be it with intent or discreetly mid-two-step as he and Daddy were pretending to be members of the Commodores (Lionel and the smiley one with the extra juicy curl) performing "Brick House." Daddy's air bass-guitar stylings paired with Marcus's full-body commitment to the funky 1970s dance moves sent Cora and me into spasms of laughter. Had the hour not been approaching midnight, I have no doubt that a highly spirited game of cards or dominoes would have ensued.

"Whew, dat was good fun, baby, but these old bones are tired," said Daddy, feeling the repercussions of some of those earlier dance moves now in his lower back. "Cora, why don't we turn in and leave these kids to talk?"

Marcus stood up from the sofa we had been sharing to embrace Daddy and kiss Cora good night after watching their finale performance of Elton John and Kiki Dee's "Don't Go Breaking My Heart." "I should be going as well. Mr. and Mrs. Sinclair . . ." He stopped, off Mommy's corrective look.

"What did I tell you about that Mrs. Sinclair nonsense?"

One hand over his heart and the other cradled within hers, he said, "Cora. I could not have wished for a better evening than this. Everything else pales in comparison. Thank you so much."

"Nonsense, son. You helped make the night something special," said Daddy. I did not need Cora's words from earlier to tell me that Daddy had developed a great affection for Marcus. It was evident. "Now, remember what I told you."

"Yes, sir, I will," said Marcus, "and I will call you soon to take you up on that."

"What secrets are you two keeping?" I asked, knowing all the while that they would not say. *Well, I'll be a #?!\*! Daddy has known this guy less than five hours and already has his phone number and they have made plans for future outings. I have lived above him for nearly a year and don't even know what the inside of his apartment looks like, much less have his personal or office phone number, for that matter.*

"Jules, ya gettin' more and more like ya motha every day, and I am not sure that's a good ting," said Daddy.

"It's a great thing, sir. A great thing, indeed," responded Marcus. *Spoken like a man who doesn't know Cora.* His arm was comfortably draped around my shoulders, and I instinctively returned the gesture, wrapping my arms around his waist throughout the conversation.

"Never say that in front of her!" I teased. "I'll walk you to the door." What a night! I wished for it never to end. I didn't want him to say good night to me because I didn't know if tomorrow would go beyond right now.

"Your parents are incredible, Jules," said Marcus. "You are really lucky."

"So I have heard a few million times, from them no less."

"Well, they are . . . and so are you."

"Yeah, I know," I said, instantly feeling the need to clarify. "I know that they are, and yes, I am lucky . . . not that I'm saying I know I am incredible, because that would just be, like, so completely obnoxious to say . . . wouldn't it?" The appearance of a smile on his impossibly perfect mouth put an abrupt end to my babbling. Once again I just wanted to freeze time and capture the moment, but I stopped taking those kinds of photos a while ago. "Was I babbling? I do that from time to time when I'm nervous."

"Do I make you nervous, Ms. Sinclair?"

"Unquestionably so, Mr. Crawford." *Snapshot . . . and the moment is gone.*

"Marcus!" screamed Cora from the foyer, forever shattering the perfection of our moment. "Where are you? Oh, there you are. I thought you had left before I could pack you a little something." Briefly scanning the numerous containers in the bag she held, I silently questioned how much she cooked and if anything was left in the kitchen for me to eat later, although I wouldn't be opposed to having leftovers with him, if he offered. "I packed you some rice and peas, yams, and a few patties. Now remember to eat the ackee by tomorrow, because it doesn't hold as long."

"Aw, Cora, you didn't have to," said Marcus, "but I'm not complaining at all. Thank you. My fridge will be happy to see some home cooking."

"Let's just hope there's some left for me or else I'll be knocking on your door tomorrow," I said.

"In that case, let's hope that everything is in this bag," said Marcus.

"Julesea, there is plenty left for you," said Cora. "You have the stew, some jerk chicken, roti."

"The stew was amazing," said Marcus.

"Then you will have to combine, now, won't you?" said Cora, nodding yes before leaning over and kissing Marcus good night. As she did, I noticed how she held his face in the same way that I used to hold Tony's—even at the end. It never occurred to me before that this gesture, which felt so natural to me, was learned from her. "Julesea, come in and say good night to your father before you go to bed."

"My word, that woman is something. I can see where you get it," said Marcus.

"And you're not afraid," I said jokingly.

"No, actually just confirms what I already knew about you."

I was lost for words again, or maybe the moment just didn't need them. So we both just allowed it to be hypnotic. The buzzing of his phone broke the trance. "You should probably get that," I said.

"I will, later," said Marcus.

"What, why are you looking at me like that? Do I have something on my face?" I asked, feeling self-conscious under his watchful gaze.

"The first time we met you smelled like Oriental spices and vanilla. The second time like gardenia. I always seem to remember you, Jules. What do you think that means?"

*That I could rest beautifully in you. From the moment I knew you lived here, I've hoped to see you whenever I enter, only to find myself crestfallen when I don't, and that scares me even more.*

"You have a good nose, it seems," was all I could allow myself to say aloud.

"Okay, I'll take that for now," said Marcus, narrowing the space between us and softly kissing the corner of my mouth. "Good night, Julesea."

# 31

## RECAP

IT'S NOT UNREASONABLE for me to think that after such an auspicious evening, he would have called or asked me out by now, is it?"

"First of all, Julesy, who goes around saying words like 'auspicious' in everyday conversation? . . . Ah-ah," said Blake, raising a finger to quiet Richard before he objected. "Clearly, you are not using the right bait. Let's rethink this whole 'unrequited love for the neighbor' thing. It has red light written all over it. Trust me. I mean, you date for a minute, the sex is good and easy, then what? You stop talking, and it makes for awkward encounters in the lobby, or you mistakenly getting off on his floor multiple times per week, walking past his door, conveniently dropping packages near his door, so of course you can't help but listen for inside noises, only to run down the hall when you hear the door starting to open."

"Stalker," sang Richard.

"Call it what you will, I'm just saying. Heed the warning," said Blake.

"I hear you, but I don't think this guy would do that," I said.

"Who was talking about him?" said Blake, slapping high fives to Richard across the table at Cub Room. A month and some had passed since our dinner and no word from Marcus. *If I were in any way keeping a record of his patterns, I would mention that he also disappeared after the first dinner with Gary.* My parents' constant

258

inquiries only underlined the fact that I had not seen him and that I wanted to.

Fatigued with my circumstance and realizing that I didn't want the scrutiny after all, I said, "Whatever, let's talk about something else, please. Something happy."

"Great! Then let's talk about me," said Blake.

"*Yes*, that's always a crowd pleaser," said Richard, devoid of any modicum of enthusiasm.

"Ignoring you. Now, that guy from Life, 'Mr. Potentially More,' is definitely worthy of yours truly. Financially he checks all the right boxes, travels quite a bit, which will leave ample time for extracurricular activities, if you know what I mean, and he's ready to have someone to come home to. Me! Although I haven't actually been to his place yet," said Blake, accepting an imaginary crown. "Oh, and the bonus is that he is sexy as hell. Usually, I am envisioning someone *like* him anyway to get through an evening, so this is a step in the right direction. My body is addicted to him, and he knows it."

"News flash, honey, it's your internal gold digger addicted to his wallet, not your body," said Richard.

"Simmer down there, ole girl. Don't be jealous."

"How is that possible? Blake, you have been leased by more than a quarter of the affluent men across the continental United States, and yet no one has opted to buy." *Damn, player, was that a bit harsh or damn?!#?* "I, on the other hand, am still with the great love of my life. Count 'em, honey, thirteen years."

"Correction, you are still with the only gay fool of means on the seaboard who is as boring and insufferable as you are."

"Okay, you two. Play nice. My inner child is cringing again," I said. "Accept it, you are both diggers. It just so happens that one of you reads books and the other enjoys looking at the pretty pictures."

"Meow, kitty. Has she always been like this?" asked Blake.

"No, I think it was all that time in London. There is something fundamentally wrong with a culture that is averse to physical affection," responded Richard. "I like it, though."

"Umph, I'm undecided," huffed Blake. "Now, where was I? Oh yes, the guy. He doesn't need me and that is abundantly clear, which makes us absolutely perfect. I could give him what he wants and vice versa," confessed Blake.

"Maybe you have met your match," I said.

"Now, when do we get to meet your match?" asked Richard, using a bread stick to point between us. "This one has piqued my curiosity. Normally you flaunt them immediately. This one is shrouded in mystery."

"Stop calling him 'this one.' You sound like Lauren Bacall sans the allure."

"I've been called far worse."

"I bet you have," said Blake. "I'm not hiding him. I just haven't had him . . . as available, that's all."

"Oh, dear. Now we must meet *this* one. A man who doesn't fall at the altar surely deserves a medal, or at the very least a parade," chuckled Richard as he emptied the last bit from his gin gimlet.

"Or something," I said.

# 32

# AND I AM . . .

SPRING WAS FINALLY in bloom in New York. *I guess that ground-hog knows what he's doing after all.* From my living room window I could see that the once-frozen lagoon across the street now had inhabitants, mommy and baby ducks swimming about to the delight of a sea of toddlers running amuck along its perimeter, with nannies and au pairs in hot pursuit. The skyline was dominated by a prism of green trees wise enough to make way for the broad array of ivory, pink, and rouge cherry blossoms on display. My friends, like many of the building's residents, had vacated the city for the weekend by any means necessary—car, jitney, or helicopter (if you were truly big money)—in order to open their country homes in the Hamptons or on Fire Island, leaving the city wonderfully desolate. *Hallelujah!*

Since the first day I arrived in New York, she has been to me like the Old Lady in the Shoe, with 18,976,456 too many children. For most of the year, I had the misfortune of being a middle child, eager to please and too often craving her undivided attention but seldom receiving it except for a few glorious spring and summer weekend months, when the elders and younguns frolicked along her coast or in the mountains. During that time, I had New York's undivided attention and could indulge in her simplest treasures without competition or distraction. Downstairs on the sidewalk, I found myself at odds momentarily with possibilities. If I turn right and walk toward Madison, I can enjoy an almond croissant with the best cappuccino on the island. Or I could walk left and cross the street into Central Park for a bagel with a smear and a black.

"Feel like some company?"

Now knowing the cadence of his voice like my own, I said, "I'd love some," and turned to see Marcus standing behind me with enough mail in his hands to convey—but not say—that he hadn't retrieved it in weeks.

"Great, I was hoping you would say that," said Marcus.

"Is that coming too?" I asked, pointing to the jumbled overflow of envelopes, coupons, magazines, and flyers.

Appearing slightly embarrassed at the accumulation, he said, "Oh, one of the casualties of my life, as it were."

"Well, then, let's see what you have here," I said, reaching for the contents and scanning. "*GQ*, yes, *Wired* boring and not a Saturday read. *Business Weekly*, still boring but okay, *Visionaire*, absolutely. *Penthouse*, really? Why?!"

"Hey, it's not what you think. One of the guys got me a subscription as a gag gift. They have great articles." He removed it from the pile. "Listen, we can call him, if you don't believe me."

"And unsubscribing was what, unconstitutional?" I said, removing it from his hands and giving the undesirables to Percy, with instructions to keep until Marcus's return.

"I feel like you're judging me," said Marcus.

"Oh, don't feel, Crawford, *know* that I am judging you."

"Why do I suddenly have this pressure to redeem myself?" he asked. "Let's say I give you the best cup of coffee you've ever had in your life and in return you keep this little incident between us."

"Intriguing. I've never had a platinum-and-diamond-laced cup of coffee before."

"Oh, it's like that?"

"Ooooooh yeah, Mr. Crawford, it's like that."

"And here you had me convinced that you were one of those independent 'I can get my own' women whose feminist sensibilities would be offended by such obvious gestures like expensive gifts."

"Only if you left it on the nightstand next to a 'Dear Jules' note saying 'Thanks for last night,'" I said.

. . .

Exiting the building, we took a right. Under normal circumstances, seeing the tourist-laden line that extended out Via Quadronno's door would have put a cloud in my day, but Marcus's company was good, so I didn't mind the wait. Having to listen to the incessant chatter of outer-borough housewives and their spawn while my system was still caffeine-free, however, was another story entirely.

"My guess is Jersey," said Marcus in reference to the talkative foursome directly in front of us. "Fort Lee. Hayworth, maybe. Even Oradell. The headbands are a dead giveaway."

"Really? I was going for White Plains. The matching mother-and-daughter ensembles scream Westchester County," I said.

"I can see how you would think that, but the color palette and overall styling are wrong; pastels and those scary big flowers like the women in our building wear are Westchester, even Connecti-cut. The fuchsia-colored bedazzled situation paired with denims currently at hand shouts Jersey refinement," he said.

"First, I commend you on your ability to be snarky. Second, and most important, should I be concerned that you know all that?" I said, snapping my fingers in a Z formation like one of the Chelsea boys.

"Never! I'm all man, baby," asserted Marcus.

Moments before reaching the counter I noticed that the couple outside on the solitary bench was preparing to leave and decided to make a dash for it. Giving Marcus instructions to surprise me, I pushed through the crowd to claim the seat before two fast-approaching Maclaren stroller–pushing mothers could plunk down. Having the finish line, as it were, in sight and a foot or so separating us, it seemed only logical to cut left quickly to block their advance and make a strong lunge for the end zone. Seconds before my body flopped down on the bench, I locked eyes with one of the mother friends but turned away before being cast to stone for treachery.

"Here you go, something for the bones and for the belly," said Marcus. "Why are you panting like that? Better question: Why are those two women giving us the death stare?"

"Might have something to do with me stealing this bench from under them."

"You didn't," he pleaded, looking back and forth from them and their babies to me. Any remorse he expected to see was temporarily halted as I enjoyed the first few sips of my cappuccino, followed as always by a little seated two-steps-of-happiness dance.

"What?! It's a tough world out here. Besides, did you or did you not complain earlier about wanting to sit outside and could not because there is only one bench?"

"It was an observation, and don't go dragging me into your sinister deeds," he said. "I'm going to heaven. I'll try to get you an air conditioner."

"I saw that, you know," I said, jabbing him in the side.

"What?"

"You mouthing 'sorry' to the cradle pushers and pointing at me," I said. "If you feel that bad you should buy them lunch."

"I could, but I won't. Did you see those ladies? One of them hasn't missed a meal in a while and I am not the one to . . ." Marcus could not finish his callous remark before being overtaken by laughter.

"And you call me cruel," I said, sharing in this most inappropriate laughter. "Thanks for the cappuccino, by the way. Did I tell you it was my favorite?"

"No, but I promised you the best cup of coffee in town and that's it," he said.

"And yet, you are having tea? How very English of you."

"Yeah, something like that. Not too great for the teeth, but it is the way, I guess. I'll have a coffee after."

"Indoctrination?"

"Completely. Each morning before school, my old man and I would have tea before he went off to work. It was our thing," he said, making invisible quotation marks in the air with his fingers, protecting the memory. "As a result I can't seem to start my day without it."

"Hmmm, that's sweet . . ." I said. "I love it here."

"New York?"

"No, this bench."

"Ah yes, the scene of the crime. Remind me to wipe it down before we leave. I don't want my fingerprints anywhere." *Something tells me that Marcus makes it a point of wiping down everything he touches, especially women, as marks of emotional evidence may prove too messy.*

"Call it what you will," I said, taking his dig in stride. "I can come here, sit, and watch the world go by . . . albeit a considerably more affluent part of the world, but the world nonetheless. When I moved back, I was worried initially that it would take some time to find a little jewel like this, but here it is right on the corner." I felt quite satisfied with my discovery.

"My nan always watched the world at sundown out on our front stoop. Growing up, I used to think that she was just there to look out for me mucking about, making sure I stayed out of serious trouble, but then every once in a while I would catch a glimpse of her face right before the sun bowed to the horizon, and she would be a million miles away. I never knew where. Never asked, really . . . felt a bit intrusive."

"My, my, you are quite the observant one, aren't you?"

"I guess you could say that," said Marcus, tilting his face to the sunshine. I could not decipher if he was doing it in remembrance of moments past or soaking it in right here, right now with me. Either way, I loved the way the rays of light made his eyes dance rapidly beneath closed lids, triggering a pulse in his concrete jawline. *Snapshot.* "Necessity, I guess. Most things in our house went unsaid. But if I looked close enough, the truth was always there, like a member of the family no one spoke to but maneuvered around. At least most of the time."

"Ha, in my family his name is Uncle Barrington," I said. "In all seriousness, I know what you mean. I learned that much later in life than you, and I don't think it was good. Growing up, I don't remember ever having the time or space to be in observance of others, much less myself. I was always surrounded or instructed in one way or the other. When it's all you know, it becomes a way of life until the day the rug is pulled from under you. Then the easy world you thought you knew shows its real self, and becomes a cold and scary place. I guess at some point, observation becomes mandatory in order to live."

"And so it does," said Marcus. "Are you going to eat that entire thing?" He was referring to the Miraggio sandwich he'd purchased for me.

"That was the plan," I said, admiring the slices of mortadella inside the toasted baguette. "Would you like a bite?"

"Well, if you are offering, then sure."

I couldn't help but snicker. "Honestly, you are not as charming as you think yourself to be," I said, raising the sandwich to his lips for a bite.

"Yes, I am," he replied with a wink.

*Yes, you actually are*, I thought, wiping the remnants of toasted crumbs from the baguette off his face.

Long after the first round of coffee and sandwiches were but a memory, we remained at Quadronno. Mostly in comfortable silence, flipping through his overflow of magazines. At some point I suggested we make our way over to the park—*that is, if he didn't have something else to do. He didn't!* "Lead the way" had been his charge, but I never could figure out what direction was up or down where Central Park was concerned. I have never actually found the stables that are said to be there, but I am confident that at some point, if we keep walking, we'll come upon it or the Great Lawn, or end up on Central Park West. Somewhere all scenic. So I suggested that we roll the dice and see where the sidewalk led, hoping that would be more than agreeable.

After weaving our way through a seemingly endless flow of joggers, speed walkers, tourists, and horse-drawn carriages, we arrived at the Great Lawn. The details of how we got there or how long it took are anyone's guess. All I know is that by the time we arrived, my lips were an unnatural shade of radioactive blue, from the patriotic Popsicles purchased along the way from a street vendor.

"This is a good place," said Marcus, indicating a clear patch of unpopulated lawn in the sun among the sea of revelers. For every New Yorker who had escaped the city for the country, there seemed to be one sprawled about today on the lawn. They were either lying out tanning, chasing after their pets, or playing Frisbee, volleyball, or soccer. The air was abuzz with chatter and laughter from all directions. "Do you mind?"

"Mind what?" I said, plopping myself down on the grass faster than he could get the words out.

"I was going to say squatting on the lawn, but I guess not. Do you want my jacket?"

"Thanks, but I'm good. This is the first time all season that I get to feel earth under my toes. Why block the connection, right?"

Standing above me and smiling down, he said, "That makes the second time today that you've said something that surprises me."

"Really, what was the first?"

"Yes, to me barging in on your day."

"I didn't know you were keeping score," I said.

"Not score, just aware of how far I have to go," said Marcus.

"That depends. What's your destination?"

"For you to go out with me."

"I guess we won't know until you ask, now will we?"

"In that case, Jules, would you li—" Marcus began but was interrupted by a tall, sweat-laden player who had detached himself from the soccer game going on a few feet in front of us.

"Crawford, what the hell?" said the swarthy man in a Barcelona jersey. "When did you get back in town? I've been calling you."

"Last night. You know how it is, haven't even unpacked, much less checked messages."

"And that cute little assistant of yours didn't give you any of my messages?" asked swarthy man (who had clearly never even bothered to commit the assistant's name to memory the way he had her measurements), stopping midsentence as he took notice of me.

"Paolo, this is Jules," said Marcus. "Cori probably did but unless it was about the VHO acquisition, then I was not focusing."

"Heard about that. Congratulations, by the way. You got the regulatory approvals to complete that in record time. Normally the fucking Belgians are a pain in the ass. So, you playing or what?"

"I hadn't planned on it. Jules and I were just . . ."

"Come on, man. We need you out there."

"You guys look solid to me," said Marcus.

"You can't be serious. Bro, we're a man down and had to call Johnston."

"Blimey hell, he's awful," said Marcus, throwing his hands up in defeat.

"Bro, I know! They have already scored on him. Little prick can barely grab the balls in his own sack much less protect the ball on the field."

"*Paolo*, watch it," said Marcus, gesturing toward me.

I said, "Marcus, go on. You should play; it sounds like fun. Besides, if Johnston"—teasingly with invisible quotation marks—"loses this no one will play with him come Monday." Selfishly, I wanted some immediate distance between Paolo the Crass and my sunny day. Maybe, if things get hot enough on the field, I just might get to see Marcus strip down. Marcus, however, was not as quick to agree and apprehensively looked to me to make double, triple sure I was fine. "Go, I will be okay. I promise. Just stay where I can see you and don't play rough with the other kids," I said, nudging him in the direction of the game.

"Okay, but let the record show, I would have much rather stayed here with you and made fun of Paolo," whispered Marcus as he bent down to place his sweatshirt and glasses next to me.

On the field he was a natural, athletic and lean with a superior agility for handling the ball. I was most impressed with his speed and ability to stop and strike in an instant, his control of the ball always purposeful and focused on scoring, not showboating. Whether you knew anything about soccer or not, it was easy to see that he was skilled. My knowledge of the game was passive at best from listening to Dad's childhood stories of playing in Jamaica or occasionally being awakened at 4 or 5 a.m. by loud noises from downstairs during a World Cup tournament, when Cora allowed him to have his friends over. However, while in London, I did learn enough about the game to differentiate between Chelsea and Manchester, and my allegiance increased from going to the club with the cutest players at the time, hence my fascination with Real Madrid always.

Who's to say what regulation time is or was, but by the time the match finished, many of the sun worshippers had left.

. . .

"Who won?" I asked, when Marcus ran over after saying the last wave of good-byes to his friends. "Without cheerleaders or a scoreboard, the whole thing is just confusing."

"You do know there are no cheerleaders in *fútbol*, don't you?"

"There should be. Everyone likes cheerleaders. So, did you win?"

"Absolutely. We made a solid rally and came back to take it by one," said Marcus.

"Good, I was concerned about Johnston."

"Ah, you have jokes! Might I remind you, you are supposed to be cheering for me?"

"I thought about that but realized you didn't need it. Johnston, he needed me," I said.

"How do you figure that?"

"Well, it's obvious that you are their leader, not in the Captain James T. Kirk kind of way but like in a Zinedine Zidane way ... Oh my gawd, stop acting like I stabbed you. Even *you* must admit that Zidane is a-m-a-z-ing. Anyway, from the moment you stepped in to play, they all deferred to you and you knew it. Johnston's contribution, however piddly, was all but forgotten."

"Jules, do you even know who Johnston is?" asked Marcus.

"No, which is why he needs me all the more, because no one else seemed to care after the crown prince arrived. Your sudden presence made him all but invisible. Can you imagine how that feels? No, you can't," I said.

"I bet you can't either."

"Not true. I have been invisible for the past two and a half years. The only reason you can see me now is that I'm back from the abyss of obscurity."

"Three," said Marcus, pushing aside a strand of hair that was interfering with my vision. "The third thing today you have said to surprise me. I like the not knowing what comes with you. It throws a proper wrench into the entire script I expect to hear."

"From me?" I asked.

"Yes, you and in general. You're so unrehearsed," said Marcus, placing his index finger softly under my chin to raise my gaze to eye level instead of the nondescript spot on the grass I was focusing on. "Don't be alarmed. It's not a criticism. In fact, quite the opposite. It's refreshing."

Wholeheartedly, I accepted the words coming from Marcus. *Trusting who he presented himself to be was natural. It's the Memorex replay of my mental state that makes for sheer and utter confusion.* Like earlier, there was no need, no pressure to talk through the quiet moments. It felt good just to be.

"What do you say, shall we start to walk back?" asked Marcus.

"I guess, but it is a shame to fold on the first perfect day. I can't believe people rush to leave every weekend, never experiencing the magnificence of New York."

"Couldn't agree with you more," said Marcus. "I remember falling in love with her from a postcard that a friend of the family sent over when I was about nine or so. It was a view of the Chrysler Building. Something about the grandness of it and the eagles, oh man, those eagles, majestic like they're daring the sky . . . I knew that I would live here. I also said that I would own that building. When I finally did get here, I knew that I would never truly leave."

"Except for work and to frolic in the Hamptons," I said, surprised that it had not occurred to me earlier. "Speaking of which, what are you doing here? Shouldn't you be there with the other power brokers doing the whole 'opening of the house for the season and luxuriating' thing?"

"Maybe, but it's not going anywhere. Normally, I go up when I have a reason to."

"I'm sure that Gary is up there right now casing your house."

"All the more reason for me to be here. Oh, and don't think you're not coming up whenever we do that shoot," said Marcus. "I have not forgotten you owe me."

"Completely selective memory . . . but for conversation's sake, any idea of when that will be?"

"Not sure, soon though. It's a rare moment I get to just have time here without meetings or preparing to fly off somewhere, so it will take some prying before I trade in a personal weekend so easily to do a publicity shoot."

"Seems like a waste, though. I mean, you have a home there, an amazing one from what Gary says, on the beach no less. I would think you'd spend volumes of time there unless you have an aversion to water, sun, and just being mellow."

"One would think, but I don't. You know what they say, 'power begets power.' Water is the most powerful force on earth, so we're good," said Marcus.

"Did you just say that about yourself?"

"Ha, that did sound brash, didn't it? I bought the house a couple of years ago because Sasha, my ex-fiancée, thought it would be a good look. The whole process took some time to configure; finding the right house on the right lot, in the perfect enclave, getting the permits to build, acquiring the art et cetera, and once it was done I had a beachfront property in Bridgehampton but no Sasha, so . . . it is what it is, a lovely house, but not yet a home like my place here is."

"Oh, I didn't know . . . about Sash—her." *I didn't know is right, but how could I have? It's not as if over the course of our two or three supervised encounters, Marcus volunteered his dating history, nor had the opportunity presented itself for me to ask!!!!!! And I am not asking now. Talk about a crap way to end the day.*

"Nothing to know really. Things happen. Priorities change."

"Sounds like a novel but for another day," I said.

"A vignette at best," said Marcus, "so don't get your hopes up. Bugger. I forgot my mail. Listen, thanks for letting me crash your day, Jules. I knew we'd be great together."

"Should I wait for you?" I asked, not entirely prepared to say good-bye just yet.

"No, no. The lift is here, you go on."

Along the way, all but unknowing, we had exited the park, passed the doorman, and arrived at the elevator, but I could not recall the path getting there. Had there been many people on the street and haphazard taxis speeding about? Yellow lights and crosswalks to be darted through? I can't recall. All I know is that the day started and there he was making it the best day. Now it is ending and he is still here. I could probably ask for more by way of violins, a fairy-tale kiss, and white doves, but I don't want us to arrive at happily ever after so soon because few are fortunate enough ever to discover what comes next.

Later that night in bed, my adrenaline was still going. A warm-water soak earlier had removed the physical remnants of our day, but my mind refused to let them be washed away so easily. It raced from context and moderation to desperation. *Today I had a carefree beautiful New York day with a nice man, no more no less, who makes me feel nervous-safe-pretty-funny-erratic all at the same time . . . I wonder if I'd make him a good wife . . . our children (Maximus and Isabel—Issi for short) will have his eyes, my smile, and a curly mane of hair that is the combination of ours . . . What if he was just fucking about wasting a day and forgets about me . . . Did I have food in my teeth? . . . OMG, what about when I tripped? He thinks I am a klutz.* The undeniable realization that I really liked Marcus sent me reeling from bed and into the kitchen for a snack. I loaded the audio player with a Funkmaster Flex mix tape and proceeded to dance myself into exhaustion. Side A was nearly done when my jam session began to lose its delusional luster.

I needed to connect with someone and get an objective take on my day with Marcus, so I dialed Richard, only to be greeted by the housekeeper at his Mantoloking home, who advised that "Mr. Boulton was entertaining at the moment but could be pulled away if paramount." *Clearly it is . . . I mean, let's examine the facts: I can't sleep and am dancing around in my skivvies to remixes of Busta Rhymes and Super Cat—clearly a matter of vast importance . . . to me.* Hanging up the line, disappointed but not defeated, I phoned Blake but was greeted by her answering machine.

Okay! Here is the downside to a single girl remaining in the city during the season. While the days are filled with possibility, the nights are quite desolate and solitary. Calling Cora was not an option, and besides, I was much too sober to fool myself into believing that she could have a sensible discussion about the prospect of Marcus and me without calling our minister to reserve a date. No, she was to be kept at bay until there was a serious development. Until such time I will just have to look for my objectivity in a bowl of mint chocolate chip ice cream.

Passing through the main hall, I thought I heard a noise outside my door. I peered through the peephole and saw Marcus milling about. Before he could ring the bell, I opened the door, having completely forgotten that I was underdressed and cradling a container of ice cream. Total "lonely girl" moment—all that was missing was a pack of powdered doughnuts and a Diet Coke!

"Wow, look at you," said Marcus.

"Yeah, there goes the mystery . . . What are you doing here?"

"Would you believe me if I told you that I got off on the wrong floor?" he asked.

"Oh, anything is possible, I guess," I said. "What's that in your hand?"

"The reason I can't claim getting off on the wrong floor," said Marcus, looking at the sealed envelope he was holding with my name written across it. "I figured you were out, so I was going to leave this under your door."

"Okay," I said, looking at the envelope with some skepticism. "Should I open it now?"

"Well, you could, but now that you are here—and wearing . . . Doesn't really matter," said Marcus, placing his hand along the base of my camisole, interlacing the stitched edge with his fingers and proceeding to stroke the delicate space of my belly that peeked out just north of my pantyline.

"Charming. Focus, Crawford."

"I am, but you are making it hard," said Marcus, his hand now working its way up the front of my body, eliciting a current of electrical excitement. "If memory serves, you were in the process of agreeing to go out with me before . . ."

"Before Paolo the Crass—purchaser of *Penthouse* subscriptions—interrupted," I said.

"So you do believe me. Yes, before that."

"Selective memory you have. I don't recall you asking me out."

"Hence the note. Not having your number made it otherwise impossible to do so earlier, and I didn't want to wait until Monday to ring."

"Well, you have me now."

Stepping within inches of me, Marcus said, "That I do, and so many things I'd like to do to you . . . Would you like to go out with me, Jules?"

"Hmm, that sounds—"

"Like what?" said Marcus, his lips hungrily meeting mine, forcing me against the door. After a few moments—my hands having traveled under his shirt down his chest and reaching the washboard of his abs—it was clear that we were walking the dangerously fine line. Mustering my last bit of strength, I pulled away.

"Stop, we can't," I said.

"I know. Not yet."

"Well, you're quite sure of yourself."

"That I am. I want to know you, Jules. When I take you, it will be because we both understand what it means, when you're mine," said Marcus. "Until then, Tuesday, dinner? I'll sort the details provided you give me your numbers—unless you prefer I continue to loiter about, but then you would have to invite."

"Of course, and Marcus, please try not to smell of another woman's perfume on Tuesday."

"Four," he said.

# 33

## ARE YOU NEW?

**N**O MATTER HOW great the weekend was or how blue the skies may be today, Mondays suck. They have to be the most dreadful of all the days on the calendar. It's as if people's mental rest on Sunday is all for the purpose of creating to-do lists that inevitably find me at the top of them. Nancy Wilson had been with us only a short time before an influx of calls from other jazz musicians, their record label execs, and reps, jockeying for them to do a limited engagement at Carly's when her residency was up. Since her debut with us, Michael had tasked me with making certain that a great volume of my media efforts went to positioning the rebirth of her career in direct correlation to her stint at Carly's.

"Put the fact that I like her aside," he said. "Cats want to be in business with you anytime they feel that the association can work to their advantage. The trick is to make the short-term success theirs and the long-term payoff ours. Make her hot, Jules."

"Any suggestions on how I might go about doing that when, one, we are not her representatives; two, they are insanely territorial; and three, she is not Harry Connick Jr.?"

"That's why you're in PR. You are in PR, right? Which means you know how to spin a point of view? Stop fretting, it's a small leap from the spin to the sell. You'll know we're onto something when Harry is seated at a table and my studio has a waiting list of booked sessions as long as the restaurant."

Getting Harry at a table was indeed doable, but I had to lure him, not invite him. As for the state-of-the-art recording studio upstairs with private sleeping quarters and a meditation room, otherwise known as Michael's Lair, I was not privy to those books, so there was no way to be absolutely certain of what would constitute a profitable return. Off the top I knew that it rented out for more than $10,000 per day session, which would make any up-front fees we were paying a performer pale in comparison.

Not endeavoring to try to rewrite the media relations book on how to successfully launch a brand in NYC, I did the next best thing and called Carly for access to her Rolodex. At her insistence our initial blow-up had transitioned from a pink elephant in the room to a camouflaged one. This, of course, pleased Michael no end. So much so that even when, against his micromanaging suggestions, I decided not to invest effort in pandering to the easy get that was established jazz lovers, in favor of some of Carly's society contacts who never ventured below Forty-second Street, he relented. My thought was that if you love Nancy, then you would find her, and they did, religiously. As a result of the buzz I had created, my Mondays had been taken over by a legion of pompous individuals who call me "DAH-ling" in lieu of my name, which they have not yet committed to memory, only to tell me what I need to do for them. Today they make up the entire first page of my phone sheet and, because each is one degree of separation or less related to Carly, I must endure. *Agony.*

"Jacklyn, what are you doing out there, dancing around the phone lines? Why is line two still blinking? Pick it up or take a message. It's driving me crazy," I said, sitting at my desk with full view of her across the doorway. I could see her doing a number of other things, but tending to the ever-ringing phone was not one of them.

"I tried, but he will only speak with you," she said.

"Well, that is not going to happen in the next ten minutes," I said, staring at the hypnotic blinking red light to my right. "Who is it anyway? Can't you just get rid of them? Pretend to be me."

"I tried that. Let me see," she said, re-engaging the line. "It's Marcus Crawford. Do you want him?"

The sound of his name seemed to ring out like a morning bell at a Tibetan temple. A sudden appearance of moisture in my palms made the phone difficult to grasp. Luckily I caught it before it dropped on the desk, then mumbled something incoherent before placing my current call on hold and sprinting into the hall to Jacklyn's desk.

"What I want is for you to lower your voice!" I said in a hushed whisper, looking up and down the hall to make certain that no one was approaching.

Michael had complained many times before about our seeming inability to use the interoffice message computer system for calls instead of yelling to each other. "Jules, why is it I can hear everything that goes on in your office when mine is on the opposite side of the building?" he would ask. My hope is that this particular moment eluded office ears, especially his. I hadn't been true to my word with Michael, nor had I worked out how I was going to tell him that Marcus and I were spending time together.

"Put him through," I said, stealthy in my movements as I crossed the threshold into my office.

"Why are you looking around like that?" asked Jacklyn suspiciously, also on high alert for matters unknown. "You're making me nervous."

"Never mind about me, just you keep doing whatever you're not doing . . . hush . . . I'll explain later," I said, pulling the door shut behind me.

Secure inside my office, I leaned against the closed door for support to quiet the strumming bass erupting from my chest. It seemed to be dictating that I skip to the phone despite my urge to keep him waiting for a few extra minutes. *You know what I always say, "Jump the first time a man calls and he'll expect you to tap-dance for life."* At the most inopportune times, the Cora-isms of my up-bringing often have the ability to supercede my own inner voice. This time, however, my nerves prevailed, and I dived right in.

"Hi!"

"Did I catch you at a bad time?" asked Marcus.

"No, well, kinda. No, not really," I said, stumbling over my words in search of a solid course. "I was just surprised is all . . ."

"Good. Let me preface by saying I know it's short notice and it's not Tuesday, but would you like to have dinner tonight?"

Searching the ceiling for an easy-spirited connection between my thoughts and my mouth before speaking, I finally asked, "Did you really just sit on hold and refuse to speak to my assistant so you could ask me to dinner?"

"Technically, no. Cori, my assistant, sat on hold awaiting you, which by the way took an unusually long time. You should con-sider apologizing to her. I, on the other hand, took a few other calls, brought peace to the Middle East and Southwest Asia, did a fitting with my tailor, and knitted a sweater before you actually came on the line."

"Funny, Crawford. I'm known for using the Middle East peace line myself."

"You know what they say about making a woman laugh, don't you?" asked Marcus.

"Not particularly," I said, twisting the phone cord between my fingers. "However, for the sake of this conversation, let's say I was curious. What do they say?"

"Actually, they is a he, and he says a woman laughing is a woman conquered," said Marcus.

"Aaah, is that your intent, to conquer me?"

"Of course, I'm a man. That's what we do. Figuring out to what degree, now that is something we'll discuss in a few years."

"Years, you think we'll know each other that long?"

"I'd put money on that," said Marcus.

"Who said that 'woman conquered' thing? I hope it wasn't your friend Paolo."

"No, although it would be fitting. It was Napoleon," said Marcus.

"Well, in that case, I must be more careful with my laughter," I said.

"When that happens I will try harder," he said.

"Honestly, you have to stop. All of this panache and savoir-faire stuff, I just don't know . . ."

"So, we'll discuss it over dinner tonight, yes?"

"Yes, okay."

I hung up the phone still laughing, walked to the window, and found myself looking again across the street below at the very spot Keith stood months before. Like the weather that day, the memory of it all is gray and hollow now, in complete opposition to how I was feeling standing here. A warm, familiar burst of excitement I believed to be long gone had reappeared, taking root in the base of my stomach and blooming through the contours of my mouth like a lullaby. Until now, I hadn't realized how much I needed him to call me. The realization scared me. Truth is, I wanted that connection. I just couldn't imagine knowingly getting back on the all-encompassing roller coaster of emotional uncertainty it required, but Marcus made me wishful, and that is something to aspire to, right?

• • •

The hours leading up to our date seemed to be an eternity delivered on the back of a tortoise. When the blessed time did arrive, I met Marcus in the lobby as agreed, wearing a mostly new—*i.e., spontaneous purchase made weeks earlier on the off chance that I would have an event worthy of such a frock*—chocolate Donna Karan matte crepe jumper. It had been my first choice, but I needed to be certain, so a few alternates (five or so) were tried and discarded just to be sure. Finishing off the look with a pair of gold strappy stilettos and a perfume spritz behind the ears, between the breasts, on the wrists, and between the legs, I was ready to go. Judging by the looks of things, however, Marcus and I were going out all right, but to separate locations. The elevator doors opened to reveal him wearing a black leather jacket, dark denims, crisp white athletic shoes, and a Yankees baseball hat.

"Jules, you're a knockout," he said, drinking me in from freshly polished berry toes to nude, glossed lips. "Are you sure you want to waste that outfit on bowling?" he said.

"Excuse me, *bowling?*" I said, the words stumbling out in my distress.

"Yes, bowling," he said, re-enacting a classic stance. "Did I forget to mention that earlier?"

"Yes, I would say so," I replied, embarrassed and uncertain. "Bowling?! I thought we were going for dinner. You did say dinner, didn't you? Should I go and change?"

"Indeed, I did say dinner," said Marcus, staring at me, amused at himself and my obvious discomfort and keenly aware of his omission. "It seems I should have been more specific."

"Understatement. Please stop laughing," I said, trying to retain my composure but feeling quite warm under the collar, in a vastly different, less hospitable way than I had earlier. "I should go back up and change. Give me a few minutes."

"If you think it will help your game, then by all means."

"Seriously, Marcus, this is not the time to challenge me. I am far from amused at the moment."

"Do I detect a temper?" he asked.

"Yes you do . . . I don't like being . . . and clearly you . . ."

"My, you are mad at me! Kind of sexy on you," said Marcus.

Standing before him, I didn't know whether to smack him in that delicious mouth that held such promise for the end of the night or to just storm off. "Come on, don't be mad. I was having some fun is all, just trying to locate your buttons," he said, stepping in closer and caressing the length of my arm and stopping just parallel to my breast, allowing his thumb to linger on the contours.

"There are far better ways to do this, you know. Being a cad is not one of them."

"I'm sorry," he said, reducing the space between us to that of a few molecules of air. "Forgive me?"

"Forgiven," I whispered.

"We don't have to go bowling. I just thought ..."

"No, let's do it," I said, regaining my composure and walking toward the door, where Percy had taken in the entire exchange. "On the day we tell the story of how I kicked your butt all over the Bowlmor Lanes, I want to make certain it is noted that I did it in Donna Karan. Ain't that right, Percy?"

"That's right, Ms. Sinclair. That's right," said Percy, directing his last comments to Marcus: "Never disagree with a woman like that, Mr. Crawford, no sir."

"Famous last words, Percy," said Marcus.

On the drive down we spoke easily about all manner of things: his athletic pursuits throughout school, all of which he entered as a walk-on only to prove himself to be the best; his fascination with collecting rosaries because, like the scent of YSL's Opium, they are one of the few memories he had of his mom; and that if his soul could sing, it would sound like Otis Redding.

Ironically enough, in all that time, never once did he think to ask me if I even knew how to bowl. Truth is, not only did I know how, but I was pretty good and determined to show him just how good. On the Saturdays when Cora was having her weekly manicure or lunch with the girls, Dad and I went bowling. Some of our best laughs and my first stolen sips of beer were in a bowling alley. Lord knows it was needed, as the man took an eternity to align his body in the perfect position to take a shot. At some point after my twenty-first birthday, I recall Daddy preparing for a shot, and just before taking it turning around to say, "Julesea, don't you tink it's tyme you order your own beer instead of drinking mine?" *Truly one of the best moments.*

Now I was about to have a similar evening with the absolute last person I would've expected to be into bowling, much less come equipped with a customized ball. In hindsight, that should have been a sign to proceed with caution, which is the exact opposite of what I did. At the beginning of the first game, I began with a serious round of trash talking, telling him that he bowled like my grandmother after he lost the first game. At the start of the second—having won and feeling pretty confident—I suggested we make it more interesting, say, ten dollars a strike. In the blink of an eye, he sank five consecutive strikes. That's when I knew that I'd been had!

"You're so not a gentleman, Crawford! You hustled me," I said.

"Hey, I was content to let you win *a game*, but then you had to go and get all big-time," chided Marcus. "Come on now. I can't be having that."

"Why didn't you mention you were on a bowling team before?"

"You didn't ask. Besides, it wasn't an official team, just my nan and a bunch of old ladies with tinted hair in matching shirts when I was younger," said Marcus, untying his shoes.

"Well, next time I'll ask you all manner of things," I said.

"Deal. What do you say we start the inquisition over a proper dinner? There's a nice little spot around the corner that is more appropriate for your outfit," he said.

Once outside, we found Carlos positioned in front across the street, leaning against the car and enjoying a drag on his cigarette. On seeing us, he put it out and went to open the passenger door until Marcus instructed him otherwise. Carlos opened the trunk, allowing Marcus to exchange his baseball cap and leather jacket for a blazer.

"Talk about hustling someone. Is it really that simple for men?" I said after witnessing this quick change.

"It is, baby. The deck is always stacked in a man's favor. Thank goodness women have a more forgiving spirit, otherwise we could not apologize enough for the glaringly obvious inequities, you know."

"Would you repeat that into a tape recorder at a later date, so I can play it for my girls?"

"Hell no. I like being in the men's club too much—great perks. As a matter of fact, I don't even know what you're referring to," said Marcus.

After walking a few blocks west we arrived at a restaurant on the north side of the street, where Marcus has a standing reservation. I made a mental note then and there that nothing in this man's world truly occurred on the fly. We were led to a corner booth in the back to a table adorned with freshly poured glasses of champagne and insalata mista.

"I hope you don't mind," Marcus said, gesturing to the carefully placed delights, "but I had something special prepared."

Feeling quite giddy and pampered, I shrugged no. The appearance of lobster, however, did elicit an interruption in his meal selections. "I'm allergic to shellfish. I am so sorry, but it's either an Epipen or hospitalization for me."

"Now that's a compromise. Asking me to give up seafood is a lot. It's one of my favorites."

"I see. That could pose a huge problem. I guess the question to be answered sooner than later is if I'm worth the sacrifice," I said.

Marcus signaled the waiter to come over and explained my situation. Within minutes the chef was tableside outlining a seafood-free feast. Approving the new menu, Marcus turned to me and said, "You're worth it."

"You don't know that to be certain."

"I have a sixth sense about things."

"Do you now?"

"I do," he said. "Don't shake your head. You'll see. I'm always clear on what I want, Jules. I want you—healthy and having eyes only for me."

"If you are trying to do a number on my head, it's working, so I beg you to stop. Marcus, I've been on the losing side of love before, and I just can't do it again."

"That's not my intent. I have a home in Bridgehampton to show for a failed leap. You have several voices in your head telling you not to trust me. I'm trying to tell you that you can, if you want to."

"Speaking of that, the voices . . . I would like to, but then little things happen like you calling the office today, and I wonder if this is all part of some play with Michael."

"Was that not the best place to reach you in the middle of the day? Have I given you any reason to distrust me?" asked Marcus. My deadpan stare triggered his memory to our very first dinner, with Gary. "Aside from the extremely poor judgment displayed earlier, for which I have already apologized . . . Jules, I don't need you to do my bidding with Mike. As for what demands he will make on you in the future, I can't say, so, see? I am actually the one at a disadvantage here. At some point you may have a choice to make, and there's a possibility that you won't select me."

"Are you sure you're not a lawyer?" I asked, attempting to lighten the mood from the suspicious air I had created.

"Listen, business is what I do, but my passion is history. That alone tells me that many a great man has been brought down by only one thing," said Marcus. "Love."

"What I *love* is that you already consider yourself great. I mean, can a person actually say that about themselves?"

"I just did," said Marcus, looking me squarely in the face, our dining table feeling more like a boardroom to close a deal. "Only question is, are you the kind of woman who can allow herself to be loved . . . or will you cut and run when things get uncomfortable?"

Although the comment was directed at me, I felt there was much more to it and hoped I wasn't wrong by saying, "One day you'll tell me about her, your mom. Okay?"

"Not tonight. I'm still trying, very hard, I might add, to impress you," said Marcus.

"You just did," I confessed. "Like I said before, you are good . . . and dangerous in a *Thomas Crown Affair* sort of way."

"McQueen or Brosnan?" asked Marcus, removing the glass of champagne from my hand and covering it with his.

# 34

## TWO MONTHS, SEVEN DAYS, AND SPONTANEOUS COMBUSTION

**W**HAT I AM not understanding is why it's taken so long to get you on the phone, Boulton," I barked into my cell. Richard had called just as I entered the main doors at Carly's. "Oh pish posh, secretary of defense, my arse, Richard. I's met a man, and he is fabulously unbelievable, so you have to help me not muck it up."

"Dear, haven't we been down this road before? Need I remind you of Keith?"

"Low blow. Besides, Keith's wrapping was fabulous. It's the creamy center that just happened to be double-stuffed."

"Hence my point. What do we know about this man aside from the fact that he is a partner at Chimera Capital, an investor with your current employer, lives in your building, has received rave reviews from your folks, collects model creatures, and knows his way around your kitchen but not your *kitchen?*"

"So you have been listening to my voice mails! Why in the hell haven't you phoned me back then? Those random e-mails were driving me crazy."

"Of course I was listening, so please don't go all pitchy on me. I just couldn't return in detail, but rest assured I am up to speed."

"Sorry about that. Your ears, I mean. You know how excited I get. So, I am not crazy then? It is odd that he and I have been dating for two months, seven days, and have yet to sleep together. I mean we have slept together in the 'Jack and Jill' sense of the word but not in the 'Tie me up! Tie me down!' way, you know what I am saying?"

"Yes, that is odd," replied Richard. "Maybe the equipment is broken or just does not work with your parts."

"Will you stop it with that?! I'll have you know that I've done the feel test numerous times and his member clearly responds to me. It's just the actual act of engaging that has proven elusive. Okay, before you ask, I'll confess that at first he tried, but I thought we should wait, which is elementary, I know. Now it's like he isn't even pressed to try again."

"Honey, when will you ever learn? Grown men don't respond to high school games."

"Old habits are hard to break, but I'm trying..." I was suddenly distracted by Michael's reflection in the window, which meant that my conversation with Richard would have to end prematurely. I watched as Michael not so subtly lurked at the door saying something to Jacklyn, most probably trying to find out who I was talking to. Far from done talking to Richard but having no other choice, I turned around to face Michael just as he was walking in.

"Finish your call. I'll wait," he said.

"Richard, someone has come into the office. Can I ring you back? Oh, when will you be out of session? Okay. Then might I see you on Sunday? Perfect, eleven a.m. it is," I said, disconnecting and giving my full attention to Michael.

"I don't know why you did that. I told you I would wait," said Michael.

"Michael, I have seen your form of *waiting*," I said, swiveling my chair side to side. "After a few seconds you'll start rummaging through my things, asking me numerous questions about what this is or why that is there, then if you still don't have my undivided attention, you'll either sit at the desk throwing those massive yet elegant feet on the corner while sucking on one of your cancer sticks or you'll walk around, only to lean over my shoulder and read my e-mails . . . sooo, basically what I am saying is, your version of waiting, Mr. Kipps, sucks."

"You know me all too well, Jules."

"I do watch you . . . like a hawk. Can't have you slipping on my watch."

"I know you do and I like that about you," said Michael, removing the aforementioned cigar from the interior pocket of his blazer.

"So what gives? Am I costing you too much money again today with my brilliant idea?"

"Not that I know of, but you just might be. I'll let you know when I get to your e-mails. Don't give me that look like you're disappointed. You would never have known if I didn't say anything."

"Thank God for Simone," I said. "At least she reads my e-mails."

"Yes, that woman covers up any number of sins for me, but she can't handle everything, which is why you'll be at my house on Saturday night. You have any plans?"

"I'm guessing not, although if I did, it would probably be seeing the last Ailey performance of the season at Lincoln Center with Joy after weeks of planning, her agreeing to come in from Jersey, and hiring a babysitter," I said.

"Good. You're not missing anything. They perform *Revelations* at the end, same as last year and the fifteen before that," said Michael. "I'll expect you at my house by seven thirty for a dinner with Nikolai Abramovich."

"What?! When did this happen? I mean, I know his party was a success and all, but I didn't know you two still talked."

"It wasn't your business to know, but if you look a little closely, you can learn something about building a bridge and creating allies."

"Don't you mean comrades?"

"Humor is not your forte, Jules. Carly and I are throwing a dinner in his honor, an official welcome to NYC, if you will. I need a focused set of eyes and ears on Nikolai and Annya, his wife. Think you can handle that?"

"Sure, I'll try," I said.

"Don't try, Jules. Do," said Michael between quick and short inhales to light his cigar. "I need to make sure there are no flies on old Nikolai."

"What is that, like KGB-speak?" I said. "What's the attire?"

"Cocktail but not black. I need you in something fetching and not so official."

"Do I get a tip at the end of the night?"

"You keep your job. Does that count?" said Michael.

"Fetching it is!" *Great, now I really do need to speak with Richard. I know absolutely nothing about global finance, Russia, and oligarchs. Talk about being a fish out of water, I might as well be a mullet in the Caspian Sea.*

After Michael left my office feeling quite full of himself, I immediately phoned Marcus. Undoubtedly he would be at the dinner, a potentially sticky situation. *If he is going and I am going, then maybe we should go together, but were we ready to be outed? Was I ready?* The few times Marcus had brought it up, I told him I wasn't ready. Selfishly, I just wanted to keep us quiet a bit longer, because I still wasn't sure we were real. He didn't agree, but reluctantly allowed me to take the lead.

I called his private line to bypass speaking with his assistant. Our cloak-and-dagger had not afforded me the luxury of visiting his office yet. I envisioned a mysterious corner space, a combination of Old World antiquities and modern collectibles encased in floor-to-ceiling windows with breathtaking views of Lady Liberty. The Bat Phone, as it were, being one of those rotary BC (before cordless) variety, shiny black with the flat circular dial, sans the finger holes and numbers tucked away in the bottom drawer of a grand mahogany desk. The ring unlike a traditional phone so as not to elicit attention, should he be in a meeting, silently blinked a red light under the desk for only him to see.

Picking up after a few rings, he said, "Marcus here."

"Do my ears deceive me or are you a bit British today?" I asked.

"Well, since Reaganomics, the pound is doing considerably better than the dollar . . . so, yes, yes I am."

"I heard. What a sad state for old George Washington," I said.

"Well, maybe you should call him and brighten his day like you do mine," said Marcus.

"Look at you, so charming!"

"Well, it's true, Veronica. You have this great way about you," said Marcus, his delivery being so natural and easy that I was not immediately certain of how to respond, so I just sat there holding the phone silently until he spoke again. "Hello? Don't be like that. I was just playing."

"Honestly, you must believe me when I say you aren't nearly as funny as you think yourself to be, Marcus."

"I don't believe you," he said. "Cori laughs at all my jokes."

"Cori doesn't count. She's a paid employee, poor woman has no choice. I on the other hand am the realest thing in your life," I said.

"Which is why I'm strongly considering keeping you around, at least that is what my nan says I should do."

"Brilliant woman she is. Speaking of that, being around and all, not your nan, Michael just commandeered my Saturday. Apparently he is throwing a dinner for—"

"Yes, for Nikolai Abramovich," said Marcus. "You going to be there?"

"So it seems. Don't act so surprised. Why are you taking Veronica instead of me?" I asked jokingly, making light of the moment as we so often do.

"Well, not exactly. I am going, but not with her," said Marcus.

"Oh, I see. Well, this is awkward, you not thinking to ask me, I mean."

"Wait a minute. Do you really want to open that up, Jules? I would gladly take you anywhere anytime, but remember it's you who doesn't want to be seen in public around familiar eyes."

"Was that a question or a statement? Never mind, it's besides the point," I said. "Can I ask who you are taking? Are you like dating or something?" I asked, my voice raising a noticeable decibel or two.

"You do realize that you just went from zero to sixty in less than two seconds. Remarkable, actually. Better than my Maserati."

"I'm not laughing, Marcus. Were you going to tell me if I didn't call?"

"Probably not, although I did think about it, if that matters," admitted Marcus. "Listen, you don't know her, just someone I met before you and see from time to time. Jules, you still there?"

"I heard you, just thinking is all . . . What else have you not told me?"

"Honestly, Jules, there are certain things that don't necessarily warrant a conversation until you are clear on what it is you want from this thing we are doing. Unless you would like to shed some light on matters now?"

"I didn't know that you were seeing other people, publicly is all, but I guess you are. I mean, it's none of my business. It's not like we're sleeping together or something."

"Would it change things between us if we were?" asked Marcus.

"It wouldn't be a declarative statement or anything, but it would clear up some lines regarding intention," I said.

"Jules, a lot of my work is social, you know that. I have never been reserved about my intentions toward you, Jules," said Marcus. "I want to be with you in every way. Say the word and we will go together."

"I can't. Michael needs me." The words jumped off my tongue before my brain could do an appropriate edit. "What I mean is, the entire purpose of me being there is to observe Nikolai and Annya. I can't very well do that if I am with you debuting, now can I? . . . Marcus?"

"You don't have a monopoly on silence, Jules," he said in a tone that conveyed his agitation with me. "Mike's a great guy, but I won't be in his shadow even for you."

"I know and I'm sorry. Truly I am, which is why I called. Not to say I'm sorry, because I didn't know I would be saying I'm sorry, but to tell you about Saturday. I guess I didn't do it the right way. Please don't be mad, okay?"

"Delicate ground it is, Jules. I just hope you understand that," said Marcus. *I understood that he was saying my twenty-something cute-craziness is wearing thin in his grown-man world.* "Moving on, we will both be in attendance on Saturday. What are the rules here, baby? What else do you need? I have another call waiting—"

"Don't say it like that, please. I need for you not to get exhausted with me, because I don't think I could bear it. Then I need for you to delete this chick's number from your phone sooner than later, although I know I have no right to ask . . . right now. Most important is I need you, okay?" I said.

For some time I had been overanalyzing, about what I wanted—what I needed from Marcus, to pacify the turbulent conditions in my head. Now, in the most roundabout way, I found my voice and was able to share it with him. My hope was that it would not be met with deafening silence.

"Okay, I will see you there," said Marcus.

"Okay? . . . Good." I held my breath for his response, hoping for something more that would quiet the pangs of anxiety creeping into my soul.

"Jules . . . nothing . . . bye," he said.

· · ·

When not overthinking Marcus, I managed to tap into my network and learn that Abramovich's wife, Annya, was a major patron of French haute couture and Italian fashion. He, on the other hand, appeared to be less inclined to anything that was not about creating additional wealth via oil, technology, communications, and multimedia throughout Russia, Asia, and blue chip holdings in the U.S., unless it measured 34-24-36, which is clearly why Michael wanted me to look "less official."

With Gary's help (i.e., editorial discount) I acquired an Yves Saint Laurent dress for the evening featuring a slim black skirt and a voluminous white silk top with an exposed back. Despite the boatneck cut of the blouse, the fabrication made the contours of my ample bust quite visible—another gift from Cora's side, of course. He finished the look off with oversize bone, gold, and onyx bangles and flowing hair.

"Honey, trust me, men like that love themselves some cascading hair, especially all this voluminousness you got going on," said Gary, running his fingers through my mane. "You sure you're not part Indian?"

"Shut up and fix my hair right, will you?" I said, playfully slapping at Gary. "Honestly, what would I do without you always coming to the fashion rescue?"

"All right, Cinderella, remember to make sure that most of it falls over your shoulder, and when he is around, toss your head and throw it back like one of them *Charlie's Angels* girls from back in the day. It will drive him crazy! Trust," said Gary.

· · ·

Arriving at Michael and Carly's building via a yellow cab to a line of waiting black sedans was a bit intimidating in itself without fixating on the fact that Marcus and his date were most likely already upstairs. When extending the invitation—or sentence, as it were—Michael never said how many people were coming. I envisioned fifty or so. Walking through the marbled entrance hall of their home and seeing the formally attired staff in tails carrying trays of champagne, wine, and hors d'oeuvres, I would say it was closer to two hundred, with the median age being north of forty-five . . . *single solitary mullet in the Caspian, I am.* The only thing missing in this swanky affair was an arrival announcement stating each guest's position and affiliation. *I imagine mine might go something like, "Ms. Jules Sinclair, dateless spinster daughter of Charles and Cora Sinclair of Virginia" or "Ms. Jules Sinclair, dead woman walking."*

Nancy Wilson was the first familiar face I saw. Having been with us for some time now, she and I had become quite friendly, so upon learning I was alone, she clipped me to her skirt hem and made some beneficial introductions. My favorite by far was to Bourjois Cosmetics CEO and socialite Chantal Chapman. Talk about a self-made woman by way of a proper assist from a tycoon husband who was more than twenty years her senior. Chantal was indeed a force of 'UES by way of Arkansas' glamour. Everything about her was a statement, from her big auburn hair to the enormous emeralds and diamonds and deathly sharp fingernails lacquered the same flaming shade as her hair and lips. Immediately upon laying eyes on my YSL ensemble, she declared that she could never wear hers again (even though Yves himself had fitted her), to which I quipped, "Thank God, 'cause I don't need the pressure!" Chantal enjoyed the unfiltered retort and declared to Nancy that I was a gem. *That's cute and all, as long as I could be the living equivalent of the 20 carats sitting on her finger. Honestly, where is security or a little person to hold her hand up?!*

"That's why I hired her," said Michael, appearing between the two of them as if they were Heaven and Earth and he the stars; always meant to be there. "Jules, you do look lovely tonight. Clearly I am paying you too much money."

"Or maybe it's not your money at all," said Chantal, "that keeps a young woman in a certain comfort."

"Unless she, being me, has a fabulous gay with divine fashion access," I said, quickly squashing the "kept woman" direction of conversation.

"Clearly more fun, just less perks," said Chantal. "Remember, it's always better to acquire, my dear, than lease."

Following a few more pleasantries, Michael made our apologies and ushered me away to the far corner of the room, where Carly was holding court with Annya and Nikolai Abramovich. Against the nighttime skyline and the amber lighting created for the evening, Carly appeared warm and ever-present, unlike the cold, old, nosy coot I knew she could be. True, we had found a way to be cordial, even faux-friendly in the aftermath of her Tony confession, but my defenses were never down around her. *Hell, if she looked close enough she would see my hand on the trigger just waiting for her to go left.* Thankfully Cora taught me to play the civility game long ago. After initial exchanges and introductions, Michael and Nikolai made their exit, but not before Nikolai properly sized me up in a manner that was at once inappropriate and completely obvious to all present, including his wife. Her blasé attitude, however, conveyed that it was expected and the least of her concerns—unlike the meticulous application of her makeup, giving her skin the appearance of the finest porcelain bisque doll.

"Jules, you look very appropriate," said Carly. "Remarkable, actually, for a woman of your age to dress so well. Your contemporaries are trotting around in little dresses that leave little to the imagination, baring their midriff. Positively gauche."

"In defense of my peer group, Carly, it's all trial and error. Fashion, as Coco said, fades, only style remains. Mrs. Abramovich, like Carly, you are quite the style icon," I said, paying specific attention to her dramatic, cobalt-blue, embellished Valentino couture gown. *Far too dressy for such an affair, but then again my job is to charm and ingratiate, not to judge.* "Where do you find inspiration?" I asked, not trusting whatever was to come from Carly's mouth next.

"Darling, when you spend as much as I do, season after season, they have no choice but to call you an icon," said Annya, so taken with herself that Carly's steely-eyed gaze escaped her. *Ahhhh, when the rich and the nouveau riche clash—what fun!*

"Well, in that case I had better do as Chantal instructed and find myself a husband of means then," I said, garnering an affirmative nod from both.

Unlike Carly, Annya is a natural beauty, brunette and buxom. She was born to extreme poverty in Slovenia the way Carly was born to extreme wealth. Legend and gossip circuits have it that she was the au pair to Nikolai's youngest child and lured him away from his wife of nearly twenty years in a matter of months. She is the stuff of gold-digging opportunistic legend and is unapologetic about it. *I must introduce her to Blake someday.*

"Jules, I had no idea you were looking to marry," said Carly, no more interested in my marriage prospects than in Annya's style status, but isn't that what polite conversation is all about, faking it? "Why didn't you come to me? There are some stellar men about."

"Of course," I said, more as a conversation point than anything else. "I used to say that I wanted a man just like my father. I have since amended that to say I want a man who my father likes. Someone who personally checks all the right boxes and a few wrong ones, yet who is strong enough to withstand my ambition."

"Rubbish, darling. No such man has ever been created. Fathers only like the ones who are reflections of their best selves," said Carly. "As for the strength, we women crafted a fable long ago to make men believe that is who they are. They are not and never will be."

"I must agree. The men themselves do not know what greatness they are truly capable of without our eyes and prowess," said Annya. "The trickier part is to continue holding the reins without their knowledge in the face of excessive power."

"Which is why you must always be stronger, craftier, more cunning than they are, dear," said Carly.

"My goodness, you both make finding the right mate sound like an Ethan Hunt *Mission Impossible*," I said.

"It is, dear. The perfect man doesn't just appear. You make him," said Annya, "but it takes far longer than five seconds."

"It takes a lifetime," said Carly.

"Okay, two questions. Is there a handbook, and whereabouts might one go to find such a man?" I asked.

"Of course not. It's instinctual. You'll know when you cross him . . . unless . . ." said Carly in a forced tone that reeked with disapproval, be it for the sentiment or the approaching guests who had captured her attention, prompting her to cross in front of me and Annya in order to greet them.

"Dah-ling, I am so glad you were able to join us. You look absolutely fabulous, so debonair. Come, come! You must meet Annya Abramovich. Annya, this is my everything, my confidant, the keeper of my world, Marcus Crawford."

*You ever have that moment when time just stops and a split second transforms into an eternity? Well, if not, here's mine.* Knowing that he was coming tonight did not prepare me for the actual moment. I had rehearsed a few times over how I would be poised and composed when we came face-to-face. Now here he stood before me but not seeing me, with Carly clinging to his left arm and Annya to the right, sizing him up like the main course. Forget the former script, anxiety was about to make me a sweaty mess, and that never reads well on silk. My breaths were coming in faster, shorter waves, a sure sign that I could not trust myself to be in such close proximity to Marcus and not reveal the true nature of our relationship.

I was so focused on flight that I collided, champagne flute first, into another guest wearing an example of the garish outfits that Carly mentioned earlier—rouching across the hips is no one's friend . . . even if you are a size 4 and have mile-long legs.

"What the . . . shit. Oh my gawd, Julesy!!!! What are you doing here?!" said Blake.

"Holy shit, Blakes. I'm so sorry," I said, frantically trying to wipe droplets of champagne from her purple strapless dress before a stain set in, not daring to look behind me and see if our collision had elicited attention. "What are you doing here?"

"You tell me. He said to put on something sexy, and I thought it was . . . well, forget what I thought. Anyway, here we are. OMG, here you are! You look so great! I am totally borrowing that," said Blake, eyeing my YSL. "You know I am borrowing that, right?"

Elated to see a friendly face that I could download to, I briefly forgot the immediate—until, that is, the sound of Marcus's laugh echoed about. "Thanks, boo, but I have to go," I said.

"Wait, not yet. I want you to meet my guy. Well, he's not my guy officially. That's what I thought this was about. Anyway, I'm working on it. You know Richard will absolutely die when he finds out that you met him first," said Blake. "That is, if the old bat will dislodge her fangs."

"Would love to. Let's go," I said, grateful to have a legitimate reason to put as much distance as possible between myself, Marcus, and Carly. My efforts to continue forward proved futile as Blake stepped into me, forcing another collision that now elicited attention.

"There you are, dear. Marcus, you know Jules," said Carly, still glued to his side. Had I not been standing there to observe this surreal moment with my own eyes, I would not have considered Blake's depiction of "the old bat with fangs" to be true, but judging by the almost total color drain from Marcus's face on seeing me, Carly was indeed a well-fanged vampire, maybe even Nosferatu. Having no forewarning as I did, Marcus nodded a polite "hello, yes, of course" that belied his traditional charismatic demeanor and robbed me of any contact. "And this is his friend . . . I'm sorry, dear. I seem to have forgotten again. What's your name?" asked Carly.

"Blake. My name is Blake, Mrs. Kipps. I am also a friend of Michael's. We have met before, remember?"

"Yes, of course, Blaaake," said Carly in an affected drawl that purposefully emphasized the lack of sincerity. "This is Annya Abramovich and Jules Sinclair." *Maybe if Blakes had added "a friend of Michael's who has never slept with him and never will because his wallet is too short, but yours, on the other hand . . ." Maybe if she said that, their dynamic would be less arctic.*

Visibly taking great pains to ignore the slight, Blake nodded hello to Annya and then proceeded to quicken the ground between Marcus and me. "Good to meet you, Annya. Jules is one of my dearest friends," said Blake.

"My, isn't the world small," said Carly, turning to me with a disapproving glare.

"You could say that," Marcus, Blake, and I echoed in unison.

I believe this is what they call a Texas Standoff. My eyes locked on Marcus, his ever so carefully on me, Carly and Blake sizing each other up. Save for the lights blinking on and off signaling that it was time to adjourn to the dining room, who's to say where the moment would go? With each step I tried to do the math. *How the? When the? WTF! Of all the men on the entire island and in Jersey, how is it that Blake and I were dating the same one? Hold up, did she say "again" as in "I have met you before"? OH MY GOD, THEY'RE FUCKING!! Why have I never heard about him before? What in the hell happened to "Mr. Potentially More"? OMG, is Marcus Blake's Mr. Potentially More?* If only I could turn to her and get the answers to the laundry list of questions in my head, but I can't. Not with Marcus at my side imploring ever so discreetly that we need to talk. *UNDER-FUCKING-STATEMENT, MARCUS!!!! Keep the champagne. I need a bottle of Jack.*

Once inside the dining room, we separated. Each guest's seat was designated by ivory textured place cards featuring their name in brushed gold script. *Richard would approve.* If the gods were crazy enough to concoct this evening, then surely they would take great pleasure in seating Marcus and me next to each other, but not if I could do a quick swap before anyone noticed. Michael was standing near the head of the table directing traffic as it were with Nikolai, who, despite being the single wealthiest person in the room, seemed to be salivating at the attention bestowed upon him far more than his wife.

"Jules, you're here," said Michael, signaling my seat, near where he and Nikolai were standing. The majority of the guests were still milling about and not yet crossed the threshold.

As Michael continued rattling on, as hosts are forced to do, about the merits of this approaching guest or that one, I was busy scouting the table for the task at hand. For, as much as I wanted to observe Marcus and Blake's dynamic, I didn't need them sitting right near me. *For fear of having an uncontrollable desire to stab him, spill more champagne on her, or lose control of my vocals and yelling "Are you fucking serious!" at the top of my lungs to the universe before the amuse-bouche is served.*

Careful not to physically disengage from him and Nikolai, I took two steps in the direction of my seat to uncover the identity of my neighbors. Annya was to my left and some man with far too many names—Sir Brandon Phillip Von Blah Blah Blah—to my right. *What ever happened to boy-girl-boy-girl?* It would be difficult enough trying to focus on "Operation Nikolai" and entertain Annya while trying not to lament over Blake and Marcus, much less having to endure the musings of some old guy who in all probability would either have ripe breath or try to touch my leg under the table.

While putting my purse down, I discreetly switched my seat for Annya's. *Something tells me that as long as his title is right, she could overlook any number of olfactory sins.* Marcus and Blake approached from the opposite side of the table to exchange pleasantries with Michael and Nikolai. I could not help but look up and notice how very *New York Times* Sunday Edition Wedding Section they were—in spite of Blake's dress selection this evening. She so naturally fit into the space at his side I'd thought was mine alone a few days ago. Had it been a different man, I would have found extreme pleasure in her happiness, but this was not the case. It was not another man. She was standing there with *my* Marcus, and I was watching it *alone*, near sickness, without the protection of an all-knowing friend or an escort to hold my hair should I need to immediately release the emotions bubbling inside. Surely this must be one of Dante's levels of Hell or maybe part of a Kundera comedy. Fact is, I am here in this moment, but there is absolutely no laughter to be had, which makes it quite apropos, I guess.

"My my, I see your keen eye goes beyond fashion," Carly whispered from behind, catching me off guard. "He is something, isn't he?"

"I'm sorry, what were you saying?" I said, taken aback by her brazen intrusion into my thoughts.

"Marcus, of course. He is impressive . . . I sense you share my sentiment, do you not," said Carly. *Definitely more of a statement than a question.*

"I hadn't noticed," I said.

"I beg to differ, my dear. I would say you have noticed a lot, as you should," she said, locking eyes with me as if she were magically scanning my thoughts. "Great potential that one has, provided it's honed properly. Wouldn't you agree?" Fearing the release of highly sensitive data, I forcibly changed the direction of our conversation and commented about the beauty of the décor long enough for seats to be taken.

Marcus and Blake were seated in the center on the opposite side of the table, close enough that I could bear full witness to their every gesture but far enough away that their words eluded me. Inevitably the moment came that she made him laugh, head tilted back, eyes closed, a slow-finish kind of laugh. The same one he has done with me many times before, so there was no question of its sincerity. I didn't have a monopoly on his laughter. The moment crystallized, forcing me from the table. *Blakes is one of my besties, and if Marcus is her "Mr. Potentially More," then what right do I have to him? She won't value him as I would, as I do. I know Blakes. She will use him until she is bored and then she will move on. She doesn't deserve him . . . but she is my friend.*

My only familiarity with Michael and Carly's home being the observatory, I found the elevator and sought solace there. Above hung a full moon, temporarily shadowed by a ring of clouds. Its presence explained to my ill-tempered tears that tonight could not go any other way than how it was.

"Are you all right?" asked Marcus, appearing minutes after I had arrived.

"I am not. I'm so not okay right now, so please leave."

"Jules, I had no idea that you and Blake were friends. This is . . . unfortunate."

"Well, that's one way to put it. A royal *fuckup* would be another. That is, if you were standing in my shoes or even cared, but . . ."

"Don't go there, Jules. Of course I care. Why else would I be up here, instead of there?"

"Are you sleeping with her?" I asked.

"Listen, you're angry and you're hurt. Let's not compound the matter by going down a road that—"

"Of course you are, why wouldn't you be, everyone else has."

"Jules, I know this is all . . . Hell, I don't know what this is but let's not say anything to make things worse," said Marcus.

"Please stop! There is absolutely nothing I can say that could possibly make tonight worse than it already is. Marcus, you are here with one of my best friends and clearly she is not a new acquaintance unless Carly was mistaken. Either way I lose."

"I prefer not to believe that," he said.

"Really, how do you figure that?"

"Truly, I don't know in this moment, but I can tell you that the last thing I want is for you to look this lovely, up here, alone, crying tears over me," said Marcus, removing his neatly placed silk pocket square to catch the trails running down my cheeks.

"Great, that makes two of us," I said, moving away from his touch in search of some perspective. "You had better go back downstairs. Your date—Blake will be concerned."

"I'm concerned about you."

"Me too."

Once I was sure that Marcus had gone, I allowed myself a final outburst before forcibly pulling myself together. What was it about me and this room? Such misery it brings every time. In the future I must make a concerted effort never to be in it. Stepping into the hallway, to my dismay, the all-seeing eye stood in wait.

"Is everything okay? I noticed you left the table abruptly and was . . . concerned," said Carly.

"With all due respect, please use another word. I have more than enough 'concern' tonight, thank you," I said.

"I see."

"I felt a bit light-headed, dizzy, that's all, and needed some fresh air," I said, patting the last bit of moisture from my face.

"And Marcus as well? Did he need some fresh air also?" asked Carly.

"I don't know, Carly. You'll have to ask him."

"I see," said Carly, promptly switching gears in favor of a lighter approach—her suspicion satisfied. "Well, I hope there's not a problem with the food. We used a new caterer, from downtown no less, but I have been assured that they are stellar. Well, we'll see, won't we?"

# 35

# SUNDAY

CAN YOU BELIEVE she said that to me? I mean, what is it with that woman?"

"Darling, Carly is the least of your concerns . . . Sorry, wrong word," said Richard, perched in his usual Sunday position at Cub Room. The chaos of my life on this day superceded his need to start off the morning with a Bloody Mary, opting instead for the clarifying jolt that a double espresso might bring. "What are you going to do about Blake and Marcus? You can't ignore the poor man forever."

"One evening does not constitute forever, Richard. Besides, I was in no position to speak last night. It's bad enough that I faked illness to excuse myself from after-dinner chatter. Addressing his ringing my bell incessantly to explain the unexplainable truly would have made me ill."

"You know, sometimes—often, actually—I think you like misery too much, dear."

"Almost as much as you like gin? Excuse me, let's not forget I'm the injured party here."

"No, you're not, Jules. You are the party with knowledge now of all the players, so therefore you have a choice! Did you hear me? There is a choice to be made, and it is yours. Question is, what are you going to do?"

"I know you think I am weak and why shouldn't you? You're

always coming to my rescue, but there is a code, you know, about this sort of thing. *Girls* don't do this to girls."

"Honey, grow up. Codes are for children and cadets. Women not only do it every day but some actually find great everlasting happiness in using their cunning to acquire the right prize. Trust me, Blake will recover," said Richard, finishing the last drop of coffee. "Is he the right prize for the sacrifice?"

"Yes, I think so, but will our friendship?" I asked.

"That I don't know. Depends on how you handle it," said Richard.

"I wish I didn't have to. Can't you do this one little thing for me?" I implored.

"As much as I would like to break Blake's face at times, this particular cut is yours and yours alone."

"Probably won't be so bad. I bet Marcus is just like the others," I said.

"For your sake, I hope so, but I doubt it. Blake is not the singularly focused, emotionally depraved creature you believe her to be. That's just her PR," said Richard. "Quite the contrary, Blake wants desperately for one of these men to legitimize her, to show her through the front door to business associates instead of dark clubs and exotic vacations thousands of miles away from their respectable lives. Your Mr. Crawford may be more than just your ideal. He may very well be hers, also."

"Why are you telling me this?"

"Because you need to know. This is a win-lose proposition no matter how you look at it. It's time to start living your life as an empowered woman full-time, Jules, and stop straddling the fence. Blood oaths and pinky swears are for elementary school. Don't you think it's time you graduated?"

## 36

# A DECLARATIVE STATEMENT

IN THE WEEKS that followed my conversation with Richard, I did allow Marcus back in, because any thought of an immediate future without him seemed too much to bear. As a show of my commitment to being fully in the space of us, thereby eliminating the need for any decoy, Gary, Carly, Michael, Messy Mitzy, Percy, Jacklyn, Ivan, Cora, Daddy, and even his friend Paolo were along for the ride—everyone but Blake, the one person who was calling to hang out and vent about Marcus dumping her. But I couldn't. I was a coward and I knew it. In my defense, I just wanted to hang on to her friendship as long as possible. I knew that ours would not survive this. I just needed a bit more time to come to terms with the choice I had made and with losing her. Following a near encounter at Barneys one Saturday with Marcus, I could no longer hide the truth.

We had just completed his selection of new Valextra travel cases and were rounding the corner to the jewelry section when I saw her standing there in oversize sunglasses and a hat, and next to her was a new Daddy Warbucks. I froze in my step, unsure what to do next. Marcus followed my gaze.

"Hey, isn't that Blake?" he asked.

"Um-hmm."

"Well, no time like the present to say hello."

"Wait, not yet," I said.

"If not now, then when, Jules? We can't pretend forever that there is no history there."

"I know, but she doesn't know about our future, exactly."

"You can't be serious, Jules. It's been weeks now and you haven't told her?"

"I didn't know how."

"Well, you'd better figure it out, otherwise we'll be ducking out of department stores all over town," said Marcus, taking hold of my hand and exiting out the Sixtieth Street entrance. "Come on, my little puppy, tuck that tail. We can look at watches later."

.  .  .

"I was starting to wonder about you," said Blake as she settled into the booth next to me at L'express. "When I called Richard, he was all cryptic and self-absorbed as usual. Something about adopting a baby and getting the house ready for social services . . . anyway."

"I know, I'm so happy for him and Edgar. It's about time. They'll make the best parents, don't you think?" I said.

"I guess. How are you?" asked Blake, indifferent to the whole situation.

"Well, that's a fully loaded question. Why don't we start with something easier? How are you?"

"I'm amazing! Getting ready to spend a glorious holiday with Stavros aboard his yacht. We are going to fly over to Nice, where we will meet his crew, then set sail for the Amalfi Coast and then to Santorini. Can you imagine the sheer fierceness of yours truly gallivanting about the Riviera!"

"I can, and I fear the damage you will do to his credit cards."

"Correction, already done! A girl does need travel gear, you know."

"Lordy. I have no words."

"I like this one, Jules," said Blake, "I mean, he is not the ideal package, but I can work with it. He's a widower and a divorcé. He's good to me and needs me in total, not just as a trophy. Did I mention he is a *widower*? Hello!"

"You did, twice," I said, anxious to pounce on any nugget of information that could potentially minimize what I was about to say. "Good to know you're not pining over Marcus."

"Ugh, don't mention that name to me. Biggest waste of time."

"Oh, sorry," I said.

"J, don't be. It's not like you're the one who got dumped. I mean, technically, I wasn't dumped, per se. We just ran our course. Voilà!"

"Yeah, that's a much better way to see it," I said. "Besides, if you were still seeing Marcus, then you would have never met Stavros and would not be getting ready to sun and fun in the South of France."

"Exactly!! So let's only speak of beauty and yummies, since I have been starving myself for the past two weeks getting this body beach-ready," said Blake. "What are you having? I know, let's do the Niçoise and split the French toast for dessert like old times."

And that was how it was for the majority of lunch. We talked about the incidentals of life and matters concerning her imminent adventure. I tried to erase Richard's observation of her from my thoughts, as it is easier to believe her isolated in some way. Stavros was her consolation prize, and only time would tell if he would be hers to keep.

"Blakes, I know you said not to speak of Marcus again, but you do know that we are neighbors, right? Which means we see one another. And we work together, so . . ."

"Jules, correction, he is an investor, so you don't actually work together," said Blake. "As for the neighbor part, well, there isn't much that can be done about that, now is there? Except maybe taking the stairs."

"Stop. He's not bad, you know. Actually, very kind and pretty great on the eyes," I said.

"Yes, therein lies the problem. It's all peachy keen until his mystery is against you, and you find yourself waiting for his random phone calls too, for which there is no rhyme or reason. The only thing that man is consistent about is his work and his horizontal stroke. Not much room for anything else, which is fine. It's his right. All I'm saying is, don't go being all fabulous occasionally making me think we could be something while knowing all along that you have no intentions of being serious," said Blake, who by now was doing very little to mask the angst that encapsulated her relationship with Marcus.

"I'm sorry, Blake. I didn't know he hurt you like that," I said, without thinking that I was about to multiply that very pain.

"He didn't hurt me. I was just sharing. Besides, it not like it's anything you need to know."

*Shit!!! It's so easy to just sit here and allow the moment to pass. What good will telling her do? In two days she'll be on an Air France flight to happiness. Why muck that up? Except the Marcus that Blake was speaking of is in direct contrast to the one who goes above and beyond to make himself available to me. The man who speaks about a future that prominently features us together. Her Marcus is not the very same Marcus who was away fishing in some remote stream with my dad days before.* "Well, um, see, the thing is . . . he asked me out," I said.

"Oh," replied Blake, visibly shaken but fighting to remain composed. "What do I care if you go on a date with my leftovers? At least you have been warned."

"Well, it's not exactly your leftovers, Blake, which by the way sounds a bit insulting to me."

"Uh, you know what I meant. What do you mean by not exactly?"

"Remember end of last year when you started dating Mr. Potentially More? Well, a short time after that I started dating someone as well. I didn't talk to you about it because . . . I don't know why, but the timing just never seemed to be right. If you must know, I didn't really speak to anyone about it because it was complicated. And you never gave a name to your guy. Even when Richard kept calling him 'this one,' you didn't say anything. Anyway, it wasn't until the dinner at Carly's that I realized that your guy and my guy were the same person. Which is why I pretended to be sick that night, so I could leave and think."

"Normally you give far more details, Jules. Why so short this time?" asked Blake with a fire in her eyes that validated all my fears.

"Sometimes the details just don't matter," I said.

"So let me get this straight. It has been weeks since that dinner, and you and Marcus have known but neither of you saw fit to tell me. Hold up, were you the reason he broke up with me? What, so he chose you over me?"

"I wouldn't put it that way," I said, but I could see Blake running the library of their conversations, whether he'd become distant or used the old standby "It's not you it's me" line.

"Are you the one that he has 'feelings for and wants to give it a go' so he can't continue to fuck me?" said Blake. "I don't believe this shit!"

"Blake, I—"

"No, just shut up, Jules. How could you wait so long to tell me? Allow me to play myself over this guy? Walking around here like you're my friend and not the scandalous treacherous bitch you really are."

"Blake, I am your friend! I didn't know what this was and I needed to be sure it was something worth—"

"Worth what? Losing a friend over? Stabbing me in the back? You fucking cunt. Well, I hope it was worth it, because you are dead to me," said Blake, grabbing her bag and running to the door.

Rising to give chase, I left a loose wad of bills on the table and hoped it would be enough to cover the cost of our meal and the free show that spilled onto the sidewalk as she was hailing a cab.

"Blake, come on, we're not in the mob."

"You should count your blessings," said Blake as she closed the door. "Oh, and since we're confessing today, I knew Tony was fucking Angie long before you found them."

Later that night, after walking more than fifty blocks home to get some perspective, I called Cora and recounted the whole dreadful experience. I shared that I was not certain of Blake's confession about Tony and Angie. She was angry and said many things. No matter how awful a friend I had recently been to her, I just didn't believe that Blake had ever been as bad to me. Cora, on the other hand, ever the skeptic, ever my cheerleader, said she believed her and never liked her anyway—something about Blake reminded Mommy of Rosalyn, her rival for Daddy's affections.

By the time Marcus let himself in, I was in bed, having a fitful time making peace between what I had lost and what I had gained. He allowed me to cry and volunteered to phone Blake, but we both knew it would only make matters worse for her, and that was the last thing I wanted. Before closing my eyes, I asked Marcus if he thought that our relationship would be cursed cosmically because of my actions. He said, "True love always prevails, Jules. We just have to make a promise to be braver and more vigilant than most to make sure the cost was not in vain."

# 37

---

# STRANGE BEDFELLOWS

SINCE THE FALLING-OUT with Blake, the friendship lines had been drawn. In the divorce I kept Richard, albeit with a firm reprimand about how horribly I'd handled things despite his sage advice. She got Joy, which I understood, as Blake was the injured party and Joy's overly maternal instincts compelled her to try to make everything okay. Older than Blake and me, she lived solidly by the Code. Sometimes I think that Joy will die on that cross. Maybe if Richard gave her the speech, there would be room enough for us both, the saint and the sinner, but until then I had my man, my work, and a new ally in the trenches.

Nancy's residency ended and, surprise, Harry Connick Jr.'s is about to start, clearly a much better proposition than having him seated at a table. Even if Michael felt averse to me and Marcus being together because of their friction, he cannot deny that in relationship bliss I am all the more better at my job. I am happy, happier than I've ever been. That ever-present voice of doubt residing in my head of past mistakes is now less, and Jacklyn especially enjoys the perk of relationship bliss as it translates to earlier days and fewer weekend calls from me. I have a new motivation: my boyfriend, Marcus Crawford. We are a couple, and that means allowances are made, his being communication and mine being flexibility. Marcus's travel remains as it had always been, intense and international. I make certain that in the times he is home, I am there as well—whenever possible.

In preparation for Harry's debut, there is a marathon of things to be completed. The slightest oversight would impact the much-delayed weekend Marcus and I have planned to spend in the Hamptons, so Jacklyn is working inside my office for the day so that we can focus with minimal distraction. Sitting opposite me at the desk, she continues to man the phones as we draft and approve an influx of media copy and interview requests.

"It's Mrs. Kipps," said Jacklyn. "Do you want her?"

"Yes. Thanks, Jacklyn. Why don't you go and do a run-through of Harry's dressing room? Make sure we aren't missing anything on his rider."

"Hi, Carly," I said, once I was certain we were alone.

"Jules, is everything all right? I hadn't heard from you, and it has been some time since Stavros and Blake left. Did you tell her?"

"Yes, she hates me."

"In time she will come to thank you. After all, had you not come to me and shared the sordid mess, she would never have met Stavros and maybe finally gotten the life she desires."

"I hope you're right, but it doesn't change the fact that I am missing a friend."

"Choices, darling. We all have choices, and you made the only one there was to make. Marcus is quite a catch. It's quite rare to find them of his caliber at the time they are ready to get serious about things, if you know what I mean. Besides, Stavros is right for her, not Marcus. I saw him drinking her in at dinner."

"So it wasn't a coincidence that they met?" I said.

"Heavens no, dear. If we left everything to chance, then her kind would rule the world, now wouldn't they?" replied Carly.

"True, I guess. Any word on when Michael is going to blow or is that one for chance? I have seen him give me *that look*, but he hasn't said much of anything, which has me quite nervous."

"Good cause to be. Thankfully, he's been preoccupied. Just know that I have given the union my blessing, which may be enough. Let's see," said Carly.

I heard the words clearly but did not have complete faith in Carly's sphere of influence as it related to Michael's territorial nature over his professional pursuits. He may not be addressing the matter directly with me but he was peripherally, which is exactly where I felt I had been pushed to—the periphery. There was something major brewing, far more important than the opening of Harry Connick Jr., but that was all I knew. Whereas I used to be part of the inner-circle think tank with him, Raymond, and Simone, I was now pushed to the perimeter, skimming at the edge of the conversation but not yet knowing fully the topic of it.

"Carly, why did you help me?" I asked.

"Preservation, dear, preservation."

"Excuse me?" I said.

"In time you'll understand, and you'll thank me," said Carly.

. . .

The day of Harry's debut found Michael on cloud 999. He was buzzing about with more exuberance than normal for such an occasion. Earlier his tailor had come to put the final touches on a white dinner jacket he had commissioned for the evening. I recognized Mr. Vintorini in the hall as I made my way down to his office. For my part, I found it most useful to provide just enough cushion in our dynamic for Michael to seek me out instead of readily showing concern for his not addressing my relationship with Marcus. Of the many lessons that Michael had instructed me in over the past year, this was by far the most useful and easiest to incorporate.

"Come on in, Jules. Tonight's a big night. You feel it?" asked Michael. He was standing before his interior full-length mirror admiring his reflection in the new jacket. "Which do you prefer: the rose or the pocket square?"

"Pocket square, more classic and understated. The whole town seems to be buzzing about Harry's performance. We even have people flying in," I said.

"That's what I wanna talk to you about. I need you to remove the people from my table. Don't cancel them, just find room elsewhere."

"Michael, that's impossible unless you want me to put them in the kitchen, and I don't think Jean would like that very much. We are above capacity for both performances, standing room only. We'll be lucky if the fire marshal doesn't make a surprise visit and shut us down."

"Sounds like a great problem to have, if you ask me. Make it work. Nikolai is coming into town."

"Okay, how many in his party? I'm sure if it's small I can reshuffle and put them somewhere."

"Just him and his second in command, Mikhail. I don't want them *somewhere*, I want them at my table ... alone."

"Okay, just so I am clear ... I'm moving five people from your table in order to make room for two?"

"That's right. Also, I need you to draft a statement for morning release announcing my newly minted partnership with Nikolai toward the global expansion of Carly's."

"I'm sorry, you're what?"

"You heard me. Nikolai wants to be in the service business and is putting a cash infusion into Carly's that will allow me to do what I want to with the business."

"So you are still set on expanding, despite what the reports showed? What happened to wanting to keep the business private, nurturing its growth and image for a while longer? At least that's what you wanted to do when Marcus suggested expansion." I added the last bit under my breath.

"Your boyfriend doesn't run things around here," said Michael, tossing the pocket square to the floor near my feet and affixing the rose to his lapel. "I brought him into this, so we take my lead. Now I want this on the local morning news show as well, so make . . . What, Jules? Is your hand broken? Do I need Simone to draft it?"

"Of course not. I just . . . You just made it into this whole us against them—against *him* thing that I completely supported. So much so that when you reamed me out for that innocent dinner with him and Gary, I felt like I had disappointed you, and even how I struggled against initially liking Marcus because I didn't want to be disloyal to you. And now . . ."

"Now what? You realize that a game is always in play and inter-changeable, is that it? Ain't that some shit," said Michael, removing the dinner jacket as he stepped away from the mirror. "Listen, Jules, you can't ever expect to know completely what the full agenda of a man is. You just have to be buoyant and adapt. Can you do that? Of course you can. Now let's get started, unless there is something else?"

"Yes, Marcus and me together. What about it? You said your-self that I watch you and know you better than most, so just let me have it. I know you don't like it. Do I need to be worried about my position here with you?" I said, emboldened as I often am by Michael's unapologetic delivery after a few moments of being on the all-too-familiar receiving end.

"Transparency is not an everybody situation, I get that. You and Marcus, I'm not pleased, but I trust you until you give me a reason not to," replied Michael. "I'm in a good mood today, Jules, so I will say this. Keep your eyes open, your mouth closed, and never forget family. We're family, Jules."

"Was there a Sicilian convention in town that I didn't know about?" I asked.

"What?"

"Nothing, everyone's going mobster these days," I mumbled, and returned to my office for the remainder of the day to work with Jacklyn, adding the new partnership announcement to our already extensive list.

Marcus was still out of town when the announcement hit, so I can't be sure if I was his first or second phone call, but I know I was at the top of the queue when I heard the short-tempered urgency in his secretary's voice as she put him through to me. And for the third time in as many months, my loyalty was called into question. Marcus felt that I should have given him prior notice: "I'm not asking for insider information but you could have said something." When I tried to explain my actions and talk about my conflicts, trying to do my job and feeling caught in the middle, he said, "Feelings are like the wind, Jules. They come and go, you'll get over this tantrum. This isn't about separation of church and state. Your oversight, as it were, could impact the business that I do." Later I would learn that the omission did impact Marcus's portfolio, though not in the way that I thought, as it was the principal piece in cementing a relationship with Nikolai that would soon put us in California and potentially cost Michael everything.

In the meantime we had the "just us times," or JUTS; precious, suddenly available weekends, or evenings that originated from a last-minute cancellation. In those times, we would lose ourselves in the kitchen, on the sofa, in the bed, or anyplace that was only about us. Marcus would speak vividly about what it was like to grow up in Boston, attending Brown, Oxford, his dreams of creating a legacy to be passed on to his children so they never had to question whether he'd existed. We developed an affinity for late-night games of strip Trivial Pursuit, and we were so good at strip Twister, it could have been an Olympic competition. With each revelation and shared insight, my respect for Marcus grew, as did my commitment.

After this blowup I make a point of being more mindful going forward, while still keeping fully focused on my work affairs. I embrace that "I" am now part of a "we." The initial phase is seamless—

attending ballet and opera openings, baseball and basketball games, fund-raisers and auctions together—I am now required to accompany Marcus to client dinners whenever girlfriends, fiancées, and wives are encouraged to provide an air of civility. We even vacation—or weekend, as it were—with his corporate contacts from around the globe. It's what his lifestyle demands. *It is a lot to be constantly "on" at that level.*

Unlike my experience with Tony, for the most part everyone in Marcus's New York scene took to me well enough. As Carly so aptly said, "Dear, it would be poor form not to," when I expressed my surprise at how smoothly things seemed to be going. The part she left dripping on the floor was "when your mate is as accomplished and connected as Marcus." All well and good, but the one thing I didn't account for was its restrictive nature, as his world frequently overshadowed any perceived needs I may have had.

The time I relish spending with my friends was reduced to a fraction and his commitments became infinitely higher priority. Every second or third week, I managed to see Richard or have lunch with Jessica, whose husband—*yes, the guy from my final interview who she wanted me to meet*—was in the financial trade as well. Richard, being in the final stages of adopting a Chinese baby, seemed to have very little time to play constant therapist to my life's predicaments. *Apparently learning Mandarin and preparing for the arrival of little Ming Thuy Boulton Davis was getting the best of him.* The one bright purely coincidental spot, however, was that Joy and I mended fences after Marcus and I ran into her one evening at 8½ as she was awaiting a dinner meeting that was unexpectedly canceled. Before coffee was served, she understood—*begrudgingly, mind you*—that we were much more than a fling.

Then there were the *like it or not* downright inopportune times, like being pressured to cancel my plans, *even a late night at the office*, to accommodate a forgot-to-mention commitment on his calendar. His seeming detachment from or noninterest in some of my affairs often left me feeling displaced and exposed, sometimes missing the self-sufficient woman I had become in London. That woman in the later stages found great value in who she was and relished always being a priority, not having her identity lost in that of her companion. Desiring not to be consumed by these thoughts to the detriment of our relationship—and feeling that I had no other recourse—I shared them with Cora, who to my astonishment was quite empathetic, *albeit antiquated*. Ultimately, she told me that it is the required cost to be with a man who is fully in his person and of a certain stature: "You don't want to be with some man who isn't rooted, Julesea. You want a man whose shadow looms much larger than yours but his heart beats for your well-being. Trust me, you'll have a much better life. Why you want to carry all that weight anyway?" were her exact words. In looking at her and Daddy, I saw this to be true. I just don't know if I want to be Cora is all.

## 38

# IN OUR FUTURE I SEE

Marcus's cover and feature did not make the winter edition of *Decor* magazine as Gary originally planned. It did, however, make end-of-summer inclusive of a four-page spread, yours truly pictured on two of them, named and categorically identified, "Marcus Crawford and mate Jules Sinclair." Cora, naturally, purchased every copy available in Virginia and demanded that Jacklyn comb the Manhattan newsstands as well for reserves. Undoubtedly one would find its way to every member of the Augustus-Sinclair family stateside and abroad within the coming days. Over dinner with Marcus one evening, she in absentia made us address the five-month-old elephant in the room.

"I was talking to your mother," started Marcus.

"When will you ever learn?" I asked in jest.

"Seriously, J, she's not that bad."

"That's because she has ulterior motives where you are concerned," I said. "Let me guess, she wants you to sign her copies of *Decor* for the girls at the club."

"Took care of that days ago. Actually, she wanted to know what my intentions are with you, seeing as we have yet to discuss them, at least to her satisfaction."

"Did she, now," I said, trying to appear as nonchalant as possible. I too wanted to know what Marcus saw in the future for us but had decided some time ago not to press the matter. Raising my hands in defense, I said, "I swear she's not doing my bidding."

"Thought never crossed my mind," he said with a wink to the contrary. "But I do think she deserves an answer—don't you?"

"Yes, I do. I just didn't want to be the one to bring it up—in case you weren't ready to discuss it is all."

"So you have thought about it?" asked Marcus.

"Of course I have. I am a woman, after all; it's part of the natural order of things. I thought about it from the moment you left Carly's without so much as my phone number. You, sir, should be counting your blessings that I've managed to keep the matter off my tongue for this long. Clearly, I'm teasing . . . sort of. I have thought about it, but only casually," I conceded.

"Really," said Marcus, placing his fork and knife down to sit upright in his chair before leaning toward me. One side of my brain immediately started to race with the possibility of *oh my gawd is he going to ask me to marry him? I'm so unprepared. Totally should have worn the other dress—photographs much better*, while the other pleaded for neutrality. But he said, "I'm not ready to get married. Maybe in a few years, but not now."

"Oh . . . is that in general or just to me?" I said, crestfallen, feeling this the only logical next question.

"Well, I don't—"

"Don't do that. You know if you want to marry me, whether it's six months from now or four years from now, the same way you know every other important step in your life long before it happens. You're a decisive planner, Marcus, so don't dance around, just tell me. I can handle it."

"I know you can handle it, Jules. I just wonder if I can handle it if my terms are not accepted," said Marcus. "Are you even ready to settle down?"

His phrasing caused me to pause. This is not at all how I envisioned the evening going. Quite the contrary, when his driver Carlos arrived at the office to pick me up, I'd been pleasantly surprised when the door opened to see Marcus seated inside to greet me. My understanding had been that he might be delayed getting to the restaurant due to a last-minute meeting but would send the car for me. On the ride to Le Bernardin, we laughed and exchanged spirited tales about the day. He spoke of needing to make another trip out to L.A., even asking if I could find a few days to join him, as this visit would keep him there for about two weeks. I didn't know the specifics, only that there was a studio ripe for acquisition.

"I choose not to think of it as settling," I said. "Yes, I can see myself married to you, but if you can't, then . . ."

"I never said I couldn't see us married, Jules. I'm just not ready in the immediate future. There is so much on my plate right now that I have to be mindful of. Can you accept that . . . and wait?" said Marcus.

"Truthfully, I don't know," I said, blatantly aware that those words could very well mean I'd leave this table a single woman once again, but I had to speak my heart. "What do I do with feeling like a fool as the years go by and all that I was has been completely enveloped by your world, with no promise of anything more than being identified as Marcus Crawford's guest? Hell, Marcus, I already feel like that from time to time but I try not to show it."

"I would never ask that of you, Jules. If you choose to give it, then that is solely your decision, but it is not what I would want or expect. Your independence is one of the things I love most about you," he said. "Jules, I know that right now you think me oblivious but I'm not. I'm aware of what I am asking of you. I know what it feels like to wait on someone only to be disappointed. I won't do that to you."

"I'm not Sasha, Marcus."

"I was referring to my mother," said Marcus. "Is there an urgency in you that needs to get married within the next year, Jules?"

"No, but there is something to be said for taking the option completely off the table. It changes the dynamic of you and me. Growing up I heard Cora and Aunt Helen talking about how no man is ever going to buy a cow when he can get the milk for free.

Please don't laugh, I'm serious. Marcus, your stance is putting me in that position now, and if I am to believe you, then I must compromise myself in order for us to work, and I don't want to do that. You would not like me for doing that, how could you?" I said, pushing my plate to the side, finally abandoning all pretense of still having an appetite, much less eating the meal.

"You know, it's been a while since I had to think of someone besides myself. Sasha was the last. In hindsight, that relationship was more about control and wanting to craft a life that perfectly fit into a frame than of focusing on the substance. I want to be smarter with you. Can you just hang in there with me?"

"Why do men always ask that and expect a yes?" I said. "Tell me why I should."

"Because you will be my wife and the mother of my children one day if I have my way. Because I am on the brink of doing something big that I have never done before, and I need you with me. Because I—"

"Shhhh," I said, placing my index finger to his lips, stopping him from completing his thought. "Don't say those three words now, please, because some part of me will never believe you, no matter how sincere. If you need me and can see me in your future, allow me to figure out what I can handle."

"It's true, you know," he said.

The air between us was noticeably strained on the ride home. I reasoned aloud that it might be better if I slept alone, just for tonight. When we began dating exclusively, Marcus and I exchanged keys to each other's apartments and had often alternated nights spent at each other's place, depending on who was the first to arrive home. I could count on one hand the number of times we had gone to bed unhappy with each other. This, however, was the first time that we may find ourselves in the same city and not sleeping together, so I resigned myself to just letting the moment breathe. Additional words could only complicate things, and the ice between us was thin enough. Inside the elevator I pressed the buttons for both floors and told him that I was tired. When we reached the seventh floor, he exited uncontested.

The darkness within my apartment felt heavy, like an old acquaintance I knew all too well and was not excited to come in contact with again. I sat by the windowsill with only the illumination from the streetlights and taxis below. *Did I overreact? Was I too calm? Damn Cora and her meddling. I was not ready to have this conversation. Better yet, I wasn't ready to hear what I already knew in my heart to be true.* One of the fundamental things that made Marcus and me great is the clarity I have in seeing him as a man and not the storied knight that had wrecked me previously. Despite what Blake imagined seeing when he was her Mr. Potentially More, nothing about the Marcus I knew said he was ready for marriage just yet. Hell, his dating a non-model civilian monogamously still took conscious effort, for which I respected him. Marriage, while a future possibility, was for now a far different story, hence me trying my best to not entertain anything other than what we have presently, but that was before tonight.

The past few hours made his position unquestionably clear, no longer a speculation, and forced me to confront the one hurdle I still had yet to conquer since Tony: trusting what I could not see. In order to be fully with Marcus, I had to trust him entirely with my heart and now my future, with no guarantee of the implied protection those vows before God and all of our friends would one day provide. Could I do that now, after my experiences in love? Could I guarantee myself that, whatever my relationship with love was in the past, I would be smarter, more realistic now? Normally, I would have called Cora to discuss my heart, but seeing as how nothing pleasant would roll off my tongue, I opted for a long, hot shower instead.

Turning the faucet to the hottest setting my body could tolerate, I sat beneath the showerhead until a dense steam enveloped me. The beads of water falling invisibly through the mist hit my flesh hard and strong, and my body succumbed to its force, crumbling from the aggression trapped inside. This was not how tonight was supposed to go. We were to fall into bed intoxicated by the cuisine of Eric Ripert and tell some racy jokes before exploring our most intimate treasures, my legs spreading, allowing him to go deeper as I got wetter. Having waited nearly three months, I was overjoyed to discover that Marcus was a skilled and unselfish lover from the start of foreplay to the climax of orgasm and well into the afterglow. Sadly, the same can't be said for his domination of the covers whenever the time to sleep came, but that too he made up for in the middle of the night, awaking as he often did to find me only partially covered. In my mind's eye he stared at me intently, as one often does when debating the merits of a big purchase or tattoo, before tracing the contours of my face or shoulders with his hands, kissing me softly and then covering me. I know this to be true because sometimes I was awake only seconds before looking at him through the cast of the moonlight. Seeing him stir, I would rush to close my eyes, pretending to be sound asleep. Given the choice tonight, I would surely offer him every cover on the bed not to have this wall between us.

The heat from the water intensified my longing, making me want him more. After a few moments I stood to locate the shampoo, only to have my heart stop ever so briefly, at the sight of Marcus, "Is there room for me in there?" standing in the open door. Watching him undress my heart returned.

"Always," I said, inviting him in yet frozen in place.

"Here, let me do that," he said, reaching for the shampoo in my left hand.

For a few moments we stood face-to-face, both holding tight to the bottle before letting go and allowing our hands to express what words could not. My body pulsed under his touch, begging for more. His lips hungrily created a trail from the nape of my neck to the base of my stomach before traveling back up and taking my mouth. With one arm Marcus lifted me waist-high against the shower wall, holding my face with the other, and entered the deepest part of me that ached to receive him. Instinctively he thrust hard and forcefully, taking possession of my very soul, until I could no longer restrain myself from crying out his name, begging for more.

To me, morning was an intruder, but it was of no consequence to Marcus as he continued to sleep peacefully next to me, the bed-linens masking part of his body and my limbs covering the rest. Somewhere around twilight, the conflicts of my head and heart had returned. For what seemed like hours I gazed upon him longingly, in turmoil. My mind struggled to answer if he was worth the purchase of my heart for a season with no promise of a lifetime. My heart screamed loudly *yes*, but it had been wrong, very wrong, before, so I waited and looked admiringly at his high cheekbones and the way they converged into a well-proportioned nose; the fully defined lips that always seemed to be smiling, even in slumber.

"How much longer are you going to look at me before having your way with me?" asked Marcus, his eyes still closed.

"Who says I'm looking at you?"

"You are. I told you before I can feel you," he said.

"Well, then, feel this," I said, playfully taking his nipple between my teeth, eliciting a slow moan of satisfaction.

"Oooh, do that again," he pleaded.

"For the record, you said, 'I always remember you.'"

"So I did," said Marcus, now fully awake and flipping me over so that he was on top.

"Hmmm, I love that," I said.

"What do you love?" he whispered, lowering himself slowly onto me.

"Feeling the weight of you on top of me, holding me, inside of me. I never want to be without you."

"Good, 'cause I'm going to ask you something. Promise you'll say yes?"

"Kiss me. Then ask me," I said.

"Do you love me?"

"Yes, I love you, Marcus," I said, without hesitation.

"Good, 'cause I could never stand being in this lifetime—in love with you as I am—without you."

. . .

"Julesea, I don't like this one bit," said Cora. "You just got to New York, now you're supposed to pick up and move to L.A. with Marcus without so much as an engagement. That's not how I raised you."

"Stop it, Mommy! I've been here nearly two years. You're overreacting. Besides, we're not moving there. Marcus has been back and forth a few times this year and may have to be there a few months or more. You know I've been out before for a weekend or two seeing him. Now I will come out for a week or so at a time, when I can. That's all."

"That's all? It's that simple, is it? What about your job?"

"This is why I didn't tell you earlier. I knew you'd overreact."

"At least someone is. What about your job, Julesea?"

"I can't win with you, Mommy—one day it is family first, then it's career," I pleaded. "I can do both. When the time comes, Marcus is going to sort it out with Michael. It's not like I leave tomorrow and am going to stay forever. I thought you liked Marcus."

"Liking Marcus is besides the point, child. Listen to me—I did not raise you to have some man fight your battles. Did you learn nothing from the other one?"

Knowing better than to debate the merits and/or shortcomings of Tony, I said, "Daddy fights your battles."

"Daddy is also my husband, so he has earned the right. You understand the difference?" asked Cora.

"This feels right, so you have to support me, okay? I don't want to lose him, Mommy."

"You can never keep anything worth having with fear, Julesea. Release that and make your decisions from a place of strength, otherwise you will be looking over your shoulder all the time making bad decisions."

"That's not what I'm doing. Do I want to get married? Yes. Trust me, if I start to feel that Marcus has no plans to marry me, I'll let go. Please try to understand. I didn't plan for it to be like this, and yet it is. I love him, Mommy, so I want to support him. And before you go there, Marcus is not Tony. He doesn't keep secrets from me."

"Every man keeps secrets, Julesea. Even your father," said Cora, still bursting with disapproval.

"You know what I mean," I said.

"And you heard what I said. I don't like this one bit." Then Cora's tone came softer, more hollow. "Promise me this, you won't walk away from your career *ever*. A woman must have something of her own to ride out the tides of life." For the first and maybe the only time, Cora lowered the veil between faithful supporting wife and the desires of a woman with dreams deferred, giving me a glimpse into her personal regret for the road not taken. *If I were brave enough, I would have dug deeper to find out why, at this particular time, the matter of self-reliance is of the utmost importance to her. If I didn't still need the illusions of childhood that had cast my parents as perfectly unblemished superhumans, I would have asked.* "The day may come, and I pray that it does not but it may, that you awake and don't recognize the man you are with. What will sustain you, Julesea? You can't run off across the world forever. You'll have to make a home sometime."

"I hear you. I do," I said. "Let's not argue about this. I leave for L.A. tomorrow."

# 39

# 1 NORTH WETHERLY DRIVE

**B**ABE, WHY IS there an oil field in the middle of L.A.?" I asked Marcus on the ride up La Cienega from the airport. Unlike my last trip in, when he sent a car to fetch me, this time he met me at the gate looking quite SoCal, if I must say—and I do. His requisite workday designer suit had been swapped for a dark blue button-down dress shirt with sleeves pushed up, dark denims, crisp white Pumas, and gold-frame aviators—all of which seemed ideal complements to the new Aston Martin convertible that transported him there.

"It's always been there, baby. Maybe you didn't notice it before."

"Still doesn't tell me why it's there. Seems quite odd," I said.

"You're odd," said Marcus, affectionately squeezing the tip of my nose, "and hopelessly beautiful. You hungry?"

"Famished, actually. You know I never eat on domestic flights. Something about the whole process just seems unsanitary."

He laughed aloud. "See? Odd! Can you hold tight for about an hour? Steven has two properties to show us. He says they're close to each other, so it shouldn't take long. Afterward I'll take you to this great restaurant off PCH, Geoffrey's I think it's called. The views are amazing. You're literally sitting right on the ocean."

"As long as I can grab a juice or something before, that's fine."

"I know the perfect place. Have you had a Jamba Juice before? Oh, Jules, it's good. Fresh fruit, sorbet, and you can get protein powder, immunity, energy . . . you'll love it. There is one further up, across from the Beverly Center Mall. We'll stop there."

"Sounds good," I said, tilting my head back to enjoy the warmth of the dry sun beaming down. Though my flight left JFK at nine forty-five this morning, New York had already felt like a sauna from the end-of-summer humidity. "So what exactly are you looking for in a property?"

"Correction, what are *we* looking for," said Marcus. "This will be as much your place as mine, so I want to make sure you're happy, okay?"

"Our place, I like the sound of that," I said with a triumphant smile. "Nice. I guess that doesn't extend to cars, huh? An Aston Martin, really? I mean, who does that?"

"Hey, I have to represent."

"That's the excuse you're using?"

"Oh yeah," he said, looking straight ahead at the length of traffic coming into view as we descended the final hill into the basin of L.A. proper.

"And this has absolutely nothing to do with you living out some childhood fantasy you had at fifteen years old about one day moving to L.A., driving a convertible charcoal-gray DB9 with a tobacco interior down Pacific Coast Highway?"

"Honestly, I must stop telling you things," said Marcus.

"Never," I said.

The first property we saw was in a high-rise near UCLA in an area called Wilshire Corridor, enveloping both sides of a quarter-mile strip that felt more like Michigan Avenue in Chicago. The unit was spacious but lacked character. It was minimal in construction with expansive windows, as requested, but clearly factory-grade. We knew instantly that it was not a contender. The second unit located on the opposite side of the same street and closer to the Beverly Hilton hotel was older, with some personality, but quite small, prompting Marcus to ask if one of the bordering units was available so that he could combine them. Neither property was, so he requested to see something closer to Beverly Hills, preferably in a small-to-medium-size building that had substantial outdoor living space and a walkable neighborhood, unlike the busy Wilshire Boulevard that defined the Corridor.

Having spent his entire professional adult life with New York as home base, Marcus welcomed the time in L.A. but needed to replicate the Big Apple's conveniences as much as possible to alleviate the unsettling comparisons that plague so many East Coast transplants. Steven had a property in mind but had to check with his office to make certain that it was still on the market: a new limestone construction with about thirty units, located on Wetherly Drive near the Four Seasons Hotel, which Marcus had been calling home for the past few weeks. Without seeing the unit, I was immediately pleased with its location because the adjacent street was Doheny Drive. For some reason—I think it was the palm trees bordering both sides—the skyline was always perfect, powder blue, encapsulating my entire vision of what L.A. is supposed to be on any given day.

In order to reach Geoffrey's we had to take the Pacific Coast Highway into Malibu. The view was breathtakingly beautiful, with the pristine Pacific Ocean to the left and rough mountains to the right. Along the way Marcus maneuvered through surfers in wetsuits, darting without regard across the road, and caravans of weekend leather-clad motorbike clubs and uniformed cycling groups. After descending a major bluff past Pepperdine University, we reached Geoffrey's, sitting at the base of the mountain etched into the cliffside. There was not a bad view in the entire place, whether overlooking the water with various boats and surfers or to my right, where Marcus sat. On the drive back, Steven called to say the unit he had in mind to show us was no longer available but the penthouse was. The price was more than Marcus had wanted to spend, but we agreed to see it nonetheless.

"It's not a question of whether I can afford it, Jules. It's a matter of whether I want to pay that much for a property that is at best a transition home," he said as we pulled up to the building. From the outside it was pleasing, understated yet elegant with floor-to-ceiling windows and architectural balconies made of steel treated for an aged bronze or rust effect. I noticed that there were two grocery stores nearby, in addition to some galleries—a promising start. When we entered, however, I felt the building's austere elegance, like one of those beyond-perfect living rooms I was never allowed to sit in as a child, or the good china that only leaves Cora's cabinet for Christmas, one of Daddy's business dinners, or to impress the girls from the club.

Inside the lobby was a security desk, positioned between two waterfalls. Every guest was required to sign in. Once inside, a key card was required to access the main floors. The two penthouse units, however, were only accessible via a personal code that was programmed specifically to the unit and then the key card. For Marcus the whole process was charming, as it became another gadget to play with. To me it was a bit pretentious, but I dared not say anything as I could tell instantly that he was smitten.

On level PH, the sliding doors opened to reveal a single corridor with bare walls, a convex skylight running the length of the hall, and two double-paneled doors to each side. The unit on the right had sold, leaving us the north-opening door, which was a good omen, or so I had been told once before—*although east is best*. The entrance hall featured an abundance of wall space, perfect for his collection of contemporary art that always seemed ill-placed in the Manhattan home and overflowed the Bridgehampton one. After a few steps we were in the main room, with an open floor plan, chef's kitchen, and an entire rear wall of windows providing an unobstructed view of the hills from Hollywood to Beverly Hills. I won't lie—that view alone hypnotized me before I was wowed by the bedrooms or Bali-inspired rooftop deck that covered nearly half of the 2,000-square-foot property. My only concern was how long it would take to make the place feel like our first home and not a faux interpretation created by an interior designer, especially with most of my time being spent in New York.

．　．　．

Later that night, seated at the hotel bar, we talked about the unit. For his part Marcus said he didn't need to see anything else; he liked it. I confessed that something about it felt forced, like all the bad superficial stuff that I had ever read or heard about L.A.

"What if I give you the majority of the closet space?" retorted Marcus with big, pleading eyes.

"Well, that's generous of you, considering the closet is larger than most people's bedrooms, so that is completely unnecessary, but thank you," I said. "Listen, it's clear you really like this place. I don't hate it. Promise. It's just not what I envisioned in the whole sunny California dreamscape, is all."

"I know you want to be in the hills . . ."

Correcting him, I said, "Not necessarily the hills. Hancock Park is fabulous, all those big historic homes and picturesque lawns. Did you know that at Halloween they block off some of the streets, open all of the homes, and thousands of kids from everywhere come through to trick-or-treat? How cool is that?"

"When we have kids, I promise. As for now, I am not one for mowing lawns, taking out the trash, and such nonsense."

"I know, which is why they have people for that now, but that is besides the point. You"— I started, before being overwhelmed by his desire for me to love the Wetherly penthouse just as much— "we love it, so let's do it."

"Ahhh, that's my girl. You'll love it, you'll see," said Marcus, leaning over to nuzzle my neck. The smell of scotch emanating from his breath delighted my nose. "Ms. Sinclair, can I take you upstairs?"

"By all means. I thought you'd never ask."

· · ·

The plushness of the Beverly Hills Hotel bed did nothing to help me fall asleep. Eventually my tossing and turning disturbed Marcus, forcing him awake.

"Do I need to ask or will you fall asleep soon?" he said.

"Don't ask," I said, sleep-deprived and frustrated.

"Cora?"

"How did you know?" I asked.

"Isn't she always the voice in your head—besides, your dad called."

I sat up in bed and reached to turn on the bedside lamp. "Really, when? I didn't know about that."

"Don't think you were supposed to. Man stuff. He called after you and Cora spoke about this—coming to L.A., what it all means. He was worried."

"I told her not to be. I know what I'm doing."

"Do you?" asked Marcus. "I promised your dad I would never intentionally hurt you, Jules."

"Really, what else did you promise him? Because I know that could not have been enough for Daddy if he actually picked up the phone. And it wasn't about *fútbol*, dominoes, or fishing," I said.

"If you must know, I told him that I would never dishonor you or his family. I said that we are building something solid here," said Marcus.

"Well, that sounds wonderfully promising!"

Lying next to me, Marcus continued: "In order not to do that, I must tell you something, and I'm not sure of how you will react."

"It can't be any worse than telling me you're not ready for marriage, so deal with it," I said, my tone laced with the bitter taste of the pill I was having difficulty swallowing. "Obviously still adjusting."

"I'm not quite sure," said Marcus. "Jules, you have this great personal inclination for the everyman that supersedes everything you do, including work. It's one of the reasons we fit so well. Together we balance the scales in some grand way. If given the choice to eliminate an opponent and see them go without, you would opt to find a compromise and spare them grief. I'm not like that, never have been. My inclination is always to identify a goal, win, and whenever possible, be the one to sink the shot. Whatever casualty is left behind is just a matter of bad planning or, worse, poor execution by the other guy—it's intrinsic to who I am."

"Jesus Christ, are you trying to make me nervous? 'Cause I'm getting there real quick."

"Jules, what do you think I'm doing here in L.A.?" asked Marcus, now sitting on the edge of the bed with his back to me.

"Exploring the film business to invest in movies and stuff so I have something to watch, right?"

"Something like that, baby," he said, inhaling deeply to decipher whether he truly was ready to part with the information being held so closely. Rising from the bed to put on his robe, Marcus walked over to the desk for perspective and context. "Yeah, I'm here to invest in the film business, but not as a money guy. I'm taking over a studio, with a consortium, and I will run it."

"Okay, that doesn't sound too bad," I said with a slight smile, sensing there was more.

"In order to do that, I need some major capital support, the likes of which I have been brokering for years now. One of those is Nikolai Abramovich."

"Michael's Nikolai?" I asked. "Michael never mentioned anything to me, not that he should have."

"Not exactly Michael's Nikolai, baby," said Marcus, partially turning around to address me squarely, "and this is where I need you to understand."

"Nikolai is a contact I have had since my days at Goldman. Unbeknownst to Michael, I put him on his radar in order to gain control of Carly's . . ."

"Wait, I'm not sure I'm following you. Why would you do that? From what I know of Nikolai, Carly's doesn't fit his portfolio."

"It's a bit complicated, but the most basic version is this. The primary reason I got involved with Carly's was not entirely to help Michael. It was to help Nikolai. At the time he was my top client at Goldman and needed coverage for some holdings, so I used Carly's as the shell for those acquisitions—acquisitions he could not directly access for reasons not important to this conversation. As a result Michael has—correction—the whole Carly's investment group now has a vote in the future of those properties. Which never should have been a problem, since I control the largest single stake. Michael, however, goes and marries Carly, which I didn't see as a problem until a year or so ago when it came time to transfer them over. All of a sudden Michael starts speaking about expanding. Together their shares outnumber mine, and Mike has gotten greedy, trying to lay claim to what was never his."

"So Michael knows about this property?"

"Yes, of course, sort of. He knows it's earmarked for me, and in return the partners of Carly's have been paid handsomely to leave it be, if you will. Using it, building on it, was never an option. Some deregulatory events have occurred, making it possible for Nikolai to knowingly retain these territories. He's grown impatient and wants the holdings before activating his resources to move forward with the studio."

"But that makes no sense. In comparison, I would think a studio far more valuable than Carly's or some land it could sit on. I mean, it's just a restaurant in Manhattan sitting on less than half a block."

"On the surface it's just a restaurant in New York, but the portfolio, the sum of its parts, Jules, is quite valuable. That's the dispute. Over the years we purchased a sizable amount of real estate in Chicago, London, Brazil, Nigeria, and parts of the Baltic, all of which I oversaw. Those lands are worth a fortune, or should I say what's underneath them. Now Michael wants to feign amnesia and build, laying claim to something that was never rightfully his. To do so undermines the value, prohibiting Nikolai from getting the reserves on each. Hell, it's more valuable to leave as open lots, forests, and dry land."

"But what I don't understand is, why would Michael do business with Nikolai?"

"Because he doesn't know about our relationship and can never find out, at least until everything is done," said Marcus.

"So then, you are not trying to kill Michael's dreams?" I asked, thinking about that first revealing discourse with Michael in my office.

"Truth be told, I couldn't care less, as long as he's not expanding into one of those locations. Ridiculous, this all is. I've done what I could to force him and the board to do their own research in order to see that we would only lose money in expanding over some supper club that would never return even a quarter of the selling or licensing costs, for that matter. Initially, Carly, like Simon, vowed to vote her proxy with me. Unfortunately, that changed after Michael leaned on his position as her husband. Which is why I went there for dinner last year and, in a moment of admittedly poor judgment, allowed it to be known that you and I had dinner days before. It was not my intent, but Mike was being Mike, pushing my buttons, and I got careless.

"Anyway, with pressure from Nikolai mounting, I was left with no other recourse than to provide him entry and sway Michael. Even with Carly's support, Mike can't hold out forever. He needs the protection, he thinks, Nikolai will provide him to fulfill his dream; buying me out, take over Carly's and expand."

"So it was you who led Nikolai to me, so to speak," I said.

"Yes, but that was a matter of circumstance, long before you and I were *you and I*. Planting seeds, you see."

"Got it. So these shares, I presume they are unrestricted, because Michael has no obvious reason to suspect Nikolai of any-thing other than being some wealthy man who is quite generous with his money and whom Michael has run a good pitch game on, I take it."

"Yes, something like that," said Marcus. "And potentially these shares could be sold or voted anytime against Michael, making him lose everything," I said. "So, are you going to push him out or just sit there and watch as Nikolai does?" I asked.

"I haven't figured that out yet. I know what I would like to have happen," Marcus said matter-of-factly.

"Listen, I know you two aren't on the best of terms right now, but he is your friend. Is it really necessary? There must be another way to get what you want, give Nikolai what he is due, and leave Michael with his dream."

"I wish, baby, but it's not that simple. Mike won't budge, and I need the alliance that Nikolai's multimedia and communication businesses will give me in Hollywood." Marcus paused to take my temperature on this line of conversation, pouring a glass of Pel-legrino. "Jules, taking over a studio is a costly enterprise, and it can't be done with haste. The shares must be purchased over time. Alliances within that machine must be built with everyone from agents to producers and countless executives. In order to do that and not lose everything I have worked for, I need resources and even more extensive relationships or else these past years have been for naught."

My mind was still racing to properly assemble the complex puzzle unfolding before me, even more so to grasp this unscru-pulously methodical and unflinching side of Marcus. "And for this dream you would betray Michael, just to get what you want?"

"Is that any different than what you did to Blake?" asked Mar-cus, with discernible agitation in his tone. "Did you not betray your precious Friend Code or whatever it is to get what you wanted?"

"That's different," I said, stung by his words. "How could you compare the two?" Since that revealing night at Carly's, Marcus had never brought up my handling of the whole affair in a manner that placed blame or criticism at my doorstep. Quite the opposite, he provided a shoulder for me to cry on immediately after Blake unleashed her verbal rant on me and when I received her subsequent e-mail from abroad telling me that payback would be hell—he just listened and said everything was all right.

"Listen, Jules, we're getting off track. I didn't say that to hurt you," said Marcus, placing his water on the bureau to embrace me around the waist. "I am telling you all this because I don't want to lie to you. But you can't push back like this. I need to know that I can trust you."

"You'll destroy him. Do you understand that, Marcus? Do you even care? Michael has his faults, yes, but he has been good to you. Please, find a way to leave him with something. His life is that place."

"It matters that much to you?" asked Marcus, now stepping back to survey my face. "Why do you care so much?"

"Because he's been good to me," I said.

"Then I will try," said Marcus.

"Don't try, do," I said. "Now let's go back to bed, please. I want to dream this away."

The lights were off now, but my eyes were wide open, surveying the ceiling. It's not that I expect Marcus to be perfect, but this whole situation makes me wonder about what is at the root of this man. Had I explained away too much of his alpha drive, seeing only what I wanted to see? He must have sensed my restlessness, because he shared one last thought before we both said good night to this conversation. "Jules, try not to judge me harshly as your inclination is to favor Mike in all of this. I know you don't think that given the chance Mike would do the same thing or worse to me in order to preserve his dreams, but he would. I know him far better than you do. I know what he is capable of. After all, he taught me how to play this game and to survive."

"I just don't want to be caught in the middle," I said, not turning to look in his direction.

"But you are, Jules. You have been since the moment we decided to make a go of things," he said, grabbing hold of my free hand that lay immobile between us.

"So I go back to NYC, work alongside him knowing that forces are conspiring behind his back, and pretend as if I know nothing?"

"Yes, until I figure out how to leave him with something, as you asked."

Of all the things that Marcus could have told me, of all the things I might have been better prepared to hear, this was not it. My last thought before falling asleep, and for days thereafter, was how I could have responded differently, if not supportively, then more neutrally, so as not to elicit the looks of doubt I saw every once and again in his eyes when addressing me during the remainder of my trip that week. At the very least, the gross miscalculations I made would never have provided the foundation for our blowup. "Marcus, is there anything else I should know?"

"No, my sweet."

•  •  •

"Darling, why do you always call me from the plane just as you are about to take off? You know I hate being rushed," complained Richard. "I know what Marcus told you is troubling—makes no never mind for a multitude. Just keep your head down and focus on doing only the job that Michael pays you for and protecting the relationship you are in with Mr. Crawford."

"Easier said than done, Boulton. I just wish I knew why this bothers me so. It's like this reveal has painted everything between us that came before in a totally different light. Before, when I looked at him, I was clear, good or bad, modelizer or not, about who I saw. Now, I don't know. You know?"

"Do you want to hear the answer or shall we continue into round two of 'This Dysfunctional Life with Jules Sinclair'?"

"You know I am always up for a good game of denial," I said in jest.

"Well, then, you are conditioned for self-sabotage, my love. You and every other girl like you who grew up watching *Sabrina* or *Pretty Woman*, swearing by a standing brunch appointment after your Saturday-morning mani-pedi. You want the fabled Linus Fairchild and Edward Lewis types for what they represent on a one-way screen, so you romanticize an ideal that is never possible, choosing instead to fast-forward through the uncomfortable bits. How much time do you actually spend in reality? I'll tell you. Zero. So when the complexities and motivations of a three-dimensional relationship with real emotions, messy motivations, and flawed human matter present themselves, you are unable to cope, leaving you no other recourse but to self-destruct."

"Well, that's grim," I said, casting my eyes downward, away from the flight attendant signaling me to turn off my phone now that the doors were closed and the plane was ready for takeoff.

"Honey, I'm a wise old gal. Shoot, I'm somebody's papa now, so I know. Step over and around, don't jump in. You've done that, it's lonely and unfulfilling. Make you a—"

"Bugger, I really have to go now. The flight nazi is giving me the evil eye."

"Of course you do," said Richard theatrically.

"Don't be like that. I have to go. Bye-bye, kiss the baby for me, bye," I said, hastily powering down my phone before the approaching attendant made an example of me.

# 40

## DOMINOES

THERE IS SOMETHING frightening about knowing too much. Independent of how much time passes before the proverbial hammer drops, you are always on edge, testing out different physical reactions and tonal inflections to convey that you are just as shocked by the event(s) as the victim.

I have been back (and forth) to New York for nearly four months now since the conversation with Marcus (and the one with Richard). In that time I've quietly observed the infiltration of Nikolai in and around the office, in the restaurant operations, around town, on the phone, and in e-mails setting up (oops, I mean cozying up to) Michael. I have seen Michael go from states of sheer elation with his chest poked out to pensive and measured in his movements and confidences, boxing mostly everyone out if their last name is not Abramovich or first name Raymond. And despite my best efforts to heed Richard's advice/warning to remain Switzerland, I have found myself making frequent overtures to ensure all that is our dynamic extra pleasant and comfortable while being careful not to ask for details. However, I can't shake the feeling that I am also making myself a sacrificial lamb. For purely different reasons, I care about the well-being of both Marcus and Michael, and in my own way I have tried to split myself as best I can to appease both—or at least give the appearance of it—but coming up horribly short, I'm afraid.

Carly's press had long been a well-oiled machine, not requiring the constant vigil it had before. Knowing this, and being preoccupied with other priorities, Michael was amenable to my taking a few days off twice a month in order to be in L.A.

"As long as your phone works and you're back Wednesday morning, do your thing" had been his parting words.

Sunday mornings through Tuesday evenings I spent in L.A. with Marcus when he was not able to be in New York, but it was shaping up that the quantity of my physical presence substantially overshadowed the quality of our time together. Like clockwork, I would land, taxi on the tarmac, and turn my phone on. But instead of a sweet note from him to greet me, there was always a While You Are Here Schedule to review of luncheons, dinners, pool parties, and screenings requiring me at his side. Knowing full well why such attendance was necessary, I seldom questioned or complained. *It seemed the least I could do given that my initial response was far from what he expected.* I will, however, confess this—my civility with some of the short, socially awkward, bad shirt–wearing, grossly unattractive chubbies sitting on large wallets and their overly silicone-enhanced, botox-injected, bleached female company did wane from time to time, but not enough— I thought—to come off as rude or negatively impact Marcus. In the few moments daily that we found ourselves alone—driving to something, coming from something, before bed or morning coffee—we seemed to be extra polite. I can't dare speak for him, but I can say that for my part, I was too aware of my limitations to encourage a conversation. Everything was moving so fast, and I didn't want to know anything further than I did, so I began framing the little dialogue we did have. Soon there was no denying that the comfortable ease that resides in the silence of a naturally compatible relationship had become strained. Anytime I felt him preparing to share whatever was on his mind regarding Michael, Carly's, or Nikolai, I would speak of everything else—my friends, their lives, their jobs, their opinions, the decorator we had hired since I conceded the reins of outfitting the L.A. condo after the first month. Eventually he stopped offering and, instead of shining a spotlight on the elephant in the room, he would skirt the matter.

"I miss being on the couch with you reading the paper, Jules."

"Me too."

. . .

Wednesday morning through Saturday evening, I was in New York, living out of my office. For whatever strides the adult me had made, my apartment (or should I say my insane closet with a kitchen) spoke to disorderly collegiate days past and to my current emotional state in trying to appease two masters. Seeing how chaotic the first mornings back in New York were for me, Jacklyn got into the habit of going to my place and gathering a few items to store inside my office. This enabled me to go there directly from JFK and get a solid two hours or more of a disco nap before barreling into my workday. Her reward for going above and beyond the call of duty was various appreciation gifts from around town: Bliss Spa certificates, Bergdorf's or Saks's gift cards, a Crunch Fitness membership, a dinner or two on my expense account. From her twenty-three-year-old point of view, she was happy to do so, as I was living exactly the life she fantasized—*the very one* that Richard had criticized on the plane. I was Audrey Hepburn in *Sabrina* and Julia Roberts in *Pretty Woman* sans the whole prostitute "safety pin to hold up the boot" thing. For her, everything was simple and free of baggage. I envied Jacklyn for that. How could it be possible that a mere seven-year age difference could render such vastly different perspectives? I bet, given the chance, Jacklyn would be clear to step over and around and leap!

"Hey, Jules. Welcome back. How was your Labor Day in L.A.? I bet fabulous. Did you see Brad Pitt? I love him," said Jacklyn as I emerged from my office after one such rest.

"No, but I did see John Taylor, still hot," I said.

"Who?"

"You can't be serious. John Taylor from Duran Duran ... 'Hungry Like the Wolf,' 'Rio' ... forget it," I said. *Clearly, seven years accounts for more than I thought.*

"Um, okay, Michael stopped by earlier and wants to see you. I knew you were still asleep, so I told him you were stuck in traffic on your way to the office."

"Rock star, Jacklyn, rock star! Did he say what he wanted?"

"Nope, only to come see him when you get in."

"In that case," I said, reaching out for my double espresso that was waiting at the ready, "I had better go see what the boss wants."

My watch showed the time to be 9:45, making the traffic alibi completely possible. Simone was away from her desk when I arrived, so I proceeded to Michael's door, knocking before letting myself in, and found him at his desk in the midst of a call. From the sound of things, he was either bored yet obligated to endure the caller or it was Carly—*like I said, bored yet obligated.*

"Jet-setter, how's L.A.?" asked Michael. "Did you see anyone famous?"

"What's the obsession with that? Jacklyn just asked me the same thing," I said.

"Well, what else is one supposed to do out there? It's a one-industry town."

"That is true. If people aren't looking for stars, they are trying to be one," I offered.

"Yeah, muthafuckers see them lights of Hollywood and get intoxicated. Speaking of getting caught up, how's our boy doing out there?"

"He's good, adjusting but overall enjoying himself," I said, feeling the hairs on the back of my neck stand up.

"Good, good. Glad to hear it," said Michael, not taking his eyes off me. "That Hollywood game is a different animal, I'll have you know. Still don't understand why he wants to explore the VC investment side of things out there."

"VC? Michael, you know they call themselves investment bankers now," I said, trying to mask my discomfort with the direction of the conversation. "'Venture capitalist' is taboo."

"So it seems. Everybody's trying to reinvent themselves these days, going from finance to studios. You know what I mean." *Definitely a statement to be avoided and not a question.*

"I guess. Are you?" I countered, attempting to redirect the conversation away from Marcus.

"Me? Just trying to survive every day holding the vultures at bay and keeping my little part of the world running smoothly," he said.

"Effortless," I said, pretending to be oblivious to the targeted statements Michael had made. "So what's on your mind, chief?"

"A few things, actually. I'm doing London. Nikolai and I have been speaking about it for some time now. Been putting some things into play."

"Nikolai wants to open a location in London?" I say skeptically. "I thought he was a silent partner like Marcus and Simon."

"Like I said before, everybody with a dollar has a voice. I'm just glad this one is in favor of supporting me and not tearing me down. What do you think? You lived there for a while, worked at Conrad before I brought you in here."

"London's great, very metropolitan, as you know. Has a huge nightlife scene with theater, music, private clubs, et cetera. It's a financial capital with a diverse group of people, many of high net worth, desperately in need of marquee restaurants with good food. Nothing like Carly's is there."

"Exactly what I was thinking. Any drawbacks you can think of?"

"Off the top I would say the temperament. If you're going to open there, design it with the spirit of a Londoner, that consumer, in mind. For example, they have a much stronger appreciation for vintage soul music than we do, so an adjustment to what talent we offer would need to happen. Don't just go and plunk a U.S. rendition there—it won't work, and the Brits will tell you quickly."

"Good point, good point. I gotcha. What else?"

"Location, something central and resurging, like here in the Meatpacking District."

"Okay, possibly Shoreditch, so let's say I did all of that, do you think it would work?"

"I have no doubt," I said.

"Great, so if I were to tell you that I am looking to break ground in a matter of weeks, September seventeenth, to be exact, on a location, what would you say?" asked Michael.

"I would first say that you are insane. Second, I would say there is the matter of local government support, permits, and union contractors to contend with, and a whole manner of other minute details that are equally as involved, requiring more than groundbreaking, especially the Michael Thurmond Kipps kind, with cameras and news outlets present. Last and most important, the time commitment. How are you going to split the time between London and here? Specifically, being away from Kaylin for such a long stretch of time? This is not something I could imagine you doing from afar."

"As to the first, maybe. To the second, all of that is long under way. Nikolai has some resources. Now, as to the last, well, that's where you come in. I want you to run point on London when I'm tied up here," said Michael.

"What?! I mean, why?" I say, torn between being wildly elated at the opportunity and panicked about the impact it would have on my life.

"You know the terrain, Jules, and you know what appeals to me. I am not saying for you to be there full-time but for a few days every other week or so, to get a firsthand look at how everything is coming along. Some of the visits we'll do together. Think you can handle it?"

"I already said you were insane, right? So I shouldn't repeat myself. Michael, are you absolutely certain about this?" I asked at the risk of exposing that I knew far more than I let on. "London is a very expensive city, and to do anything close to what you have created here is—wow, I can't even imagine how expensive it would be, the type of financing needed to pull it off."

"You let me handle that. As I said before, I've got deeper pockets now. I'd need you there on the ground, ready to go, by September eleventh."

My mind was racing as I sat there before him, drumming my fingers along the desk. What an opportunity; overseeing the debut of a restaurant from the ground up would be a major enhancement to my career. Cora would be thrilled, but the explosion in my relationship? I had already put an unfathomable distance emotionally between Marcus and me, but now I would be putting a physical one there as well. Realistically, there was no way I could go to L.A. as often, and not at all until this project was completed. Hell, I was barely making the five-hour flight. There was no way I could handle the twelve hours from London to L.A. direct. I didn't need to consult anyone to know that the ramifications of this would mean the end of us, and there was one thing I was absolutely certain about: Losing Marcus as a result of a direct action on my part has never been an option.

"Can I get back to you about this?" I said, getting out of my head and refocusing on Michael. "I need to speak with Marcus first."

"Really? I didn't know things between you two were so serious, to the point of discussing the merits of smart career decisions," said Michael, rather snidely. "I wonder how often he returns the courtesy?"

"We are serious, I'll have you know. Why else would I be back and forth to L.A. as I have been?" I said. "Trust me, it's not for the smogged-out air and wheatgrass shots."

"Well, let's hope he knows that," said Michael with a detectable cut in his tone.

"Huh? Why would you say something like that?" I inquired.

"Oh, nothing. Just guy stuff. You two talk and let me know. I'd like a decision sooner than later."

Getting back to my office, I asked Jacklyn to ring Marcus. This was the kind of news I'd prefer to discuss in person, but that would mean keeping it to myself until week's end when I got to L.A., and that would be impossible to do. I'd go positively mad, so why risk it? As I waited for him to answer, my thoughts returned to Michael: how opening in London like this so soon seemed irrational and unlike a decision that he would make cavalierly, but then again maybe it is not, if he has the opportunity and deep-pocketed support. Problem is, I knew the motivations of that support, so I couldn't help but think Michael was being positioned to be in over his head real soon with what he would come to owe Nikolai if—scratch that—when he defaults on the only collateral he will have left: his interest in Carly's and its holdings. I knew for certain that if backed into a corner, Michael would readily sell his interest in the holdings before parting with Carly's.

An hour or so later, Marcus called back. He'd been in the midst of a morning tennis match and left his phone in the athletic club locker. Having played an energetic match and won, his spirits were high, so I jumped right in with my news, leaving no room for him to interject until I had completed all I needed to say and laced it with so much enthusiasm that he would find it hard to offer no support.

"Well, that is some news indeed," he said, his demeanor calm, giving nothing away and offering less. "Is this what you want to do?"

"Are you kidding me? It's a huge opportunity. I can't believe you didn't tell me that London was happening after everything," I said, bouncing in my chair. "I am over the moon at the possibility of it. Aren't you?"

"I can see how you would be. It just seems like a piss-poor time to be away, you know?"

"I do, but Michael said it would not be permanent. Mostly when he is unable to be there, you know, for a visit here and there to make sure all is in line. I mean, I know this cuts into our L.A. time, but it's not forever. Besides, we are great at long distance," I said, my tone having lost its earlier excitement as I listened closely for any warning that Marcus's response might provide. Yet it still offered none. "We can handle that, right? Of course we can!"

"Yes, of course," he said. "Listen, I have to get out of these clothes. I'm going to be late for my doctor's appointment."

"I didn't know you had a doctor out there. Is everything okay?"

"Yes, just some routine stuff, a few tests, nothing serious. Let's you and I discuss this in person when you arrive. Okay?"

"Sure. You'll let me know if there's a problem or anything with the doctor, right? I didn't know—"

"Indeed," he said, hanging up the phone.

"Okay, bye then. I love you," I said into the dead receiver.

# 41

# DETONATION IN 3 . . . 2 . . . 1

HERE'S THE THING *with being on cloud nine—it's not real and can never be sustained. It's a euphoric state of mind that can dissipate as quickly as it appeared, leaving the victim crashing down to earth, much the worse for wear.* Marcus had not been as excited about the news as I'd hoped, but it was far better than it could've been, so that was something. On Saturday, we would discuss the slight adjustments to be made here and there. To me, it seemed only right that, given the amount of time I'd devoted to being with him in L.A., he could put himself in London when I am there or back in New York into our old life. Easy. But first I needed to tell Michael the good news.

Simone was now at her desk, smartly dressed as usual in a black sheath dress and matching cardigan with her red-lined Prada reading glasses balanced on the bridge of her nose. In the years that I have been here, it is fair to say that the only speck of color the woman owns outwardly is those glasses. Although I am convinced that she wears racy pink, red, and animal-print lingerie under her work staples. *I mean, she must, no woman can live by black, gray, brown, and dark blue alone—not even a native New Yorker.*

"Hi, stranger, is the boss in?" I ask, making my way toward his door anyway.

"He is, but now is not a good time," she says, causing me to stop. From the interior I can hear Michael's raised voice, and it's explosive.

"Who is he yelling at?"

"Not sure. He told me to jump off the line," says Simone.

"You're totally lying, Simone. I know you know. You had to put the call through, so come on, dish! Who is it? Last time I heard him like this, he was going in on Carly over Marcus."

"Well, this time he's going directly to the source. He is on with Marcus. You still want to go in?"

"Hmmm, no," I said, feeling in my bones that something about this was far from coincidental. "When Michael has had a chance to calm down, tell him I came by to discuss London." Better to make a hasty retreat and call Marcus. But no sooner did I turn to leave than Michael opened the door, obviously charged and ready for battle.

"Simone, get Nikolai on the phone," he said, before laying eyes on me. Then—"Jules, how long have you been out here?" He looked suspiciously from Simone to me.

Before Simone could interject, I said, "Just got here," shooting her a quick look to silence any commentary she might give to the contrary. "Came by to let you know that I am on board for London."

"Really?" asked Michael with a slight amount of disbelief. "And Marcus is aware of this?"

"Yes, of course. We spoke about an hour or so ago. He didn't have any objections. We just need to work out the details, you know, time together and stuff, when I get to L.A. in a few days."

"Ha, well, look at that shit. With you he's all calm and amenable. With me he is in hysterics, threatening shit like he is running things. I guess that's to be expected with everything he's dealing with right now," said Michael.

"That does not sound like Marcus at all. He's done a lot to make this possible—what do you mean 'everything he's dealing with?'" I asked, remembering that he was at the doctor's, a matter that seemed to have slipped his mind in earlier conversations. "What do you know that I don't? It's the third time today that you have made some offhanded comment or other about him."

"Jules, it's not my place to say, but I can only imagine how difficult it is for Marcus to keep things straight, trying to take over Inception Studios, dealing with Blake and the baby. Now this. No wonder he was unglued with me on the phone. You going to London had to be the last straw."

"Wait, what are you talking about?" I couldn't believe I had heard correctly. "Blake and what baby?"

"Michael," said Simone, rising from behind her desk, attempting to halt the impact of his words. "Don't—"

"What, Simone? Jules is family. If I don't tell her, then who will? Clearly not Marcus."

"What baby, Michael?" I yelled.

"Jules, lower your voice. I hate to be the one to tell you this, but Blake has a baby and Marcus, well . . ."

"You're lying," I said. "Why would you say something like that, Michael? That's crazy. Blake and Marcus haven't seen each other in more than a year. You're mistaken. Take it back."

"Wish I could, baby girl. Shit, I'm sorry. Maybe I shouldn't have used those words exactly," said Michael, "but that seems about right. Her daughter is a couple of months old, so . . ."

"Michael, STOP IT!" yelled Simone, coming from behind her desk to my side. "Jules, honey, are you okay? You don't look so good. Why don't we sit down?"

Brushing her off, I said, "Simone, why is he saying that?" But she had no words to offer, only her arms to hold me up with. "Michael, why are you doing this?"

"I don't want to see you throw your life away, Jules, on a guy like that. I told you I didn't like it when you started dating, but I remained silently supportive. Now, with Blake and the baby, I can't stand by and watch."

Grabbing my stomach before retching, I said, "I think I'm going to be sick." I broke away from Simone and ran down the hall to the restroom, throwing myself over the nearest vestibule and trying to empty my heart of the shards.

"Jules, you all right?" said Michael from the other side of the stall.

"GO AWAY, Michael. I don't want to hear you anymore. Just go away."

"Listen, I know you're upset, but I am not the one you should be upset with. I am shocked as well." My sobbing turned into accelerated short breaths. "Jules, it's going to be okay. You go home, rest, and just focus on London. It's exactly what you need to put all this behind you, you'll see. Okay? Jules, are you listening to me? Let me hear you."

"Yes, when do we leave?" I asked.

"That's my girl. I'm bringing you in on Tuesday the eleventh, remember. You can rest up. I get in later in the week. We'll paint the town."

"Okay," I said weakly from a crouched position on the floor.

"A word of advice, write this whole situation off. Don't talk to him. Delete him from your life from this moment on. I told you he'd turn on you, didn't I? Forget him, he's not worth it."

"Okay."

"I'll send Simone in to check on you. Carly and I have plans for the theater tonight, so I have to go."

"Okay."

•  •  •

Night had fallen by the time I awoke on the sofa in my office to persistent knocking at my door. The details of how I had gotten there were jumbled. My eyes swollen, nearly shut from a torrential cry, my heart shredded beyond recognition, I had nothing more to say, nothing to give, so I just lay there wishing whoever it was to go away and let me be. After a few lighter knocks, the door opened to reveal the shadow of an all-too-familiar figure who deserves far more from our friendship than the persistent drama I seem to consistently bring: Richard.

"Oh, dear," he said, rushing to my side and kneeling to help me sit upright. "How long have you been in here like this?"

My voice hoarse and cracked, I said, "I don't know. Simone brought me in, I think. I don't know. What are you . . . ?"

"Jacklyn called. What happened?" asked Richard.

"Marcus, he . . . I thought we, but he—" I stumbled over my words as the thoughts ran together. I couldn't bear to hear the truth come from me, so I just shook my head and closed my eyes.

"He what, dear? Is he okay? What happened?" asked Richard, brushing the matted hair away from my face. "Let's get some lights on in here." The harsh glare made me wince, forcing Richard to dim them to the glow of a candle. "Do you want something to drink? Let me get you something."

"Blake has a baby, did you know?" I said.

"Yes, poor child, and I do mean that, baby, but let's get to that later, under better conditions."

"It's Marcus's."

"You can't be serious," exclaimed Richard, standing at the bar, stunned. "Why would you think such a thing? She has been abroad with her Greek traipsing the globe for nearly a year. There is no way."

"Yes but the baby—"

"With Stavros—"

"No! Michael said it's Marcus's. That it's a girl a couple of months old and it's Marcus's," I said, waiting for Richard to refute my words, but he didn't. Instead he said "oh" and went silent, quietly doing the calculations to determine if there was a possibility that maybe just maybe Marcus could be the father to Blake's baby. "Have you seen them?"

"Afraid not," he answered, sensing it best not to contradict the probability of events.

"So it's possible," I said, choking back fresh tears.

"Jules, anything is possible, I guess. What did Marcus have to say?"

"I don't know. Haven't spoken to him. *Not* speaking to him," I fired back angrily. "What could he say? It's unexplainable."

"Dear, I am not making an excuse for any of this because I don't know the facts, but at the risk of upsetting you further, and that is the last thing I want to do at a time like this, I just have to believe that there is an explanation."

"But I heard them arguing before Michael told me."

"I don't know what to say, but there is a certainty about the two of you, so I must believe that there is a logical—oh dear," said Richard, looking at me crumbling under the weight of my despair. "Tell you what, let's get you home, out of these clothes, and into a nice hot shower. Everything is better after a shower. I'll even make you something delicious to eat, maybe some soup and my famous grilled cheese," said Richard. "You'll like that, won't you? Yes."

"Okay."

The only thing the shower did was make me more tired. I had no energy to do anything, so Richard helped me into pajamas and put me to bed with a bowl of tomato soup and a grilled cheese on a serving tray, which remained untouched. Before falling asleep, I asked Richard if he'd checked the machine just in case Marcus had called. He had not—another sign. Richard pleaded with me to call him, but I refused. What would I say? How much more pathetic could I look than by calling him about something he didn't even deem necessary to tell me but confided to Michael? Tomorrow would be better.

When tomorrow did arrive, I can't say it was better or worse as much as I willed it to be better. Yes, I wasn't crying, and I was dressed well in advance of Richard, sleeping on the left, the side of the bed that belongs to Marcus, but my spirit was parched and desolate. *How much I love this man—my best friend. The only person I can count on every time and yet here I am again making the same demands. Poor Jules, in a traumatic state with no regard for anything that may be happening in his world, always taking.*

When Richard awoke, I focused on rising to the occasion of being my best self in order not to bring on his looks full of sympathy and concern. I channeled the old Jules, surprising even myself with a genuine laugh over coffee when he confided that sleeping over was not the purely selfless act it appeared to be. Apparently, little Ms. Ming had a serious set of lungs and liked to raise the roof into the wee hours of the night, every night. Last night was the first time in the months since they had adopted her that he slept soundly.

"Honey, there is a reason the laws make it difficult for gays to adopt. I don't have the constitution for the upkeep. When can I just buy her a car and send her off to live in careless disregard for the privilege she has been brought up in?"

Independent of how many off-color comments I may make about my folks, I know that I am lucky to have been brought up in a family like ours. Having this frame of reference, I felt for the first time in our long friendship that I had some valuable insight to offer Richard as he and Edgar went through their parenthood journey. We spoke about the balance and compromises that parents make willingly and the ones that they must never make, like finding personal time to keep the romance going. Lord knows I heard enough and saw the loving results of Cora and Daddy's "couple time." Richard at one point brought me to laughing hysterics as he confessed to feeling that with Ming, he had unknowingly signed up for a lifetime of never winning the argument—which was starting to make him question his professional competence. I did enjoy the image of Richard becoming frazzled, but the thought of a baby girl, any baby girl, infuriated me. Little Ming, by sheer association of gender and age, forced me to think about what Marcus and Blake's child could look like. What her name could be. Most important, it reminded me of how horribly cheated I felt not being the first, the only, to bare his offspring—but I did not reveal any of this to Richard. I knew that had I given any hint of instability,

Richard would have remained at my side until the next day's flight, which is exactly what I didn't want. I needed to be alone, and he needed now to be with those who needed him most: his partner and daughter.

Once alone, I allowed myself to own my anger. Yes, I was dev-astated at Marcus's betrayal, but unlike with Tony, where I felt sorry for myself for far too long, I didn't feel self-pity this time. I knew that I had done nothing wrong to warrant this. I was angry as hell, and with each moment and no phone call, my anger grew. *This was not the man I knew. Did he change or did I make him over into someone he never was?* Strangely, in the midst of it all, there was a strength brewing in my rage that I'd never felt before. No longer did I feel the need to run and hide in a story line or country foreign to me. Hiding was the last thing on my mind. Quite the contrary, my life was the main event. I needed to see him and understand how he could do this to me. And with that fire, I boarded what was intended to be my last flight to L.A. Prior to takeoff, I sent him a text to say that I was coming in earlier than normal and would just as well take a taxi from LAX. I gave no details as to which flight, because I didn't want to see him before I was ready, nor did I trust myself to leave a voice mail potentially alerting him that something was wrong. Looking back, I wonder if Marcus ever really stood a chance to explain himself after my ambush, as he would later call it.

. . .

During our argument, he said that I'd made up my mind long ago of his guilt, so what was the point of continuing to go through all this? I said because it was the very least he owed me. And so we went the course, putting all our cards on the table. He told me that he was blindsided by Blake's pregnancy after learning about it one evening at dinner with Michael. To hear him tell it, it was innocent enough, and he thought no more of it until Michael made mention of the child's age, noting that he found it questionable that Stavros could be the father, given his advanced years and the timing. Taking this into account, Marcus attempted to contact Blake numerous times, to no avail.

When they did speak, Blake was less than accommodating. *Given how things had played out between the three of us, how could she be anything less?* Marcus, unable to bear the thought of having an unclaimed child in the world because of the abandonment scars he will forever carry from his own mother's desertion, volunteered to take a paternity test. Blake apparently agreed, claiming it was the least he could do. And all this, says Marcus, snowballed into the most destructive storm when Michael, by way of Annya, who unwittingly spilled the beans, learned that Marcus and Nikolai had not only known each other for years but were business partners.

Well, it didn't take Michael long—not having the complete story and believing Marcus to be his adversary—to determine that one way or the other, Nikolai was doing Marcus's bidding and trying to steal Carly's right from under him. Feeling duped and needing to act quickly, Michael committed to London, thereby securing something substantial. In the process, knowing what he knew of Blake's situation, he decided to leave a lasting calling card for Marcus: personal ruin.

Quite rich in loftiness, I said, "You should consider writing a screenplay instead of taking over a studio." I lashed out, fueled by pain and anger. *He's lying.* I remained unconvinced (unable to hear) that the victim in all of this was in fact Marcus. So when he stormed out, not to return, all I had were the fragments of our argument, his defense, our history, my baggage, and my love for him to replay.

Indeed, it is a horrible thing for a woman to be left alone with only her thoughts at any time, but especially in a town like L.A., where there are no streets to walk and get lost in. So I returned to

New York for a day, busying myself with all sorts of maintenance details to keep occupied, inflict pain, and force escape. There was the spinning class in SoHo, head-to-toe waxing with Ella, followed by a mani-pedi and threading on the East Side, a wash 'n' set uptown with the Dominican girls, and some quality time with a friend, who knows me better than most, in the Village that rendered me drunk enough to go blank but not enough to reduce me to a blubbering idiot—*I think.*

"I see you've started without me," said Tony, strolling into Frank's Bar and sitting down.

"Yeah," I said, sprinkling salt on my hand in preparation for a tequila shot. I know it's odd, but he's the only person I wanted to talk to, that I could stand to be around. "Something like that— ugh! That's good," I said, biting into the tart slice of lime.

"How many up are you?"

"I don't know, not many. Ask the bartender, he'd know," I said. Tony tapped the bar, indicating that he wanted to catch up.

"Damn, J—you know tequila is not my drink, but here goes nothing," he said, quickly throwing back three shots. "So you wanna tell me what's going on or should we just sit here?"

Fighting back tears, I said, "Can we just sit for a minute? Just need to be next to you for a bit, okay?" In between drinks and water chasers, I recounted the sordid tale of Marcus and me. He listened to everything until he was certain I'd said all that was to be said.

Shaking his head, he said, "You know, in my entire life I don't think I'll love someone more than I love you, Jules. That's real talk. I don't know which is worse, seeing you hurt like this and knowing that once I caused you similar pain or realizing that you are in love in a serious way, with someone else. Don't say it. I know it's selfish, but it's what's up."

"I'm sorry," I said, realizing how unfair it was for me to unload all this on him.

"Don't be," he said, signaling for another round. "Love is a good thing and I want that for you—always have. Just wish I could've ... Never mind. So, this dude, Marcus, left, you left, and here we are."

"Yep," I said, looking him in the eye, toasting and downing. "And I just feel lost—empty, you know? Like there's a huge chunk of me that's just out there and I can't put my arms around it—I can't find it. *My heart*—it hurts, and I'm so scared that it won't stop this time."

"J, you know I chased you for a few days after the whole Angie thing but stopped when I thought about what it all meant for us, why I did it, what would happen if I got you back, and that whole shit was crazy, yo. I wasn't ready and I knew it. I wasn't ready to love you with that all-encompassing kind of love you expected. I still needed to do me, and I know that sounds fucked up, but that's the truth. I'm telling you this to say, go easy on yourself, baby, this is the first blow, your emotions are racing all over the place and your mind hasn't even had a chance to catch up and figure things out. Give it a few days. Then you'll know what you need to do. Just ride that shit out. Hell, love is the biggest wave we'll ever get, better than any I've found surfing," said Tony, pushing my hair away from my face to dry my tears. "Damn, you're pretty."

"And *you* suck. I can't believe you stopped chasing after three days," I said, between laughter and tears.

"Hey, I didn't say it was three days, although that sounds 'bout right. *I'm just joking*—see, you can still laugh. All's not lost. I did it because I love you just that much, Jules Isabel Sinclair—I had to let you fly, knowing I'd never get you back," confessed Tony.

"Did that mean you had to go and tell *Carly* all about it?! *My God, that woman!*"

He laughed uproariously. "Ahhhh, shit! Yo, Carly is not a game! You hear what I'm saying? But her heart is in the right place."

"Yeah, I've learned that. She helped clear the way initially for Marcus and me."

Everything else that evening was a blur. By the time I boarded my flight on Tuesday morning out of JFK, anyone looking at me could see that I was the human equivalent of rubble inside, but it didn't matter. My only thought being to sleep the full five and a half hours it would take to get to London and revisit some old healing haunts. Whatever sleep nature did not provide, Ambien would. An hour or so before landing, I awoke with a tear-streaked face after having a lovely dream of Marcus and me sitting at Via Quadronno, sipping cappuccinos and laughing. It seemed so real. I could touch him, feel the moisture of his skin, smell the Hanae Mori cologne we'd picked out at Fred Segal the week before.

I was devastated to be awake and have to confront reality all over again.

# 42

## LONDON CALLING . . . AGAIN

**2001**

**B**UT MY LIFE is an ocean away, and if I knew how to stop looking outside of myself for answers, I could tell him that and get
out of my own way. *What would I say? I'm sorry—for what? For
not believing you? How could I even go down that road when I didn't
even know what the truth was?* Michael says it's his child. Marcus
says it's not, and under different circumstances, I would be inclined to believe Marcus, because that is what my heart wants
so badly to do. Experience, however, had showed me the cost of
blind faith, and while the time with Tony was good, it was also
a reminder. I don't want to be that fool again, I said to Richard
one evening later that week on the phone from the hotel when he
called to check in on me. During which time I also recapped my
time with Tony.

"Jules, please tell me you didn't do something irrational like
sleeping with the ex to get over the . . . You know where I'm going
with that, it's supposed to rhyme."

"Oooh, death to the great gay rapper once and for all," I joked.
"Relax, Richard. I know where you are trying to go, and it's un-
necessary. Tony and I did not sleep together. Although I am sure
I tried at some point. From what I can recall, I was wailing about
Marcus, then I remember seeing Ivan or Percy, one of them, and
that's it. When I awoke, we were both on the sofa fully clothed, all

buttons and zippers intact. I put him in a cab, and that was it. He did smell nice, though!"

"Oh, don't we all! Well, it seems people do grow up. Imagine that, there is hope for you yet, Jules," said Richard. As it stood, he was still the only person in my friendship/family circle who knew that Marcus and I were having problems. "Is that happening anytime soon?"

"I'm *trying*."

"Stop *trying* Jules, and do! Honey, you can't keep doing this to yourself," said Richard. "One way or the other, you have to know the truth. Marcus says that it is not his child. Do you believe him?"

"Yes, I mean I want to, because I want to be happy, but it does not add up. Why would Michael say that it is? Why would Marcus not tell me unless he was hiding something?"

"How would you have handled it if he had come to you?" asked Richard.

"I would have listened. Together we would have figured it out," I said.

With extreme reserve Richard asked, "Are you sure about that, dear? Correct me if I'm wrong, but didn't he come to you before with a highly sensitive matter and you were not as accommodating?"

"Entirely not the same thing," I said emphatically.

"I disagree. It is exactly the same thing, Jules. He trusted you once and you—"

"Stop, please don't say it. I know what I did . . . but this—" I paused, divorcing myself from the unjustifiable. "Michael is not just my boss, you know that—he's like a mentor. It all was just too much, like designer trail mix, it was . . . all wrong."

"I'm not saying that what he may or may not have done is right, but it is comparable."

"So what do I do? I can't go apologizing for something that I still don't have answers to," I said.

"Then do the only thing you can do. Go to the source and get your answer, honey."

"I told you. I'm not ready to talk to him."

"I'm not talking about Marcus. Call Blake. She is the only one who knows the truth."

"Are you insane?! I am the last person she wants to hear from after what I did to her. I mean, it's bad enough that I broke up the relationship she thought she had with him, but now I could potentially be standing in the way of her child's relationship with her father," I said. "You're not mad, you're certifiable!"

"It's the only way, and it's long overdue," said Richard. "The fact that you two girls could not get past unknowingly dating the same guy is beside the point. True, you should have been more brave in your dealings with her, I have said it before. But you girls were best friends long before Marcus came into the picture. At the first onset of friction, you threw all of that away instead of dealing with it head-on. Aren't you tired of doing that, Jules, with every relationship in your life? What happens when the day comes that you elect to throw me away?"

"I would never, Richard, never," I said. "Besides, I haven't spoken to Blake in forever. I wouldn't know how to reach her."

"Easy, dear, you call her," said Richard. "I just happen to have her number on hand, unless of course you would prefer to see her. That is possible too. She is in London right now, has been living there for some time, according to Joy."

"What would I do without you, Boulton?" I said, chuckling aloud.

"Thankfully, we will never have to find that out, now, will we?"

"Never," I said. "Good night, my friend."

I paced around the number Richard had given me for some time, staring it down like a fighter preparing for battle. I rehearsed what I would say and how I would say it many times over before picking up the piece of Sofitel stationery it was written on and going over to the phone. Independent of how she would respond to me, I would remain calm. There was no expectation of getting the friendship back, as I didn't believe that was due to me—but I was entitled to hear the truth.

After the first ring, a heavily accented Indian-British house voice greeted me—"Good evening, Giannakopoulos residence." Having thought the number I dialed was her direct line, I was taken aback, forcing the voice on the other end to repeat, "Hello? Giannakopoulos residence. Is anyone there?" After identifying myself and whom I was calling, I was placed on indefinite hold. At first I reasoned that Stavros's home was enormously large and for some reason not equipped with an intercom system, causing a delay in locating Blake. Then it occurred to me that, while I may want to speak with her, she may not want to speak with me, which was well within her rights. I was about to hang up when the voice returned, informing me that the lady of the house was putting baby Catherine down for the evening but would be available for tea tomorrow, if my schedule permitted. On hearing the name of my hotel, he confirmed that Blake knew the location of the Sofitel St. James, and would meet me there at 14:00. Hanging up the phone but still holding the receiver, I dialed Marcus's number, but was overwhelmed by a surge of panic in my chest that forced me to hang up before it rang.

. . .

Impossible. Of all the days and times to be running late, this is most certainly not the one. On Saturday, the site manager from the new property location called first thing to do a last-minute run-through before Monday's ceremony with Michael and Nikolai. After he assured me that the meeting would take less than an hour, I agreed, believing I had more than enough time to return to the hotel for afternoon tea with Blake. What I did not anticipate was being stuck in a massive gridlock of traffic, rendering me nearly twenty-five minutes late. With no mobile number for her, I called the hotel after the first five to alert her to the delay. The young woman at reception delivered a return message to me of "Not to worry, take your time," allowing me to breathe calmly until I realized how truly late I would be. My only hope was that Blake would still be sitting there some forty minutes later.

Nearing the roundabout at Piccadilly, I jumped out of the cab before it came to a full stop and sprinted against a traffic light into the hotel, looking from left to right. The girl at the front desk who'd fielded my earlier call saw my distress and directed me to the high tea room. Huffing and puffing, I ran into the parlor to find Blake alone, looking more refined than ever in a black puff-sleeve blazer, fitted indigo jeans, and drippy striped T-shirt. There was a stroller at her side with the opening covered, concealing baby Catherine's face and my answer. At seeing me, Blake rose awkwardly, smiling as I approached. Were we to hug, shake hands, or just nod? Uncertain of protocol, we did an awkward combination of all three.

"Wow, you look great," I said, "but you always did."

"Thanks, you too," said Blake, giving me the once-over. "Jules, you look amazing, but you were always fit. Your hair is still crazy beautiful. I always wanted those big curls."

"You're one to talk. I always wanted your perfect straight locks. Never satisfied with what we have, are we?"

"Never," said Blake. "Remember when you put that Japanese straightener in your hair—talk about a big mistake. I think I cried more than you."

"Oh, I know! Remember how self-conscious I was about dating Tony because he had more hair than me, and you said, 'Honey, dreadlocks don't count as hair. They're more like spiritual ropes to grab on to.'" We both said that last part in unison, clasping hands, losing ourselves in memories of great times past. "Oh, Blake, hair wasn't my only mistake, you know. I was bloody awful to you, and I am so very sorry."

"You were once, I'll give you that. But you were amazing the other ninety-nine times, Jules, so there is nothing to forgive."

"You don't have to be kind," I said. "You owe me nothing."

"I'm not being kind. I'm being honest. If it weren't for you, for us, for New York, *and for Marcus*, I would not be here, living the kind of life that I only dared dream about but never thought I might have one day. Not with the way I was going."

"Yeah, about that," I said, directing my comment toward the stroller. "Catherine—I mean. I didn't know, and then to find out from Michael. I was just blown away, you know?"

"I know! Who would have imagined me, pregnant, a proper mum, living in England. Insane!"

Perplexed by her response, I was unsure of how to delve further, so I erred on the side of caution and followed her lead. "Richard said the same thing."

"I bet he did, that old gay bag. How is he? I miss him. I miss you. Joy says he has a little girl around Catherine's age, God help that child. She'll be the only Barry Manilow–loving, overly articulate preschooler on the Upper East Side with a strong affinity for bridge and bourbon. Clearly she will need friends that money can buy. I can only imagine what else the old girl had to say."

Inhaling deeply, I said, "Well, in light of things, not much, as he's spent the majority of the past week consoling me." I stopped before feeling like a fraud. "Oh, Blake, let's not do this! Let's not talk like old times and pretend that you don't know why I'm here. I know you do. You must! I need to know whether you think I deserve to or not. Catherine and Marcus."

"Oh, Jules, I am so sorry for that. I was just upset. The weight wasn't coming off, and you know how I am about the chub—does a number on my head. My hormones were everywhere. I wanted to punish him for coming between us and I wanted to hurt you, although I missed you, because you were supposed to be there for me.

"Remember, we were going to raise our kids together—then everything changed," said Blake. "Knowing what I know now, I wish so very much that I could take it all back. The time I wasted feeling spiteful when everything I had ever wished for was right there with Stavros and here with Catherine." She pulled back the blanket and lifted the child into full view. *Oh my goodness, what an angel, all chubby with big brown inquisitive eyes, rosy cheeks, and a few raven strands at the crown. There were things about her that seemed like Marcus—her mouth, her nose maybe, but I couldn't be sure. His hair was dark blond, as was Blake's, but maybe there was some latent genetic thing manifesting in Catherine to produce her dark coloring. Who can tell anything about kids at this age?!*

"Would you like to hold her?" asked Blake, and she passed her over to me before I could object. "Ahhh, look at that, she likes you." Witnessing my awkwardness, she added, "You won't break her, I swear. Believe me! She won't bite as much as gnaw and drool."

"Am I holding her right?" I asked, shifting to find the right position as Catherine squirmed in my arms. Sensing my discomfort, she took the lead and smiled a gummy saliva-filled grin that melted my heart and calmed my nerves. *How could I ever—no matter what—how could I deny this angel from having the best, most loving of all, especially supportive parents like I had?*

"Blake, she is heaven. Of course Stavros would accept her, how could he not with this little face. Yes, yes you are," I said, playfully bouncing her up and down.

"He'd better accept her. She's just as entitled to his fortune as his other kids. I don't care what his ex says. Why, what have you heard?"

Caught off guard by Blake's comment, my grip slipped. "Oh shit, eek, sorry! What are you talking about?"

"What are *you* talking about, Jules?"

"Catherine, is she Marcus's child or not?" I asked, clearly so there could be no mistake this time. "Blake, I'm dying here."

"No, why would you ask that? Listen, I know I was wrong for allowing Marcus to take the paternity test, but I wanted to make him sweat a bit. Then Stavros found out and, well, let's just say he didn't approve. He said I was being childish. Maybe. Anyway, I thought to tell Marcus, but he forbade additional contact, so I told Michael before things went any further."

"I am *so* not following this," I said. "Are you saying that Michael knows Catherine is not Marcus's baby?"

"Of course he does. He and that old bat even received the birth announcement."

"I need you to start from the beginning—and make it simple," I said.

"Let's see, a few months ago Stavros and I had dinner in Knightsbridge with Michael and those Russian friends of his, Nikolai—don't trust him, by the way—and Annya. She is fierce, I love her! I was big as a house—you know, the unattractive stage of pregnancy—and a little extra cranky about everything, Little Miss Thing holding my body hostage, did I mention that?"

"Blake, focus," I said, having forgotten her predilection for unnecessary commentary when asked for specific information.

"So . . . Michael and I get to talking. He said something snippy about Marcus being slick and his blatant disregard for other people, yada yada, would serve him right. I didn't give it any thought again until Marcus started calling a few weeks ago demanding—you know how entitled he can get—to know about the baby. I didn't appreciate the intrusion or his tone, for that matter, so I told him if he wanted to be sure, then go ahead and get tested," said Blake, reciting the entire saga with all the salaciousness of a tele-novela. "You must believe me, Jules. I never thought he would take a paternity test, especially after I said the baby was not his, but he didn't believe me. So I called Michael to clear things up since they talk all the time. *Uh-oh*, what's wrong? You're twisting your hair. That always means trouble."

"Karma," I say, trying to suppress the dual desire to laugh and cry. "Oh, Blake, this life thing is so not easy."

"You're telling me. I mean, what crazy universe would trust yours truly with raising a child? I just don't know," she said.

"Well, know two things, lady. I am so very sorry for not being more respectful of us. I should have mined this dynamic, especially when a complication arose. Second, and most important, be careful. Michael is not your friend—nor mine, for that matter. He is only about self."

"We all are, Jules," said Blake with a laugh. "That's the one thing I have come to know up close and personal. We all just want the best the world has to offer that we believe will make our lives the most. The only hope is that the pursuit leaves minimal carnage. If you remember that, most things are forgivable."

"What about broken trust?" I responded, thinking about Marcus and myself.

"Just requires more work and a little bit of luck," said Blake. "Look at us. We're back together."

Amid a haze of cucumber sandwiches, scones, and a year's worth of delayed gossip, the afternoon zipped by. Blake and I had so much to catch up on. She and Stavros were planning to get married during the holidays in order to have Catherine baptized in the Greek Orthodox Church, despite very vocal objections— to the religious conversion, not the marriage—from her Mormon parents. London was not her ideal location, and she longed to return to New York, but would stay for now because it worked for Stavros's primarily Europe-anchored business. Within the next year or two, they planned to have another baby, bringing the Giannakopoulos brood to seven—two expensive ex-wives and a future missus committed to making her predecessors look like bargain shoppers.

Oh, how we laughed and caught up. I told her about my splitting time between New York and L.A., the offer from Michael, and his sinister role in Marcus's storming out. The latter of which she did not see as a problem. Apparently a monthly walkout was par for the course for her and Stavros. She said he, like Marcus, will always find his way back home. *How could they not with women like us!*

Soon the time had come for her to return home, as Stavros was adamant about having dinner together nightly. Before leaving, I promised to attend the wedding and she promised not to breathe a word of Michael's deception to anyone, allowing me space to deal with him in my own way, in my own time.

. . .

The feeling of laughing and crying—*otherwise known as being on the verge of a breakdown*—returned almost immediately after Blake and baby Catherine's departure, so I decided to take a walk for some fresh air. Starting on the desolate streets of Piccadilly, with its grand architecture, I found my way to Covent Garden, amid the hustle and bustle of shoppers, theatergoers, tourists, and schoolchildren. The noise and congestion were welcome accomplices to the matters in my head. With each step and sidestep to avoid colliding with a passerby, my life started to make sense, the comedy of errors abundantly clear.

On the one hand, I can accept that it was all worth it to see Blake beaming as she was, but then I think of my heart and the toll it all has taken. What cost is too much? Why is being a woman in today's world so hard? I have to believe that despite Cora's quiet longing for something proprietary, a career, given the choice she would not change her course because she has been loved abundantly and has lived happily, a comfortable, purposeful life. What has my purpose been? To be a pawn for others? Working toward their life's happiness while mine lies undefined?

When I lived here, I came to know what I wanted, and then I went to New York to live it. Somewhere along the way I lost track.

I got caught up. Michael's and Marcus's purposes became more important than mine. Michael's because he controlled my career. Marcus's because he holds my heart. So I gave everything away to both of them without holding firm to the things that are important to me. I gave away my power and caved to the fear of disappointing someone or getting hurt again, only to end up near ruin . . . *and starving!* But I'm going to get it back as soon as I get a bite to eat.

## 43

# FATHER KNOWS BEST

THE PANGS OF hunger in my stomach intensified with each passing block until I looked up to find myself standing in front of Mr Jerk, a Jamaican restaurant located in the heart of Covent Garden on a busy side street just down from the Donmar Warehouse theater. This has to be a sign, I think to myself, so I enter and order some stew and coco bread at the counter. Normally this place is busy every hour of the day and night. This evening, business was only moderate, allowing me to slide into one of the orange plastic booths and eat comfortably before walking back to the hotel. Awaiting my food, I pulled out my phone to make the only call that mattered. It's just after lunchtime in Virginia, so he should be in the office.

"'Ello, dis is Charles."

"Daddy," I say, instantly relieved at hearing his voice. "I messed up."

"I was wonderin' when you was going to call me," he said. "You ain't kill no one so da rest is fixable."

"How? What do you know?"

"Marcus called me the night ya two had ya roar. I was just waitin' for ya to find yur footing and pick up the phone. Poor fella, dem crazies bombin' the towers didn't make it any betta."

"Is he okay?" I ask, longing for any insight as to his well-being. We hadn't spoken in a week, and that was killing me.

"He's goin' to be fine, just like you if ya two kids can calm ya'selves down and take responsibility for one another. Makes no damn sense."

"That's easier said than done, Dad. Thank you," I said, looking up to find the waiter placing my order down.

"Where you at? Who ya talkin' to?"

"I'm at Mr Jerk, Daddy, getting some food," I said. "A lot of things were said and done beyond whatever he may have told you. I just don't know if we can get back to where we should be."

"Nonsense. You are exactly where you are supposed to be, at the fork in the road, faced with decidin' if this is the one love worth fightin' for. That's where you are. So which is it? What cha' gon' do?" demanded Charles.

"I'm trying to figure that out now," I said.

"No, you're not. You already have, girl, so stop foolin' ya'self and delaying ya life. Nutin' is wrong wit lovin'. Above all, builds character. Look at what it did for me and your mother. You tink witout that woman I would work so hardt to be a success? No, I'd be right there back in Jamaica playing in some roots band content wit a spliff and a Stripe, but I'm not." Hearing me laugh, Daddy continued, "That's my girl. Your spirit ain't broken if you can still laugh, and that is something to be grateful for. What do you want?"

"I want to be with Marcus," I confess.

"Then what you doin' in London in dat fake Jamaican restaurant instead of Los Angeles with Marcus, where you belong? Jules, I don't know everything, but I know some tings were said or done to make ya both run. Marcus is a solid man—a little light but a good fella nonetheless. I know he'll always provide and love you, if you allow him. The hardest ting for any man to do is lay hisself bare for anyone to see, especially the love of his life, but he'll do it for the right woman. It's scary as hell. Accept him. Stand by him. Don't try to change him."

"But what about me?"

"That's the only thing you can control. Stop fightin' wit ya'self, expectin' someting that is against your spirit. There is nutin' in ya upbringin' ya need to rebel against. What's there to prove? I know how we raised you all sheltered, provided for, and with unending love. Most of dat is good, some of it wasn't. All of it was for you to know what 'the most' feels like and never do without it. Dat's yur birthright as a woman—as my child. You've always had a choice, we madedt certain of that. Why you choosin' to work on two separate paintings for your life instead of focusing on one masterpiece?"

"When did you get so smart?" I said, smiling broadly.

"Happenedt the day you were born, bunny."

"I love you, Daddy," I said, choking back tears.

"Right back at you. Now get ya'self off dis phone and get home," he said. "I'd feel real guilty about goin' on dat fishin' trip up to Oregon wit Marcus next month while you two like dis, but I will. You know how I love my fishin'.'"

He was right. Fathers often are, saying little but saying the most when needed. I know what I want, and that is to be with Marcus for as long as fate will allow. Placing our relationship above all else doesn't diminish me, and if it does, the only judge and jury that matters is me. The rest will fall into place—it always does. *Leap and the net will appear.*

Arriving back at the hotel, I stop by the front desk to notify them that I would be checking out first thing in the morning, and if they could arrange transport to the airport, that would be great. Reviewing my reservation and seeing that I was leaving nearly a week early caused a moment of alarm for the desk manager.

"Ms. Sinclair, I do hope that nothing is wrong," he said, knowing that I was a New Yorker and thinking falsely that the World Trade attacks could be the cause.

Inhaling, I said, "No. Everything is perfect, actually. It's just time to go home is all."

"In that case, we look forward to seeing you again on your next visit."

# 44

# HEATHROW AND LAX

SECURITY AT HEATHROW was something out of a George Orwell movie. In order to make the 8:20 a.m. flight, I was advised to be at the airport four hours prior to departure, given the additional security precautions and that I was flying international. The night before, I didn't sleep. After packing, I sat to write my resignation letter. In light of everything, whether Marcus and I work or not, there is no way I could continue working for Michael knowing what I know. It's one thing to be caught in the crosshairs of dueling fire. It is quite another to be walked up to and cut down in cold blood for the sake of sending a message. And that is what he did to me, ignoring the fact that I was not some nameless person but an employee, a friend, a protégée. Over the years Michael had taught me many invaluable things. This, however, was not a lesson I wanted to incorporate into my life or business. True, I would again have to live off my savings, but thanks to his and Carly's generosity by way of salary and a rent-free apartment, I have time to find the next-best job, be it in New York or permanently in L.A., if Marcus will have me.

Two checkpoints before reaching the interior of the airport, only to stand in the security queue for a full hour and then some, before dashing down the causeway as my name is being announced over the loudspeaker, then reach the gate moments before the door closed—no small feat. *First class, as they say, does have its privileges.*

Finally secured in my seat, I started to unpack my purse of the in-flight reading selections I'd lifted from the hotel and pulled out the very envelope that was supposed to be given to the front desk at the time of checkout and delivered to Michael's room before he left for the groundbreaking this morning, which was to begin in about an hour. *Oh well, serves him right.*

Leaning my head back into the seat to decompress, I was startled by the ringing of my phone. My instinct was to just turn it off without looking, until I glimpsed Michael's name flashing across the screen. *Seems only fitting, I guess, for it to end this way. As Richard would say, "the dramatics."*

"Jules, you coming down? I'm waiting," asked Michael.

"Don't. I'm not coming, Michael," I said. "Tell me this, did it give you pleasure to see me like that?"

"What are you talking about?" he asked.

"Why did you lie to me about Marcus being the father of Blake's baby?"

"I didn't lie, Jules. Never said it was Marcus's. I said—"

"But you led me to believe it was the truth. Right there in front of people for everyone to hear, and then you encouraged me to leave. I trusted you, Michael! Why? How could you do that *to me?*"

"Jules, it's complicated," said Michael. "I'll explain it later. What's that noise behind you? Where are you?"

"I'm at the airport."

"This is not a game, Jules. What are you doing at the airport? Get in a car right now and make your way to the site. I'll meet you there."

"No. I'm out, Michael. I quit."

"You can't be serious. All this over Marcus? He's a big boy, Jules. He can handle himself, trust me. This little show of solidarity you're displaying isn't going to win you any favors. I should know. I was loyal to him for a long time, showed that kid the ropes, and he left me high and dry. You should be thanking me."

"You're wrong, Michael. Marcus didn't leave you empty as Nikolai plans to when he calls in that very sizable loan he's given you. The only reason you have New York and London is because of Marcus," I shot back. "All of that land was never yours in the first place, and you knew it but you got greedy. You got greedy and you got played."

"I see, Boy Wonder has been talking after all," said Michael, regaining his composure to make a valiant show of things.

"Yes, that's what people in relationships do, Michael—they talk. But we stopped doing that because of you. Because I gave you an importance you did not deserve. Marcus promised me that independent of what happened, he would protect you—leave you with something," I said. "And for what? Look at what you've done to him. Look at what you have done to me."

"Damn it, Jules, I didn't plan for things to go down like this, shit just happened. What can I say? I'll fix it after the ceremony, I promise."

"Is that all you have to say to me? Oh my gawd, what a fucking ego you have. I trusted you from day one. Why would you be so careless with that?" I was so focused on Michael that I didn't notice we were ready for takeoff until the flight attendant approached.

"Ma'am, I must ask you to turn your phone off," she said, neatly attired in a red Virgin Atlantic flight suit.

"It's off," I said, snapping the phone shut and tossing it in the bag below. "It's over."

I once heard someone say, "I don't know what the future holds, but I know who holds it." Looking through the window as we taxied down the runway, I was secure for the first time in the answer: ME! I hold the keys to my future.

# 45

## DEEP BREATH

As we turn off La Cienega onto Burton Way, the driver alerts me that we are minutes away from the condo. Looking out at the palm trees, thinking about where I've been as I enter this thirty-something journey of my life and how much I've grown, I know I have much to be proud of.

*I swear that woman has a sixth sense or else she has wired me with some type of tracking device.* Two blocks before we reach Wetherly, Cora phones.

"Hi, Mommy, what's going on?" I say in the most pleasant, peaceful tone I can muster as not to elicit any unsolicited commentary.

"Today was your groundbreaking, was it not?" asks Cora. "How did it go? You didn't call me."

"I wouldn't know. Wasn't there," I say, realizing that she was opting to engage in a different kind of fishing expedition instead of being direct.

"Umph. I heard that could be a possibility. So you are back in New York, I presume."

"No, Mommy, I'm in L.A. Is that a problem?"

"I see. And you are sure about this?"

"Yes, I am sure," I affirmed, my resolve giving way to the motivating feelings behind my admission. "I probably will never be able to explain it in any way that will make you understand, so I won't even try but he . . . Marcus matters, and I want to be there if he'll have me."

"You sound sure of yourself."

"I am, Cora."

"Then go get him. I would have done the same thing for your father if that Rosalyn had"—she paused to laugh at her own repetitiveness—"you know the rest."

"Oh, *I do*," I say. "Mommy, what if he's not there or doesn't want to hear what I have to say?"

"Then you wait until he is. You wait until your heart tells you it's time to let go. That is the very least that true love deserves."

"Miss, we are here," interrupts the driver.

"Okay, I have to go now. Let me call you later. I love you."

"I'm proud of you, Julesea—Jules."

# 46

## OTIS REDDING

**M**Y INDIFFERENCE TOWARD this hallway since the first day Marcus and I walked in is magnified today. Like most things in L.A., it feels ostentatious—boldly trying to be something it's not. (Kind of like me, I guess.) The overly modern furnishings encased in an I. M. Pei-esque (but not really) construction make it feel cold and austere rather than the luxury advertised, and today even more so. The clickity-clack of my heels on the marble floor sounds like a death march instead of a return to love. What if he is not here? What will I do? I mean, I'm ready, but what if he needs more time? Can I wait like Cora says? I hope so. *I'm here, I'm here!* I repeat the words to myself in front of the elevator, unable to actually step in. A cute couple and a single woman with a purse dog come up as I stand there. The doors open and I nod them off. *I'm here,* but I just can't get my feet to work. I can feel the security guard staring at me, which is kind of pissing me off. Can't he see that I'm also middecision here? Whatever, no big deal. I'll just walk over like so, press the button like this, and get in. See. No big deal.

Putting the key in the door, however, is another thing entirely, so I stand again, awaiting divine intervention. Then I remember a mantra that served me well once before:

*I long to be the woman who is loved passionately and deeply by a successful man who can provide for me in all ways that matter in this life. A woman who realizes that happiness is not a choice between this or that but an accumulation of moments experienced and shared. I want to be the woman who knows when to let a love go that existed in rose-colored glasses and to walk into a true love that requires no special frames to be alluring. I want to be the woman he chooses to remain faithful to and committed to even when things aren't going smoothly. I want to be the woman whose eyes hold his future.*

I can tell from the stillness that greets me at the doorway that no one is home. There is, I think, a hint of his cologne in the air, but that could just be my imagination, so I go further in. Marcus's gym bag is not in the hallway where it normally is, but then again I can't remember if it was there on the night he stormed out. The living room offers me no clues, as it's clear the housekeeper has been in to sort the mess we made, as she does twice a week. Placing my purse on the chaise, I go into our bedroom, stopping by the bed to trace the outline of where he usually sleeps before going to the closet. Everything, as far as I can see, is in its place: his watches on the center island displayed next to his collection of sunglasses and readers. There are no noticeable gaps to say that clothing was once here but is now gone—even his toothbrush and shavers are here. All is in place awaiting Marcus's return. Now all I had to do was join them—and wait.

The flight and drive in were easy compared to this. Hours had passed since I arrived, bringing an end to the day, and still Marcus hadn't come home. Calling him would be of no consequence, because whatever it was that would be said deserved more than a faceless delivery. If there was convincing to be done, then he needed to see my face, see that he possessed my heart without question.

The time idling was doing a number on my head, every little noise making me jump with nervous anticipation, thinking it's his key in the lock. It's unbearable! I walk over to the audio system, press Play, and crank up the volume for company. Otis Redding's rich voice fills the house, and I am hearing Marcus's soul if it could sing. I allow myself to get swept away in the melody and the understanding that for him to have been listening to Otis, he must be breathing us, reliving us. That's something to hold on to. The song abruptly stops. He's here. Standing before me. He sees me. I open my mouth to speak—but he motions to me to stop, and walks over.

"May I?" Marcus asks, taking me by the hand, and leading me into a slow dance.

"Yes," I say, trying to swallow the knot in my throat. "I was scared—"

"Shhhh, shhhh, listen," he says, pulling me to him tenderly as Otis starts to sing, "I Love You For More Than Words Can Say." Reciting each line softly in my ear, Marcus sings tenderly as he holds me tight, until we melt into one. My heart overflows, begging never to let go.

> *Honey living without you is so painful*
> *I was tempted to call it a day*
> *You've got me in your hand, why can't you understand*
> *I love you baby, for more than words can say*

I bury my face into the warmth of his neck, and exhale for the first time in a week, knowing that I desire to be only where he is, that no one, and nothing will ever matter more than what we create together. I'm dancing with my purpose. Every other word from him battled the other to express all that is in his soul, while not betraying the man, he believes I need him to be. I feel the force of his heart, beating ferociously against my chest. *I have no doubts. I trust this man and all that is to come between us.* Tilting my head up taking my future into full view, I wipe Marcus's tears and meet him in song.

*You've got me in your hand, why can't you understand*
*I love you honey, for more than words can say*

"If you'll have me," I say.
"I do," says Marcus.

## The Beginning

# Acknowledgments

TODD HUNTER—MY EDITOR and Jules's champion. Thank you for providing the platform. Your support means a lot.

Aunts Ollie, Almetta, and Vivian—you've championed me since '74. There are no words to convey how blessed I AM as a result!

Joy Leton—you, who always believes I can do anything. Reachin' kid, that's why I love you.

Rodrigo Santoro—you and I, words can't express. You live in my heart, obviously. Really . . . Seriously, Dynasty!

Lisa Rudolph—If asked to write about you I would start with "You are woman phenomenally," but I think that's plagiarism and Ms. Maya ain't to be crossed!

Leeya Myown—Little Goddess, always remember that you are light and all things are for you, so dream with your entire being and enjoy.

Richard Harris—too many firsts were with you, my friend. I honor you the only way I know how—everyday!

Nicole David—How can one so small hold up so many? Very blessed am I to be among the lifted.

Shohreh Aghdashloo—It's not right how very hard I crush on you, but I do. You, my dear, are grace, sophistication, and purpose.

Mikki Taylor—for inspiring me from afar, to showing me how to be a commander in chic everyday. J'adore!

Star Jones—Lady, I've watched and learned. Thank you, for all.

Brad Zeifman—come on now, amazing (you are)! Thanks for always having a song ready. We'll work on pitch and tone soon.

Janice, Bradley, and the Most Handsome Jerry Lewart—you gave me Sag Harbor. Thank you!

Ambassador Shabazz—your friendship and counsel is prized. For all that is, and all that is to come, I celebrate you!

The village that keeps me together—Tiffany Persons, Lakisha Bellamy, Jessica Teutonico, Bryce (OMG!) Wilson, Gino Columbo, Michael *"Who Me, I am French"* Sanka, Haydn Wright, Robert Marinelli, Ryan Tarpley, Shawn Howell, Judi McCreary, Brian Braff, Nancy Seltzer, Wes Carol, Adrienne Alexander, Robyn Price Pierre, Matt "Chuck" Davis, Tatiana Litvin, Arnold Robinson, Karen Earl, Jarrett Mason, Pat Green, Karen Cummings-Palmer, Claire Thomas, Amy Elisa Keith, Cheryl Francis Herrington, Michael Broussard, Kynderly Haskins, and Debra Langford (!).

I LOVE YOU ALL, clearly!